HELL IN RAGS

VB Scott

NO BARRIER
Publishing

No Barrier Publishing

CONTENTS

DEDICATION

To Watership Down by Richard Adams, the book that absorbed me so deeply that I practically ignored my vacation in Hawai'i while devouring it. It's my favorite book on leadership, found family, and seismic societal shifts.

To Hell in Glass, a Japanese metal song by Das Feenreich. The vibe and composition were the foundation I carried with me for years before constructing an entire narrative around the musical structure that led to Hell in Rags.

To the world in poverty. May we rise up against the rich and powerful before it's too late, and all of our dystopian nightmares come to pass. DO NOT LET THEM WIN.

CONTENT ADVISORY

The following book contains:

- Bloody violence
- Strong sexual content (lightly graphic)
- Pervasive strong language
- Non-graphic allusion to rape
- Non-graphic attempted rape
- Torture
- Suicide
- Misogynist slurs
- Non-graphic fear of child harm

Underfoot Gangs By Sector

[Sector Alpha: Female Gang Name, Male Gang Name]
Sector A: Onyx Orcas, none
Sector B: **Brass Bulls**, none
Sector C: Diamond Ducks, Maroon Mongeese
Sector D: Crystal Crackers, Iron Iguanas
Sector E: Violet Vipers, Acrylic Kicks
Sector F: Sapphire Snakes, Mammoth Tusks
Sector G: Luscious Lemurs, Green Marines
Sector H: Murder Minks, Horned Tornados
Sector I: Tiny Elephants, Super Sparkers
Sector J: Crooked Crows, Granite Gophers
Sector K: Quartz Queens, Silver Falcons
Sector L: Royal Rabbits, Purple Rams
Sector M: Black Hippos, Street Snappers
Sector N: Smoking Toads, Giant Judges
Sector O: Thirsty Thorns, Bullet Dogs
Sector P: Velvet Sharks, Puffin Punks
Sector Q: Flinty Frogs, Jagged Jaguars
Sector R: Vermillion Voles, Scare Bears
Sector S: Rocky Truncheons, Love Lions
Sector T: Killer Kittens, Ivy Dragons
Sector U: Cheep Chicks, Slippery Eels

Sector V: Dynamite Guppies, Lance Brigade
Sector W: Ember Elves, Cursed Ravens
Sector X: Ghost Foxes, Fire Ants
Sector Y: **<u>Denim Demons</u>**, Hammer Nails
Sector Z: White Whales, Emerald Eagles
Upcity: **<u>Ruby Riders</u>**, Idle Batemans

PART ONE
TRASH CANS

Chapter One

BRASS BULLS

REGINA RONDEL HAD NEVER smelled sewage in her life. If she'd recently eaten anything, her stomach would have been empty, its former contents adding to the stench. Sickening squelches came from somewhere off to her side. Her arms ached at the joints, tied back tight by rough, scratchy rope. The smell and sounds forced her mouth to open, but nothing came out but a painful, abdominal-squeezing heave. Unfortunately, plenty rushed *in* and made her even more nauseous. An open palm smacked her across the face.

"Shut up, Upcity baby," someone growled.

Regina opened her eyes to disorienting dimness. Candles offered their low light to small areas around the room, but she had a hard time seeing the faces of the people standing around. One of their flickering heads moved in her direction.

"Aww, the 'pretty one' finally woke up. Don't faint again, bitch."

Regina frowned in the darkness. Mocking her appearance... She'd heard it from her gang for months because she couldn't come up with the funds to get the plastic surgery they required in order to rank up. Barely hanging onto their small apartment in the lower sections of the Upcity, Regina's parents promised to do everything possible to save up for the operations, but they couldn't afford it at the time.

"I think she needs a little kiss where you hit her, Vela," a voice said from across the room.

The woman that slapped her, "Vela" apparently, bent and gave Regina's cheek a wet kiss, followed by a thick, hard lick from jaw to temple. Regina shuddered and yanked her head away, which earned another slap.

"Soon you'll be begging for anything other than pain, princess," Vela whispered, then darted her tongue into Regina's ear before standing up. Vela moved on to two other shapes that were in as vulnerable a position as Regina.

Vela slapped each of them in passing, then took up a position against the wall. A new figure materialized from the shadows. They raised an object to one of the candles, lighting a torch, illuminating an oddly regal face—sharp points, a grim line for a mouth, yet her eyes appeared wise and calculating, even in the fiery light.

The woman brought the torch to Regina's face, then to Regina's gang sisters. She brightened their backs, their tailored leather jackets.

"'The Ruby Riders.' Cute name, girls," the woman said.

"Found'em down in the markets," one of the anonymous women circling them commented, then slapped the back of the middle Ruby Rider's head. "Fuckin' *hagglin'* with our stall."

Tiffany, the middle sister, raised her head.

"You wanted more than the dirty trash ca—"

The woman slapped her again, then grabbed Tiffany's hair and yanked her head back.

"Upcity *brat!* Fuckin' slummin' down here, wantin' to trade the same as—"

"That's enough, Ezzie." The regal woman took an authoritative step forward. "How big is your gang, girls?"

"Big enough to wipe you off the map, sewer trash." Brittney, the last of their trio, spit at the regal woman's foot.

Vela kicked Brittney in the side, tipping her over.

"Still a layer to go before you reach the sewers, princess. What do you say to a little spelunking to go along with your slumming; complete the experience? All the better to share with your sisters..."

"Come on, Vela, let's just let them go," a new voice said.

Vela exhaled and her head swiveled to a part of the room unseen.

"Our Queen of Compassion, ladies. Shut the fuck up, Rina, or you'll take the same bath."

Regina heard Rina mutter "bitch," but she didn't say anything further.

"What do you think, Brace?" Vela asked the torchbearer.

"High price to pay for slumming... But what else can we do to keep you little brats from returning?"

"Please don't kill us!" Tiffany squealed.

"Well, that's usually the best way to keep you people away from here," Brace said. "But that'll just mean more unwelcome visitors if we kill you. We don't need the police all up in our business."

"Wait until the Riders hear what you've done..." Brittney sneered. Regina almost yelled at her to stop making things worse, but she didn't want another slap for the trouble. She'd never really liked Brittney, anyway.

"I don't think you know who you're *talking* to, doll," Vela said, then kicked Brittney in the stomach, forcing her to vomit.

"Fuckin' 'Ruby Riders.' Tch!" Ezzie spit on Brittney's jacket. "What does that even mean? You pink virgins have no idea, do you? You just thought of the first thing that came to your rich, vapid little minds because it sounded cool, didn'tcha? Brace, I'm with Vela. Let's string these bitches into the sewer."

Brace lowered herself to illuminate Brittney's silent tears.

"She looks like the type that would come out angrier, more vengeful. She might even inspire her virgin friends to attack us, for all the good *that* would do."

"Fucking right, ugly bitch," Brittney said, then winced as Vela placed her foot on her head and added a little weight.

"Then we have *you*," Brace said, shifting the light to Tiffany. "Already pissed yourself. You'll be easy."

"I— I didn't..." Tiffany whimpered.

"Smells like rich piss to me, boss," Ezzie said, pushing her knee into Tiffany's back.

Brace finally brought the torch to Regina. "I like the quiet ones most..." she murmured, almost as if she didn't want the others to hear. Then, she *did* whisper, "which one of your sisters would you sacrifice so you could go home?"

Regina peered at her miserable sisters as Vela and Ezzie lightly tortured them with prodding and poking. While she didn't like Brittney personally, nothing she'd ever done warranted a *death sentence*. And poor Tiffany—the initiate tasked with bringing back a "treasure" from the Underfoot—she'd only recently healed from her surgery, finished the week before. She hadn't yet had a chance to show off her *second* new parentally-gifted car to the upper level male gangsters, the Idle Batemans.

What if Regina got away? She was already on thin ice. The Ruby Rider leader routinely threatened to kick her out for not having the surgeries like everyone else. Regina was the lowest-residing member of the gang, despite her tenure as a reliable lieutenant. There were always new, far-more-affluent members to recruit, and their leader grew impatient with Regina's lackluster performance in improving her class and status to meet the gang's lofty standards.

Maybe, if Regina proved her value by saving the new blood...

"Lower *me* into the sewers," Regina said. "Free those two first..."

"Oh, *thank you*, Reggie!" Tiffany cried. "Thank you thank yo—"

Ezzie socked her and pushed her down next to Brittney, right into the puddle of vomit. She squealed until Ezzie put her foot on her head, like Vela to Brittney.

Brace smiled slightly, then whirled around.

"Rip off their patches and gag them, Bulls, then bring them to the outhouse."

More women than Regina could count converged into the candlelight and grabbed at the three Ruby Riders, tore off their gang patches, then dragged them outside. The ancient streets were filled with the disgusting resident trash cans. Steam released from mazes of pipes from the metropolis above, and added to the gagging, horrid smell no better than the room they exited.

"Don't forget to blow out the candles, Rina," Brace called back to one of the last women to exit.

The light in the streets glowed only marginally better—lit by braziers and mints of candles. Rina nodded and went back into the room.

The rags Brace's gang wore were held together in the back by their own patches: The Brass Bulls. The leader of the Ruby Riders warned them to stay away from anyone wearing that branding, due to troubling reports she received from her contact in the Underfoot. Unfortunately, Brittney wasn't paying attention when she picked a fight with their stall over trade-gouging the rich.

The Brass Bulls dragged the Ruby Riders through the street, not hiding their activities from the denizens. Most never bothered to look in their direction, some ignored them if they did, and only a couple showed anything resembling compassion but went about their lives, nonetheless.

Regina raised her head while being pushed along, trying to catch a glimmer of light, some *hope* in their dark environs, but all the skyrises and endless flying vehicles of the city, combined with pipes, tubes, and nets suspended above, blocked any natural light from reaching the Underfoot, like the depths of the ocean where sunlight died.

Objects occasionally landed in the nets, and scavengers climbed to grab the bounties—mostly discarded food and garbage from the residents above. When the scavengers came down, they shared the partially-eaten, dropped food with children. Regina dry-heaved at the sight, but with the gag in her mouth, she started choking.

Rina, who had since caught up to them, responded quickly. She pulled the gag out, then rubbed Regina's back until the heaving stopped.

"Thank yo—" was all she managed before Rina stuffed the gag back in. Her expression wasn't malicious, though, unlike Vela and Ezzie as they kept watch over their prisoners.

Dismay flooded Regina as they neared a *literal* outhouse—like in those old Westerns from 200 years ago that their private school played to kill time and feel better about their lots in life.

Brace pounded on the locked door.

"Occupied!" came a woman's reply.

"Are you a civvie, or in a gang?"

"Civvie, ma'am!"

"How much longer are you going to—?"

A dirty woman came out, still pulling up her rags. Brace grabbed her by the arm and scanned her back for patches, then let her go.

"Thank you, ma'am!" the trash can called over her shoulder.

Vela put her foot on the outer wall of the outhouse. She kicked and knocked over the tied-together planks to reveal an uncovered manhole rimmed with sludge that Regina couldn't look at for more than a second before gagging again. Tiffany and Brittney had similar reactions as the three of them were lowered to their knees.

"Tear these prissy pussies up, ladies," Brace commanded, then turned to converse with someone a few feet away.

The Bulls gleefully tore the clothes off the Ruby Riders, leaving rags behind. Vela ran her hands over Brittney's exposed skin that wasn't still covered by underwear. The Riders braced for the assaults that were sure to come, but Rina stepped between them.

"Brace didn't say anything *further*, Vela."

Vela scowled, murder in her expression. Brace came back and Vela stood down, though she kept a hard stare on Rina.

"We've got ten minutes," Brace said. "Tie ropes to their bonds."

Brittney and Tiffany squirmed and fought to no avail. Regina put a brave face on and didn't fight back. Brace smiled and came over to pull her gag out.

"I said I'd do it, *only* if you free them first." Regina kept her voice low as Brace had done in the room.

"Listen, 'Reggie,' I don't know if letting them go teaches the right lesson," Brace said so everyone could hear. "I think all three of you should take a bath, experience *true* slumming, then I can sleep knowing you three will do everything in your power to warn the Upcity to stay out of the Underfoot once and for all."

Before Regina could protest, a stern voice came from behind the group.

"What is this, Brace?" A male police officer came forward. He was the most hopeful thing Regina had seen in years, but Brace gagged her again before she could exclaim her joy to be saved.

"Thieves, Officer. Just teaching them a little lesson. They stole from the Clinics near the Elevators."

"Oh yeah? Where's the stuff?"

"We already returned it to the Doc. Best not to delay his treatment schedule when he's only down here for a few hours."

The officer looked over the Riders. Was he ignoring their pleading eyes? Or could he just not see them in the dim light?

"Alright. Just don't 'accidentally' let go of the rope like you did last time. We never recovered that guy."

"He tried to kill one of mine, Officer. He deserved it."

"Sure enough, Brace. Thanks for helping out the Doc, but don't get any closer than that to the Elevators, you got me?"

Regina couldn't believe it when he turned his back on them and disappeared through the circle of Bulls. Several of them gave varying silent gestures of derision to his back, then returned their attention to the Riders.

"Now, where were we?" Brace grinned.

"You were going to let them go, and do whatever the *fuck* you have planned for me."

Vela put her foot on Regina's shoulder and threatened a rough stomp.

"You're going to *wish* all we wanted to do was *fuck*."

"They get it, Vela," Brace said. Vela backed up with a sneer. It was incongruous, seeing such a rancorous, foul brute wearing the prettiest face of them all—for Underfoot standards anyway. All but Regina in the Ruby Riders were far more beautiful, thanks to their surgeries. If Regina got out alive, she'd surpass all of the degenerates standing around her... If she could beg her parents just a little harder next time...

Brace studied Regina's face again, which made her squirm.

"I wonder, dear Reggie... Or should we call you 'Raggy' now?" The Bulls laughed and plucked at the Riders' rags. "You seem so eager to save your sisters. I wonder if they feel the same about *you?* Hm?"

Brace turned her gaze to Tiffany and Brittney.

"Well, girls? Would you take a dip to save Raggy?"

Of course they wouldn't, but it still hurt how quickly Brittney shook her head, never looking at Regina. Tiffany did, but with pained eyes; empathetic, yet fearful. She shook her head after "apologizing" wordlessly to Regina.

Vela laughed, followed by Ezzie, then the rest of the Bulls howled. Only Rina and Brace didn't.

"What a tight-knit family you have, Raggy," Brace lowered herself to Regina's eyeline again. "You still want them to go free?"

Regina's lips quivered as she cast a scowl to Brittney, then nodded beneath Brace's gaze.

"Rina, take a couple Bulls with you and escort those two cream puffs to the Elevators. Run them through the *real* slums on the way. But they're going to watch Raggy take a bath, first."

Regina fought against the restraints but only managed to fall over. The street always seemed wet and musty, like rotting trees, the smell that sometimes drifted into her bedroom window from the vast forests covering the landscape between cities.

Vela and Ezzie tied a rope to the bonds behind Regina's back. She didn't think her joints could ache any worse until a pulley they drew down from above the outhouse lifted her in the air. They maneuvered her six feet above the hole. She wasn't prepared for how putrid it smelled: magnitudes worse than the room she woke up in, and the open air of the dark streets. They hadn't even lowered her yet.

The Bulls closed the distance inch by inch, twisting the knife. Tiffany muffled out cries, and Brittney finally looked sorry. Or was it relief? Rina and the two volunteer Bulls turned the Riders from the spectacle and pushed them away.

The rope stopped to where another inch would have put Regina's shoes in the muck around the rim. Brace snapped her fingers and the Bulls pulled the rope back up, then grabbed Regina's legs and swung her away from the hole.

Vela righted the outhouse over the hole. Several trash cans from the sidewalks ran to form a line to use it.

After they fully untied Regina, she winced and rubbed her aching arms. Brace stood in front of her, then wiped a thumb along Regina's cheek, rubbing away the tears.

"The Ruby Riders don't deserve you, Raggy. Come see what it's like in a *real* gang."

Chapter Two

SLUMMING

SABRINA LED THE TWO princesses to the true slums, off the main thoroughfare on the way to the Elevators. They were intensely ashamed of their exposed rags and kept moving their hands and arms to cover themselves, despite the protection of their luxurious, still-intact underwear.

"No one cares, Rubies. But if it makes you feel better, you could trade for a blanket off any of these old folks."

The haughty bitch, the one who quickly betrayed her sister back at the outhouse, scoffed and spit—a nasty habit for such a pretty creature.

"Keep your disgusting shit away from us, trash can."

Sabrina sighed while the other two Bulls pushed the women on harder.

"Pretty brave words come out of you—when there aren't so many Bulls around. But then again, you *did* spit on the boss's foot..."

The braziers illuminated huddled masses along the side streets and alleyways, waiting for the scavengers to bring down net scraps, or trading items of little value for other items of little value. Dirty children ran in and around even dirtier adults. Most were orphans. Sabrina's heart ached whenever she saw little girls alone. She hoped they'd survive, as she had, until they were old enough to be initiated into a gang. Otherwise it would be a lifetime of abuse and terror, followed by an early death.

The weaker, younger of the two Riders gave Sabrina a little smile.

"Thank you. For stopping that Vela from…"

"Pay attention, princess," Sabrina said. "We're going this way for a reason. Your sister sacrificed herself, and I don't think either of you understand the gravity of that. You're going to learn *something* from your little escapade today."

Sabrina and her sisters roughly guided the women through the dregs of humanity—weaving around box shanties and open sleeping areas, the swarms of people trying to get their hands on cleansing wipes from the scavengers, the dark alleyways filled with whores of all sexes who traded for food scraps, and the over-capacity Clinics with Doctors from the Upcity (mostly nurses but for the once-a-week visit from esteemed doctors).

Police presence in the Underfoot mostly existed to protect the Clinics. Even better-protected were the Elevators—guarded lethally to keep unchipped residents away. Only a few officers ever forayed into gang territory if they were *allowed to* by the leaders. They often did nothing, but in rare circumstances, their electric guns and air of authority came in handy.

"How do you people *live* like this?" the spitter sneered.

"Shut up, Brittney," the rookie said.

"What did you just say to an officer?" Brittney lunged at her sister. The Bull let her go, and so did the other. Brittney slapped the rookie, who took it like a baby and teetered back into an onlooker, who shoved her away.

Sabrina got between the women, staring into Brittney's enraged eyes while the rookie put on a show to get around and continue the fight, even though Sabrina wasn't trying to hold her back.

"Is that how you earn respect in your baby gang?" one of the other Bulls commented behind Brittney.

"What, better to be like your 'Queen of Compassion' here? The weakest bitch in your whole—"

Sabrina admired Brittney maintaining eye contact, but it was broken when the nearest Bull grabbed her by the hair and yanked it back to growl in her face.

"Don't you *ever* speak ill of Rina, got it, cunt?"

Brittney bared her teeth through the pain. "I don't give a fuck about any of you. You're *all* filth."

The Bull almost scalped the bitch, but Sabrina held up her hand and motioned for Brittney to be let go.

"So much hostility for an Upcity Princess," Sabrina said. "Some of the gangs down here would snap you up in a heartbeat, if you could survive their initiations. But I think you're all bark and no bite, little bitch."

"Yuh—yeah? I'd beat *your* ass, 'Rina.'"

"After that display at the outhouse, I highly doubt you have the fortitude to—"

"Where does a trash can like you learn such big words?"

Sabrina cracked a smile. "I like this one the more she yaps, ladies."

The Bulls scoffed and shook their heads.

"Tell you what, babe. You knock me on my ass and I'll take you right to the Elevators. No more lessons, no more *trash* your poor eyes need to suffer. I'll even fetch you a relatively clean blanket so the Elevator operators won't gawk at your new ensemble."

"I don't want anything from *you*, but if I can beat one of you Bulls I'll get promoted for sure. Tiffany, you're my witness."

Sabrina glanced over her shoulder at Tiffany's shocked expression taking in the exchange. Brittney slapped Sabrina's cheek before she'd even turned back, followed by another panicky slap when she did face her, as if the second one would do the trick.

The Bull behind Brittney stepped up and grabbed her manicured hand. Brittney tried pulling away but couldn't match the strength of the grip. The Bull closed Brittney's hand into a fist for her and squeezed it. Brittney winced as a fake nail detached.

"Like *that*, pussy," the Bull said, then let go.

"You're— You're not going to hit back?" Brittney asked, her haughtiness draining before Sabrina's eyes.

"Your true colors are showing. I take back what I said—no one down here would take yo—"

Brittney punched Sabrina's cheekbone, hitting the eye socket. It wasn't all that hard, even with the surprise factor. Brittney's face crumpled and she held her shaking hand. A quick tear rolled off her cheek. Tiffany came around and hugged her, moving her away from the three Bulls, then turned to face them.

"Is that offer still open? If *I* knock you on your ass?"

"Give it a try, rook," Sabrina said.

Tiffany squared up, ready to charge forward. Sabrina tried not to laugh at her slender, soft fingers curling up into a fist—better than Brittney's, anyway. At least Tiffany was prepared to fight with honor.

She took a step forward when a mass flashed before them and smashed into the street, covering Tiffany and Sabrina with blood and gore. Tiffany held her hands to her head and screamed at the puddle at her feet, while Sabrina just looked up. Scavengers were already climbing up to repair the net. Bounty momentarily rained down on the Underfoot from the hole the Upcity suicide had caused. The whole street of people converged on the garbage, food, and possessions of the body.

"Don't let the Riders get swallowed up!" Sabrina commanded the Bulls, who nodded and fought to reach them in the ensuing chaos.

She reached down in the scrum and pulled out a purple paisley necktie, formerly wrapped around the dead man's throat. She looped it around her fist and searched for other treasures dropped from the net or by her fellow frantic residents. A discarded, dirty blanket… Perfect.

Sabrina ventured to the safe perimeter of the Elevators about a quarter of a mile away, where the Bulls held Brittney and Tiffany. She flung the blanket at Brittney, who let it fall to the ground.

"Someone will pick that up within seconds. Cover your shame on the way home or don't, we don't give a fuck. You, Tiffany… Come here."

Tiffany stepped forward with caution. Sabrina handed over the tie. Tiffany took it gingerly, confused.

"Doesn't matter where we live, rookie. Life sucks for us all."

Sabrina motioned for the Bulls to relax and they left the princesses to have their chips scanned for their passage into the Elevators. She flashed their gang sign when Tiffany looked back, and the Bulls parted ways.

A FORT OF CARDBOARD, ornate with its little window openings, cut out by Sabrina's cherished, nine-year-old unofficially-adopted daughter, waited for Sabrina to come home. They didn't have many neighbors, since they lived close to the fouler-smelling area of the sector. Others made that choice as well, but not many managed to stay long. The elbow room was nothing to sniff at though, Kirsten always joked.

Sabrina kissed Kirsten when she entered, running her fingers through her knotted hair, then hugged little Panda tight. Panda was eager and squirmed out of her embrace to light up her aromatic candle, a monumental find. She only ever lit it when all three of them were in the house. Panda gasped.

"What happened to your eye, Mom?"

"What? Let me look at that, Sibby," Kirsten said, bringing the candle up to Sabrina's eye. "Did you get in another fight with that Vela bit—woman?"

"It's alright. Doesn't hurt at all."

"That's going to turn into a black e—"

"I've had them before, K. It'll happen again. Anyway, I'm starving. I hope you found something to eat, because I was...occupied."

"Mm-hm..." Kirsten sighed.

Panda went to her corner and brought a kerchief to her parents, filled with half a cut of fatty prime rib, cold and pink.

"Better hold that over the candle, Pan. Did a scavenger give that to you?"

Panda nodded.

"What did you trade?"

She shrank back and stared at her feet, shy and nervous. She only had one shoe.

"What did I tell you about trading your foot coverings? Cutting your feet is a death sentence. What do I have to do to make you remember?"

Panda cowered behind Kirsten's leg, peeking out to assess how angry Sabrina really was. Two years before, Panda had been foolish enough to stand in front of one of the steam pipe openings, even though they'd warned her of the danger. Sabrina dove to push her out of the way at the telltale *hiss* of a coming blast and received a nasty burn on her calf for the trouble. She'd yelled at Panda, about how they couldn't bear to see something happen to her, but her love twisted to desperation and escalated. Conditioned by a lifetime of violence, Sabrina slapped Panda when she didn't promise quickly enough to never do it again.

She immediately regretted it, showering Panda with affection and apologies. Sabrina cried that night as she told Kirsten what she'd done—how she couldn't believe what came over her. She'd always promised herself she would never hit her children like she'd suffered. Kirsten soothed Sabrina with understanding and together they discussed better ways to convey to Panda how much they loved her, but also, how much more careful she needed to be.

Sabrina picked up Panda from behind Kirsten's leg and hugged her, stroking her black hair. While Panda sniffled and apologized quietly, Sabrina cocked her eyebrow at Kirsten.

"Did you see? Was the scavenger local? Maybe I can get it back?"

"It's okay, Sibby. I'll talk to the family over by the outhouse tomorrow. Their son has grown a lot this year, maybe they haven't traded his old shoes yet."

"Sounds good. Panda, thank you for getting dinner tonight. Cook that up a little more, please, then let's eat."

She set Panda down, then sat in the corner as the shack filled with meaty aroma, the first time in months. Sabrina pulled a bottle of nutritional pills from her inside pocket. They were the only thing no one ever traded in the Underfoot. They could be found in the weekly supply drops from the Upcity, or given out by the Doctors, and there was enough to go around—for now.

Sabrina spent a couple of late nights a week searching the streets for the freshly-dead and taking their pills, if they weren't already gone when she found the corpses. If she happened upon nearby children, she'd share some of them, but she couldn't afford to give them *all* away with her own family to worry after.

Kirsten tore a hunk of meat with the least amount of fat off with her teeth, then took it out of her mouth and passed it to Sabrina. Sabrina pushed a pill into the center of it and handed it to Panda. They did the same, splitting the remaining meat into two hunks. They wiped the grease off their fingers, then Kirsten produced her own surprise, a square of chocolate with an almond and bite marks on only two of the four sides.

No one had any clue why the Upcity was so keen on never *finishing* anything they ate. However, chocolate was rare enough to find in the nets. Scavengers often ate them immediately, but if someone below the nets noticed the find quickly enough, they'd trade for the right price. Sabrina lifted her brow to Kirsten as Panda savored the square like a little mouse.

Kirsten made a motion with her hand, pushing her tongue against her cheek and with a sly smile. Sabrina scrunched her lips and rolled her eyes, but returned the smile. She'd have done the same thing. It wouldn't have been the first time.

Panda snored softly while Kirsten held Sabrina in her arms on their nest of blankets. Sabrina ran her fingers over the back of Kirsten's hand, her eye throbbing lightly as it swelled.

"I heard more about her today, Sibby," Kirsten whispered, inches from Sabrina's ear. "The Denim Demons are making their move…"

"Mmm... I've heard the rumblings, too. But it could be weeks, months even, before they reach our sector."

"Do you think Brace will have a plan for—"

"I don't know. She probably thinks we'll just beat their asses and that'll be that. That's *definitely* how Vela and Ezzie would go about things."

"What are you going to do? Let them battle? Then join the Demons once the dust settles?"

"I couldn't just stand there. Vela would kill me. I'd look like a betrayer."

"But... Isn't that the plan?"

"It'll take more careful planning than that, K. The Demons won't accept me without a show of faith, and I have to keep up appearances as long as possible with the Bulls."

"How are you going to do that?"

"I'll need to find some way to contact them beforehand."

Kirsten's hug tightened around Sabrina's chest as if holding a teddy bear for comfort.

"It's alright, K. Olive is a saint. She leads with love and compassion, not fear and intimidation. Every gang not led by assholes will want to join her. She gives so many spoils to others. I heard she's never had a defector..."

Kirsten's breathing grew heavier into Sabrina's hair, already asleep.

"Never talks down to her ladies..." Sabrina murmured, "never lets them attack each other... Never lets them rape, despite the pillaging..."

She sniffed, remembering how she'd come upon Vela seven years before, raping a young woman who got too close to the Brass Bulls' headquarters. Sabrina was a rookie, then—she had no status to challenge Vela, and even if she had, Vela would have torn her apart. When the Bulls broke their meeting that night, Sabrina rushed outside to find the woman. She was right where Vela had left her, catatonic. Sabrina dragged her out of sight of the passing Bulls. She took care of her for a year before the woman spoke a word, simply telling Sabrina her name: Kirsten.

"Olive...would...never..." Sabrina whispered, right before sleep took her.

Chapter Three

LIVE

OLIVE PUSHED AN ELECTRIC baton into the neck of the Thirsty Thorns leader, incapacitating her after an exhausting battle. The Denim Demons cheered, each one holding their own conquests by the raggedy collars, bodies slumped against their thighs. Olive nodded to her second-in-command, Twill, to tie up the leader like all the others, then signaled for the Demons to wake up their prisoners. Light slapping of faces ensued. If water was easier to come by, she'd use it for waking up the unconscious.

The Thirsty Thorns' leader, Mika, came to. She glowered at Olive, for all the good it did her. Olive gave her a sympathetic look, then turned to the larger squad of defeated combatants.

"I'm so sorry it came to this, fellow warriors. But I offered peace, supplies, and high spots within the Denim Demons through your leader, but she let pride stand in the way of your progress. She spit on my extended branch; slapped away my handshake. The benefits from keeping you under her thumb, never earning more, were seemingly too great."

"She's l—" Mika started before Twill, Olive's enforcer, gagged her.

"This battle was regrettable, my friends," Olive continued. "But no one died. No one ever dies in my battles. Do you know why? Because I believe in lifting each other up! We'll never have better lives if we're always fighting over territory *here*, scraps of shit *there*, turning on each other, always looking up with envy, feeling sorry for ourselves... I promise better lives for us all! For all the Underfoot! We don't need to live above the nets to be happy! We just need compassion for each other! I offer the Denim Demons' hands of friendship to you all. Shake your combatant's hands and we will share our bounty with you, as you are one of *us* now. Join us to spread love and eradicate inequality!"

The Thirsty Thorns' leader strained to shake loose of her constraints, but Twill and Olive blocked her from her former subjects' view with their legs. Twill kicked back, silencing her struggling. More than three quarters of the Thorns shook the hands of the Demons, and were immediately untied. The Demons' support members brought forth jiggers of white wine, meat morsels, and wedges of lemon. The display of wealth resulted in almost all of the rest of the sisters shaking hands, and they partook.

The ex-Thorns were ordered to stand and splay their legs to have the measurements of their waists taken, along with their inner and outer seams. Support Demons lugged sacks of reconstructed, patched jeans into the crowd and assisted each other in matching their new sisters with their forever uniform. The Denim Demon patches were pre-sewn into the seat of every pair.

Five Thorns remained after the new converts were led away to prepare for their initiations, each with a loyal Demon watching over them. If they were bitter for missing out on the meal, they didn't show it. Olive approached each one and gave them a quieter speech. One of them shook her Demon's hand, and earned an embrace for it. The Demon led the former Thorn away for dinner and jeans.

Olive admired the last four most of all. Loyalty was the most valuable commodity in the Underfoot—the *only* way to survive. Unfortunately, the precious trait also made it hard to turn to another side. Almost impossible. It was no less than a small miracle that Olive had managed to turn Twill. If that hadn't happened...

Twill had been a most loyal charge to her former gang, never swaying to words, gifts, or Olive's attempted wiles. In fact, Olive had given up on her, after having assimilated the majority of her gang into the Denim Demons already, until Twill brought the last handful of her former gang upon the Denim Demons for a surprise attack. Twill had the upper hand in size and strength, being taller and broader. Olive wore the bruises and soreness of their altercation for weeks after. But Olive got lucky when ducking a right hook from Twill and, unfamiliar with the territory, Twill fell over an ancient guardrail—there to protect from falling into the mass of snaking, lethally-hot pipeworks that ran the Upcity.

Twill caught herself from falling to her death with the wet ground. The panic in Twill's face as the sludge came away in her hands in clumps compelled Olive to act without thinking. She dove to catch Twill's hand before she slipped into the chasm, bracing herself with the lower part of the railing. She couldn't get Twill out alone and almost dropped her, but her Denim sisters rushed over quickly enough to bring them both back to safety.

Twill constructed her own jeans as a show of allegiance that night.

Olive looked over the remaining four Thorns, proudly defiant. Unfortunately, she couldn't simply let them go free. Like Twill had, others would attack, and Olive wasn't naïve enough to believe her luck would save her every time that happened.

Olive motioned to have the women taken away for more convincing later, then she turned her attention to Mika.

Twill ungagged her, and the two of them were cursed from the top of the towers to their feet. Olive let her vent, now that there were no Thorns left to defend her.

"You twisted my words, bitch. I said I needed time to call a meeting of the Thorns. I didn't refuse *shit!* We always vote before a big decision."

"I think you meant 'voted.' The Thorns are finished," Olive said. Democracy had its time in the United States. But the people living higher up in the towers didn't get to where they were, creating a new country of ultra-wealthy megalopolises, by voting and acting like a collective—they manipulated, cheated, forced, coerced, conspired, paid more, stepped on and *over* people. They had no regard for their fellow man in reaching their goals.

Olive did care about people, but she wasn't content with coalitions, arguing, debating, and delaying in the name of explaining shit way above the heads of the people that needed her help; the ones truly affected. The gangs either accepted her many offers of friendship, or they foolishly threw their might into her concrete wall of support and *still* joined her in the end.

Except for a few pigheads here and there...

"Well, as the last member of the Thirsty Thorns, how do you vote *now?* Come join me where I'll respect and use your leadership skills, or lose rank and suffer the initiations of a new gang. Careful with your answer, though. I'll just be after those gangs soon enough..."

Mika only glared in stubborn defiance.

"Twill, escort her out of the sector. Make it *clear* what'll happen if she tries to get back in."

Twill nodded and dragged Mika off, ignoring the barrage of curses. Olive sighed and ventured through the intersection as the gangless came out in search of anything that might have been torn or dropped during the gang battle. She put her hands on children's heads and the shoulders of the old folk, giving them all sympathetic smiles and promises of a future less bleak and painful for them all.

Olive and her next four strongest Demons brought the remaining Thorns to the sector's supply pipe, where a large crowd of gangless huddled around, elbowing and pushing to get closer to the weekly drop. Olive addressed the Thorns.

"What was your gang's protocol for getting supplies, ladies?"

"First come, first serve. Cut in line, take what's mine."

"Cute. Did you follow these actions simply because they rhymed?"

The Thorns exchanged uneasy glances. Clearly they were never allowed to question their leader or the status quo.

"We do things differently in the Denim Demons. Watch with me."

Olive whistled, causing her captives and several gangless to startle. Two dozen Denim Demons materialized from the edges of the crowds, then forcefully pushed their way around the opening to create a small barrier. The gangless were too weak to fight back, but they at least stopped fighting each other for positioning, instead turning their impotent wrath on the Demons.

Objects clanged and tumbled against the pipe, the music of supplies dropping. The first crate landed on the ground and exploded open. Demons pulled it aside and quickly separated the contents into categories. Another crate hit, and the process repeated.

Even more Demons arrived and held up the barrier while others sorted. After the tenth and final crate shattered, the gangless were about to break through the barrier. Olive whistled again, cutting through the din. She nodded to her Demons to start distributing the contents to the crowd—giving them out based on perceived needs: feminine supplies to women; toys to children; safety-shaving kits to men; cleansing wipes, used clothing, and nutrition pills for all.

No one was hurt, like what happened in the usual, unsupervised scrums. Supply drops in certain sectors were often fatal—children trampled, possessions stolen while attentions wavered, old folks thrown aside by the young, people taking more than their fair share, leading to murders. In the Denim Demon's care, no one got nothing, and no one was ever hurt.

Once the Demons finished and the crowd dispersed, most with grateful smiles, Olive wasn't surprised to find sneers on the faces of the four Thorns.

"Good going," one said. "Now you have nothing for yourselves."

Olive smiled and motioned for the women to be brought along with her on a little stroll. They went to the other end of the sector, the former border of the Thirsty Thorns. The Demons herded the scavengers away from the nets, then one of them climbed into the net and motioned overhead.

A flying vehicle grew larger as it lowered to the Underfoot. The Demon grabbed hold of a cold pipe and unhooked a corner of the net. The vehicle lowered a half-car-sized chest through the gap. Once the Demons below unhooked it, the vehicle raised and left. The net was re-secured and the scavengers were freed to go about their business. The Demons picked up the chest like a casket and carried it to the center of the Thorns' old headquarters. All the Demons and new initiates gathered.

Inside the chest were flashlights, bottles of wine, sealed packages of meat, bundles of vegetables, bags of fruit, recycled linen, cleansing wipes, and blunt weapons. Several Demons swiftly grabbed the weapons and took them out of sight. At the prospect of receiving such fresh goods, three of the four Thorns shook their captors' hands and were treated to new jeans. The last one remaining kept her frown. There was always one...

Olive brought her to meet with Twill upon her return. A handful of Demons carrying the weapons joined them as they ventured where the Thorns dared not go—the territory of the male gang of the sector. The Demons had already negotiated peace with them before overthrowing the Thirsty Thorns, in exchange for the weapons. The last Thorn scoffed once the men left with their death-dealing equipment.

"What the fuck was *that?*" she yelled.

"Let the men fight the men," Olive explained. "They'll thin themselves out eventually. They let us do our thing, and we didn't have to sell our bodies."

"They want our bodies and territory eventually. You think the other gangs don't want to avoid selling themselves or losing their territory?"

"We offer stability in the streets, less challenge to their 'authority.' A full ego goes a long way to placating them."

"Still doesn't solve the rape—"

"We have more than enough willing Demons to supply pleasurable nights after dances and hangouts. I spend an extended amount of time with each sector's leader to negotiate harsh treatment for rapists. Men will sign almost anything for the promise of willing participation in their fantasies. If we give them power, they don't have to *take* it."

"That's too easy..."

"Such are men, sweetheart. But it's worth it to make the Underfoot a better place to live for all. You can either live in fear of them, or use their nature against them."

"What if—"

Twill interrupted.

"The last male gang who broke their promise to us lost access to our women and the weapons, and they were defeated by their rivals soon after. When words and honey aren't enough, we do not tolerate them. I trust you have no more questions."

Olive put her hand on the skeptical Thorn's shoulder and held out the other. She looked down at the open gesture and kept her hands at her side.

"I want to be with Mika. Will you let me go?"

"You're an amazing sister. Mika is lucky to have you. You were worth the effort, my dear. Here." Olive handed over a full lemon and a carrot. "Twill, see that she's reunited with Mika, please."

Twill nodded and escorted the girl away.

Olive went back to the headquarters to rejoin her gang, who were in the middle of introducing themselves to their converts.

"Welcome to the Denim Demons, my new friends." Olive quieted the crowd for one last speech. "I'm sure you're all tired, but your initiation begins tonight. You will split up to visit all your sector's fellow residents to verify they have nutrition pills. If they don't, you are to give them some of yours. Seek children and old folks first. When you run out, you may come back here for a rest. The initiation will continue tomorrow morning."

Olive trusted her lieutenants would sort out the groans of inconvenience and went into Mika's former quarters with a Demon and a sack. They collected loose fabric and objects of value, stripping the place bare. In a little nook behind Mika's nest, Olive found a sheet of paper. It was rare to find loose paper in the Underfoot, and even rarer were writing utensils. The image on the paper had been drawn in thin streaks of blood. It was a portrait of the final Thorn who had refused to become a Demon, laid out nude in the nest. The face detail was amazing—a real labor of love, important enough for Mika to have used her own blood to draw it and risk infection.

Olive's heart sank. She shuffled out of the quarters, the paper in her hand. Twill entered the headquarters, a lemon and carrot in her hand. She nodded solemnly at Olive.

Olive sniffed away a tear. Their proactive presumption had been based on real events—the rejects coming back for a final attack: revenge. Three Sectors had launched attacks behind the Demons' backs, resulting in unnecessary injuries and even a couple of deaths. Before they planned their attack on the Thirsty Thorns, Olive and Twill had discussed a new rule to definitively end any final, desperate attacks from opposing gang's remnants...

Olive fell to her knees as regret filled her chest. Tears plinked the paper she held, the blood too old and dried to smudge; they'd been together a long time. Several Demons immediately surrounded her to keep anyone from seeing their leader's show of emotion.

The portrait was so beautiful, turned all the more tragic knowing the loyalty of the subject. Olive kissed the paper, then folded it and put it in her back pocket. She wiped her tears with her shirt of rags and gathered herself in time for Twill to break up the circle. Olive embraced her tight. Twill rested her chin on top of Olive's head.

"Tell me they didn't suffer..." Olive whispered.

"They didn't suffer, Liv."

Olive pushed out of the embrace.

"Don't *ever* call me that again."

Olive left the headquarters and sought to give out the rest of her nutrition pills, as well as the items of luxury she found in Mika's room.

Chapter Four

ZEALOTS

A NIGHT FILLED WITH uneasy dozing gave way to a stiff morning and a foot pressed into Regina's shoulder.

"Up and at'em, princess," a voice said. How could it be morning if there wasn't enough light to see the person's face?

When she didn't immediately get up, the woman standing over her grabbed her by the rags and lifted her up, then dusted her off in a convivial way.

"There we go, Raggy. Ready for your initiation?"

"I haven't agreed to anything. I'm your prisoner. ...Right?"

The woman only turned Regina around and pushed her towards the herd of Brass Bulls. They spoke conversationally in small groups. Some sneered at her arrival.

Regina rubbed her hand against her face where Vela had struck and shuddered at the memory of the wet lick that followed.

"Don't be a baby, Raggy. Showing weakness will get you killed down here, and we won't interfere if someone challenges you," her guide said. "Hide that shit."

Regina lowered her hand and took in her surroundings. Braziers and candles illuminated the space, a hollowed-out section of a tower foot. A giant slab of concrete blocked the entrance of the stairway to the Upcity, crushing the flight so no one could climb or get around it. A small folding table in the center of the room bore plates of food scraps and rotisserie rats.

A dry heave escaped, even as she tried to hold it back. The Bulls' sneers turned to flat-out disgust and their rumblings against her presence grew. Regina shrank into herself, hating the intense scrutiny of the bloodthirsty trash cans.

The one she remembered as Ezzie, recognizable for her short stature compared to Vela and Brace, grabbed a rat and a handful of food and brought it to Regina, thrusting them at Regina's chest when she wouldn't take them.

"We know you're too good for this, princess, but it's a goddamn feast to us. Eat before I give you a *real* reason to get plastic surgery."

Except for the rat, the food was indistinguishable. All she could identify among the mass in the dim light were bite marks...

"The fuck are you worried about, huh? All you Upcity assholes have your teeth cleaned every day, don't you? Where do you think this came from?"

Regina took the food (and the rat by the tail), if only so Ezzie would leave her alone, but she stood with her arms crossed, waiting for Regina to eat.

"The rats are checked, Raggy," her guide said. "You won't get a disease from them."

"I'm... I'm a vegetarian," Regina lied.

"For fuck's sake, you goddamn baby," Ezzie fumed, then snatched the rat away and tore into it as she made her way back to the leaders.

Regina regarded the unappetizing handful, realizing the Bulls weren't going to stop staring at her until she took a bite. Gingerly she brought the least mushy piece to her lips and bit down. It wasn't as bad as expected, which kept her from heaving, until the light from the nearest brazier glinted off a long hair, revealed from within the part she'd bitten off.

Instead of getting angry at her for spitting it out and dropping the food, the Bulls laughed and turned their attention away from her at last. The woman to her side picked up the scraps and ate them like it was nothing.

"There— There's a fucking hair in that!" Regina said.

"Mm. So? Probably came from some pretty Upcity bitch, yeah? Maybe it's even one of yours. Why are you so grossed out by your own kind?"

"That's not—"

Brace called attention to the room. Flanking her were Vela and Ezzie, and the one they called Rina stood slightly off to the side.

"Good morning, ladies. Recruiters, we need you to venture into the other sectors. I want bad bitches capable of knocking people on their asses. Stay away from Sector D for now, the Crystal Crackers are losing ground to the males over there and it's getting more violent than usual. I want to see which of them are still standing before we bring them to our side."

A quarter of the women nodded and left.

"Vela needs some volunteers to deal with the males trying to grow a pair over *here*. There's only five of them attempting to reform after the last time we fucked them up. There'd better be zero by tonight."

Half the remaining Bulls raised their hands. Vela picked out a dozen, seemingly at random, and they left the building.

"Ezzie has volunteered to keep the clinic-to-Elevator street cleared for the Doctors. Remember they toss out pills on their way home—get as many as you can, and *don't* bother them during their shift." Brace gave the crowd a look of warning, then Ezzie took half of the remaining Bulls.

"It's Rina's week to gather supplies. Word is the drop will happen in five hours. Get those fucking plugs, ladies; I don't care who you have to knock over to get them."

Almost all the others followed Rina out. Regina assumed gang life would be different in the Underfoot, she just didn't know it was going to be so violent. The worst the Ruby Riders had to deal with was an occasional slap from a lieutenant for insubordination—rare enough on its own. She'd only ever witnessed four slaps; one was for her, from their leader when they'd convened after their scheduled round of plastic surgeries and Regina hadn't complied. For her disobedience, she'd also been tasked with "guarding their territory" while they shopped for their new leather jackets, simply taking down Regina's measurements and shoving it towards her when they got back—just like Ezzie had begrudgingly given her food a few minutes before.

"For the rest of you, we're taking these initiates to Sally's unveiling."

Regina noticed there were some youngish women without patches standing around, a Bull close to each of them. The woman to Regina's side clasped her hands and stamped her feet in a giddy delight.

"What? What does that mean?" Regina asked.

"I can't believe Brace approved. I thought she'd reject the idea out of hand."

"You're Sally?"

She only nodded, then ran to thank Brace. She left the building right after.

"Come on, virgin," Brace called to Regina. Apparently Brace would be her Bull escort. Regina wasn't sure if the special interest Brace seemed to be taking in her was a good thing or not...

Regina took a few hesitant steps towards the building's exit, eager to get away from the reek of the place for the only slightly-more-bearable smell outside.

"Where are you going, Rag Doll? Over *here*."

The rest of the room converged to Brace by the food table.

"You babies take this leftover food and pass it out to the gangless."

Regina regretted her wish to leave—the people outside smelled worse than the Bulls' headquarters. Were none of them using the cleansing wipes? Her private school always made such a big deal out of their monetary donations going towards the supply crates to the Underfoot. Why had she given away her money if they weren't even going to *use* the supplies she bought for them? She could have saved that money to get the surgeries she needed! Or at least a cute wrap for her steering wheel to make her parents' regrettable choice of the car they'd gifted her for her sixteenth birthday a *little* snazzier.

Though none of the trash cans in the streets stared at her underwear exposed through the rags, Regina blushed the entire time she went back and forth from the building to drop off food. The relatively low light provided good-enough cover, but the heavy, humid air licking her skin was uncomfortable, to say the least.

"Alright, good work, rookies," Brace said. "Let's head out."

Regina followed closely behind Brace as she led them on a long walk through the streets. She couldn't believe the fear and respect the Bulls inspired as they moved among the populace. No one ever backed away from the Ruby Riders. In fact, they often gravitated to their beauty and style, wishing to join, wanting to fuck, whining to hang around their superior presence.

She especially envied all the extra attention her sisters received from the Idle Batemans, once their surgeries healed. They were guaranteed protection and money if they made the right connections. The surgeries helped hook them up while they were young, ensuring financial stability so the Riders could focus on their gang activities and other hobbies.

Regina painted for her main talent. She often stared out her bedroom window at the expanse of trees that covered as far as the eye could see outside of the megalopolis. She brought out the shapes in the canopies with her brush. Whenever she visited one of her higher-up sisters in the towers she brought along her supplies to capture the distant megalopolises from a new vantage point.

She long suspected one of the only reasons their leader kept her around after the surgery issue was for her skills as a portrait artist. She'd painted each of her sisters, and they displayed them with pride in their homes alongside their wealthy parents' extravagant paintings. Regina hoped to someday be the caliber of artist that everyone's *parents* would hire to adorn their mantlepieces—paid work, not just favors.

Something Regina noticed as she followed the Bulls was the lack of artwork, at least what she could see near the braziers. Evidence of past art was ancient and indistinguishable, or graffitied over long ago, before spray paint supplies disappeared.

"You're quiet," Brace said, startling Regina out of her thoughts. "I like that, but it also makes it hard to trust you."

"Why do you need to trust a prisoner?"

"Don't pretend you aren't drawn to my gang, princess."

"As soon as you let me go, I'm history."

"I let you go last night. It's not my fault you can't navigate for shit down here. You want to take off? Go ahead."

Regina hadn't considered she could have left at any point, but it was a humbling remark—go where? She had no idea of the street patterns. The tower feet were unidentifiable. If she saw the Elevators she'd bolt for them, but what if they were miles away? It already seemed like they'd been walking that long...

"When are you going to escort me back to the Elevators, like the other two?"

"When I think you've learned enough about life down here. Maybe you can convince the Upcity to send better, more plentiful supplies. Maybe you'll warn people up there to stop treating us like a tourist attraction. Maybe you can put in a word at the hospitals to send more volunteers."

"I don't have any contacts for that kind of—"

"Contacts are everything. Cultivate them. Cherish them. Never betray them. You never know when a contact could save your life, alert you to danger, cause a mis-shipment *here*, a strategic assassination *there*. Contacts in the Upcity are worth a hundred supply crates."

"You... You expect me to be your Upcity contact?"

"Don't flatter yourself, sweetheart. You'd be one of many. Doesn't mean I can count on all of them. Only a couple are really useful—the ones I know actually *care*, outside of any monetary gain. And for that, all I can do is show you my world. You can do with it what you will."

Regina couldn't help feeling a little flattered, regardless. That was a level of trust and responsibility she still hadn't earned in the Riders, despite her tenure and how well-liked she was with most of her sisters. Her interest piqued in Brace.

"Why do they call you 'Brace?'"

"Because you'll have to when you enter my nest."

Regina sucked in air and nodded, then looked away. She supposed it made sense there would be a lesbian or two in a gang of women, but it was strictly forbidden in the Upcity, gang or no.

"I saw that. They don't like it down here, either. Religious zealots are one of the only organized groups in the Underfoot that isn't a gang, though they operate like one. They're the reason we're going to this unveiling."

"What do you mean?"

Brace nodded ahead to Sally standing in front of a blanket hanging above a brazier. A crowd of people stood around it in a semi-circle. That cop that didn't help the night before stood by her side, swinging his electric baton with his other hand on top of a holstered electric gun.

Regina supposed there wasn't much to get excited by in the Underfoot. It was the largest gathering of people she'd ever seen outside of a baseball stadium, but she couldn't imagine what Sally could have done to bring such a crowd. As they got closer, though, she recognized the gigantic smile on Sally's face—the smile of someone who would soon be perceived; her soul laid bare for all to gawk at. Regina felt similarly when she'd presented a portrait of her favorite celebrity to her class in elementary school.

The expression looked so goofy and lame on a woman as old as Sally—early to mid-twenties, most likely. If she were a true artist, she would have been trained early, most likely starting in kindergarten when washable paints would be made available from—

Regina shook her head. That line of thinking was ridiculous. These trash cans had no education system, no art supplies, no... Was this why Brace brought Regina here? So she'd lobby for art supplies to be included in the crates? What good was art down here? They clearly didn't value it when they let it get torn up, discarded, and tagged. It would be yet *another* waste of money. The kids would probably eat the paint, and they'd break down the canvases for their braziers or torches.

Brace instructed the rookies to stand with their backs to the blanket. Regina wanted to see the unveiling, but Brace turned her firmly in place, then went down the line, whispering in each of the girls' ears. She ended on Regina.

"You stand here and protect this with everything you've got. If you get knocked on your ass, you're out. If you hit anyone back, you're out. If you react, *their* agenda wins. Let our cop friend handle the aggressors."

"Why would there be aggress—"

The blanket tickled the back of Regina's neck with a whoosh. She watched the sea of eyes take in the sight behind her, whatever it was. There were nods, neutral faces, smiles, frowns, anger, shocked eyes; whatever Sally had done inspired a wide range of emotions. Regina remembered her first unveiling, met by robotic applause from the whole class, like they were instructed to applaud no matter what. When she thought harder about it, wasn't that the same reaction—same rhythm of disinterest—that so many of her Ruby Rider sisters had to their portraits?

Most of the onlookers clapped and cheered, which made the angry faces stand out starkly. Regina could see they meant to *show* their anger. The mass lurched forward, pushed by the furious. The good among them tempered the surge by grabbing and pulling their rags. Soon fists flew in the crowd. The cop kept his ground, but pulled out the electric gun.

Regina took the moment before chaos fully broke loose to look over her shoulder. Sally beamed next to a canvas of patched-together white rags, and an ugly amalgamation of various media—yarn, string, grease, charcoal, blood, colored textiles too small and useless for anything else. The portrait explicitly depicted two women in congress. It was hard to tell who they were—neither of them looked like any of the Bulls, but with the poor rendering, they could have been anyone.

It was hideous, like a four-year-old had been given the technical ability to *do it* but the lack of artistic skill showed their true age. Regina squinted, hoping she was only missing details in the low light, but no, it was just...awful! Who did Sally think she was, smiling next to an abomination like that? Had she no shame?

A wet splat met the canvas, followed by another. The cop grew agitated for the first time.

"Hey! That's a waste of food, you ingrates!"

Sally's smile melted, and Brace's face morphed to a sneer. Regina followed the murder in Brace's eyes to find a group of zealots pushing forward through the crowd. They were too close already. One punched an initiate on the other side of the semi-circle and she landed square on her back. Brace moved to help her up, but the initiate rose and plugged the hole before she got there. Brace backed up with a little nod.

Blows landed against the semi-circle. Regina reluctantly hooked her elbows with the other initiates to strengthen the line. More foodstuffs flew over her head, but Regina couldn't hear the splats for the zealots screaming in her face, pointing, spitting, pushing... She took a strike in the stomach that would have brought her to her knees if she hadn't been linked in the chain. Once she'd straightened back up, she had a strong urge to bite off the finger of an old hag, wagging it way too close to her face.

A far more aggressive man pushed the old woman aside and punched Regina in the forehead. Sparkles of light flitted before her eyes. The chain held her up. All across the line, others received blows.

The idiot cop finally started poking people with his electric club from over the initiates' shoulders. He began on the other side, though. Regina absorbed more hits than she'd ever thought she could handle, before he managed to poke his way over to her side so people backed up.

A hunk of something splatted into her hair. It was cold and actually felt better than the throbbing heat of her forehead as it dripped onto her face. A torch flew above their heads and landed against the canvas. It didn't catch fire, but it caused the corner of the canvas to disconnect from a tie and swing down into the brazier, which greedily devoured it in a manner of seconds.

Regina expected Sally to be a pool of tears. Surprisingly, although her smile had disappeared, Sally gathered her poise and drew her lips into a hard line as severe as Brace's. Another cop arrived from a side street and joined in the crowd control. Brace led the initiates to help the people that had fallen down in the scrum outside of the circle. A few yelled epithets at Sally while they turned tail. One tried to strike

Brace, but she leveled him with a short punch from her hip, shocking in its speed and power.

Regina hoped that the victim was one of the assholes who punched her. Despite her best efforts to remain detached and keep escape to the Elevators as her top priority, there was an unfamiliar feeling stirring within her. Was it just satisfaction, seeing the damage she suffered redistributed? Or was it something vicarious?

Chapter Five

MOTHER

SABRINA ENTERED HEADQUARTERS WITH her arms full of supplies and laid them all on the table along with her volunteers' spoils. On the way back from the drop zone, Sabrina strategically let certain objects drop at the feet of people who needed them.

Vela approached, wearing some nasty bruises on her face from her fight with the men. She'd likely taken all five on at the same time, Sabrina reasoned. Vela was like that. She huffed her disappointment at Sabrina's pile. Sabrina ignored her and brought cleansing wipes to some of the rookies who'd suffered the worst of whatever happened at Sally's unveiling.

Brace yelled at everyone to shut up and gather around the line of initiates. She went around clapping them on the backs and congratulating them on protecting their future sister, Sally, until she came upon one in particular. She stopped in front of the initiate and dropped her head sadly.

"Bridgette, I admire you for standing right back up in line when you got knocked down, but I need people that can *withstand* any punch. You need to start the initiation again, but I want you to practice with Vela."

"No, Brace," Sabrina said, stepping forward, quite aware of Vela's hard stare. "I'll train her."

Brace squinted. She hadn't really seen Sabrina that day except in quick passing. Her intense gaze settled on Sabrina's black eye.

"Hmmph. *There's* a sister that can take a hit. Alright, shadow Rina. You'd better be ready for the next initiation, runt. You'll only get one more chance."

Brace was about to dismiss them when Vela unexpectedly strutted from around the table to Sabrina.

"I pray, tell us how you earned that black eye, Rina. Are we to believe you suffered it at the hands of those weaklings in the street? Or was it someone worse? Like a pink pussy, weaker than our Raggy over there?"

Sabrina straightened her back, ready for Vela to test her.

"Hey!" one of the two Bulls that had run the errand with Sabrina piped up. "Vela, I *told* you those were *sucker* punches. The bitch had no honor! Sabrina didn't fuckin' *flinch!*"

"Yeah? Maybe she'll take—"

Before Vela could get in her own sucker punch, Brace materialized between the two of them and grabbed Vela's fist out of the air.

"All that adrenaline from fucking up the men is still coursing through you, I see. Go to my nest and I'll leech it out of you."

Vela gave Brace a quick, devilish smile, scowled at Sabrina, then stormed over to the section where Brace slept. Brace turned and put her hand on Sabrina's cheek, comforting but all too brief as she let go to circle the room, congratulating and thanking everyone for the day's hard, painful work.

The failed initiate gravitated to Sabrina, who tested the rookie's stance and strength immediately with a little shove of the elbow. She caught herself mid-stumble, then stood respectfully next to her like it had been *her* accident. Sabrina smiled and put her hand on the woman's shoulder.

Brace dismissed everyone. Sally broke free and ran out of the building before anyone else. Brace caught Sabrina before she could follow.

"Hey, Rina, take Raggy with you. She would have fallen, too, if it wasn't for the linked chain."

Sabrina nodded and left the building, only slightly aware of the two initiates trailing her. They weren't important at the moment. Two blocks away, Sally had a little nook in a building that she'd used to create her artwork. They found her huddled into herself rocking on the balls of her feet, shaking and sobbing.

Sabrina put her back against the wall and slid down to a seated position next to Sally. She stroked Sally's warm, sweaty back.

"Get away, I don't have anything."

"It's just me, Silly."

Sally sniffed without looking up.

"I don't like that nickname anymore, Rina. You're making fun of me like everyone else does..."

Sabrina grabbed Sally's shoulders and guided her into an embrace. Sally sobbed and clutched Sabrina's shirt. Bridgette lowered herself in front and put her hand on Sally's shoulder. Raggy stood off to the side, hugging her arms, still overwhelmed by the new environs.

"I thought it was pretty," Bridgette said.

"You didn't even see it, runt." Sally frowned.

"No, but I saw your smile. It must have been pretty—to make you so happy."

Sally snorted in spite of herself, but her quick smile fell away again as she shook.

"You don't get anything for rubbing shit on your nose, Bridgette," Sabrina whispered. "You still have to withstand a punch. But I'll make sure you pass the next initiation. You can go home."

"Where's that?"

It was Sabrina's turn to laugh. "Good point. I meant head-quarters. Brace will let you sleep with us until the next initiation. Go on, I'll see you in the morning."

Bridgette left and Sabrina ran her hand over Sally's forehead, pushing hair out of her face.

"What did it look like, Silly?"

"I said—"

"I heard you. You don't get to choose your nickname. Tell me what you made."

Sally hesitated, then pushed up and sat next to Sabrina's side now that she'd calmed a bit.

"It was nothing special."

"Tch!" Raggy had a look of disgust while emitting the sound. Sabrina looked up at the Upcity citizen with silent anger. Clearly Raggy thought she was outside of earshot, as she cleared her throat and took a few steps away in evident shame.

"Fuckin' rookies." Sally laughed; it was such a pleasant sound after all the sobbing. Crying could get one kicked out of the Bulls. Any other lieutenant witnessing such a display would make sure of it. Only Sabrina kept their secret shames—their broken bursts, their momentary lapses—locked up in her heart. She wasn't blind to the way so many looked up to her, or how Vela and Ezzie noticed the same and couldn't wait to find a reason to get her exiled. All they had to do was knock her on her ass, but they never managed it, and every beaten attempt brought Sabrina closer to Brace in terms of respect.

Sabrina imagined that if she *wanted* any sort of power, it would be relatively easy. The women responded to her love and toughness better than the fear that Vela and Ezzie inspired. Brace somehow managed their three clashing forces expertly. Sabrina respected Brace's strategic leadership, and even though they needed Vela's strength, she hoped one day Vela would be disgraced and exiled.

If Vela and Ezzie weren't in the equation, Sabrina wouldn't be looking to join Olive. She would plead for mercy for Brace once the Denim Demons had conquered their way through the sectors to theirs. She would protect as many Bulls as she could. That wouldn't be so hard, at least from the rumors. Olive was love personified—never killing, always sharing, teaching, helping all regardless of their status, gang or no.

If anyone was to ever negotiate with the Upcity to allow people to move up from the Underfoot, it would be Olive, not Brace.

"Hey Raggy, get your ass over here." Sabrina gestured for her to sit down.

She took small steps, reluctant. Tired of waiting, Sabrina yanked on her rags to force her to sit in front of them.

"You ever tell anyone—" Sally began to threaten.

"She won't, Silly. This one knows true loyalty. Didn't you see her yesterday save those other two? What a brave sister she'd be, if she could only take a punch."

Raggy stared at her lap, not expecting a compliment after being talked to so roughly a second before.

"I took several hits today—"

"Not without the link," Sally said. "You think Brace was the only one watching? We all watch out for each other... Even when our world is crashing down around us..."

Sally sniffed again and Sabrina rubbed her shoulder.

"Stop crying, Bull. What did you think of the artwork, Raggy?"

"Could you not call me that?"

"Gotta earn a nickname. If you don't like that one, do something besides walk around like that. I can't believe you didn't take the time to sew up some patches last night."

"Sew?"

"For fuck's sake..." Sabrina chuckled, causing Sally to laugh again.

"What the hell's it like up there, Raggy?" Sally asked, pointing at the concrete blocking their view of the megalopolis above.

"I... I don't know how to answer that... Like, it's light, at least..."

"We know what light is, asshole. I'll show you tomorrow," Sally huffed, but there was still a smile on her face.

"I mean, even at night. We have lights in our homes. There are headlights from the vehicles flying endlessly along the layers of highways."

"Why do you people throw so much shit into the nets? Don't get me wrong, it's better than rat, but I don't *get it*."

"...We're told that everything in the nets is recycled or reused. It's cheaper than what they charge to pick up refuse from bins. I don't know. I don't make the rules. Why pay for something we don't have to?"

"If you go back, can you throw out some stuff that isn't half-eaten? Maybe some other *fancy* stuff? Like nail clippers?"

"Goddamn, you see a kid score a nice find and now it's all you want. Our nails are fine," Sabrina said and mussed up Sally's hair.

Raggy seemed pensive, like she wanted to say something, but thought better of it.

"What is it?" Sabrina prodded.

"Would... Maybe... I could get you some art supplies..."

"That's sweet, but after today," Sally shook her head, "fuck art."

"No! You can't give up just because of that! Didn't you hear the cheers in the beginning? Just because *I* wouldn't have painted two wo—"

"Shh!" Sally cut Raggy off. "It's not important what it was. Anyway, it's not about that. Other people got hurt because of me..."

"Wow, it was *that* powerful?" Sabrina whistled.

A Bull, only two years into her tenure, approached their huddle from the street. Sabrina didn't know this one as well as the others, because she gravitated to Vela. She flashed their gang sign, to which Sally and Sabrina responded in kind.

"Heyo, Rina, Sally. Either of you take dibs on Raggy?"

Raggy hunched her shoulders and hid her expression. Sabrina didn't blame her.

"Doesn't work like that, Erin. You need to *ask* first."

"Not according to Vela..." Erin muttered.

"Yeah? Tell Vela to say that to my face. In the meantime, ask, then be on your way."

"Hey Raggy. You like women?" Erin prepped her hair with a little palm push, and pulled down on the bottom of her rag shirt so Raggy could assess her chest size. At least she tried words first, instead of violence.

"Nuh... No..." Raggy said, too quiet for Erin to hear.

"Come on, look at me, rookie. I'm really good in the nest, Vela says so. And for an Upcity girl, I'll be *really* generous."

Sabrina covered her mouth. Erin was indeed cute, at least in so far as she kept her face clean with wipes daily. Sabrina touched Raggy's foot and pointed for her to address Erin again, properly. She peered up quickly and back.

"I don't like girls," she answered at a higher volume.

"Fuck." Erin dropped the pose and her shoulders slumped. "What about you, Sall—"

"Me neither, Erin. Sorry."

"But, Brace said... Your art!"

"It wasn't about *that*. I just made it for... Alright, fine! I made it for Rina! It wasn't meant to be sexual, though. It was... It was just about *love*, is all..."

Erin blinked a few times.

"Well, *Rina*, are you going to just sit there, acting like this doesn't turn you on? Hmm?" Erin exaggerated an aggravated pose of sensuality. Sabrina burst out laughing, which made Sally and even Erin chuckle.

"Is Vela busy? Why don't you just stay with her tonight?"

"She's fuckin' Brace right now. She almost punched me when I asked to join… Don't know why, it wouldn't be the first time. Maybe because it was with Brace?"

Sabrina whistled again. She pointed at Erin for effect when Raggy cringed.

"Another brave sister. I'd fight side by side with you any day, Erin. But maybe tonight have a date with your fingers, and try the new recruits next week? I heard the recruiters bragging about a big haul."

Erin waved her hands as if to discount all that, since she was horny *now*. But she smiled and flashed their sign before walking away.

"Are you all so fucking crude all the time?" Raggy whined.

"Why, who's listening?" Sally smiled and gesticulated.

Satisfied with Sally's change in demeanor, Sabrina shimmied up the wall. She helped Sally up and hugged her. Sally signed off and left for her nest. Raggy looked up expectantly, but Sabrina didn't indulge her, crossing her arms instead. Raggy sighed and climbed onto her feet.

"Suppose one has to earn manners here, like anything else."

"Earning is so much more gratifying than having things handed to you."

"I'm not in the mood for a life lesson."

"No, but maybe you're in the mood for something cold to hold against your face? You're swelling up."

"I can take care of myself."

"Not down here, you can't, princess."

Sabrina clapped her hand harder than necessary on Raggy's shoulder and guided her towards a sparsely populated alleyway.

"Would you all stop calling me that?"

"Stop calling you 'Raggy,' stop calling you 'princess.' Acquire the guts to say that to everyone at headquarters and you might get somewhere. Careful that your nickname doesn't become Whiner."

Raggy jerked her shoulder out of Sabrina's guiding grasp and walked ahead a few paces out of reach.

"I said I don't like girls. I don't want you touching me like that…"

"I was only… Okay. Fine. *Good*. Set your boundaries early, speak with your whole chest. Brace will respect that."

"I don't care what Brace thinks about me."

"Oh yeah? Be thankful *she's* taken you under her wing; that it wasn't Vela or Ezzie."

"Where are we going?"

Sabrina skipped ahead, exaggerating that nothing bothered her. She brought Raggy to a line of pipes behind some rusty sheet metal. Wrapping rags around her hands to avoid a deadly cut, she carefully moved the metal away.

"There aren't many pipes in our sector that run cold, but two of these do."

"Which ones?"

"You want that handed to you, too? A child would have figured it out by now."

Raggy found the correct ones after a few mistakes and hisses. Without asking what to do, she leaned her face against the cold. Sabrina did the same for her black eye on the other pipe.

"*Our* gang's 'mother' figure is second in command," Raggy said while she rolled her face on the cool relief.

Sabrina closed her eyes. Raggy hadn't earned any sort of explanation for the way things were in the Brass Bulls, but it didn't stop her from thinking about how Vela jumped ahead of Ezzie and Sabrina during yearly promotions. Ezzie wasn't as disappointed—the two's work was violent and any day could bring a natural promotion; being number three wasn't as bad as number four.

Brace valued Sabrina's opinions when it came to gang business, but her voice was usually ignored or smothered by the other two.

In the Denim Demons, every voice was important. Olive listened before she made decisions. She would see Sabrina's dedication and smarts, and instead of exploiting her, she'd be valued and heard.

Chapter Six

GHOSTS

OTHER THAN DRY BLINKS, Olive's eyes hadn't closed for hours. She slapped her own face twice and sat up, arching her legs over the rim of old blankets in their nest. Olive scratched her scalp as she ran fingers through her hair. Twill stirred and groped for Olive to come back. Her nail caught in Olive's armpit hair and Olive yanked away her torso with a wince; the cost of not deserving to be touched.

"It was the right decision, Li—Olive. Come to sleep."

"Why didn't I see the fucking grey area?" Olive's tongue scraped against her chapped lips. She reached for a bottle of wine and swished it around.

"Mika threatened the Demons the entire way to her fate. So did the other one. They would have come after you. They could have been the ones to break us..."

"Maybe so. What if I'd made that decision before taking *your* gang? Huh, Twill? Would you be happy with my black and white decision *then?*"

"This was *our* decision."

"Fuck that. *My* words are what matter. It was *my* decision."

Olive again pulled away from Twill's probing fingers and stood up. She grabbed the bottle and left without covering her body or answering Twill's protests. Demons filled the temporary headquarters near capacity, old and new members, sleeping, or rustling together quietly so as not to disturb their neighbors.

She took another swig and stepped around them carefully, since the candles had been dowsed at nest-time. She stepped outside to take in the humid air on her freshly-wiped skin. A few gangless looked her up and down in their slow passing but didn't dare get close to her. It was impossible to tell a person's mental state in the Underfoot, and an unfamiliar naked woman with a glass bottle wasn't anyone *she'd* approach without protection.

She ran a hand over herself in the low light, disturbed by how similar her body was to Mika's lover—slightly better fed than their sisters, so their ribcages didn't stick out quite so prominently; their shoulders carried more confidence; their face crinkles from smiling so often; even the little trail of hair from their navels, left a little more unkempt, but luscious. Olive still marveled at the detail Mika had conjured from her *blood*.

In a way, the Denim Demons were built upon Olive's bloodshed, and she often bled so they wouldn't have to. Until Twill came along, she took part in the duels and all the singular challenges across a battlefield without hesitation. An enforcer hadn't been needed because of the relative poor condition of the other gangs and their leaders. Was it needed now?

She took another drink and leaned back on the wall in front of a brazier. A hunched, rag-covered mass approached, unrushed in their gait. Olive's eyes followed the silent worker as they deposited a chemically-enhanced log into the brazier, then shuffled to the next one.

Such a simple existence... What drove them? They were given lighters and the wood supply by the government to keep the Underfoot lit. Beyond that, her contacts in the Upcity never elaborated on whatever agreement they had with the workers. Credits had no value at the base of the towers—there were no electronics to keep them, disperse them, or use them.

As the log burned, the space became hotter. A slick sweat beaded along Olive's skin. The wine began its muddy work in her mind. The portrait of Mika's beautiful, loyal lover wouldn't leave her thoughts. Her fingers traced along her upper leg, against the edge of hair, and she quivered despite the heat in front of her.

On the way back to the nest, she stumbled too close to some of the Demons. She ran her hand over their precious heads to lull them back to sleep. One couple peeked out from their rags and offered her shelter in their nest, but she only patted their hands and moved on, back to Twill.

Olive licked the back of Twill's salty neck and kissed along her collar to her shoulder. She expected Twill not to react as quickly as she would otherwise, especially with the way she'd left things, but the wine made Olive a little more insistent than usual. She kissed Twill's back, to the crease of her armpit. Her head dug and lifted the arm, the hair beneath tickling her nose as her lips traveled around to Twill's breast. Twill finally stopped pretending to resist and lifted Olive's mouth to hers. Olive took a swig of wine and shared it, their lips pressed tight to seal any spillage.

Twill's fingers journeyed with haste to Olive's spread legs. Their lips brushed each other's between their hot breaths passing back and forth.

"Twill," Olive breathed, "no...more killing..."

Twill didn't waver in her work. "It may not always be a choice..."

"We...*always* have a...choice."

Twill expertly edged Olive along. Olive bit into Twill's neck, apologizing to the skin with her tongue, only to repeat it again like an abusive lover. She clamped her lips and shud-dered.

Olive tipped the wine bottle to Twill's lips, then shifted in the nest to reciprocate.

THEY SPENT THE NEXT day stabilizing the sector and placating the men. Olive did her duty in that department as well as on the battlefield—seeing to the leader before and after nego-tiations for their gangs to co-exist.

Negotiations didn't end one sector at a time. Olive had to recruit the best-looking Demons to backtrack to previous-ly conquered sectors and make sure the men didn't break their promises. The Demons typically swept through a sec-tor, then utilized the converts to protect the newly-acquired territory. Olive worked it out with her Upcity contacts to add a new monthly drop zone to that sector, and left one Demon officer behind to keep the sector in line and oversee the distribution of spoils.

That evening Olive ventured to the newly-conquered sec-tor's Elevators under a cover of rags and waited for her con-tact to arrive along with the Doctor shift change. The contact wore an olive-colored set of scrubs as a signal that could only be seen close to the lights of the Elevators. Olive followed the procession, maintained by police officers and volunteer former-Thorns. They'd grumbled at the demeaning task but it didn't take much coercion when Olive promised a small square of chocolate once they returned to headquarters.

The olive-scrubbed Doctor gave a quick scan of the area around the Clinic tents. If Olive didn't get her attention at that moment the Doctor wouldn't come out again until the end of her shift, and if she missed her then, it could be a week before they returned.

Olive pulled a set of jeans from her overly-ragged ensemble and held them up for the contact to see the name stitched on the seat. The Doctor noticed, nodded, and held up seven fingers, meaning Olive had to allow seven people into the Clinic before crawling beneath the tent's back flap. The contacts were terrified of showing preferential treatment in front of the officers. They never elaborated with Olive *why*, only to say the government didn't take kindly to their resources being used more than the barest minimum.

After seven patients entered and exited the tent, Olive slid under the back and immediately pulled off all her clothing. The Doctor ran her hands over vital areas and did a fast checkup since she was using her breaktime to create a lull in clients.

"Should I tell them to make this sector a regular stop?"

"Yes, please. We'll move on to the next one very soon."

"Before I came down here today, I overheard that the med service lost a vehicle and they can't track it. That usually means it crashed out in the Forest, or in the Underfoot. Keep an eye out for it."

"Is there a reward for finding it?"

"Of course not. At least not for you. But if I nudge an officer to a potential crash site, I could get an extra day off for my assistance."

"Well, that doesn't really give *me* much of an incentive..."

"What would you do with *time off?* All you people do is exist down here. Imagine not having to go to a fucking job every day..."

"Yes... Imagine that..."

"Anyway, nothing says the *contents* of that vehicle have to be returned..."

"Ahh. You could have just said that instead of bringing the attitude—"

The Doctor's prodding turned painful. Olive took it in silence. Some of her contacts got off on their power over the Underfoot, even when they weren't that many levels up in the Elevators themselves.

"You're as healthy as someone down here can be. I can give you five pills and a swat on the ass on your way out."

"This turned feisty on a nail's head. Give me the pills."

Olive dressed and crawled out. She passed the pills to five teenage girls on her way back to headquarters, making sure they saw her face. She told them to hang around the edges of any woman they saw wearing jeans if they hoped for a better life, and if they asked nicely they could get a free plug from their matron.

After meeting up with Twill, she passed word to her relay network to be on the lookout for any crashed vehicles. Olive found it hard to believe a crash would go unnoticed or un-gossiped about, but if it had only been the night before, the Demons had time to pounce on it.

"If you really want to find it first, we should search tonight," Twill said.

Olive didn't sleep at all the night before. After she'd taken care of Twill she simply went back to sweating on her side of the nest, eyes wide open as that poor woman's face hovered a few feet away, translucent but unmistakable. Twill had slept much better, and if the day before hadn't happened, Olive would trust Twill one-hundred-percent with carrying out the task.

It was still secondary to the murder Olive had greenlit, but she had lost trust in her closest ally and most satisfying lover she'd ever had. The fact that it wasn't technically even Twill's fault further haunted Olive's conscience. Twill was just doing what she'd been ordered to. The lack of remorse she showed, though...

Olive enlisted a dozen women who claimed to be well-rested and they set off in pairs to find the downed vehicle. If Twill was bothered by not being paired with Olive, she didn't show it.

Olive passed the time searching with Senna, a Demon recruited a sector only a couple before the current one. She asked about life in her previous gang and what she thought of the Demons so far. The woman was as starry-eyed as most of them whenever they got to spend time alone with the boss. The ones that seemed unimpressed with her were the ones Olive found *most* useful.

They searched for hours, asking questions of the wanderers who moved between sectors. A promising lead led them back to Senna's original territory. Olive thought that fortuitous and she was a little excited to potentially get to the vehicle first. Although others would hide the best of what they found and pretend like it was untouched, Olive only wanted to get there first so she could reward her gang properly, equitably. Jealousy would never be stamped out, but in a pseudo-meritocracy, it could be tempered.

A crowd of people gathered up a side street. Olive filtered through the side to find a group of Demons assigned to the sector standing around a car. The scavengers had already repaired the netting above, and no one dared touch the car or its occupants for fear of what Upcity folk could do to them—people who weren't even considered citizens in the government's eyes.

Olive approached the car, her worry increasing from the smoke rising from the point of impact with the street. A middle-aged man slumped in the driver's seat, his face covered with streams of blood. A woman about Olive's age frantically spoke into a little square in her hand and shook the man's shoulder with the other.

The woman saw Olive and leaned out of the broken window.

"Stay away, trash can! Like I told the rest of you, you touch us and our company will see to it you get dropped from the highest tower!"

"I'm just making sure you're okay, miss. Where there's smoke, there's likely to be—"

"You don't know shit about cars, dirt magnet. Once my alert goes through, you all better be gone!"

"I'm not going to hurt you. There's no frequency down here. Can we just move you over to the side, out of the wreck? My gang will protect you, I promise."

"You trash don't care about us, you just want our stuff. Stay the *fuck* back! My daddy will have you hunted down if you touch me."

Olive put her hands up. "Is that your daddy? Is he alive?"

"No, he's just a trainer. I think he had a heart attack…"

More than the brat being pulled to safety, Olive *did* want to remove the contents of the crashed vehicle before the whole thing burned up. She motioned for the Demons to surround the car.

"Hey! What did I say? They'll kill you all if you take one step closer!"

Olive also motioned for a little crowd control, to keep the unpredictable gangless away. The woman couldn't do anything, but Olive didn't want to make her harrowing experience any more nightmarish if she could help it.

The woman's squeals of protest echoed through the street as Demons converged and pulled her out of the car. The rest of them covered the vehicle like ants, searching for valuables of any kind. All the electronics were ignored—without electricity in the Underfoot they were useless, and batteries were non-existent but for the ones installed in the flashlights gifted by the Upcity, which were designed to serve *only* that purpose.

The woman screamed, but they were far enough away from the Elevators that no police officer would hear her. Still, a small, petty satisfaction spiked in Olive as she put her hand over the woman's mouth. It was plain in her eyes that she thought Olive's "dirty hand" was more dangerous than the crash she'd endured.

The Demons dragged out the man and confirmed he showed no signs of life, then they stripped off his personal belongings and clothing and piled it all neatly to the side. One of the Demons brought his identification to Olive and she looked it over with her flashlight.

"Here, sweetheart," Olive said as she slipped the ID into the woman's pocket. "Would you stop fighting? We're not going to hurt you. What's the code to get into that trunk?"

The woman shook her head defiantly.

"We can get into it without the code. Cutting through the backseat is easy enough. I'm just trying to save time before that fire spreads."

"You trash don't deserve what's in there."

Olive snapped her fingers for the Demons to tear through the back.

"How do you know anything about—" the woman started-ed.

"It's not the only vehicle I've come across. What's in there, Senna?"

Senna stuck her head in the back of the vehicle and talked to the Demon squirming into the trunk area, then relayed back that it was medical supplies.

"That explains why the Doctor was interested in finding it..." Olive said under her breath. "Senna, come hold our Up-city friend while I take a look."

Olive passed the woman off and directed the Demons to bring the goods back to the sector's headquarters. The woman screamed and pushed out of Senna's inattentive grasp, running up the street, hoping to skirt the gangless. However, they herded her against a wall and converged. See-ing their hands rake down her clothing to take the precious fabrics terrified Olive that they might not stop at the clothing.

Senna ran into the throng, shoving her way to the woman. Olive's heart rate increased when she saw Senna's fist raise and pound down somewhere in the mass of people.

The Demons dropped what they were doing around the vehicle to help, but Olive signaled that they should protect the goods, then pushed through the throng herself. She found Senna and the unconscious woman and pulled them out, then indicated for Demons to herd the mob out of the street.

Olive dressed the woman in the man's clothes, since she was only left in a set of impossibly luxurious underwear. Everything had been torn from her body, including her jewelry and piercings. Senna brought an alcohol wipe from the medical supplies and Olive cleared the blood off the woman's ears.

"Why did you punch her, Senna?"

"She was panicking and making it worse."

"You could have put yourself between her and them."

"For that *bitch?* She's lucky I did *that* and didn't leave her. Calling you garbage..."

"They're just words, Demon. We could have earned this one's favor. Now she'll slander us in the Upcity. You've set us back years..."

"Fuckin' bitch deserved it."

Olive sighed and dropped her head.

"Coordinate with the sector to get these supplies to headquarters. Give out half to the gangless." Olive stood and glared into Senna's eyes, rendering her sheepish. "Don't ever hurt an Upcity citizen. *Ever!*"

Senna couldn't meet Olive's eyes after that and went about her task. Olive braced herself for what she had to do to get the woman to safety. She grabbed an arm and pulled it over her neck, then lifted the woman's torso to lay across her upper back and made for the Elevators, about a mile away.

Heavily-weaponized guards grew noticeably restless at her approach, raising their weapons. Her legs shook with the exertion. No one rushed to help the woman—they were only concerned with non-citizens attempting to get into the Elevators. A police officer cautiously stepped to her.

"Stay back, trash can. She can wait for the next shift of Doctors."

"This woman is a citizen, officer. Please take her home. I also have the coordinates to the vehicle she crashed in, and the name of the Doctor who alerted me to find it."

"Where's this one's identification?"

"Unfortunately, I found her *after* she was stripped of her possessions."

The officer bent to observe the woman's face.

"Did you rough her up?"

"...She...panicked. I...knocked her out."

Another officer approached and ran a scanner on the back of the woman's hand.

"She's a citizen, alright. Reported missing yesterday."

Olive was exhausted, and not only from the journey carrying the heavy woman. Lack of sleep caught up to her and she staggered to the ground, only mindful not to let the woman's head hit the street.

Sure of the woman's citizenship, they showed more urgency in getting her to the Elevators. Olive collapsed on her back. A ring of guards and their electric batons filled her vision.

"Do you know the penalty for touching a citizen?" one of them asked.

Olive tightened her lips. She may not have deserved what she was about to endure for that woman in particular, but she did for the two women who materialized behind her eyelids as she closed them to accept her fate.

Chapter Seven

CHALLENGE

REGINA KEPT HER SIDE-EYES and head shakes better hidden as the days passed, especially when in the vicinity of Vela and Ezzie. Rina hadn't hit Regina yet, which puzzled her since she thought Brace had been quite clear on toughening her up. All Rina did was show Regina how to stand and focus her center of gravity. She eventually explained that protecting the face wasn't the priority, it was withstanding the blow; they all bore their scars proudly. She wouldn't mangle Regina's face in "practice" because that simply wasn't the goal, but she couldn't expect the same of others.

Regina didn't particularly care for Rina's soft touch. Brace's mix of tough love and violent admonishments intrigued her more; the results were immediate and obvious, and there wasn't a lecture at the end of them.

Sally found Regina nibbling at the only edible-looking thing from the breakfast table, avoiding bite marks like they were diseased. Sally grabbed the scrap Regina had been working on before she put it back on the platter and ate the whole thing in two bites.

"Don't be wasteful, Upcity runt. Any more than you already are, I mean. Come on, I was too busy to take you to the light the other day, but we have some time now."

"I know what light looks like."

Sally slapped the back of Regina's head, not as gentle as she thought it would be based on Sally's soft breakdown the night of the unveiling.

"Hey, Brace, I'm ready!" Sally called across the room.

Brace nodded, finished her conversation with Vela, then came over to Regina and Sally.

"Bringing the Rag Doll, Silly? Fine, but she's *your* responsibility. I've got shit to do."

"Just taking her to the light."

"Well, Raggy," Brace started, "we're going to be passing—"

"Stop calling me that!" The words exploded out of Regina's mouth. She hadn't even *planned on* saying anything—she would have suffered the nickname until she left the Underfoot—but it was wearing on her, being equated to them; one of them.

Half the Bulls were out on tasks. Regina wished Vela and Ezzie had been out, but they came to Brace's side in a blink.

"Say that again, runt," Vela growled.

More than blurting out a challenge, she was even less prepared for something physical. However, she remembered how Rina stood up to Vela the other day. If she was ever going to earn their version of "respect"...

Instead of cowering, Regina set her feet and back like Rina taught her. Her expression betrayed fear against the façade of defiance, but it was dark.

Vela smiled venomously and cocked her arm back. Regina flinched in expectation of the coming blow, but Vela stopped a couple inches from her face.

Vela and Ezzie laughed derisively and walked away. "Fuckin' Rina," Ezzie said. "If *we* were teachin' the bitch she'd be ready to take a hit by now."

Regina shrunk before Brace's neutral stare.

"Don't start shit you're too scared to finish, Rag Doll. If I wasn't here…"

"You'd be Vela and Ezzie food," Sally finished. "Come on, I really want my bath today!"

Brace brushed by Regina. She gave a little "hmmph" when Regina didn't budge her stance from the hard shoulder. Regina interpreted it as approval, at least, and trailed Brace into the street alongside Sally.

"Anyway, what I was about to say, *Raggy*," Brace continued, "was we have to pass the Elevators to get to the next sector. Are you going to bolt?"

She…didn't really know. The more time she spent around the Bulls, the more she learned about herself—what she would and wouldn't do for her own gang. Of course the environment was horrible and she wanted to be out of it sooner than later, but something inside her said she had more to learn from Brace, as long as she did a better job picking up on Vela and Ezzie's trigger points and how to avoid them.

"I…won't bolt."

Brace clapped her on the back. The blow stung her skin, but earning a smile from that hard face dulled the pain.

Regina regretted her gung-ho attitude when they crossed the street border of the next sector. Rival gang members stopped what they were doing to follow the three of them, until Brace paused to have a conversation with them.

"What are they talking about?" Regina asked Sally.

"Telling them we're only here for a short time."

"Telling? Or asking?"

"Bulls don't ask, Raggy."

When Sally didn't elaborate, Regina noticed the gang back off, malice in their expressions and postures lessened. It was hard to tell whether they acted out of fear or respect, as the low light didn't reveal anything else. After a moment, Brace beckoned and they continued on while the gang dispersed.

"Sounds like some Upcity shitter crashed his vehicle way over in Sector O."

"So what?" Sally said. "If it didn't crash in ours, I couldn't care less."

"Something delicious came out of it, though. Apparently that cunty, deluded Olive got the fuck shocked out of her at the sector's Elevators—killed one of the two passengers, it sounds like. She barely got out of it alive. Wish they'd just stomped on that bitch's head and been done with her, but maybe now her gang's push will die before it really gets going."

"Who's Olive?" Regina asked.

Brace caused Regina to shrink from her furrowed brow.

"Was that not enough context? Aren't you educated, princess?"

"I may have been more educated at age *six* than you are now, but that doesn't mean I know all about what you trashy bitches do down here—other than fuck each other and subsist on..."

Brace closed their distance. The stink of her breath stung Regina's nostrils, and her eyes watered as she fought to hold back a sneeze, defaulting to grasping her nose between her thumb and index finger.

That was the worst thing she could have done.

Brace grabbed the raggedy collar of Regina's shirt and twisted it so tight that the fabric began to choke her off.

"We respect bravery, and you've proven you have it. We'll respect you speaking up for yourself, when you prove you can back it up. What we don't respect is speaking derogatorily of your sisters without a hint of jest."

"I don't talk shit about *my* sisters," Regina managed as pressure threatened to close her windpipe. "But you're not one of them. None of you are. I'll talk down to every person here, because I *do* look down on you. You're as interesting as the shit in the nets ten stories below my bedroom."

"The *mouth* on this one," Sally whispered from Regina's periphery. "Brace, let me fuck her up."

"Wait for the initiation, Silly. If she survives, maybe she'll back up her brave, *stupid* words. Give Rina the benefit of the doubt that she'll turn this pink pussy into something of substance."

Sally punched Regina's arm anyway, and Brace let go of her vice grip. It was utterly shocking how much a simple arm punch hurt and how long the pain lingered.

"I got the information I needed. I'm going to find my contact, offer my condolences to the dead citizen's family, and a promise that I'll finish the job on that Denim Dipshit."

Brace glared at Regina. How did she know—?

"*Because*, Ten Stories, what did I already tell you about Upcity contacts? We massage their egos and they continue to interact with us. Now go take your bath and if I see you at headquarters tonight you might earn back some of my respect."

Brace left, not even with a hard brush off. Somehow it felt worse that she didn't. Regina shook her head at Brace's turned back and muttered under her breath about the value of that respect when her hair tightened against her scalp and her neck was yanked back. Sally slapped Regina's face twice, harder than the Ruby Riders' leader had ever slapped her.

"Your insults touch us all, *princess*. You don't like Brace? Fine. You show her *goddamn* respect, though. You've seen how much Vela hates Rina? Guess what? She still respects the *fuck* out of her. We wouldn't *be here* otherwise."

Regina struggled against Sally's grip and tore the hand away from her scalp. A clump of hair remained entwined in Sally's fingers.

"All this shit about respecting each other," Regina snarled, her show of force and anger dampening the fire on her scalp. "Violence isn't respect. I respect sisters who support me and don't *hurt* me."

"We're not in your little pussy world of rich bitches."

"You wouldn't ever *sniff* my world if we didn't come down here to experience this zoo, you fucking crybaby."

What the fuck was wrong with her mouth? Was the gutter trash drawing it out of her? The week before she would never think to rub someone's face in their emotions.

The dip in Sally's expression from righteous anger to unexpected betrayal stung. Regina knew better, but it escaped her, nonetheless. She was lucky the initiation buffer protected her from a full-on conflict—

Sally's expression went as dead-eyed as it had when she stood by her burning canvas. She shifted her stance, just as Rina surely taught her, too.

"You're absolutely right, Reggie." Regina couldn't explain the swell of emotions she felt at hearing her real nickname again, especially from anyone in the Underfoot, but that fleeting feeling of recognition was quickly buried by guilt over Sally's shimmering eyes. "I was a baby the other day. I didn't face the consequences of that. Hit me."

"That's fucking absurd. I'm not going to hit you."

"You think I'm a coward. That I'm softer than you. Maybe I am. Prove it. Knock me on my ass and I'll take you to the Elevators. I'll even give you your hair back."

Regina peered down at her hair still in Sally's fist, and smiled at the absurdity of the gesture. Sally's tears finally spilled out with a reciprocal burst of laughter. The tension between them disappeared.

Regina wanted to move past it and see what was so great about "the light bath," but Sally grabbed her sleeve and pulled her back in front of her.

"Hey, I challenged you in front of the Diamond Ducks. You need to hit me."

"Fuck that. I don't want to."

"You don't get it. Brace isn't here. They'll attack me if you don't hit me."

"What the hell does two sisters from another gang arguing have to do with—"

"You're not my sister yet. You don't have patches. If I lose my challenge to an unpatched runt they'll kill me on principle."

"You're making shit up as you..." Regina trailed off as unfamiliar gang members surrounded them, their neutral expressions drawn downwards.

"Hit me, Reggie. And if it's a little slap I'll level you. Your hit needs to draw blood."

"I hate this fucking place," Regina muttered as she squared up. If the gang hadn't drawn in, she would have ignored Sally's inanity, but as ridiculous as it was, this was life and death...

Regina raised her arm but realized her palm was open. She'd never hit a sister, and she'd only been slapped. Forming a fist felt foreign.

"Don't tuck your thumb in your fist, dummy. You'll break it," Sally whispered. "Whatever happens, don't hold your hand like a baby after you hit me."

Regina tried to remember Brace's movements when she knocked out that protestor. Her punch had been from the hip and only traveled a short distance. Regina fired her fist into the center of Sally's face.

Sally's head snapped back, but her body didn't move. When she straightened her neck, blood already ran from her nostrils into her mouth. The Diamond Ducks murmured their approval at both Regina's punch and Sally taking it. A grotesque grin parted Sally's lips. Her teeth were covered in decay or blood, or, most likely, both.

Regina went from staring at Sally's teeth to the dark ceiling dotted with twinkling stars. Maybe it had all been a bad dream?

The pain at the back of her head and the side of her face disavowed her of that notion. Laughter and cheers filtered through the ringing in her ears. Sally's face appeared above hers. A few of the Ducks clapped Sally hard on the shoulder with wide smiles as they passed by to leave. Sally didn't budge from the hits, like they were flies landing on her back.

"Are the Brass Bulls lowering their initiate standards?" one Duck chortled and moved on with her quacking sisters. Sally only maintained Regina's eye contact.

"Is this crybaby worthy of your respect, Reggie?" Sally asked as she extended her hand.

Regina remembered Rina's lesson and refused the hand she hadn't earned. She got up with her own remaining, wobbly power. Her face twitched. The other side would have a matching black eye. Fuck it; she would have surgery soon enough.

"Show me what light is like down here, Silly."

SALLY EXPLAINED THERE WERE five areas across the twenty-six sectors perfectly positioned at certain times of day for the sun to shine between the towers and through the nets. They were like little vacation spots for the Underfoot. Sally pushed her way through the trash cans, cutting in front of the line to put her face under the one-by-one foot square beam of light interspersed by the shadow of the netting.

Sally's complexion was dishwater grey, as were all the other people who only absorbed five seconds of Vitamin D before being shoved aside for the next in line. Sally held someone at bay one-armed for an extra ten seconds before moving aside. She'd kept her eyes tightly shut, so Regina never saw their color. Her rats nest of black hair and puffy, bleeding face was hard to keep eyes on. Responsibility for the damage filled Regina with remorse.

"Get in here, Reggie," Sally said. "Let me see your pretty face."

Sally pushed someone aside and stood Regina under the light.

"Aside from the coming black eyes, you have a nice nose. I'm glad I didn't hit it."

Regina squirmed loose and stood off to the side while Sally exchanged heated words with the line. Somehow Sally won the argument and people stifled their complaints while she rejoined Regina.

As they walked back to Bulls territory, Sally asked what it was like receiving formal education. It was hard to describe—like trying to explain how one learned their mother tongue.

"You know, Brace is educated," Sally said matter-of-factly. "Just because people don't attend an Upcity school doesn't mean they can't learn to read. Most of us just don't want to."

"Where do you get books? I haven't seen a single one."

"They're as rare as unopened chocolate. Brace took one from a defeated gang and forced their leader to teach her how to read. She teaches any Bull that wants to learn but doesn't require it."

"Can't have too many smart people under your...control..." Regina put her foot in her mouth again. Each time tasted worse than the last.

Sally punched Regina in the arm, hard as usual.

"I'm going home, Reggie. The Elevators are two blocks that way, then a quarter of a mile. You'll feel the air get cooler."

Sally didn't wait for a response, or to see which way Regina's feet pointed.

Chapter Eight

Messages

SABRINA WAITED IN LINE all day. Her Doctor contact gave a shake of the head when she spotted Sabrina at the shift change, meaning there would be no chance of cutting in line. If it had been any of the other leadership, they wouldn't accept that answer. They'd push through to the front, and their patches would give them prioritization.

Contacts were as varied as the people in the Underfoot. Some were tough and hard to squeeze information from. Others could be skittish—scare them once and they'd disappear to other sectors. The Doctors knew how dirty the Underfoot was, so tit-for-tat rarely happened.

What the Doctors had were antibiotics, nutrition pills, information, and a gift for stating the obvious: how unhealthy they all were.

At the end of the shift, Sabrina's contact exited the tent and stretched dramatically, an indication to meet her near the Elevator gates. Sabrina left the groaning line and threw a blanket over her head. She waited by the exit, slightly out of sight of the guards, then her contact stopped short and put her back against a pillar to smoke a synthetic stick. Smoking wasn't allowed on the Elevators and she had a long trip ahead of her.

"Your hero almost died," the contact whispered. "I heard she tried to rush past the guards to jump on the Elevator in Sector O. Killed a man and brutalized his charge after their vehicle crashed."

"Killed? Are you sure? Olive would never do such a thing."

"Just relaying what's being passed between the volunteers. Someone said it was all a lie; a show of force to keep the line between the guards and trash cans reinforced since there had been some slippage."

"People are getting on the Eleva—"

"Don't speak that thought into existence, Rina. They're dying for their *attempts*. And even if they got on an Elevator, it scans for chips the entire trip. The training videos they make new volunteers watch explain that if we lose the hand with the chip in it down here, to *never* get on until proper authorities can install a new one."

"What will happen?"

"Whatever colorful thing you want to believe that causes instant death."

Sabrina retreated into the blanket with a shiver. She wished she could simply run off to join Olive, but even without her patches she was known by enough other gangs' leadership to be spotted along the way. If Brace ordered a ganghunt, Vela or Ezzie would easily catch her.

"Can you give a message to Olive?"

"No. I like being on this side of the city. The other side is shit. They don't even have a handbag shop in that tower. Plus the view is lame. All the mountains are on *this* side."

"Mountains? Handbags?"

"Tch. Sorry. Anyway, just because I can't give the message to Olive, doesn't mean I can't pass it along for other volunteers to spread. There are *some* who like visiting each sector at least once a year to stay updated. Crazy bitches."

"Tell her she has a friend in Sector B. I...I want to help her..."

"Help her what? Lead *trash cans?* What does it matter who leads who down here? The scraps are the same, the lines to see us will never get shorter, and the guards are only going to use increasing lethality with each foolish attempt to board an Elevator. Why the fuck would anyone want to 'lead' this place?"

"Maybe our reasons are as foreign to you as mountains are to me. What if you didn't have them?"

The Doctor sighed and blew out the last of the synth stick smoke. "Our walls can show anything we want. It doesn't compare to the real thing, though. I'd still get used to it, even if it was fake."

"Your walls...show?"

"Forget it, Rina. Here, I saved what I could. The red ones are antibiotics. Jeez, girl, your nails are really gross. When you use wipes, get them in there. Or cut them. You're only spreading misery down here."

The Doctor left curtly. Sabrina took the blanket off her head and handed it to a kid as she left the lineup area. She found Raggy a couple dozen feet away, assessing the guards, taking a few steps, then peering back towards headquarters. Sabrina watched her battle indecision, but kept a distance. Finally, Raggy stopped by an officer. Sabrina moved within earshot.

"...them I'm safe. Working on a project to get art supplies added to the crates."

The officer roared with derision, then nodded. Raggy turned away and began the walk back. Sabrina followed close, then tugged roughly on her sleeve from behind. Raggy spun around and braced for unexpected violence.

"You could have been jumped a dozen times since I spotted you, Raggy. Go alone into another sector like this again, and you won't be coming back. Oh wow, who fucked up your face? Vela?"

"No, it was Sally."

"What the fuck are you embarrassed about? Sally's stronger than she seems."

"I didn't think she was strong enough to flatten me out... But she did."

"Were you standing like I—"

"*Yes*. I think your teaching is bullshit. Vela and Ezzie think so, too."

Sabrina took a deep breath. "Just because Brace said to follow me, doesn't mean you have to. Maybe she'll respect you more if you seek one of those two out of your own will..."

"I'm so fucking *sick* of all this 'respect' talk."

"Well, you still have mine for turning around back at the Elevators." Sabrina clapped Raggy's back and moved ahead, lest she find any new reason to use a fist rather than an open palm on the Upcity Whiner.

Sabrina handed out pills on the way back to headquarters but kept a few antibiotics for her family. Panda got a second shoe to protect her feet but if she traded them again, it would be nice to have them in an emergency.

Outside headquarters, Brace conversed with Vela and Ezzie. Sabrina hung back, not interested in talking to them at the moment. Vela and Ezzie nodded about something and went inside. When Brace turned to follow, a sudden flash of movement from across the street caught Sabrina's eye. A blanket flew up and a woman emerged, running straight for Brace's back with a pointy object in hand. Sabrina charged without thinking.

"Brace!" she cried when she wouldn't get there in time.

Brace spun around and backed up quickly, providing enough space and time for Sabrina to tackle the woman from behind. Sabrina pounded the attacker down with her fists. The onslaught of knuckles earned some satisfying grunts, until the woman swung the sharp object around to slash across Sabrina's face.

"Fucking *bitch!*" Sabrina muttered through struggles to get the woman's wrist under control. The two rolled over and the woman put her weight into her arms in a drive to stab Sabrina through the heart.

She wasn't very heavy, and Sabrina crossed her arms to protect her chest. She maneuvered the woman's arms so they crossed as well, taking away her leverage. Sabrina let her drop closer and butted her skull into the woman's nose. The sharp object clattered to the ground accompanied by a scream of pain. A mass of movement engulfed the woman's upper body and she crashed to the floor nearby. Sabrina blinked to find Raggy had draped a blanket over the attacker, entangled her, and rolled the cursing heap away from her. Vella and Ezzie converged to secure the capture. Ezzie pushed Raggy away hard, sending her sprawling and crashing into the empty food table.

"Don't ever take away someone else's victory, runt," Ezzie growled at Raggy, then they took the attacker outside to the room the Bulls had held the Ruby Riders.

Brace helped Sabrina up and clapped her on the back in thanks before following Vela and Ezzie. Several other Bulls rushed to be a part of the torture for information. Blood rolled over Sabrina's eyebrow into her eye from the cut along her forehead. She tasted iron running into her mouth from the cut over her cheek. At least the bitch had missed her eyes...

No one helped Raggy up, who seemed to be lying in a daze of confusion. Sabrina dropped down next to her splayed body. Sally and Bridgette did the same, followed by all the initiates who weren't allowed to take part in the torture.

"Ezzie's such a bitch," one of them muttered, and the others nodded agreement.

"All of us are, runt," Sabrina said with a steadying breath. "She'd still die for you."

"That's bullshit, Rina. Nobody helped you except *Raggy*. Fucking cowards."

Sabrina might have gotten up and punched the girl on the edge of the group if she had a little more energy.

"They knew I'd win. My sisters trusted I'd save Brace. *Brace* trusted me."

"Your sisters left you to die," Raggy finally piped up, though she didn't rise from her sprawled position.

"Not all of them..." Sabrina said, feeling a little warmth at being able to say kind words.

Raggy shifted to get up. Sabrina put her hand on Raggy's knee and gave it a squeeze before tilting back on her arms.

"I'll forgive you runts for your words. That was your first experience with our real world. Always keep your eyes and ears open. Always be ready for a fight."

"I've heard other gangs aren't like this," one of the initiates mumbled.

"Other gangs aren't on the top," Sally said. "This is your life now, runt. Get used to it or leave before the next initiation. Once you're in, you can't leave."

If Sally wasn't there, Sabrina might have taken that opportunity to give a little acknowledgment to Olive, maybe earn a few new backers when the time came to do whatever was necessary to help the Denim Demons succeed in taking over Sector B. It would be the greatest challenge Olive would face on her journey across the Underfoot, no matter how many gangs she brought into her loving arms.

Though, of the Bulls she didn't want to overcommit and kill themselves in defense of their territory, Sally was Sabrina's favorite. Maybe it was time...

"There are some gangs out there who lead with something other than fear and violence. A lot of us don't get the chance to choose where we end up—recruitment is based on where we're born."

"That's plain enough," Raggy butted in. "How is it the softest of you lot is the *only one* covered in blood after shit like that assassination attempt?"

Sally had the same urge to inflict violence that Sabrina had nearly succumbed to a minute before, tensing at Raggy's criticisms. Sabrina put her foot on Sally's and shook her head.

"Whatever you all think of me, soft or not, we all need to be able to take the pain they deal," Sabrina said. "Remember that the next time you look at me with pity, or, God forbid, feel the urge to blurt out shit like Raggy just did in front of a Bull. We prove our worth by standing alone, *together*."

"I can't do anything *right* here, can I?" Raggy blurted again.

That inspired a murmur among the initiates echoing the feeling. *Good.* It would be far more difficult to convert them if they were as hard-headed as true Bulls. Sabrina was going to let it go at that point, but she had a thought about how she could change things, right then.

"Thank you for your help, Reggie."

She witnessed a smile from their captive for the first time.

"She's got a nice smile, doesn't she?" Sally said. "I'm sorry I had to wipe it off earlier, Reggie..."

Sabrina sighed and a warm feeling grew. "Thanks" and "sorry" were hard to earn for any initiate. She held out her hand for Reggie.

"I'm Sabrina." Reggie shook reluctantly, as if she didn't understand what had just happened. "If you still want Vela or Ezzie to teach you—"

"No!" Sally interrupted. "She doesn't need those two. See what she did to my face?"

Sally leaned over to show the other women.

"That was her first punch ever! Imagine if she were to take this fucking seriously and stop complaining all the time!"

"Did you show Reggie how to punch like that, Rina?" Bridgette asked. "Can you show *me?*"

Fuck. Always back to violence in a snap. Well, Sabrina didn't expect converting her sisters would be that easy...

BRACE AND THE OTHERS returned to the headquarters after Sabrina had sent the initiates to collect food from the scavengers. Erin, the cute horndog from the night of Sally's unveiling, stood close to Sabrina as they waited for Brace to announce their interrogation's findings. Sabrina smiled and Erin grew bashful all of a sudden.

Brace raised her hand for quiet.

"The Sapphire Snakes send me their regards. Time to send ours. Rina, you have the honor of choosing a Bull to join you in retaliation for what that bitch did to your face."

"Pick me, pick me, pick me," Erin whispered to herself.

"I'll fight with ya, Rina," Ezzie proclaimed.

"Take me with you, Rina," Sally insisted. Everyone in the room but Brace, Vela, and Reggie raised their hands.

Brace cut the clamoring off again. "Who's the lucky Bull, Rina?"

Sally was already bonded to Sabrina. Ezzie fought without nuance and would never turn on the Bulls. Perhaps a sister she didn't know very well yet could be swayed with a little alone time.

"I choose Erin as my sister in revenge."

Instead of erupting, Erin only nodded solemnly under Brace's gaze, though Sabrina noticed her fingers curling in and out with nervous energy. A few nearby Bulls clapped Erin on the back.

"A brave choice, eh Vela?" Brace nudged Vela and she chuckled. It reflected well on Vela that Sabrina chose one of her recent initiates.

"She likes a third in the nest, Rina. Better watch out!" Vela said to a round of laughter.

Erin's shoulders drew down and she held her fingers behind her back. Apparently she was more outgoing in a smaller group.

"Alright, Rina," Brace said, "The Snakes operate out of Sector F. They may have been acting on someone else's behalf, according to that slutty serpent we strung up in the sewers. Kill a Snake, kill a Denim Demon if you see one, as unlikely as it would be for them to be this deep, then come back here for our next event.

"In the meantime, I want every single Bull and all your initiates to run a sweep of our sector. Act with extreme prejudice against anyone with a patch or mark that isn't one of ours."

"Before you all go," Sabrina said, "please partake of the food we gathered for your hard work today."

Sabrina grabbed Erin's hand outside the headquarters and pulled her swiftly to the outhouse. The structure had been knocked over by Vela and a taut rope hung through the middle of the manhole. With no nearby alternatives, many people had used the hole since.

"Help me get her out," Sabrina instructed a confused Erin. When she hesitated, Sabrina added: "It'll be easier to find a high-value target if we bring her with us. I haven't visited Sector F in years."

When they pulled the naked Snake up, Sabrina couldn't believe what her sisters had done to her. Using the weapon she'd used to attack, they'd cut up her back and buttocks, and the way they'd hung her ensured the open wounds would be covered in piss and shit.

"How many wipes do you have, Erin?"

"They're mine. I'm not wasting them on this bitch. Besides, I haven't wiped my face yet today."

"You look very pretty right now. You don't need them."

The easy compliment did the trick and Erin handed over a fresh wipe. Sabrina had several in her pockets. She wiped the girl's bloody face while Erin grumbled and wiped off her back.

The Snake was dazed; she'd likely given up on life. Sabrina slapped her cheek in a soft but steady rhythm until her eyes focused.

"Can you dry swallow?"

She shook her head weakly.

"Erin, run and get some water from a steam pipe scavenger. Hurry, please!" Sabrina turned back to the Snake. "What's your name?"

"S-s-s-stevie."

"Was that hiss on purpose? Hey, wake up, Stevie. I have an antibiotic for you. Just let me clean up these cuts."

Sabrina finished scrubbing Stevie's back in time for Erin to return with water cupped in her hands. Sabrina hoped she'd had the good sense to wipe off her hands first...

"Here you go, Stevie. Take this pill. There you go. Thank you, Erin. Come on, we'll get you something to cover up with on the way to the next sector. We need to be out of here before the Bulls start their sector sweep."

On their way out, Sabrina kept her eyes peeled for a dead body, just like when she went pill hunting. Close to the sector's border, a heap of a former person lay next to a brazier.

Sabrina stripped the body and dressed Stevie in the rags. There were no supplies to salvage otherwise.

Sabrina breathed relief when they entered Sector C. The Diamond Ducks saw the patches and nodded approval for their passage. They wouldn't all be easy like that, though. Only Sectors A and C had a legitimate reason to begrudgingly befriend the Bulls thanks to Brace's ultimatums.

If they weren't hassled, it could take a day to get to Sector F and back, and Sabrina was already tired. She took Erin and Stevie to the local steam water supply and got her own drink to take an antibiotic for the cut on her face, then found a place to nest for the night before they'd cross into Sector D. They restrained the weak Snake with the blanket so she couldn't run away.

"Let me keep you warm tonight, Rina," Erin whispered as she spooned into Sabrina's back without asking. Before she could even object, Erin was snoring into the nape of her neck.

Infatuation could be useful, or deadly, depending on how Sabrina played it in the coming days...

Chapter Nine

EASY OR HARD

OLIVE OCCASIONALLY GROUND HER teeth as her body suffered the reverb of her punishment. She still heard the crackle of electricity flowing through her skull. Her skin vibrated randomly, as did the back of her eyes.

She refused Twill's advances in the nest, instead sleeping with Demons she knew didn't enjoy the company of women simply so she wouldn't have to deal with fingers trying to snake their way to caress her breast.

Her first order of business upon returning from the Elevator incident was to collect their supply of electric batons and throw them into the deadly-hot pipeworks on the edges of the sector.

"I still don't think that was a good idea," Twill had said after the last one clanked down to its demise.

Olive took Twill aside and warned her not to contradict her within earshot of the others. She addressed the rest of the Demons once they returned to headquarters, laying out her expectation that they begin training their bodies to both give out and receive blows. She'd had enough of death, and less-deadly force was the new directive, but would require individual strength to enforce; to sustain without dying themselves.

To demonstrate how serious she was, she invited Twill to punch her in front of everyone. Twill absolutely refused, despite Olive's earlier insistence not to contradict her.

Olive refrained from lashing out and instead chose a larger woman from a recent conquest to come up and punch her. Before the woman made her way to the front, Twill leaned over for only Olive to hear.

"Just because those barbaric Bulls do this shit..."

"The closer we get to Sector B, the more important it'll be for all of us to toughen up. The things I've heard they do to messengers and assassins—each *other*... We have to match their strength."

"Olive... Do you still not understand why I, of all people, joined—"

The rookie stopped in front of Olive and waited for the directive to hit. Olive pointed at her chin and braced for it. The rookie drew back but the blow didn't come. Twill had hooked her arm into the rookie's, turning her around.

"You hit *me*, Demon. Our Olive has suffered enough this week."

"You're making me look weak, Twill," Olive muttered. The rookie only showed confusion between the two of them.

"Your XO just gave you a command, Demon. Hit me." Twill put her hands behind her back and didn't flinch at the coming blow. The rookie apologized profusely, even though Twill didn't move.

"Good hit, rookie. You! Over there. Your turn. Get up here."

While the two traded places, Olive stood next to Twill to whisper: "If I can't take a hit from my own people, they'll all think I'm wea—"

"Do not say that word about yourself, Olive. Understand something—you're our leader and you need to keep your goddamn brain intact. And... I'll be *fucked* if you're the only one who suffers for what I did to those two women for our cause. Now leave and prepare to take over the next sector. I have a gang to toughen up."

THAT NIGHT OLIVE WENT to Twill's nest. She let out a pained hiss when Olive put a hand on her shoulder and yanked it away. Olive shifted to put her back into Twill's. If she couldn't spoon, she still wanted to be in contact.

"I love you, Twill," Olive said.

Twill shifted and Olive thought she might not say anything. It was the first time Olive had ever said it to anyone. Anticlimactic was an understatement. Olive sighed and curled into herself, worried that she'd damaged something by refusing Twill's advances since the electrocution.

Twill's feet caressed Olive's calves and her back softened.

"You were the one to lead me from my life's cycle of violence," Twill whispered. "You're the only hope for the Underfoot. I'd die for your noble cause, as readily as I'd die for you. If despair ever took you, it would take us all."

"It seems violence has found you again... How is this any better?"

"It's...different. It's worth fighting for, what you're doing. It's not mindless."

"It's all tainted..."

"The Thorns will be forgotten, Olive. No one even knows except you and me, and I'll take the secret to my grave."

"Why does that still feel...wrong?"

"Because you're Olive. That isn't your world. It's mine. I don't want to be a part of it anymore, but it's my place. I'm your shield. And... I... I love you, too."

Olive's tears spilled over her nose into the other eye.

"Can I hug your legs tonight while I sleep?"

"...why?"

"I imagine that's the only place that doesn't hurt, and I must hold you all night."

Olive didn't even wait for an answer. She moved around and entwined her arms with Twill's legs, kissing the fuzz along her calves, then resting her open palm on the side of her lower leg. Twill placed her hand on Olive's hip and they fell asleep together, yin and yang.

IN THE MORNING THE Demon scouts from the relay network met with Olive and Twill in their most-recently conquered sector. The news skewed bad.

People believed the rumor that Olive had inflicted violence on a citizen, that she may have even had a hand in downing that vehicle. There were rumblings that she sent an assassin against the Brass Bulls' leader. A smattering of newly-acquired Demons were reported to have robbed several families in the next sector—the one where negotiations would be taking place later that week.

The only good news: a message passed from the Doctors that Olive had an ally in Sector E. That excited her enough to send Twill on a fact-finding mission and shore up the support. The sooner she began strategizing against Sector B the better.

It was a little overwhelming to tackle all the problems at once. Olive took a break in her nest to read the faded and battered copy of her favorite book, which described the lives of rabbits in conflict. She'd read it before getting her hands

on one of the circulating copies of an animal encyclope-
dia and thought the book had been about real people who
lived outside hundreds of years before. Somehow, learning
they were cuddly little fluff balls spoke to something deep in
Olive—that she didn't need to be physically strong or violent
like Twill or Brace or the other handful of gang leaders who
ruled with fists and fear. Other ways were possible...

And yet she'd still succumbed to the pull to kill—always
the easiest solution past a certain point. Suddenly the words
beneath her flashlight tasted of poison. They weren't for her
anymore... Could never be again...

Olive resisted the urge to toss the book into a brazier and
instead walked outside the headquarters in the direction of
the sector where her charges had supposedly robbed regular folk. On the way, she came upon a young girl, maybe
twelve-years-old, trying to read something from the light of
a brazier, uncomfortably sweating from having to stand so
close to the heat.

"What are you reading there, sister?" Olive sat
cross-legged to the girl's side.

"A story about kids saving the world. They're tricked into
running simulations by the adults that aren't *really* simulations, because they don't believe the kids could handle the
damage genocide would do to their minds in reality, and the
adults are too cowardly to do it themselves. It's called a Game
but the writer was just being ironic."

"Wow. How long have you been reading?"

The girl shrugged. If she knew words like simulation, reality, genocide, and ironic, she must have been reading for
years. Olive had found a book in a dead man's hands when
she was about six. She stared at it cover-to-cover for a year
before she came upon a living person with another book
open by a candle. She asked what her own book was supposed to do, and the old man had kindly set her on his lap
and showed her what reading was.

The book she'd picked up was the rabbit book.

Olive put her flashlight on top of her well-worn copy, and handed them both to the girl. Her eyes were wider than her mouth. Nobody gave either of those objects away for free in the Underfoot. Olive stood, placed her hand on the girl's shoulder for a little squeeze, then continued towards the next sector without a word.

ESTABLISHED DEMONS HAD GATHERED the five trouble-makers who'd robbed a street of families in the neighboring sector. The goods were laid out on the sidewalk—hairpins, pills, food scraps, plugs, yarn, rat skewers, and broken plastic cutlery.

"Do you sisters not appreciate what I give you? Why would you steal from those less-fortunate than yourselves?"

"Because it's easy," one of them said. Olive admired directness. Usually.

"I know the draw of the easy way, sisters. I regret every time I've taken that path. The easy thing for me would be to exile the five of you. It's much harder to believe you'll change.

"The hardest thing for *you* is facing the consequence of your actions, and sticking by me afterwards. Can you do it? Let's find out."

Olive directed her loyal Demons to give the offenders physical deterrents in the vein of how Twill had begun training everyone. It wasn't enacted from a desire to dominate them. If they could take the beating and remain with her, she would trust them more in the battles to come.

They each took a hit to the stomach and face. Olive hugged the first in line and rubbed her back.

"Easy or hard, sister?"

The girl got her breath back and stiffened. "Hard."

Olive kissed the top of her bent-over head and moved to the next one, who's answer was the same. The third one bolted before Olive touched her. A Demon made a step to chase but Olive told her to leave it alone and continued with the next two girls, who both chose to stay.

"I'm so proud of you, Demons. Gather up what you took and return all of it. I'll see you tonight at headquarters."

OLIVE CONVERGED AT THE border of the next sector's male territory with several officers. She never used the new recruits for the pleasure missions because it took time to relay to the Doctors that she needed sex infection vaccines to inoculate not only her gang, but the male gangs as well. It could take an extra month for the next supply drop to include a parcel of syringes. The number of deaths from infection in Olive's home sector decreased dramatically, and the surrounding, conquered sectors followed suit.

A representative of the Purple Rams offered escort to an open space with an escape route, a stipulation Olive insisted on, since not every gang played nice from the beginning.

The male gangs trafficked in drugs and employed most of the scavengers, keeping choice finds for themselves. Olive got them to loosen their iron grips on the goods by sharing spoils from her supply drops. The men also used the goods to trade in women, and when Olive willingly offered that in order to keep the peace, they had fewer reasons to hoard the wealth and the lives of those beneath them improved in increments.

Olive still hadn't discovered a way to eliminate drugs from the equation. She couldn't necessarily begrudge the users who were only trying to escape the misery of existence in the Underfoot. God knew she stretched herself thin as it was, to not *also* have to placate the thousands of gangless who would either never be accepted in a gang or flatly refused to join out of some strange sense of pride that Olive would never understand.

At the meeting place, the leader of the Rams shook Olive's hand. Just like all the others, his gaze drifted to the shape of her jeans, and what lay beneath the shirt of rags. She'd yet to meet one who really listened until they got to the topic of vaccines and the timing of the scheduled visits.

The truces were the worst part of being a leader, but they had to happen before negotiations with the female gangs started. Most sectors' male and female gangs had uneasy coexistences with each other. The threat of rape could be tempered by the threat of disease and retribution. Some female gangs were dependent on the drugs and that was just fine with the men that took advantage of both their need and their bodies when they were high.

Olive's experiment with inoculating the men and reducing their impulses to rape seemed to be working so far in the other sectors. The Rams were already on the path. All she had to do was come back once their leader was inoculated and seal the deal in his nest. It was a small price to pay for peace, she reasoned. She had plenty of wine to drown out the taste of them, plenty of wipes to clean up afterwards, and the special supply drops provided pills to keep unwanted pregnancies at bay. Pregnancy was a seventy-thirty proposition of death for both mother and child in the Underfoot... It was no wonder their population was declining.

The one thing Olive looked forward to in getting closer to Sector B was the knowledge that Brace didn't negotiate with male gangs. They simply killed them in Sectors A and B, and rumors were they'd be taking on C and D soon. Olive's negotiations with the female gangs would be harder because of it, but it would ultimately prove beneficial to avoid the other aspect and focus on more important matters. The sooner those sectors fell, the quicker she could staunch the killing.

Having agreed on the vaccine exchange, Olive led the Demons out of the male territory. They draped blankets over themselves to hide their jeans and wandered around to get a sense for the gangless in the new sector. There weren't many differences between the sector populations, to untrained eyes anyway, but there were variants based on what the Upcity tossed into the nets around their sections. Some of it was food-heavy, so the gangless weren't as thin. Some tossed cosmetics more than others, so the women attracted men from other sectors. Fabric was richer and stronger in certain areas.

Olive grew up in a sector that tossed books more than others. That tapered off at a certain point that no one could explain, but once that happened, books became valuable displays of wealth. However, it didn't take long for most of her sector to trade them into further sectors for other goods. The books dispersed naturally. Gangs had gone unnamed until enough leaders learned of colors, stones, and animals from their tattered contents.

After giving a plug to a teenage girl and her excess rags to an older man in need of cover, Olive started her way back to the safe sector. An arm reached out of a small alcove in the base of a tower and yanked her inside, pressing her into the ground on her back.

"Fuckin' Denim Demon." The man's hot, rotten breath filled her nose as his hand covered her mouth. "We ain't waitin' on *your* terms. The Purple Rams don't do what cunts dictate."

Olive didn't recognize his voice as their leader; perhaps he was a disgruntled lieutenant familiar with the negotiations.

"Rams *take* what they want." He pressed his chest into her torso to keep her pinned and fumbled at her jeans.

"Now I see why you chose jeans. Too tight to get into without your permission? There's ways around that, bitch." He brandished a sharp object. Olive tried to shake free but he was quite a lot heavier than her. He held her head down with one hand while the other slipped the blade between her hip and jeans, then ripped down, cutting the denim along the outside seam along with her thigh. The cut felt colder than her skin, freshly exposed to the air. Her hips swiveled to get away from the blade but that only played into his goal of tearing the fabric away from her groin.

Olive tried clawing at his eyes but his reach was too long. She pounded on his arm but his muscles and his angle of leverage were too rigid to budge. With half of her jeans still not making it easy for him, he set the blade down next to her thigh in a haste to position himself better. His thrust stopped short, as he received penetration instead of achieving it. He looked down. Blood poured down Olive's arm, as her hand tightly grasped the object's base, the rest invisible, plunged into his abdomen.

The painful pressure on her head lessened, but all his weight fell on top of her. She vomited when her hand followed the blade *into* his stomach. Olive squirmed out from his weight, then twisted her torso to throw up some more. Her tattered jeans were caught beneath his legs. She yanked the fabric and fell onto the sidewalk outside of the alcove from the force. Blood streamed down her leg and dripped from her hand.

Olive untangled the fabric of the jeans from its clump and tied it above the gaping wound, then grasped the cut edges at her waist to hold her remaining pants up. She stumbled from shock and nearly fell into the street again. People ignored her. A couple of nearby women with patches sneered at her, then laughed at her cut up jeans. Olive mustered herself and limped as quickly as she could to safe territory.

At the opposite corner of the sector she found the technicians who collected steam and dripping water from the cold pipes for drinking. When she got there, her entire leg throbbed, the wound itself undeterminable, lost under the oozing red. She gave a square of chocolate to them for a bucket of precious water to be poured down her leg. The sight of the bloody stream and the cut it left behind made her so nauseous that she lost consciousness.

Chapter Ten

BULL RANCH

AFTER SABRINA LEFT THE headquarters, Brace came over to put a hard hand on Regina's shoulder. She whispered that she appreciated Regina stepping in to help their Rina and not to let Ezzie's words get in the way of helping sisters in the future. Regina stifled her indignant response to the hypocrisy. Then Brace shifted to put her arm around Regina's back and led her outside.

"How do you feel about getting laid tonight, virgin?"

The question jarred Regina into speechlessness.

"Not from *me*. I heard you don't like women. That's fine! We have a coupling tonight. Need to release some of the tension around here—after an attack like that and all."

"A...coupling? Like a dance?"

"Sure! Gotta keep the men from thinking violence is the only answer to their urges. We cull the violent ones and nurture the ones who don't want to dominate us. They're *adorable*."

"I've...never heard you talk like this. Are you okay? Did that assassination attempt scare you?"

Brace's good humor disappeared, replaced by a look of malice that made Regina squirm. The Underfoot was making her ignore her inhibitions; forgetting how precarious her situation was.

Then Brace smiled again. "Ten Stories, when someone comes *at you* regularly, you just appreciate life a little more each time. I get to fuck and sleep another night away. Come with us, Doll."

Regina's fascination with the Bulls was similar to how she enjoyed zoos, and this coupling was yet another thing to learn about them. She certainly didn't want anyone to take her virginity, but at least with the way Brace talked, it sounded like she wouldn't have to worry about any aggressive advances.

She followed the Bulls through the streets to another building with men hanging around outside, leaning on the walls and playing games with little objects on the sidewalk. Were they gambling, placing bets, making deals with one another on who should get who? At the sight of the Bulls approach, they all stopped their activities and stood at stiff attention that made Regina think of the space force cadets in classroom visuals.

"Hello, boys!" Brace said. "Everyone clean tonight? Who needs cleansing wipes? Ladies, pass them out.

"We've got a special companion with us tonight! Who wants to spend the evening with a pretty pink Upcity pussy?"

The men clamored in place, their hands shot into the air, and there were shouts of "me, me me!" Regina's neck shrunk between her shoulders. She made to turn and run when a brick wall stopped her. She looked up to find Vela grinning at her.

"They won't hurt you, Rag Doll. If they do, all you have to do is get me or Ezzie's attention and we'll make him pay. Permanently. Have fun!" Vela didn't leave it as a choice, instead spinning Regina back around by the shoulders and positioning her next to Brace like a prize to be auctioned off.

"Any other virgins here?" Brace addressed the line. One guy got a ribbing from the men standing nearest to him. They shoved him forward in all his shyness. His neck disappeared just like Regina's did. Brace leaned over to whisper to Regina.

"He's more embarrassed than you. He won't try anything unless you tell him to. Take his arm and go anywhere you like in the sector. We'll see you tomorrow morning, Ten Stories."

Brace gave a nudge and Regina caught herself after a step. She realized she hadn't met a single man in the Underfoot other than the police officer. Another learning opportunity. Another animal subject...

Regina put her arm in the crook of his and guided him away from the eyes and hooting of the rest of the men and Bulls.

Regina broke the ice. "What's your name, virgin?" He winced and muttered something she didn't pick up. "Oh. I'm sorry. I think those Bulls are rubbing off on me. We don't talk like that in the Upcity. It's all new to me."

"...I'm Virgo, until the guys give me a new name."

"Mmm. It's so strange what kind of information trickles down here. Like, how the hell would any of you know the stars otherwise?"

She couldn't tell if his quiet was from her question or shyness. "So, Virgo, where do you like to go down here? That dark street? *That* one? Or that even *darker* alleyway? Do you ever stare at the braziers like they're movies?"

The mocking went right over his head. "There's a place in Sector A, where I grew up... Only *I* know about it."

Regina grew more amused with each step they took without any follow-up.

"Well, are you going to take me there?"

"Oh. I was just answering your question. I'm too big to fit in the crevice anymore. It led outside."

Regina sputtered and stopped. "Outside? *Outside* outside?"

"Yeah, but it's all trees. You can't really go far without the trunks swallowing you up."

"Wow. That air must have been *fresh*. I would have stayed out there if I actually lived in this horrid place."

"There's nothing out there, though. Water? Food? The light hurt my eyes too much. And what if I got lost?"

"Mm. I guess so... Ironic that you could die out there. They planted all those trees between the megapolises to *save* us, and the planet or something. I don't know, I wasn't paying all that much attention in History."

"History? What history?"

"Uh... It's knowing about the cities and how they were built. *Why* they were built."

"Why was the Underfoot built?"

"Oh. Um. Remember, I wasn't really paying attention, but... The Underfoot is the prison system."

"Prison?"

"Um... A couple centuries ago they started putting criminals down here. You're all descendants of them. There aren't many crimes committed in the Upcity anymore, since everyone has enough money to pay off fines or buy justice."

"So... We'll eventually die out?"

"I doubt it. You trash cans seem to fuck like rabbits."

"Rabbits?"

"Alright, enough History. I'm...getting a little hungry. Do you know where we can get some food that isn't from the nets?"

The look on his face indicated she was crazy, so she led them to a nearby net. Scavengers with full pockets climbed down and announced to the group of waiting trash cans what they'd procured. One lifted up four inches of an unfinished submarine sandwich still wrapped in plastic. Regina pushed ahead like she'd seen Sally do and said she wanted it, and that she was a Bull. The scavenger told her to turn around. When he didn't see any patches he scoffed and kept the offer open to others.

Regina didn't have much on her other than her rags. After a quick pat-down for something, anything to give away, she stopped at her hair. She had hairpins still tucked above her ears. She took them out and offered them.

"Anything else?" the scavenger asked.

"I could punch you out."

He laughed. "Just like a Bull, but no. Add something to those hairpins and it's yours."

"How about a quarter roll of thread?" Virgo said from Regina's side.

The scavenger took the trade and moved onto selling the next object. They found a brazier and sat down against the wall. Regina snatched the sub out of Virgo's hand when he went to take it out of the plastic.

"When's the last time you washed your hands?"

"This morning. I used my last wipe."

"Mm." Regina tore the sandwich in half and handed him the part with bite marks. "I've got an extra wipe. I'll give it to you once this little date is over."

"This is a date?"

"What did you *think* it was?"

"The way the guys described the 'Bull Calls'—Brace just chooses the pairings, and they find a nest and...you know..."

"Fuckin' Brace. Why does she need to control *every-thing?*"

Regina *was* at least thankful that Brace wasn't just joking around pairing her with a virgin. His shyness kept his eyes off her most of the time. While her face wasn't plastic-attractive for the men in the Upcity yet, she did draw their eyes elsewhere. If she'd been wearing something more form-fitting, and not draped with rags, she wondered if Virgo would still be averting his eyes.

After the meal, she handed him the extra wipe and they began the walk back. His head was slumped a little differently than simple shyness, so she asked, "What's wrong?"

"Nothing... I just... They're going to expect me to 'report' how it was. They always share details after the couplings."

"Charming. Just make up whatever you want, Virgo. How would they know if you're lying or not? Repeat what you've heard before."

He shrugged and moped onward. These were the men Brace cultivated? She'd heard that after her surgery, she'd have to fend men off, and they wouldn't be shy about fighting for her. Previously she thought that would be the most off-putting part of dating, but Virgo presented a worse one—pity over conquest.

"Virgo, are you fishing to fuck me?"

He winced again, a most annoying habit from a man.

She didn't really consider herself a true virgin. The Ruby Riders had toy parties once a month where they bought each other the funniest shaped toys, in which the winner went home with a fancy bottle of lubrication to go along with the prize-winner. They'd all won at least once, and the toys were never thrown out the window...

Despite that, she didn't want to feel a weak man like Virgo inside her for her first *real* sexual experience. She did have a little pity for him, though, as repulsive as the thought was. Maybe he was just down on his luck, never getting picked by Brace, or whatever reason he could possibly still be a virgin with the easy practice of "coupling."

"Have you ever even...*felt* a woman?"

"No."

"Well, I could tell you what it's like, if you want your lie to be more effective."

"That's...a good idea."

Maybe he *was* really just fishing with his pity?

"Okay. It all feels like skin. The skin between my legs is wet, but that's it. It's nothing special. It smells different, but I don't know what you might have down here to compare it to. Mention the nub at the top of the opening and they'll believe you were with a woman."

"There's no change in texture? What about the hair?"

"What does my hair have to do with this?" Regina put her hand to her head.

"You know, *down there.*"

"Oh, shit. I never thought of that. We get laser surgery young in the Upcity. You mean women don't *shave* down here?"

"Laser surgery? Shave?"

"Oh God, what a horrid existence you people suffer..."

An idea came to her the more she thought about describing her body and how inadequate her explanations would ever be.

"Hey, Virgo. You want something none of your friends will believe? Follow me."

She took him to the place Sabrina had consoled Sally. Regina put her back to the wall and pulled Virgo in front of her. She lifted her arms.

"Reach into my sleeves and feel beneath my arms."

No one had ever touched her hairless armpits. She didn't expect his trembling hand to tickle so much. She involuntarily dropped her arms and her wrists hit him on the shoulders.

"Fuck, that was weird." Regina shuddered out the residual ticklishness and they tried again to the same results. Despite that, Virgo had a big grin. Warmth radiated from Regina's chest from the unplanned touch of a man. She supposed one more little touch wouldn't hurt...

She grabbed his hand and scrutinized his nails under the brazier light.

"Don't scratch me, Virgo, or I'll push you into that fire and step on your chest until you burn to death."

He swallowed and nodded. Regina was equally elated that she could mimic a Bull so well already.

She guided Virgo's hand beneath her rag shirt. She still had her underwear on, even though it was the same set from when she first came to the Underfoot. She let his hand squeeze her chest over the fabric. It was soft linen; not as high a thread count as the richer women, but still softer than anything anyone would ever get their hands on in the Underfoot.

The pressure of his hands warmed her further.

"Feel good, Virgo?"

He nodded and exhaled. He'd been holding his breath the whole time.

"They're probably going to ask about the other place, aren't they?"

Regina shocked herself with the comment. What was she doing? Did she *like* it?

She guided his hand over her panties so he could feel the front of them. Something lurid was taking over her senses...

"Hold your arm up," she commanded. As he bent his arm at the elbow, she kicked her leg up to rest over his arm. He wasn't expecting the action and nearly dropped her before he realized what she was after. He pressed his hand against the wall to support them both. "Stay above the fabric," she whispered.

Her eyes closed and she rested her head on his shoulder. He had no idea what he was doing but it still drove her desire for more than his clumsy touch. She pulled his free hand away to hold her firmly as she maneuvered the space between her legs to meet his hard protrusion, still protected by three layers of fabric.

His breathing sped up, so she grinded against him harder to be sure she could finish before or at the same time, but it was too late. He winced, and she was okay with that one as his breathing hitched three times. When he started to lean away from their embrace she seized his hand and placed it back between her legs, still over the fabric, and she ground herself to her own completion a few seconds later.

Virgo slowly lowered her leg and shrunk into himself, as if greatly ashamed.

"All the other guys may have been inside a woman," she said through steadying breaths, "but you're the first to feel the underwear and unshaved armpits of an Upcity pink pussy. They're going to be jealous as *fuck*."

"Yeah, I guess they are. Thanks. Am I...still a virgin?"

"Mm, no idea. Did it feel good, though?"

"God, yes."

"Then who the fuck cares?"

He walked off like an excited child before stopping around the corner and poking his head back.

"Hey... During the next coupling, can we have another date?"

"Sure. Looking forward to it."

Regina didn't plan on still being down there by then, but why rain on his parade?

When he disappeared, she leaned into the corner of the wall and checked for anyone close by. She couldn't see anyone beyond the brazier's light, so she put her fingers between her legs, beneath the fabric, to earn something more satisfying. Her eyes fluttered as the sensations intensified, then her heart seized at the sight directly in front of her: Vela, breathing heavily herself, her arm leaning against the wall to Regina's right, trapping her in the corner. She pulled her hand out, ready to push her way out of Vela's block, but Vela snatched her wrist and brought Regina's fingers into her mouth. Vela moaned while her tongue ran over each finger, sucking them clean. Regina felt her dinner threaten to escape, but feared if she threw up in Vela's face, she'd be killed.

"I've never had Upcity pussy before, either. You're the best thing I've ever tasted, Rag Doll."

Regina shivered in fear. How long had Vela been listening? *Watching?*

"No, no, no, baby," Vela's tone softened, and she pulled Regina's head to her hard chest. "I won't hurt you. Let me finish what you started, baby. You'll never look at a man the same again, I promise."

"I'm...I'm...I'm not..."

"Oh, I know, baby. I know. But you've never been with one. I won't force you to do anything for me. But let me show you what it's like. Just once."

Regina's opportunism peaked along with her piquing curiosity, and was that...also arousal? Or just the tingling sensation of fear electrifying her skin?

"Vela...if... If I let you, will you promise to never hit me?"

Vela brought Regina's face to hers and she put her mouth on Regina's cheek as if she was going to lick or kiss, but she only rubbed her lips over it as she whispered deep from her throat with need.

"Yes, yes, baby. I'll never hit you again. I won't hurt you."

She was on her knees and removing Regina's rag pants before Regina could respond affirmatively to the deal. Could she really trust Vela wasn't just saying that to get what she wanted? The fact Vela didn't expect *her* to do anything in return was a convincing point...

Vela caressed the underwear like it was the most precious material in the world. Her touch wasn't clumsy in the least. It was already doing a far better job than Virgo, and all she was doing was marveling at the fabric. Regina reluctantly hooked her thumb in the band of her panties and revealed her smooth front. Vela's mouth went to it immediately. Her tongue tickled, but in a much better way than when Virgo had touched her armpits. Her legs quaked, and Vela worked with it. Her smile was rare enough to see in any other circumstance but mocking and jovial threats. Regina couldn't stop staring at Vela's lips.

"You want these, don't you?" Vela whispered into the surrounding skin, her mouth causing little spasms in Regina. She *still* hadn't touched her where it mattered, and *it didn't matter* as Regina convulsed anyway. Vela caressed Regina's thighs, cupped her butt, and *eased* the orgasm along so Regina somehow didn't collapse to her knees.

Vela rose to Regina's face again.

"Oh baby, have I got things to show *you*."

Vela's lips met Regina's and their taste didn't make her as ill as she would have imagined, not to mention how surprisingly soft they were, despite Vela having such a dirty, violent mouth.

"Mmm," Vela moaned, then broke off the intense closed-mouth kiss. "I won't bite if you come to my nest tonight, Reggie baby."

She bent down and pulled Regina's pants back up. Vela gave a quick kiss on the cheek which Regina could feel her smile through, then left back to headquarters.

Regina started getting her breath back under control, but she remained frozen, stuck in a confused state of fearful shock and recent ecstasy. Her underwear was incredibly uncomfortable. Her arms seemed to have been stuck in the same position as when Vela took the fingers out of her mouth. In fact, had she moved at all since Vela cornered her, other than to lower the band of her underwear? She vaguely remembered her pants being pulled back up. Would she have even been able to do that on her own if Vela hadn't done it for her?

Once she finally gained a modicum of control over her legs, Regina shuffled her own way back. When she reached the headquarters, it was mostly empty. The Bulls were still out with their couplings.

Regina glimpsed the cardboard enclosure around Vela's nest. Regina's *temporary* nest was on the other side of the floor. Her feet carried her to her own nest but she kept looking over at Vela's. Struggling with indecision, she removed her wet underwear and put the pants back on. It was a freeing feeling, the looseness. She hid the underwear in a corner of her nest, then added the bra next to them and lay on her back in her pile of rags. As stimulated as she was, she fell asleep as instantly as if she were in the safety of her old bed, ten stories above.

PART TWO

REGRESSION TO THE MIDDLE

Chapter Eleven

UNFORESEEN

Sabrina woke to a pleasant, cool sensation. A dark shape hovered over her and caressed a wipe along the slash on her face. It took a disorienting moment to realize it was Erin, who hummed a lovely little tune of nothing.

"This'll be the best fucking scar in the gang," Erin whispered when she noticed Sabrina's eyes were open. "Even better than the ones Vela hides..."

Sabrina got up and turned away from Vela's biggest fan, but still thanked her for cleaning the wound. "Did you clean up the Snake, too?"

"...She's being a baby. She pushed me away."

"That's only natural. What we did to her..."

"Fucking deserved it," Erin muttered and got up to kick at Stevie's feet. "Wake up, S-s-s-snake. I don't know why we don't just kill her now, Rina. Why are we going to their turf?"

"Because Brace thinks she's still hanging in the sewer. She was going to send her body back to their gang as a warning, or she would have cut the rope. We have to take out a different Snake, maybe a higher up one."

"And a Demon, too, right?"

"If we find one..."

Sabrina took them to a nearby net and gathered scraps of food to fuel the day ahead, then they continued onward to Sector F. Each Sector had a main thoroughfare that was easier to traverse and avoid attracting attention from rival gangs, but they were still watched.

It wouldn't be until they got to Sector H or so that the Bull patches would mean nothing. Before that point, a pair of Bulls proved reason enough to give space—as long as they minded their own business.

Sector E seemed to be in a name competition with the Sapphire Snakes, as they adopted the moniker of the Violet Vipers. The Vipers wore strips of fabric wrapped around their arms like snakes as their patches. Sabrina had expected to see lots of them, but was surprised to find them all clustered in a circle, ignoring the street. She angled her little group over to them and their voices became clearer.

"No one in Sector E wants to help your stupid asses!" one shouted.

Sabrina decided it would be best not to poke her head over any of their shoulders to see who they were talking to, when another shout caught her ear.

"Demons aren't welcome here!"

Sabrina's sensibility evaporated as she wheeled around and pushed her way past a pair of surprised Vipers. In the center of their circle was a big Denim Demon with bruises on her face. A Viper stood on either side of her; one punched her in the shoulder while another targeted her lower back. Why was she just taking it? She was bigger than all of the Vipers, some *combined*, but she took easily block-able pot shots.

The Bull patch on Sabrina's back kept them from touching her as she stepped into the ring.

"What's going on, Vipers?"

"Butt out, Bull. She's trespassing and making up shit about having an ally here."

"Why would she make that up?" Sabrina got closer to the Demon, strategically turning her back so the other women got a good look at the Bull patch.

The Vipers sneered and mustered their courage for an all-out attack, done playing games. Erin pushed through and joined Sabrina's side. The Vipers' aggressive postures relaxed and they backed away at that.

One of the Vipers asked if there were more Bulls. Sabrina shook her head.

"All of you get out of our territory. We have enough Vipers in a two block radius to fuck you all up. If you're not gone by the time we get back with the rest, we will!"

The Vipers backed up but stayed a few feet away in a line. Sabrina tentatively slipped her arm through the Demon's to guide her towards Sector F. It was a moment before she remembered Stevie.

"Where's Stevie, Erin?"

"I'll get her. Meet you at the border."

The Demon pulled her arm out and muttered thanks for the assist.

"What is a Demon doing so deep in the Underfoot?"

"I'm wondering the same thing about a Bull. I heard you don't venture past C. Why haven't *you* attacked me yet? Or rather, why didn't you let the Vipers finish what they started?"

"I know the Demons are peaceful. You look like you could have taken them all on. The fact that you didn't fills me with such hope! I'm so glad to hear you have an ally in Sector E, too."

"I think I've been misinformed. They were more violent than any of the other sectors I've passed through."

They reached the border between E and F, and as they waited, Sabrina took in the Demon: a head taller, with broader shoulders, her jeans stretched taut against thick thighs.

"Listen, Demon, this is so grea—"

"Good thinking, Rina!" Erin said from behind. "Take out a Demon and Snake right away, then we can go home!"

She flung the Snake down and squared up to the Demon. Sabrina's lips quivered in a laugh to see the height disparity, but respected Erin for not letting that deter her.

"Come on, Erin, no need to—"

"Hey!" she snapped and shirked away from Sabrina's placating reach. "Don't interrupt a challenge!"

"No! It's not that eas—"

Erin packed a lot of unexpected strength into a push. Sabrina stumbled over Stevie and fell on her butt on the hard ground.

The Demon kept her eyes on Erin, content to take the first punch. Did the Demons duel, too?

Erin unloaded a punch that caused the Demon to take a step back and touch the spot reflexively, eyes almost comically wide, but she caught herself and squared up. If it was any other time, Sabrina would have been so proud of the power housed in that small body. Vela really did teach her well... Erin readied herself for the counter, striking a strong stance and putting on her best grimace of intensity.

The Demon turned around and walked away.

Erin cried out and demanded she stop and answer. Sabrina scrambled up and put her hand on Erin's chest to hold her back from an advance. Satisfied that Erin would stay put based on her confused expression, Sabrina ran to catch up to the Demon. She touched her elbow to get her attention. The Demon wheeled faster than expected and Sabrina was on the ground again, the only recognizable sight tinged with a red glow from nearby braziers. Or was it blood?

The Demon materialized over Sabrina with a sad look on her face.

"I'm...I'm sorry. I thought the other one was going to sucker punch me..."

Sabrina's only reaction was to put her hand over her left eye. The hit had been so hard she was still recovering from the shock, her mouth hanging open as her face slackened to internalize all the force she'd just absorbed.

"I... We're not supposed to..." the Demon said before Erin jumped into her torso and brought a double-fisted hammer swing down on her head. The Demon staggered back and grabbed Erin's shoulders, then flung her into a growing crowd of people.

The towering Demon stooped and put a hand on Sabrina's shoulder. "I'm sorry you're a Bull."

With that she turned and ran before Erin recovered, pushing away the onlookers who caught her. When it was clear the woman was not only too big, but too fast as well, Erin stopped her pursuit and came back. Frustrated tears fell off her cheek. She rubbed them angrily away with her sleeve and sat cross-legged beside Sabrina.

"That— It doesn't count, right? She broke the challenge! I won't tell anyone you fell... That wasn't *fair!*"

Regret kept Sabrina on the ground even after the shock of getting knocked flat subsided. What a shitty turn of events. Why couldn't they have all just *talked* for a minute?

Sabrina sighed as her focus shifted to the feeling that something might be seriously wrong with her eye—Erin seemed off-center, although sitting squarely beside her. Sabrina held her hand over her eye, as if it was the only thing keeping her from losing it. With the other hand, she reached out for Erin's. Erin grabbed it and hugged it against her cheek, then kissed the heavily callused knuckles and placed it in her lap, holding it firmly.

"I won't tell..." she whispered, tears pushing out again. "I promise."

"Stop crying, Bull," Sabrina whispered, though her voice cracked.

An unfamiliar woman came into Sabrina's view. "Need an escort to the Clinic?"

"We don't need your help, S-s-s-snake b—" Erin started before Sabrina squeezed her hand hard.

She got up and braced herself against Erin's shoulder, then held her hand out to the Sapphire Snake, who took it reluctantly. She hadn't seen their back patches yet.

"Listen," Sabrina said, "Stevie needs your help. She's over there. She needs more antibiotics. I'm sorry for what we did to her."

The Snake froze in place. She was obviously only on patrol and hadn't expected to run into two Bulls and a near-dead Snake. She didn't seem to have close backup. Sabrina used that moment of fear. She directed Erin to retrieve Stevie, then addressed the confounded Snake.

"Hey... I need a favor from your gang, since I brought the assassin back to you. When the Denim Demons come through to negotiate, *please* ally with them. They're going to have trouble with Sector E. It's in all of our interests to cooperate with the Demons.

"Will you please tell your leader?"

The Snake didn't respond clearly, cut off by Erin dumping Stevie in her arms.

"Two for one, Rina. It's these S-s-s-snakes' fault you've been hurt so badly in the last two days. Let me fuck them up for you."

"Nuh...no." Sabrina's lips quivered as the pain in her eye persisted and she struggled to hold back a wail. "Go, Snake. Get out of here! Help your sister!"

Erin gave an unnecessary shove in the back to the healthy one, as if to get in a "last word." Sabrina took Erin's hand and led her back to Sector E. At the border, Sabrina leaned on Erin's confused shoulder.

"Sister, you... You have to get us through here. I...can't see to my left."

Sabrina *could* see the battle playing out in Erin's head through her hesitation. They were disobeying Brace to return home without enacting further revenge, and Sabrina had been knocked on her ass *twice*—by that Demon and Erin. Sabrina didn't mind disillusioning Erin of her competence as a Bull leader, or losing her unfounded infatuation, but prayed in her moment of weakness that Erin would remain loyal—or at least be enticed by the opportunity of superseding her sister enough to see her home and formally disbarred.

Erin blew that expectation up by kissing Sabrina on the cheek and promising to protect her through the Sector. She tightened her grip on Sabrina's hand and led her swiftly through the street. A block from the border, a large contingent of Vipers stood. Erin veered to go around a less-travelled block, but more Vipers materialized to hem them in.

Erin's palm grew sweaty and their grips loosened. Sabrina knew what went through Erin's mind before she even made the decision. She opened her mouth to issue a challenge but Sabrina let go of her eye to clamp her hand over Erin's mouth.

"I'm already out of the Bulls, Erin," Sabrina whispered. "Slip out of here. Go be with your sisters."

Erin tore her head out of Sabrina's hold.

"*Our* sisters."

Sabrina tried to ignore the dismay at her sight loss once the removal of her hand confirmed it.

"If you still believe that, as your XO I *command you* to escape while I distract them. Get the fuck out of here, Erin!"

Erin took a quick look around at the converging Vipers, then she surprised Sabrina further with a kiss on the lips.

"I'm not leaving you, Rina." Erin spun around and put her back into Sabrina's. "I'll protect your left side."

Sabrina clocked the enlarged fists of some of the Vipers concealing thin pipes behind the fingers.

"They have pipes, Erin. Take those out first."

Erin's back stiffened, pushed off, then came back. She'd struck the first blow, judging by the wet sound of a Viper hitting the ground. Sabrina was pleased that one of the pipe-bearers on her side attacked first. She caught the fist and leveled the attacker, then bent to pick up the pipe and threw it as far as she could so that it clattered into the next sector. The Vipers hesitated at the quick loss of a weapon and two fighters. Brass Bulls never used weapons, despite their opponents always trying to gain any sort of upper hand.

A mass pressed hard into Sabrina's left side: Erin catching a running Viper and reversing the momentum. A pipe rolled out of the Viper's hand after Erin rendered her unconscious with a punch to the side of the head. Sabrina flung the pipe into the mass of feet, then Erin helped her scramble up in time for the next round of Vipers to rush them.

Between punching their faceless assailants, Sabrina and Erin routinely reached behind each other to verify they were still there. Erin's open hand on her back reminded Sabrina of the way Kirsten would touch her after a hard day's work. The thought brought a new desperate thought that fueled her fighting fire: she *had* to see Panda and Kirsten again. No one would take care of them if something happened to her.

Unfortunately, the sheer number of Vipers countered Erin and Sabrina's devastating blows. Worse, exhaustion caught up to them much faster with all the extra movement of repositioning and remaining vigilant; much more taxing than standing in front of an opponent one-on-one when both know what's coming.

A pipe fist hit Sabrina above her forehead hard enough to cause blood to spill from split skin into her good eye and she staggered. Erin caught her with her own back and pushed Sabrina up to her feet—the only thing keeping Sabrina upright. They were officially losing, and she was about to get Erin killed in the process, and for what?

A commotion rose above the din from Sabrina's right. A woman a head taller than everyone else bulled through the mass of Vipers. The brief reprieve allowed Sabrina to wipe the blood out of her eye to see more clearly that the Denim Demon returned. No longer passively taking pot shots, she made the Vipers cower in fear of the damage she inflicted.

The Vipers who'd been hanging around the back of the mass changed their priorities to helping their fallen sisters up and away from the fray. Sabrina dropped to her knees, utterly spent. Erin put her hands in Sabrina's armpits and lifted her, then ran them through a gap in the Vipers' defense. With a nauseating swivel, Sabrina looked back to see the Demon following closely behind. They crossed the border to Sector D and the last few chasing Vipers slowed and hurled curses and shouts at the retreating "cowards" to never step foot in Sector E again.

Sabrina could hardly keep her legs beneath her, so the Demon helped Erin with the burden of dragging her to a relatively safe alcove off the main street. Once they rested with their backs to the wall, Erin startled them with a sob before she covered her mouth. It was too dark to see any damage, but when Sabrina put her hand on Erin's forehead, it was covered with either sweat or blood. She sniffed her hand, and it was both.

"I was told Bulls don't cry," the Demon said as she caught her breath.

"She's not crying," Sabrina mumbled, her energy too low to speak clearly. "It's the joy of surviving another day..."

The Demon left it at that and pressed her head against the wall.

"I'm *so* glad you came back," Erin's voice cracked. "Now you can complete my challenge and I can avoid exile."

Sabrina sighed and put her hand in Erin's, entwining their fingers.

"No one's going to exile you, sister. I promise."

"I don't want your promise. I have to prove myself."

"None of them were there." Sabrina put her other hand on Erin's chin and drew her close so she could squint in the faint red light to gauge her reaction. "I don't think you took as much damage as me, but you took enough that they'll buy that you fulfilled the second half of your challenge."

Sabrina let go and leaned back again, too exhausted to partake in further debate.

"Why did you come back?" she asked the Demon.

"Olive might have exiled *me* if I told her I left behind people who saved me from those Vipers."

"You...speak directly with Olive?"

"I'm the XO. Twill." She offered her hand to Sabrina for a shake, which Sabrina returned and matched the strength behind it.

"Tell me when you've got your breath back, *Twill*. Then you need to hit me." Erin spoke without looking in Twill's direction; it was simply a matter of fact that it must happen. Nothing Sabrina said could dissuade her true Bull heart *or* head.

"I have to get back. I don't have time for your violent nonsense."

Erin exhaled like she was ignoring the words and preparing to take the hit. Sabrina took advantage of her expectant demeanor and told her to stand outside and ready herself, then leaned to Twill.

"Get back to where? Which sector are you in?" Sabrina prodded.

"We'll be taking over Sector L this week."

"You're going to have your hands full with A through E, I can tell you that. I put in a word for you in F. I hope they listen. Sectors I and H are *friendly* rivals, not outright enemies. Win one and you win both. I wish I had more info on the others..."

"...Why are you telling me all this?"

"Twill, I think they fucked up the relay. Your contact wasn't in E, it was *B*. *I'm* the ally. I...may not be useful after today. I've...failed every possible test since..."

Twill rustled in her rags and pulled out a small roll of bright fabric. It reflected the small amount of light in a silver glow.

"I was to give this to the new contact. When we come through, we'll do everything we can to make it peaceful, but if there's fighting, we'll count on anyone wearing a patch of this to help us."

Sabrina nodded and pocketed the roll. She shook Twill's hand again. "Thank you, sister, for coming back for us."

"Thank you for your support, sister. I look forward to the day we work together side-by-side."

Sabrina tried to get up but fell back into the wall. Twill helped her up, then they went out to meet Erin. As before, she squared up, ready to take a hit.

"Just hit her in the stomach, and it'll complete the challenge," Sabrina whispered. "Make it hurt if you want her to relent."

Twill did as asked. Erin doubled over but stayed on her feet. After a moment overcoming a dry-heave, she stood straight again like she was ready for another. Twill put her hand out for a shake. Erin looked at it for a moment. Sabrina worried she'd have to explain they wouldn't be alive without Twill, and that killing a Demon was no longer on the agenda, but Erin finally shook it. She put visible effort into out-gripping the woman almost twice her size. Twill only smiled, then turned to leave. Erin shouted for her to wait, then ran to a pile of fabric near a brazier. She unceremoniously pulled the blanket from around the dead body and handed it over to Twill, pantomiming covering up her jeans for easier travel between sectors.

Twill thanked them both with a nod, then left. Sabrina put her arm around Erin for support as they watched her disappear into Sector E. Sabrina began to turn away when Erin brought their lips together and held them there. She put her arms around Sabrina's neck and insisted the kiss not end.

Sabrina had no energy to resist, but the kiss did a remarkable job of helping her forget all the pain in her face and body. She tasted dried blood from both of their lips pushing through their slightly open mouths.

Erin broke it off, mercifully, put Sabrina's arm over her shoulder, and led them back in the direction of Sector B to meet their fates together. But on the way, the least Sabrina owed Erin was an explanation for her treasonous actions...

Chapter Twelve

CANTANKEROUS

OLIVE WOKE INSIDE A busy tent. As she oriented herself, a Doctor examined a patient, discharged him with a handful of pills, then ushered in another one. Olive's lower back hurt deeper than skin and muscle. Her right leg throbbed. She lifted a blanket to discover a long row of stitches.

"You can only be in here for another few minutes, then you need to move on," the unfamiliar Doctor said to Olive while probing the new patient's ribcage and back. "I recommend you keep weight off the leg so it can heal faster."

"Why does my back hurt?" Olive asked as she got up gingerly.

"I don't know. If you want a more thorough exam, you'll have to get in line. I staunched the bleeding when your friend rushed you in here, but haven't had time for a genuine inspection."

"I'm sorry for the trouble. Do you need help cleaning up?"

"She already did that. She's been waiting outside. I gave her antibiotics and wipes for you. Now I think it's best you move along. I don't like patients cutting in my lines."

Olive limped out among the long queues of gangless. She looked around for Twill but there were no exceptionally tall women standing in wait, nor were there any Denim Demons. An unfamiliar woman approached and put her hand on Olive's arm.

"Feeling better, then?"

"No..." Olive winced at the lower back pain that wouldn't go away even as she stretched.

"Come on, let's get away from the crowd." The woman offered her shoulder for Olive to lean against. The crowd parted, but Olive couldn't tell if it was for her or the woman. Then she looked down to realize her jeans were actually gone, replaced by rags that parted along her leg to allow it to breathe.

Confusingly, the woman led them to a building off the main street. She tried to deposit Olive near a mint of candles but Olive resisted.

"I'm...sorry. My back... I don't think I can sit."

The woman nodded and held out a steadying hand while Olive eased herself against the wall. Olive asked the woman who she was. She rolled up her sleeve to reveal a crude scar of a rabbit carved out in her skin.

"Royal Rabbit, hm?" Olive had mixed feelings—they were the gang who they were to negotiate with once the Purple Rams situation cleared. "Am I... Is this sector L?"

"Mmhm. You're in my territory, Denim Demon. I found you with half of your jeans torn off, but I recognized them."

"But I was in Sector M... Wasn't I?"

"Let me start from the beginning. I found a Purple Ram dead on my street. Based on the state he was in, he'd been doing what Rams *do*. I followed the blood trail from his stomach, and then your leg, all the way into Sector M—where I found you lying face down near a pile of garbage."

"I was near the water techs when I... I don't remember any garbage..."

"It was *near* there. Based on your back pain... They must have dumped you off after—"

"Please, don't..." Olive held up her hand as a pained tear rolled off her jaw. "So then you brought me here? Why not just leave me in a Sector M Clinic?"

"I said this is my sector. The Doctors make way for Rabbits here. You needed to see someone. Fast."

"Thank...you," Olive's head dropped and she pressed her palm into her eyes to prevent more tears from rushing out. Regret piled up in her chest as she questioned every decision she'd made since the battle of the Thirsty Thorns.

Her attempt to hold back caught in her throat and sobs burst out anyway. The Rabbit put her arms around her and guided Olive's head to her shoulder. She stood there patiently as Olive shed her sorrow and pain.

"My Rabbits killed the water techs. Then we brought two of ours to Sector M to train new techs. They're all women."

Olive didn't know what to do with that information. She didn't care about the techs that hurt her; she had no place for people like that once she'd push through the sector, but... Olive extended her arms, separating from the Rabbit's embrace, a hint of disgust crawling along her lips over the killing, regardless.

"Are you close with the Demons' leader?" the Rabbit asked.

"...Yes," Olive whispered, then sniffed and rubbed her face with a sleeve.

"We've seen the gang's progress and what happens with the men. I want to propose a different tact in Sector L."

"What do you propose I pass on to her?"

"What that Ram tried last night? It's almost *daily* for the gangless here, and my weaker Rabbits. I don't think you're going to get anywhere with them. The vaccines will only make them bolder."

"You want to...?"

"Negotiations are a waste of time. I need help to wipe out the Rams. We'll join the Demons, as long as we can stay in our home. I know the Demons spread out..."

"Demons don't kill..."

"Your leader is going to have to get over that if she plans to push further. K, G, and A through E are going to give you all hell. None of them will accept peace. The Bulls are dug in from A to C, and I've heard D has been given an ultimatum to join as well. The Demons can't afford to risk a protracted war in the middle."

Olive couldn't decide if she should drop the charade with the Rabbit, then bring up the new information with Twill later. But could they afford "later?" Who knew how much time Twill would be away seeking the contact in Sector E?

Was she even in any position to argue with the necessity for brutal solutions, having suffered from that very situation and needed saving? She needed the sectors to need *her*, not the other way around...

Thinking about the destruction wrought by men, she remembered the seeds she'd been sowing by pawning off the weapons—allowing the men to defend against each other while also satisfying their base needs so they'd leave the women alone. Olive needed to harness her advantage.

"What's your name, Rabbit?"

"Ren."

"Ren, what if we could get what we want without dirtying our hands?"

OLIVE REINFORCED WITH HER Madames the priority to make the men happy and solidify their commitment to the women in their sectors, then they had the male gangs send volunteers from Sectors M through Z to destroy the Purple Rams for their transgression.

It was a quick but bloody affair—they had weapons and the Rams didn't. Olive and Ren had the drugs collected and centralized. Olive wanted to throw them into the sewers, but cutting off the supply so suddenly would cause nothing but misery. By centralizing, the Demons and Rabbits planned to wean the citizens to sobriety and earn their allegiance if they returned to functionality. Anyone who resisted conformity would suffer for their vices eventually, when the drugs never resupplied.

The victorious men were treated to women from different sectors than their own on their ways back home. They were told to remain available in case they'd be needed again, and almost all of them seemed eager for the prospect of glory and happily received rewards.

Twill returned after the battle was over and said nothing about the decision Olive made. She only relayed the information about their new ally in Sector B, not E—the best thing Olive heard all week.

The first night Twill was back, Olive wouldn't let Twill touch her, nor show her the leg wound—claiming to be sore from a slip on cement near the water pipes. The next night she feigned tiredness, even though she lay awake the whole time. The third she simply "felt gross" but refused Twill's offer to personally wipe her down from head to toe. The fourth she drank too much wine to force herself to fall asleep.

In the daytime they worked with the Rabbits to set up negotiations with Sector K, fraught with peril as that would be. With Twill by her side, Olive was more confident and didn't feel as vulnerable, but that still didn't allow her to let Twill's affection through. Whenever they were alone, Olive would push Twill's hand away.

Even as the pain in her back lessened, imagining what had happened to her, along with her memories of the Ram on top of her—every sensation, from panicked fear to her fingers in his intestines—wouldn't go away, no matter how much she drank to forget. Twill made a comment that there wouldn't be enough wine to share with the new sectors they conquered if Olive continued.

The night before the Sector K negotiations, Twill didn't even bother coming to their nest, and that hurt Olive more than she expected. She *needed* Twill close by to feel safe, even if she couldn't handle her touch yet.

Olive left the Rabbit's headquarters and asked a sentry if they noticed which direction Twill had gone. After wandering and meeting a few more Rabbits along the way, Olive realized Twill had just gone to get water. At that, she held back and found an old docking platform to sit on and wait for Twill to return. Being near the water pipes was the last thing she needed.

With the stitches, she'd been avoiding wearing jeans, relying on a loose skirt of rags that split along the side. As she dangled her legs over the edge Olive swore she felt blood running down the length of them, dripping off of her toes. She rubbed her hand along her thighs, but she was dry. Even along her stitches nothing seeped out. She leaned back on her palms and stared off into the darkest corner along the street. The things haunting her kept adding up...

Something brushed her foot and she reflexively kicked out. A hand caught it before it connected with anything. Olive leaned forward to Twill.

"I'm sorry. That was a refle—"

"I know."

"I... I thought you might have...left."

"Why would I ever leave the Demons?"

That stung. Before, Twill would frame their relationship on each other, not the gang. Was it a passive aggressive swipe at Olive not returning her affections? Twill was far more direct than that...

"The Purple Rams. The killing..."

"That's *your* hangup. I would have made the same decision."

"Good." Awkwardness filled the air and Olive forgot why she even came after her.

"Do you need help down from there?"

She did, but didn't want anyone touching her, even Twill.

Especially Twill.

"Why don't you tell me about the Bulls?"

Twill leaned her hand on the platform edge, her thumb lightly touching Olive's thigh. It wasn't lost in Twill's eyes when Olive scooted away an inch.

"They pack a fucking punch, Olive. The smaller of the two that I met nearly knocked me over, and it took all my power not to react too much. Then she took a hit that has won battles for me. The *smaller* of the two! Tunnel-visioned on her goal, cantankerous. She demanded to take my hit *after* we were at peace, to satisfy their code, then she helped with my travels like it hadn't even happened!"

Olive let that wash over her. Such news was daunting, even with the knowledge that at least one of them was on their side.

"Two of them nearly held off an attack by all of the Violet Vipers. They might have succeeded if I hadn't crippled one of them..."

"You just said—"

"Our new ally, I meant."

"You *crippled* her?"

"Yes. I'm not proud of it. I didn't mean to. It was a reflex."

"Is this going to be an issue going forward?"

"She's on our side still. I... Even with what I did to her she's still eager to help us. I respect her greatly."

Olive leaned her elbows on her knees and scratched her itchy scalp.

"If one of them will turn, perhaps others will..."

"I would not count on much help, besides the one I gave the bright fabric to. But...I know she'll try."

"All of that said, how are we going to—"

"We'll need to think on it. None of it matters if we don't *reach* Sector B. We can't afford to look that far ahead yet."

Olive thought about the cantankerous one.

"There have always been rumors about the Bulls' love for challenges..."

"They are not overblown, and they take them as seriously as you take not killing."

Olive sneered at herself; she'd already crossed that line twice. The Bulls had more integrity than she did...

"What do you think of using their challenges against them? What if the leader allowed a negotiation by way of a one-off challenge?"

"Olive, I'm going to say this as gently as I can. The *small* one would break you in half with one blow. If that's anything to go by, their leader could kill *me*."

"Can you... Can I train for this?"

Twill shook her head. "The Bulls train, even before their initiations. If you aren't killed, there must be a return blow, which they learn to take as well as they can dish out."

Twill took Olive's hand and used unexpected strength to not let Olive pull away.

"Your hand would break against their leader's face, and she wouldn't even react to it."

"You're exaggerating."

"I'm not. I'll prove it to you. I want you to hit me as hard as you can."

Olive used her other hand to yank away from Twill's grasp.

"No. I could never hurt you."

"You're right, which already proves my initial point, but... I want you to get out whatever has made you hate me this week."

"I don't hate you."

"Then why have you been—"

"I can't tell you, Twill."

"Tell me with your fist."

Olive smiled a little at that. "That's stupid."

"Not to Sector B. But regardless of that, if it's the only way you'll touch me, I'll welcome your fist."

"Love makes us do stupid things, doesn't it?" Olive ran her hand over Twill's healing cheek from the hit she took from the Bull.

Twill put her hand on Olive's thigh. Olive picked it up and moved it aside, but kept her hand on top to run her thumb over.

A slow recognition seemed to cross over Twill, that it wasn't touch itself Olive was rejecting, but *where*. Olive couldn't keep pushing Twill away like that, for Twill's sake, or her own. She resolved to hold her hand more, and perhaps the nauseous feeling she had from being touched would finally go away.

However, she *did* need help down from the platform and her pride backed off enough to allow Twill to put her hands into her armpits and lift her down like a child. Before, Twill might have given a playful caress over Olive's chest before letting go, but Twill respectfully avoided the excessive contact.

Olive looked up into Twill's eyes and took her hand, leading them back to the Rabbits' headquarters. Twill said she'd help keep watch and Olive went to their nest alone. For the first time in a long while Olive slept easier, knowing her partner would watch over her.

Chapter Thirteen

PRIDE

VELA ACTED LIKE SHE hadn't nearly melted Regina the night before—mind and body. She didn't even make eye contact during the morning meeting. That distance initially confused Regina but she was ultimately relieved that the encounter might just blow over and be forgotten. Although... She'd had a dream that took things *further* than they'd ended in real life, in which Regina took up Vela's offer to join in her nest. She hadn't woken up with revulsion, which did nothing more than perplex her. Perhaps a day apart was what she needed for a full reset.

Regina ate around bite marks of scraps while Sally taught a group of initiates how to take punches in Rina's absence. The next initiation was only a couple of days away. Rina hadn't really done much with her, but Regina couldn't really blame her, what with the whole assassination and revenge thing.

Ezzie paced around the initiates, nodding or shaking her head at Sally's lessons, but she didn't interrupt, either. Regina bolstered her insane state of mind and ambled over to the Bulls' number three leader. She offered Ezzie the rest of her scraps, who stared for a moment, then wolfed them down.

"Thanks, Rag Doll. Instead of tossin' it half-eaten out a fuckin' window, then lettin' the Scavengers get their nasty hands on it, then lettin' it trade more filthy digits 'til it arrived here, you gave it right to me. How'd that feel? I could fuckin' kiss you."

"Please—don't," Regina said a little too defensively. Ezzie squinted at her, then a smile broke across her hard face.

"Hey, I can get you alone time with one of the men. One who might know a little more about what he's doin'. There's one stud that really knows how to work it around—"

"That's... Why would you think I need *that?*"

"That look on your face. You did somethin' you can't tell if you liked or not. Trust me, bein' around all these muff divers day in and day out, some of them not shy about propositionin', it gets temptin'. Sometimes you need to get somethin' more substantial inside you to push out those feelin's, am I right?"

"You're not— That's not why I came to you. I want you to teach me. Sally's busy and Rina's gone."

Ezzie brought her arm up and extended a punch in a flash. Regina flinched despite the blow never landing.

"That's reason number one I can't teach you. Reacting like a coward before a blow's even landed means you'll lose like one. Did you see Rina fuckin' flinch when Vela did that the other day? No, you didn't. But even if I could teach you how not to react, how to take a hit, and how to punch, none of it matters because of the second reason."

Ezzie didn't elaborate and turned to walk away. Regina caught up to her and put her hand on her shoulder. She spun and Regina ducked another fake blow.

"It's not about avoidin', runt."

"What's the second reason?"

"You up for a little trip?"

"What else do I have going on right now?"

"That's *also* part of the point. Come on."

Regina followed close behind Ezzie as she made her way to Brace and Vela having a little meeting by the front door. She let them know she'd be taking the Rag Doll for a walk. When Regina passed through the door, a hand brushed hers. She looked back to see Vela and Brace still talking without acknowledging her.

Ezzie carried herself with impossible confidence, a hammer among an ocean of nails. She never moved around anyone, walking through trash cans without breaking stride. Regina feared she would be broken in two if she were to take an actual punch from the human wrecking ball. Anxiety over her decision crept in…

A horrifying thud, followed by a shower of debris hit a spot just off the main street, a couple dozen feet from them. A rush of people converged on the site. The net above had been caved in by something. Scavengers moved quickly to repair the nets while the trash cans ran away with their garbage treasures. When they dispersed, nothing but a mass of gore remained.

"Why'd you stop?" Ezzie asked, then took a quick look at what froze Regina. "Oh. What the *fuck* do you assholes have to be so sad about?" Ezzie shook her head and continued on.

Regina caught up, but was unable to tear her eyes away from the body until they'd physically lost sight of it. Ezzie laughed when Regina's face wouldn't loosen up, even some blocks later.

"Hey, Rag Doll, when you get to that point in your life, could you strap some good stuff to your body? Or if you know anyone thinking about taking the plunge, stick a fuckin' candy bar in their pocket. Write 'Ezzie' on it first."

"Sure…"

"What a downer you are. Oh, ha! I love a good pun."

"Noted."

Ezzie punched Regina's arm "playfully." It felt like the six-month check-up exam—the kind that squeezes to check blood pressure, crushing the very blood vessels together. Regina knew she'd only receive more mocking laughter if she rubbed it, so she ignored it; pretended it didn't hurt.

Their destination turned out to be...the Elevators?

"Okay, Raggy, you pay close fuckin' attention. I'll show you why I don't take you seriously. It has to do with your hand."

Ezzie placed her palm on Regina's back and shoved her forward.

"Go on. Go put your hand on the Elevator and come back to me."

Regina frowned but walked forward. An officer stopped her by extending his electric baton but didn't turn it on.

"You're not as dirty as the others. Hold out your hand."

He scanned the back of her left hand and the little device flashed *green* with a corresponding positive *blip*.

"Says you're down here for...vacation? What the fuck?"

"Suh...something like that. It was a joke by my—"

"Alright, it's legal, it's just... Well, I'm sure you've had your fill of this garbage dump, eh? Move along."

Regina stepped past the armed sentries, then looked over her shoulder at Ezzie, who motioned for her to keep going. Regina put her hand on the Elevator door, then returned. The officer grabbed her shoulder as she passed.

"Hey, did you forget something?"

"Yes, I did. I've got to go grab it before one of those trash cans keeps it for themselves."

"Yeah, they'll do that. Hurry back or you'll have to deal with the scanning again at shift change."

Ezzie leaned casually on a barrier that separated the path for the Doctors from the "wrong side."

"What was that supposed to prove?"

"Watch this."

Ezzie hopped the barrier and strutted coolly towards the Elevators. The officer didn't speak to her, only immediately delivering a shock from the baton. Ezzie miraculously shrugged it off and kept walking forward. A second, then third officer joined and shocked her to a standstill. A fourth came round and hit her in the stomach with a club, then swung it across her face, knocking her on her back. All four guards grabbed her arms and legs and dragged her away, leaving her in the middle of the path from whence she'd come. A warning to others?

A group of trash cans converged on her, but Regina scattered them before they could tear at Ezzie's rags. She grabbed Ezzie's wrists and pulled her away from the path to a safer spot off the main street, next to a brazier. There was a dead body on the other side of it.

Ezzie didn't respond to prodding or light slapping. Unsure of how long she'd be out, Regina put Ezzie's head on her lap and pulled out a wipe to clean the angry welt forming along her cheek. That carried over to clearing dirt from the rest of her face. It was nice to see her skin without the layers of filth. Her nose was crooked but everything else would pass for low attractiveness only a few levels above them.

Regina tossed the soiled wipe into the brazier. It flashed bright for a second before returning to normal.

"Are you gonna kiss me, Rag Doll?" Regina jolted at Ezzie's open eyes. Ezzie gave a quick, easy smile, despite the tightness she must have felt in her face. "I don't like girls, so don't even try it."

Regina returned a little smile of her own and eased Ezzie into a sitting position from her lap.

"How long did I stand?"

"It took four of them to knock you down, even with those electric clubs."

"Nice. Wait'll the Bulls hear about *that*."

"So... What was that supposed to prove?"

"That this isn't your life. You can escape anytime. You can go lay your head on a... What did Brace call it? A *bed? Pillows?* We're nothing but a curiosity to you."

Regina folded her hands into her lap and didn't argue.

"Didn't think someone like me would notice?" Ezzie reached out and pushed Regina's shoulder. "We're not a fuckin' *zoo*, bitch. If I was in charge I would have dipped you in the sewer, then marched you straight to those Elevators. I don't know what Brace wants out of this, but you could never survive the initiation. I don't think she expects you will, either. You're supposed to *leave*."

"Maybe I want to prove something..."

"There are no 'maybes' down here. All those women gettin' ready for their initiation have been goin' through it their whole lives. But let's say you don't get knocked on your ass—you *still get to go home!* This is our LIFE. You don't get to come down here with those other pink pussies and decide you can be one of us.

"I will *fuck you up* with a challenge if Brace is stupid enough to let you in. Not that Brace would be stupid; *you* would be for playing along that far."

Regina shimmied up the wall and Ezzie stood.

"Don't take it too hard, Raggy. You *acted* like a sister when you helped Rina, even though she had the upper hand. You *acted* like a sister, draggin' me away from those opportunists by the Elevators. I heard about Sally's challenge, and you took it like a sister would, despite the result. And for whatever reason I'll never understand, you just walked back here from touchin' those goddamn Elevators.

"But you're *fuckin'* weak, you're too pampered, and this isn't your fuckin' home. Do you need a third reason I can't teach you nothin'?"

Was this what *pride* felt like? To open her mouth after all that, knowing Ezzie was one-hundred-percent right, and say: "Why don't you fucking hit me and get it over with?"

Ezzie mimed another hit, but Regina didn't flinch. It surprised her more than it did Ezzie.

"Are you challengin' me, runt?"

"...Yes."

"Are you expectin' I'm gonna hold back because I like you?"

"You like me?"

Ezzie's chest shuddered, her lips quivered, then she burst out laughing—just like Sally had...

"I like your sense of humor and pride, Rag Doll. But I don't hold back. Not even for pretty pink virgins like you."

"You're... You're stalling, Ezzie. And did you just insult Sally?"

Regina had lost control of her tongue along with her common sense.

The mirth flushed out of Ezzie's face, and the shadows from the brazier gave her a sinister quality that Regina had to will herself not to back away from.

"Don't bring my sisters into our challenge. This is between you and me."

Regina raised her chin and squared herself, offsetting one foot to brace against the coming blow.

"No, no, no. I can't hit you in the face without Brace's permission. Like I said, I don't know what she sees in you, but I'm not risking my life in the Bulls for it."

"So much talking for a—"

"It'll be stomach hits. Get out of that ridiculous stance. You go first, virgin."

Ezzie's stomach was as hard as Sally's face, despite the lack of bone structure. Regina's fingers seemed stuck in crooked positions after the strike, but she muffled an outcry and slowly flexed her hand back into shape. She expected a smirk or laugh from Ezzie, but she only stood there, waiting for Regina to square back up.

Regina tightened up and braced, but it was all in vain. Her food scraps came out all over Ezzie's feet as she crumpled around Ezzie's fist. Regina's feet lifted off the ground with the hit. When she landed, she desperately gathered her remaining awareness to keep from falling over or losing her footing. Regina willed both feet to stiffen once they met the ground, and concentrated on her breathing so she could straighten her back. Despite the horrible tightness around the spot that Ezzie had tagged, Regina only needed a few seconds to *look* like she was ready for another.

Ezzie laughed and clapped Regina's shoulder almost as hard.

"You know, Raggy, you almost make me wish you didn't have that fuckin' chip in your hand. Come on, Doll."

Ezzie laughed again when Regina could only take slow, steady steps to keep from falling over. She had to remember how to walk, and Ezzie wasn't helping.

INSIDE THE HEADQUARTERS LATER in the evening, the Bulls gathered for dinner. Ezzie stopped outside and lit a torch from the nearby brazier, then beckoned Regina to follow her. She halted in front of all the sisters and held her hand on Regina's shoulder.

"Brass Bulls! I want you all to see somethin'!" Ezzie grabbed the bottom of Regina's rag shirt and lifted it over her head, exposing her bra-less torso to the whole group. "Look at this fuckin' welt on our Rag Doll! She took my hit without fallin'!"

Ezzie dropped the shirt back and cheers greeted Regina for the first time in her life. Genuine ones, anyway—not the polite, almost forced applause from her art showings in school. Her face flushed hotter with pride than from getting unexpectedly exposed. Brace and Vela clapped their hands on each of her shoulders to add to all the other stinging areas of her body. Vela didn't walk away like Brace. She leaned over to whisper to Ezzie.

"Why do I get the feeling you held back?"

Ezzie squared up immediately, pushing Regina off to the side. The two titans exchanged blows. Their feet didn't move an inch, nor did they react to their freshly-bleeding faces. Vela barked a laugh and hugged Ezzie tight.

"What a true hit! Reggie, you have my respect—Ezzie *wasn't* holding back."

A new cheer rose and all the Bulls in the vicinity clapped Regina along her shoulders. She surmised her whole back would be more swollen than her stomach in the morning, but she kept on smiling through every whack.

When the boisterousness died down, a hush fell over the floor. Erin entered the headquarters. Regina stood expectantly like everyone else for Rina to come in so she could share their news, but Erin was alone. Her expression was hard, her face battered.

Brace went to her and looked her face over with Ezzie's torch.

"What a *battle*, sister! Where's Rina?"

Erin stiffened her back and held her chin up.

"We were successful in our mission, Brace. Two Sapphire Snakes and a Denim Demon are dead in Sector F. And we fucked up a *whole lotta* Violet Vipers!"

The cheers were louder for that news than they'd been for Regina, but it was a silly thing to get jealous over. However, it *was* an intoxicating feeling, being on the receiving end...

"Wonderful, Erin. Where's Rina?"

"You should have seen her, Brace. She fought harder than I did. She took every hit better than I could have. She just...took *more* than I did..."

Brace ran her thumb over Erin's cheek, like she'd done for Regina the first day they met. Her thumb glistened from the torch light for a brief moment.

"She's... Our Rina is in a Clinic..."

Vela came forward and stood next to Brace, scrutinizing Erin's face.

"You're lying," Vela whispered, but the floor was silent enough for everyone to hear.

"I'm... I'm really not... Vela..."

"I know you, Erin..."

"I'm... Bulls, I'm not lying about Rina. She withstood it all. Every blow." Erin's shoulders slumped. "*I*...failed. They knocked me down."

The Bulls behind Regina gasped in a way that reminded her of pearl-clutching Upcity women.

"Fuh... Five times..."

Regina expected another round of gasps, but the silence was worse. An intense hate flashed in her chest to see Brace and Vela back up from Erin like she was diseased vermin. Did they not hear the first part?

Ezzie moved between Vela and Brace and turned Erin around for the crowd. She grabbed Erin's patch and removed it in one stitch-tearing motion. The sound echoed across the floor louder than Vela and Ezzie's dueling blows.

Ezzie threw the patch against the concrete slab in the stairwell. Without the patch, nothing held back Erin's sobs.

Brace came forward and put her hand on the back of Erin's neck.

"Sector B is no longer your home. If we find you here tomorrow morning, you know what will happen to you."

Erin nodded and pressed her palms into her eyes. Regina noticed Vela's expression soften for a second, but it almost immediately stiffened. Erin retook control of herself, straightened, then left the headquarters.

Regina found Sally shaking her head sadly.

"What happens if she's found tomorrow?" Regina asked.

"Every member of the Bulls takes a shot at her. If she survives, she's back in."

"If not?"

"I just *said*, Reggie. If she *survives*..."

"*Has* anyone ever—?"

Sally huffed and walked away.

Chapter Fourteen

RAGING BULL

SABRINA STAGGERED THROUGH THE lesser-traversed side streets of Sector B, circuitously making her way home. When her cardboard home emerged from the darkness, a figure ran to her. Kirsten hugged her tight. Ignoring the groan that escaped from her lips, Sabrina returned the hug and leaned onto her wife, ready to fall asleep in that moment.

Kirsten pushed out of the embrace and held her at arm's length.

"Where the *fuck* have you been, Sibby?" She gasped. "What happened to your *eye?*"

"Just a fashion statement, K. I'll be fine."

Erin had threatened a scavenger from Sector C with a beating for a clean scrap of fabric that she'd tied around Sabrina's head to cover her eye.

"Sibby, it's... Panda..." Sabrina's grip tightened over Kirsten's forearms. "I can't find her... She hasn't come back since yesterday."

Sabrina wasn't home during the day often, but when she was, she kept an eye out for Bulls, lest they discover where she lived. She'd noticed an older man had taken an interest in watching their home over the last year, but always at a distance—he disappeared whenever Sabrina stepped in his direction. She'd procured a pipe from Brace for a favor then and put it inside for Kirsten to use in an emergency.

"Why did she leave?"

Kirsten let go of Sabrina's arms and pulled her by the elbow closer to their home, out of anyone's earshot.

"She was going to look for *you!* I told her to stay home, but I dozed off and when I woke she was gone. If you hadn't disappeared for so long..."

Sabrina closed her eye and exhaled. She clenched and uncurled her fingers repeatedly, making a decision. She turned to investigate the direction from which the man always watched them.

"Where are you going?"

"To do what you couldn't in all this time."

"That's not fair! I stayed here in case she came back!"

Sabrina tore her arm away from Kirsten and stormed off.

"Sibby!"

Up around a corner, where the smell got worse, she didn't see the man. She didn't know exactly where *he* lived, but there wasn't much of the sector left past a certain point. Sabrina ventured deeper into the darkness, scraping her left hand against walls to keep her upright and her right eye trained down the likeliest alleyway. A giggle came from a doorway up ahead. Sabrina's step increased. The smell tickled even her well-worn nose.

Sabrina felt around in the impossibly blacker darkness inside the doorway. Another giggle confirmed she was on the right path, though, and it sounded an awful lot like Panda. A faint orange glow illuminated around a corner ahead. She rounded it to find a little room with a few scattered candles. Panda sat on the man's lap while he held an open picture book in front of her.

So many emotions flooded through Sabrina, like a fist to the heart. She didn't quite know what she was going to do in the first few steps between the entryway and the man. The fear in the man's eyes as she closed the distance didn't bode well for him...

"Hi, Mom!" Panda said.

Her daughter's sweet voice was the only thing saving the man's face from becoming a smear between her palm and the wall.

"Look at this! It's called a... hore... horse. It's a *horse!* Look at its crazy legs, Mom! Look!"

Sabrina's lips curled involuntarily in a wave of disgust *and* relief. She lifted Panda off the man's lap into the crux of her left arm. She felt around the seat of her pants for evidence of evil and stared at the man's crotch to make sure there was nothing peeking out of his rags. The pants were dry, and the man shook his bearded head like he knew what she'd assumed.

"She wandered in here yesterday. I didn't see either of you outside your home, so I just wanted to keep her safe."

Sabrina's face contorted, searching for the lie so she could end him where he sat.

"You didn't check inside? My wife never leaves home without me..."

"I've seen the way you both look at me. I would never poke my head in uninvited."

"So, your plan, if I'm hearing you correctly, was to keep her here and never bring her home." Her sore knuckles cracked and flexed.

"No! I *did* check once already, and planned to periodically. I was going to bring her when I saw one of you outside."

Sabrina's neck creaked as she assessed his potential lies. She didn't know if she could have held back as long as she did without Panda hugging around her neck. The man cowered as she took a step and jabbed his chest. "Don't you *ever* touch my child again." A tear rolled out of her eye and her vision blurred. The man noticed as it dropped onto the page of his book.

"What's wrong, Mom? Why are you crying?"

Each breath squeezed Sabrina's eyes tighter in anger—anger that she couldn't take the man at face value, and anger that a prospective life with the Denim Demons couldn't start from killing.

The man stood up slowly.

"Here. Take the book. She really loves the pictures."

Panda let out an excited gasp and snatched the book. Sabrina couldn't see her daughter's expression, but the speed at which the book opened indicated she was familiar with what it was: it couldn't have been a last-second ploy to fool Sabrina when the man heard her approaching.

"Show me another animal, baby," Sabrina whispered. "From the book."

She heard Panda's little hand slide across a page.

"S-s-s-snake. They don't have *any* legs."

"Another one, baby." Sabrina couldn't stop crying, and she didn't know why anymore.

"Grr-aff."

"Gira—" the man started to correct, but he cut himself short when Sabrina shook her head sternly at him.

"What's your favorite?"

"The panda, of course. Look at how cute it is!"

All Sabrina could see was the edge of the page from her right eye.

"I see it, baby," Sabrina whispered. "It's so cute."

The man's face showed relief that he wasn't about to die, but not too much that he looked like he was getting away with something. Sabrina cleared the lump out of her throat and straightened her back.

"What do you want in exchange for the book?"

"Nothing. Our world needs more readers."

Sabrina hugged Panda tighter to her side. One of the book's corners stuck into her neck since Panda wouldn't close it. Sabrina went to leave, then stopped in the entryway. She turned to the right to see over her shoulder.

"If... When I or my wife are home... Would you... Can you teach her to read?"

He nodded solemnly. She reached into a pocket for a small square of chocolate and tossed it to him, then felt out with her right hand along the corridor until she saw the dull red glow of light from the alleyway.

Sabrina set Panda down in the corner after Kirsten got out all her hugs and a hundred kisses.

"Use your aromatic candle, baby, then you can look through the book some more."

Sabrina grabbed Kirsten's arm a little harder than she should have and led her to the other side of the box.

"You're hurting me, Sibby."

Sabrina held out one of their normal candles and pulled the rags back from Kirsten's arm, exposing little spots of dried blood on the inside of her elbow crease. Kirsten yanked back her arm and frowned.

"We worked so *fucking* hard to get you off this shit," Sabrina whispered. "You've been sober for two years."

"When you didn't come back, I couldn't handle it. It was the only way I could sleep."

"Our baby could have been kidnapped or... Fucking hell. How fucking dare you?"

Kirsten took a maddeningly defiant stance, like she thought she had a right to use while Sabrina was away.

"K, I could have fucking *died* yesterday, and you were just going to sit here while a stranger held onto her. If you're using, I can't trust that Panda is safe with you."

"Neither of us are safe without *you*. Where were you? How did you get hurt? Why can't you quit that fucking club and stay with us?"

It was an ancient argument, and it never ended with a victory on either side. It was worse that Sabrina had to work every day with Kirsten's rapist in order to maintain status, procure favors, and enforce better treatment throughout the sector. Their lives would be much harder if Sabrina wasn't in the Brass Bulls.

But there was a light at the other end of the Underfoot, and Sabrina only needed a few more months until she could breathe easy under the banner of peace carried by the Denim Demons. Until then, she had work to do, and she couldn't have Kirsten siphoning away attention from something so important to all three of their lives.

"Where are the other needles, K?"

"I don't have any."

"Bull-fucking-shit. Give them to me."

"Sibby, I promise you..."

"*Do you?*"

Sabrina tore through the rags and debris accumulated in the corners of their home. She scattered their nest. Panda put down her book and gleefully helped destroy their property, although she had no idea what they were actually looking for. Frustrated at not finding anything, Sabrina grabbed her tearful wife and felt over her rags, squeezing every inch of her with a grip she regretted but for the lesson that needed to happen.

"You're...hurting me, Sabrina," Kirsten whispered, but she remained motionless as Sabrina continued her search.

Sabrina would have stopped, if she didn't suspect there was a reason Kirsten spoke up at that moment; used her real name. Sabrina squeezed around Kirsten's ankle and her hand crushed thin tubes against Kirsten's skin. She tore the rags covering her leg and snatched the pieces of needles.

For the second time that day her child kept her from harming another person. She held the pieces in her right fist and shook them in front of Kirsten's face, then punched the wall to her left, her fist going straight through. She didn't feel anything, gone numb to the rage coursing through her since learning Panda was missing, and the exhaustion since Brace's attempted assassination.

Panda ran around to hug Kirsten's leg and hid her face from Sabrina.

"You watch our baby, K. I'll be back. Don't *ever* lie to me again."

Sabrina kicked through the mess and left.

THERE WERE NO DRUG dealers in Sectors A and B. Brace wouldn't allow it. Sector C had a stronger male presence that ran the drug trade there and in D. They were supposed to never set foot in B and were watched closely by Bulls at the borders.

Sabrina stormed across the border to a group of three men she recognized for their gang patches—the Maroon Mongeese. She threw the needle pieces at their backs, then unloaded her rage on them. All three hit the ground before they knew what happened. She rained fists on their prone faces and crushed their hands when they tried to shield themselves.

After rendering them unconscious, she dragged each of them to their Sector's Clinic and left them in a pile by the tents. Then she found the nearest Diamond Duck member and pointed hard into her chest.

"Keep your fucking male gang in line, Duck. You don't want the Bulls deciding our alliance isn't useful anymore. If I find drugs in B again, I'll personally come after *you*, and the Bulls will rampage through here like we did with A."

Whether it was the woman's fault or not, Sabrina pushed her shoulder hard before heading back to the border. The Duck fell on her ass but didn't say a word out of fear. When Sabrina crossed into B, she noticed Erin, who appeared to be leaving, her head and shoulders downcast. She dragged her feet without acknowledging Sabrina.

"After all we went through?" Sabrina smiled and waited for Erin to turn to the sound of her voice. When she didn't, Sabrina noticed her patch was gone. She rushed around and put her hands on Erin's arms to stop her.

"What is this? What happened to you? Where's your patch?"

Erin slowly raised her head and smiled beneath tear-saturated dirt.

"You're safe, Rina. They can't exile you now."

"What do you mean?"

Erin's face crumpled for a moment, but she fought it back. Sabrina hugged her tight and ran her fingers through the back of her hair, catching in its knots.

"I'm sorry. Oh, fuck, my hands are covered in... I'm sorry, Erin. Let me help you clean up."

"It doesn't matter. Let me go."

"To where?"

"I don't know. Maybe... I'll join the Demons. Or the Rabbits. I don't know. All I know is I'm done here."

"That's shit. You're a fucking Bull. You've never hit the ground."

"I did." Her incongruous smile grew sadder. "Five times."

"You didn't! *I* did!"

Erin brushed by but Sabrina wouldn't accept that.

"Did you... Why the *fuck* would you do this? The Bulls are your whole life—"

"No, Rina. They're yours. I was only in for two years. It's okay. I'll land on my feet somewhere."

"This is wrong, Erin. Come on, I'll explain to the Bulls what happened. I was planning to anyway."

"Don't. How can you work from within for the Demons if you're thrown out of the Bulls now?"

Sabrina took Erin's hand and pulled her to a hidden alcove off the main street. She put her arm on the wall next to Erin so she wouldn't tear off in a fit.

"We could have worked together. You're well-liked in the Bulls. This was a *stupid* decision."

"I... I only wanted to help you. Everyone looks up to you—except Vela, of course. You can do so much more than I can. Maybe... I can help you by joining the Demons?"

Sabrina sighed and shook her head. It was actually a perfect idea, but she would have preferred it more than anything that Erin didn't have to disgrace herself to her sisters. It was a horrible lie Sabrina now needed to carry. Erin had impressed at every turn, and it was tying Sabrina's insides in knots, not just to lose such a good sister, but to realize...she'd *miss* her.

The last day played in her mind. Erin acted selflessly to protect her, and felt like the only person Sabrina had left to trust. If she was willing to do all that, surely *she* would never lie to Sabrina. Erin would follow her to the ends of the Underfoot, it seemed.

Intense feelings pushed out from Sabrina's heart. She'd been betrayed three times that day, and only one person thought of *her*, showing her devotion in the most devastating way imaginable for a Brass Bull.

Erin made to leave, but Sabrina put her hand on Erin's chest and pushed her back into the wall. She didn't remove her hand, instead repositioning it over Erin's heart, which beat as fast as Sabrina's.

Their faces were puffy from the fights, painfully swollen, and Sabrina's eye throbbed horribly, as if her heart had moved into her skull and beat behind the eye cover. Sabrina leaned over and kissed Erin's neck. They'd all tasted grime their whole lives; it meant nothing to her, to swallow it with the mix of sweat, saliva, and other secretions on Erin's skin. Sabrina licked Erin's whole neck as her hands explored beneath the rags.

Erin returned the groping, and tugged Sabrina's head back by her hair so she could get at *her* neck.

Once their rags were off, Sabrina kissed over Erin's many bruises, and Erin reciprocated. Erin was a rougher lover than Sabrina expected, having slept with Vela for at least a year. However, she responded positively to Sabrina slowing her down and using her pressure differently.

Some time later, they lay on a pile of their rags in a loose embrace.

"Well, fuck," Sabrina said. "Now you're leaving..."

Erin ran her fingers over Sabrina's collarbone, then traced lightly around her heart.

"Now I have extra incentive to come back with the Demons."

Sabrina kissed the top of Erin's head.

"Give Olive all the information you need to push this place to peace. We may have to fight Brace, Vela, and Ezzie, but if I can turn the others..."

"Stop talking about it, Rina. Just let me enjoy our time together before I have to leave."

"What did Brace give you? Until tomorrow morning?"

"Mmhm."

"Then let's make our time together count."

Chapter Fifteen

DESERVE

IN A SHOW OF good-faith negotiations with the Quartz Queens of Sector K, Olive planned a special event for them, the Demons, and the Rabbits. They set up tables to pass out choice items from the scavengers and the special crates equally, regardless of status. The gangless were invited to attend as well, and were given priority in medical supplies and food. They administered vaccines to all in a little tent. Adults enjoyed jiggers of wine, and children partook of squares of chocolate.

Twill recruited more volunteers from the males to patrol and keep hostile elements away from the festivities. They had enjoyed sex with other sectors' gangs *so much* that it took no effort to convince them of Twill's direction that they make sure too many men didn't flood the streets at once and scare off the women, from gangs or otherwise.

A police officer ambled around the event but didn't bother anyone. Olive glad-handed with the Queens and Rabbits, learning about their cultures and inserting careful words for how their lives could be improved, all without conflict.

She wasn't prepared for bloodthirsty talk among the Queens' leadership that they wanted to be rid of the males, just like the Purple Rams. It was painful but necessary that Olive tamp down that talk. She couldn't afford an all-out war with every male gang in every sector. Keeping them happy was a delicate balance, knowing full well if they really wanted to they could end all life in the Under-foot.

Her defenses tasted of bile. She'd already compromised on that principle—why didn't the Queens or any other sectors deserve the same freedom that the Rabbits had been afforded? Gangless men raped far less than the gangs, and the gangs had a nasty habit of spreading drugs, which weakened entire sectors.

Olive couldn't talk about it with Twill—it would invite having to explain what happened to her that night in Sector L; having to justify why she'd ever allowed pre-emptive killing again—especially after the turmoil it brought her to have Mika and her lover killed.

Twill often came upon Olive in a zoned-out state, simply standing and staring. She chalked it up to being tired and waved off concern with a smile, then she'd hold Twill's hand to keep questions to a minimum. She even kissed her on the cheek the night before, but feigned sleep quickly after. Twill found her in such a state at the event and lightly shook Olive back to attention.

The leaders had all gone in different directions. Olive went to check on the gangless, to make sure they were getting what they needed. A commotion came from one of the tables a Demon tended and where two males stood arguing. She had loads of cleansing wipes.

Olive asked what was going on, and the men answered that the woman wouldn't give them more than five like they asked.

"There are a lot of people in this sector, sir," Olive said. "We have limited supplies and we just want to make sure everyone gets an equal amount while they last."

One of the men crossed his arms and his rags pulled back to expose a scarred carving on his forearm: the Granite Gophers, male gang of Sector J.

"This bitch gave that old woman over there ten."

Olive smiled and leaned on the table like a bartering merchant.

"Are you an old woman in need of ten cleansing wipes? If so, I'll hand them over right now."

"You're supposed to be handing out supplies equally, like you *just* said. Why's she decide that someone gets more than everyone else? That's fucked up."

"Just admit to me that you're an old woman, not a Granite Gopher," Olive raised her voice for the Queens and the men in Sector K to hear, "and I'll give you more wipes than everyone else. It's not favoritism to those who genuinely *need* more."

"I shouldn't have to explain myself to a fucking outsider who kills defenseless people and steals their shit. These people don't have the sense to know where it comes from, but I do."

Twill appeared in Olive's periphery. Olive waved her fingers for Twill to stay out of it.

"You've been misinformed. No one has died under my watch. We don't steal anything. This has all been collected legitimately. Are you going to admit you're an old woman now? Or are you here to ruin the good time of people who have nothing, unlike the *Granite Gophers*, who take everything by force of rape and violence?"

Some of the Queens shouted that Olive spoke true, and the Rabbits concurred. The two men seemed to have very little sense of self-preservation, as they didn't cower and run away before they'd be attacked. Instead, incredibly, they struck the first blow by flipping over the table, scattering the wipes all over the ground.

Olive rushed to push back the people converging to attack the men, holding a circle of them at bay. Twill helped to staunch the violent surge.

Olive decided to change tactics in addressing the men who had taken up fighting stances.

"Do you really need the wipes? Please tell me the truth."

The one she'd been talking to sneered with contempt.

"Please, just leave," Olive whispered. "I can't control all of them."

"It seems you've finally seen the point, Denim bitch."

The men straightened and strolled away like it was nothing. The allied gangs stepped aside to allow them to walk out. Olive sighed and helped pick up the table and wipes when someone shouted in the direction the men had gone.

"That's right, get back to your sector, Gopher trash cans!"

Olive snapped up to see the police officer pushing one of the two men in the back. The Gophers didn't take kindly to that, stopping in place and staring angrily into the officer's smug face. The officer erased their defiance with a blow from the electric baton. The companion shit-stirrer punched the officer to the ground. A melee erupted around the three of them, with Queens, Rabbits, and the male protectors raining blows on the two Gophers.

Olive shrugged out of Twill's grasp on her shoulder and ran into the middle of the fight shouting for peace. She ducked down between legs and found the officer unconscious in the middle of the mob. She grabbed his wrists and pulled him away from danger. Someone fell on top of her and knocked her down, smashing her nose into the ground.

She blacked out.

Olive winced awake on a hard surface as Twill ran a wipe over her face. She tasted blood and her eyes were puffy. Twill shook her head lightly when their eyes met.

"You need to stop getting involved, Olive. You have an entire gang willing to take blows for you."

"Did the officer get out safely?"

"Yes. I pushed him off towards the Clinic. It was his fault the whole thing happened."

"No, it wasn't. The event was *my* idea."

"Don't start with that bullshit line of thinking. You planned something peaceful to help the people in the sector and those fucking Gophers ruined everything from there."

"Right." Olive got up and pushed past the low dizziness it caused. "It's everyone *else's* fault."

She hopped down from the table and forgot about her leg. She hissed and jumped back to sit on the edge.

"The Rabbits used some of the medical supplies to re-stitch a couple of those," Twill said. "Are you... Do you *like* all this pain?"

That deserved a hard stare, maybe even a slap, but it would require more explaining to Twill as to why that set her off more than she was willing to dive into—it was a valid question, with how she acted of late... "What about those two Gophers?"

"Dead."

"Fuck."

"They des—"

"Shut up."

Olive got down from the table carefully that time and limped away from Twill. She didn't deserve Olive's irritation, but it was too hard to suppress.

Olive sought Ren and the leader of the Quartz Queens. The Gophers were gearing up for a fight, and the two female gangs wanted to give it to them.

Olive was sick of the fighting; the gang leaders could see that in her broken nose and limp, but she pushed forward anyway. She asked them for a day to come up with an alternative.

Through her relay network she gathered the leaders of the male gangs in already-conquered sectors. She asked them to spread word through the remaining male gangs, to speak on the best parts of allying with the Denim Demons. They were allowed to defend themselves if negotiations and presentations broke down, but she only wanted them to pitch, then bring back the results before any next steps would be taken.

The Rabbits and Queens remained skeptical of the idea, but allowed it to play out. While they waited, Olive went into Sector J for reconnaissance. She hung around street corners, listening to chatter and observing the gangs' movement patterns.

After half a day of sleuthing, she exhaled frustration when she found Twill looking around for her. She grabbed Twill's hand and led her back to the relative safety of Sector K.

"I don't need you to be my shadow, Twill."

"Your body says otherwise."

"Maybe I need this. How can I connect with the deeper sectors if I don't know anything about their lives?"

"All of this is for nothing if you fall. There's no one to take your place. It'll all go back to the way it was..."

"Then I'm *fucking* failing!"

Twill put her hand on Olive's cheek but she pulled her head away.

"That's the last thing I need right now."

Twill didn't hesitate to grab Olive by the arms and lift her off her feet, carrying her to a quiet alleyway. Olive squirmed like a child to get out of her grip, pushing Twill's torso to get away. Twill placed her down carefully.

"Maybe that's the *only* thing you need right now. You haven't said you... You haven't even *touched* me since I came back, other than loose handholds that feel like you'd rather be holding a diseased rat."

"You won't understand, and I can't tell you. All I can do is move forward. It's that simple. Now if you actually want to be a help, we need to elevate leaders who can continue my legacy—one for each sector."

"Talking about a legacy already... Do you have a death wish? If you can't tell me what caused this change in you, at least tell me that's not your end goal, or an allusion to some last ditch strategy that you're going to pull without telling anyone."

Olive looked away from Twill's concern. "I don't want to die, but... I would if it were the only way to peace."

"You've proven already it's *not* the only way. Despite your weakness recently, we can get things back to the way they were. People will forget the bad once you deliver them better lives."

Hearing the word "weakness" was both hurtful and accurate, in several ways. If it was true Twill suspected what happened, was she judging Olive? That seemed a horrible thing to think, but Olive could have done things to avoid it... She had the power of a near limitless supply of women to protect her. She had clout with the few authorities that deigned to deal with the Underfoot. She had the ear of *most* of the men.

Their biggest asset as they went deeper into the Underfoot could become a liability. So much of their cooperation came from what she did with the male leaders in their nests. She was more than willing to use her body to improve the Underfoot, so why did that night mess her up so badly?

Twill reached for Olive's hand.

"Please, Twill. Stop trying to touch me," she whispered.

"...What did I do?"

"Nothing. It has *nothing* to do with you. And all these little attempts to talk aren't helping me."

"How can I help you, then?"

"Do what I asked about the promotions. Tell me who you think can lead the sectors, and we'll go from there. I'm going back to the negotiation table."

Twill hesitated, but finally left. Olive leaned against the wall and let out slow, steadying breaths. Avoidance of talking about what happened did nothing to keep her from thinking about it.

She lowered to the ground to hug her knees. Even closing her eyes did nothing to keep her from seeing their faces: the dead Ram, the water techs and Gophers, Mika and her lover, and the casualties of the battle with the Rams. Trying to stuff it into the past like Twill wanted wouldn't help in the least. Olive would be forever haunted, and she deserved it, whether it could be argued that any of them had or not...

THE NEXT DAY OLIVE traded a fresh carrot to an old man for his food scrap and nibbled on it while she waited for the Queens to make a final decision in their headquarters. Twill left early in the morning to meet with the leadership all the way back to Sector Z.

After an hour of waiting, the Queens' leader agreed to ally with the Demons thanks to Olive's peaceful attempt at dealing with the men and for helping the gangless better than they ever had. They had the stipulation that they remain their own gang still—like the Rabbits.

Olive didn't like that. All the gangs before the Rabbits joined willingly, or were forced to join after a deathless battle. If she suddenly let the two gangs act independently, there was potential for other former gangs to fight to re-form, and the gangs further in the Underfoot would all expect the same deal.

If she'd found the sectors in better condition when she arrived, she might have gladly accepted. Instead, she explained to the Queens and Rabbits they needed to wear denim and join up if they wanted the benefits she'd presented, and to share in the spoils of the Upcity.

Of course Ren felt betrayed, and the Queens wanted another day to think about it. Olive followed Ren and explained her reasoning, all the while thanking her for what she'd done for her that night. Ren gruffly insisted she needed time to think about it, as well.

Olive went to her own headquarters and cleaned her leg and face. Close to dinner time, a scout asked Olive to come outside by the brazier to meet someone. A woman stood with her hands on her hips, her posture confident beyond measure, despite the beatings evident on her face.

"What is this? *You're* Olive?"

"Yes. What can I do for you?"

"Damn, I thought you'd be bigger than Twill. You *do* look like you've been in some scraps, though."

The woman held out her hand for a shake, which was crushing in its strength. Olive whistled and shook it in the air while the woman smirked.

"That's pretty soft for a leader. I'd like to feel Twill's hand after that sad display, if you don't mind."

"Twill's not here... Uh. Who *are* you?"

"I wish to join your Denim Demons, and help you bring peace and love to this godforsaken Underfoot. I'm here on behalf of my Rina, a leader in the Brass Bulls. Name's Erin. Tell me what initiation I need to pass and let's get this movement moving!"

Chapter Sixteen

INTOXICATION

RINA RETURNED TO HEADQUARTERS and recounted the Viper battle to the whole gang, who gleefully ate up every detail. Afterwards, Regina and the other runts were led outside for one last lesson before the initiation. Rina smiled with pride at Regina's story of standing after Ezzie's punch, not that Regina felt she had that much to do with it.

Other than a quick brush off at the morning meeting, Rina didn't mention why she wore a rag around her eye. While the initiates worked on pushing each other out of their stances, Regina sidled next to Rina and asked her what happened to the eye.

"Just worry about yourself, Reggie."

"That's a little callous coming from my teacher, isn't it? How am I supposed to avoid such an injury if you don't share how it happened?"

"Come on, you're not going to have to go through initiation. Brace is just putting the fear of the Underfoot in you."

"I don't have to prove myself again to you, not after Ezzie. I want to see that I can do it."

"Admirable, but not worth it. You can't be a Bull, anyway, even if you succeed. You've got to go back home someday. You're a Ruby Rider."

"Not necessarily. I don't have enough money to move up."

"You have to pay for promotions? And *you* don't have enough money? I thought everyone above *never* had to worry about money."

"It's a bit more complicated than that, okay? Jesus, can't you just hit me or something? I'm going through the initiation, I don't care what anyone says."

Rina clapped Regina on the back, though not as hard as the other women did.

"If words were all that mattered, you'd already be in. Look, if you want to get punched, I can't technically stop you, and if you won't listen to me, fine. Now your stance looked okay. Let's see how your arm strength measures up."

Rina held up her palms and Regina boxed at them for a while. After some time and sore arms, Brace assigned the initiates to shadow Bulls in their tasks.

At the end of the day, Regina flopped down in her nest, exhausted. A hard day's work was new to her, but it was exhilarating. Her whole body tingled as she stretched and relaxed her muscles. She drifted off to sleep despite the noise from the Bulls milling about the headquarters.

She woke to a rustling, a pressure on her back. The candles had all been snuffed and the Bulls snored throughout the floor. A heavy, rough hand caressed from her thigh up to her shoulder.

"I missed your skin, baby," Vela purred. "Your smooth, soft skin."

Her hand found the gap between the ragged shirt and pants to caress Regina's side. "Your nest is too small. Let's go to mine. It's covered, too. I like a little privacy."

"I'm sleepy, Vela."

"That's okay, Reggie. Go right back to sleep. I can work with that."

Vela's hand moved on to grasp the waistband of Regina's pants. She pulled them partially down before Regina put her hand over Vela's to stop her.

"What's the matter, baby? I thought you liked what I did the other night? I hope you know all I want is for you to feel good down here—and *there*. It's not all punching and fighting. We all need a release every now and then."

Regina froze again, as she had before. Vela's voice tickled her ear in a not unpleasant way. Her hard hands knew what they were doing. More than Regina cared about the thought of being with a woman anymore, she didn't want everyone to know about what happened, or get caught doing stuff out in the open.

"Please, Vela, don't...touch me. Please go to sleep in your own nest."

"As you wish, Reggie."

Regina couldn't believe she agreed that quickly—she feared she'd have to be more forceful in either words or actions. However, Vela didn't simply let go of her pants and leave. She shifted down to the small area of exposed skin along Regina's thigh and kissed it, pressed to leave behind a cool spot of saliva, *then* put the waistband back where it belonged. She patted the spot where she kissed and got out of the nest.

It had tickled in that nice way again—unexpected and lovely. Regina rolled onto her back and stared into the black. It seemed like she lay there for an hour. Why did she feel a little warm from being the second-highest ranking Bull's object of affection? She wasn't attracted to Vela...she didn't think. But two things were undeniable—Vela had made her feel *really good*, and it felt even better to be *wanted*—like when the Bulls congratulated her on taking Ezzie's hit.

There was a third reason, more shallow than comforting: Vela was like an insurance policy; protection if something were to happen and she needed real help in the Underfoot. Rina was injured, no matter how much she deflected. Regina may have won Ezzie's respect but she seemed like the last person interested in protecting anyone but her sisters. Brace was a wild card.

Of the four leaders, Vela was the safest to rely on. Feeling good seemed like a small price to pay...

Regina couldn't believe she lifted herself out of the nest, or that her legs took her cautiously around snoozing Bulls to Vela's nest. Then again, she'd been doing things she couldn't believe she'd ever do all month. Vela didn't stir when Regina entered, but she wasn't snoring.

Regina lowered herself behind Vela's back and spooned into her. She snaked her hand up Vela's thigh and beneath her rag shirt. Her armpit hair caught Regina off guard and she yanked her hand away, in fear that a man had snuck into the nest.

"Why'd you stop?" Vela whispered. "That felt good."

"I... I guess it makes sense that you're not..."

"You're not going to touch me because I'm not smooth like a child?"

"Sorry. I've just... At least... Like *this*, I've never touched a woman."

"Clearly. Why don't I show you?"

REGINA HAD NEVER SWEATED so much in her life as she did in Vela's nest—even as she recovered from Ezzie's hit, or while she was being lowered to the foul black hole of the sewer. Vela fell asleep quickly after they were done, but Regina couldn't close her eyes, overstimulated in so many ways.

She got up carefully, but Vela seemed to be a heavy sleeper. She thankfully didn't stir even with a bit of accidental jostling. Regina slipped on her rags and crept outside Vela's nest covering. A wall where there shouldn't have been a wall nearly knocked her on her butt. She squinted in the dark and recognized Brace's hair, although not much else was discernible. Regina's heart sped up faster than what Vela had provoked in her only a short time before.

Brace grabbed Regina's shoulder and guided her outside to the nearby brazier. She leaned against the wall and smiled, a rare sight.

"Didn't think you were taking to us *that much*, Ten Stories."

Regina only stared into the brazier, not at all sure what to say to the Brass Bulls' leader. "How did you know?" was all she could manage.

"My room is right next to Vela's. All that moaning was getting to me—wanted to see who was keeping me up. Thought she was with a new Bull, moving on from Erin's exile. Never expected it would be *you*."

"Oh."

Brace's smile remained, but she shook her head to go along with it.

"What the *fuck* are you still doing here, Reggie?"

"I thought you forgot my name..."

"I don't forget anything. I didn't forget your shaking ass when we had you three Riders in our jail. It's not lost on me, all the little ways you're trying to prove yourself to us. Maybe I should rephrase my question—*Why?*"

"You wanted to show me *real* gang life? Well, you did. It's... It's intoxicating. I feel more respected, more...*loved* here than I did in the Upcity. I...I honestly don't know if I even want to go back sometimes. A little bit ago…with Vela? I saw my-self staying here."

"You can never be a Bull, my dear." Brace said it so casually, Regina didn't think it was condescending; it was just a fact to her.

"Because I can't knock anyone over?"

"No, that's not the point. No one knocks *us* down. *That's* the point. It would take years for you to gain enough strength—"

"I know how strong you all are, you don't have to keep reminding me. My stomach still hurts from Ezzie. But the more I'm around all of you, the more I wish I'd been born here."

"That's a strange wish. You know how many people in the Underfoot would kill to have been born in your shoes?"

"And yet people up there are hurling themselves off the towers, almost every day from what the others have said. We all live in our own little cages."

"Mmm. Hasn't taken you long to become more worldly. Hey, if you want to join another gang, you could make it. I've been told the Royal Rabbits just killed all the Purple Rams in Sector L, *finally*. So…you know, if you've decided you like women—"

"I haven't decided anything."

"Anyway, the point is: you can join other gangs down here if this is the life you want, but two things: it can never be with us, and all of them will require that you cut that chip out of your hand."

Regina held up the back of her hand and ran her thumb over it. The chip was a tiny, flexible material that didn't leave a physical trace. She wouldn't even know where to cut it out, if she chose to. Despite her hedging towards staying, could she really leave behind her parents and the few Ruby Riders she actually liked? Sacrifice a steady future with one of the upper level Idle Batemans who'd fall for her plastic face, once she could afford it?

Regina chose to change from the overwhelming subject of her potential futures to the one she was being adamantly denied.

"What did it feel like, Brace? Turning your back on Erin?"

"Don't twist words to make something more than it is, Ten Stories. We have rules, and she broke them. There's nothing more to it."

"You didn't like her?"

Brace looked towards the main street where the trash cans meandered all day and night in search of scraps.

"I don't have the luxury of liking anyone. I can like things *about* them, respect them, admire them, even. But I can't let feelings get in the way of running this gang. It's not personal. Erin was a good Bull, and I respect that she admitted what happened. She could have kept it quiet. Vela is a great Bull, but if she were to fall down, I would have to exile her, too."

"All because of—"

"You're not going to make me feel guilty about the life we've chosen. This is it."

Regina still had something to prove to these hard asses. Or maybe herself... Either way, she'd lose her burgeoning self-respect if she didn't try.

"I'm taking part in the initiation. Even if I can't be a real Bull."

"It's not going to be as easy a stroll in the street like Sally's unveiling. There may be deaths..."

"Seems like any hit could lead to that. Why would this be any more dangerous?"

"If you want to join in the initiation, I'm not going to stop you. But neither am I going to give you information beforehand. The other women won't get that luxury, either. Stay here, go home, or follow us tomorrow. Do whatever the fuck you want, Reggie."

Brace punched Regina's arm and went inside. When she disappeared through the door, Regina rubbed her arm. She was still wide awake—possibly more so than before—so she decided to take a walk.

For all the time she spent in the Underfoot, she hadn't gotten used to the smell, but it didn't repulse her like when she'd first stepped off the Elevators. As she ambled past the moaning malaise of open-air trash can sex and pain of untreated ailments along the streets, she thought about Brace's words: "There may be deaths..."

Maybe she'd see what the initiation was going to be, and decide to run away if it really was that dangerous. But if something were to happen to her down in the Underfoot...

Regina took up a more determined pace and found the Elevators. She paid attention to which point the scanning device registered the chip. The officer let her pass, but not before a judgmental shake of the head at her appearance.

The Elevator's curved door slid open and she leaned back against its spacious, cylindrical inner wall. She squinted and shielded her eyes at first—the bright white light of the ceiling's fixtures were painful.

When she could open her eyes without grimaces, she was flabbergasted by the amount of dirt and grime covering her rags and hands. Her nails were blackened. Her formerly-white shoes were caked with all kinds of questionable colors. She lifted her shirt and Ezzie's welt was an angry purple that covered half of her stomach.

The Elevator stopped at floor ten and the door slid open. If it had been a normal workday, the Elevator and halls would have been jammed with people, but at such an ungodly early morning hour, the area was empty. Somehow there was still an endless line of flying traffic outside as she walked along the skyway towards her home. She stopped to stare out the window as the vehicles traversed between towers and the other cities in the distance. The dense Forest below stretched out in all directions, covering the landscape not occupied by the compact, tall, brightly-lit structures.

Regina tried to imagine the Underfoots of the far off cities. Underfeet? She chuckled to herself. Did they have their own, unique ecosystems? Undoubtedly. How fascinating would it be to travel to each one and compare notes?

Perhaps if she decided to pursue her doctorate, learning to survive in such an environment would be a valuable asset when it came time for grant requests to travel and observe.

Regina leaned against the window with her grimy, chipped hand. A series of warning beeps went off behind her. She turned and looked down to find a Servo-tron that had been cleaning up her dirty footprints. It bumped into the back of her leg until she moved. It extended a mister to spray her filthy handprint, then another extension with a cleaning rag rubbed the spot dry. The butler bot followed her as she continued home, cleaning up after each footprint.

When she arrived at the door to her home, the Servo-tron bumped into her leg again. It scanned her hand, then printed out a fine in her name for dirtying a public space. She didn't have her wallet on her—it was long gone after her clothing was torn off by the Bulls that first day. She also didn't have her identification card to scan the front lock, either.

Regina knocked on the door and waited. The Servo-tron bumped again, waiting for her to pay the fine. She knocked again, then pressed her ear to the door. The Servo-tron cleaned where her dirty hair touched and printed a new fine.

"Get the *fuck* away from me, you piece of *shit*."

It only beeped disapprovingly at her and printed out a fine for swearing in public.

"I'm gonna fucking *break* you, assh—"

The door opened to reveal her frightened parents.

"Hi!" Regina waved and took a step before the bot shoved another fine into her hand.

"George, tell this disgusting woman to... Reggie?" Her mother's eyes must have finally adjusted to the hallway light...and the dirt.

Regina looked down and rolled her eyes. "Ah, fuck. Yeah. I know."

The bot insistently printed another fine and pushed it against her thigh. She ground her teeth as she snatched the paper out of its little claw, then in sudden, newfound defiance, she picked up the Servo-tron over her head and threw it back down the hallway. That felt *much* better. Its little legs extended out of its side to right itself, then it zoomed back towards them with a new fine printing. Regina pushed her parents inside and slammed the door behind her.

Her mother ran for a trash bag. Her father went to start a pot of synth-coffee as Regina was forced to strip, putting her rags in the bag. Her mother gasped at every bruise and welt. Before she could toss the rags out the window into the nets below, Regina stopped her mother, grabbed the bag, then went to the bathroom to take a long shower.

She washed everything three times, and used a scrub brush to get underneath her finger and toenails. Cleaning her mouth never felt so good. Her hair smelled like roses and cinnamon, not dead rat and musty grime. As she stared into the mirror, brushing her hair out, she found herself wondering what Vela would think of her, right then. Would she actually consider the bruises sexy? Vela had gone wild just for Regina's hairless body. What would she think of the smells and clean skin?

The draw to return to the Underfoot hit harder than she expected. She dressed up in a particularly expensive outfit with multiple, semi-mismatched layers. It wasn't practical but she had her reasons: new underwear, shorts, a skirt, a dress, a light sweater, a small leather jacket, and two layers of socks. She fastened a pair of sandals to a loop on one of the three belts she wrapped loosely around her hips, then slipped into a new pair of black shoes she'd never bothered breaking in.

Regina met her parents in the living room over coffee and presented a new lie for why she'd gone to the Underfoot, and why she was going back—getting a head start on applying for her doctorate. She explained the colorful bruising all over her face as just having run into things since it was so dark down there.

Her parents were so beside themselves for her initiative that they were rendered speechless and changed the subject. They asked if they should continue saving money for the plastic surgery. Regina thought about it for a moment, then nodded. She'd hate to change her mind later and come back to nothing. It was important to have more than one insurance policy—Vela could die in the blink of an eye.

Before leaving, Regina grabbed another garbage bag and filled it with luxurious food and drink. She filled a backpack with art supplies.

She kissed her parents 'goodbye,' then went back out into the hallway. The Servo-tron hadn't left, and it printed new fines for her behavior. She kicked it aside and went back to the Elevators. After pushing the button for the lowest sub-level, she stripped out of her new clothes and traded them for her rags.

The officers didn't know what to make of her coming off the Elevator in her attire. When she had disembarked with Tiffany and Brittney, the officers gave them a long list of waivers: acknowledging that they were taking responsibility for whatever happened in the Underfoot and wouldn't sue the security forces for not acting. They didn't bother her this time.

Idly, Regina hated the thought that an officer might have stepped in when they were taken by the Brass Bulls.

She hated the thought of going back to the disgraceful ignorance she and the rest of the Upcity lived in.

Chapter Seventeen

LIES

Sabrina woke with Kirsten in her arms, and Panda curled up against her thigh in their nest. She lay still, savoring the familial closeness. Despite residual guilt from the tryst with Erin, Sabrina felt more caring toward her wife. She understood why Kirsten had acted the way she did, and she apologized for leaving so long without informing her of the mission that took her out of the Sector.

Panda hardly stirred as Sabrina picked her up and placed her in her own little nest in the opposite corner. Sabrina crawled back into the bigger nest and kissed Kirsten on the forehead. Kirsten sleepily moved to find Sabrina's lips, and they remained together for several moments, relieving the bad blood from the other day.

Sabrina grew bold with the intimacy and tried something Erin had shown her. She had to clamp her hand over Kirsten's mouth as she moaned, and that made it all even hotter. Once she finished, Kirsten slipped back into slumber with a smile.

After dressing, Sabrina put half a soft banana on an upturned box for Panda to eat when she woke up, with a nutritional pill stuffed into its center. Sabrina smiled at the sight of the animal book open to a page of ocean creatures. Learning about animals in the Underfoot was meaningless, but when Panda grinned as she studied them, Sabrina couldn't help sharing her enthusiasm. Panda even showed her mothers how to read some of their names, how to sound out the letters.

For the most part, the gang names didn't really *mean* anything. She didn't know what a Bull looked like anymore than a Demon or Rabbit, let alone the accompanying words before them. When she put pictures to names with her daughter, though, she wondered how many gangs would change theirs? The Diamond Ducks or Granite Gophers would likely be the first...

Sabrina leaned over and kissed Kirsten goodbye.

"Love you, Sibby," Kirsten murmured.

She went outside and walked to the main street to relieve the shift of another Bull. They flashed their gang sign before separating. Within the hour, Sabrina was met by an odd sight—Regina walking around the gangless with a bag, handing out food items from *sealed packages*. Sabrina accosted her.

"Is that Brace's supply of—"

"What? No. Brace has stuff like this?"

"She gets things from her contacts sometimes. Only shares on special occasions. What are you doing with all that?"

"I went home and brought it back. It wasn't doing any good in our refrigerator."

"Your what?"

"Never mind. Do you want to help me? I've never seen smiles as wide as when I started handing things out."

"I'll make sure no one attacks you. Can't believe it hasn't happened yet..."

Regina shrugged and kept moving. Sabrina thought to ask Regina about what else she'd brought.

"Hey, did you bring back any books?"

"No, but I brought some art supplies that Sally can use."

"Oh. Are you going back soon—leaving for good?"

"I don't know. Maybe. It depends on what happens with the initiation later today. Is there something in particular you want?"

"Just something with pictures. For my dau— For my daily reading. I want to learn."

"You don't know how?"

"Hey! *You* don't know how to please a woman, so don't give me that look."

Regina took on a cute, bashful little smile at that.

"Oh my G— I thought you said you didn't like—"

"I'm just learning things, too, Rina. I don't know if I do. I just... Vela is—"

"What the *fuck? Vela?*" Sabrina stopped walking and blocked Regina's path. "You fucked *Vela?*"

Regina sneered and stepped around her.

"Reggie, you don't understand, she's fucked up. She takes things, she doesn't ask—"

"That's what all of you Bulls do. And, I don't know, I kind of liked that about her. I never would have done it except for the way she—"

"I don't want fucking details. She's dangerous, is what I'm saying. She'll hurt you—"

"All you people *do* is hurt each other. What the hell's your problem, Rina? You sound like you're afraid of her."

Sabrina wasn't afraid of Vela, only what she did to others. It was a fucked up feeling to be thankful for having found Kirsten because of her, but Sabrina would have let it all go if it meant Kirsten wouldn't have experienced Vela's violence.

She could forgive Regina's ignorance if she hadn't taken on a more petulant nature of late, as if Sabrina had done something to piss her off.

"Look, Reggie, ultimately... Nothing that happens to you matters to me. You get to leave anytime you want. All of us are nothing to you, so I'm sorry that means I have to make you mean nothing in my life in turn. I have problems that are more important than babysitting you. But if I can warn you against—"

"Babysitting? That's a good word for why I don't like being around you. Like you're everyone's goddamn mother. I have a mother, and she sucks. You're a different kind, but you're no better."

Sabrina's eyes fluttered at the idiocy and pushed past it, not giving it the breath it didn't deserve.

"If I can warn you *against* something avoidable, I will, but only this once. Vela is a dangerous bitch to know, even if she 'likes' you. When she hurts you, don't come looking for your 'mother' to soothe you and tell you it wasn't your fault. Because *now,* it is."

Sabrina brushed past Regina's shoulder. She was getting much better at standing her ground, and even giving a little back. In a way, Sabrina looked forward to seeing what Regina would do at the initiation, but until then she'd go back to her post and watch out for gang spies. If Vela already poisoned Regina, it would be worthless bringing her to Olive's side.

Her head rolled back as she remembered Erin. She'd been attached at the hip to Vela—one of the last people she thought would have turned if she'd been asked only a couple months before. Sabrina experienced a bit of envy that Erin had the freedom to just join the Denim Demons, without all the subterfuge and danger of being caught out by the Bulls.

After a while of mulling things over at her post, Sabrina determined that if her tough words didn't sink into Regina, she would still never turn her back on someone in need of love and support. *Olive* would never do such a thing.

Sabrina joined Vela, Ezzie, and Brace before the Bulls and their eager initiation hopefuls. Brace quieted them inside the headquarters and took her place front and center.

"Today we march into Sector D to help the Crystal Crackers with their 'man problem.' The Iron Iguanas are pushing their drugs to too many people, and they're getting rape-happy. I'm told they're getting it out of their system before those Denim Demon bitches show up and take over.

"Fucked as I'll be before the Demons bring that shit *here*, I'm not going to stand by while people are raped and the Bulls can stop it. The Crackers have also agreed to bolster defenses against the Demons from within Sector D if we solve their 'problem.'

"Officers and the most experienced Bulls will watch you runts tear apart the men. Ezzie has a list of Bulls who will stay behind to guard against anyone looking to take advantage of our absence."

Ezzie pointed out those who would stay behind, ending on Sabrina with a poke in the chest.

"Sorry, Rina," she whispered.

"What the fuck is this, Brace?" Sabrina said, ignoring the other Bulls' shocked stares.

"You need to heal. You're no good to anyone in a battle with the damage you've taken lately."

"When has that *ever* been a consideration?"

Vela moved forward, ready to challenge Sabrina with the slightest provocation. Sabrina looked past her as if she wasn't there.

"You think I'm weak for losing my eye; for letting that Snake cut me while I saved you? Is that it, Brace?"

Brace straightened her back and nodded. Sabrina's hackles raised, until she realized this gave her a chance to be alone with some of the Bulls, her own body and ostracism to use as a painful demonstration of the life they'd devolved into. She could twist this to Olive's advantage.

"Fine, Brace. But you fucking *challenge* me first, before you put me on the sideline. And *fuck you*, Vela!"

Vela cracked her knuckles with a venomous smile. She took a step forward but Brace put the back of her hand on Vela's arm and guided her aside. Brace strode and squared up in front of Sabrina.

"You first, Brace."

She didn't need a moment to hedge—Brace punched Sabrina in the stomach with her right hand, then across the right cheek with her left.

She hit harder than Vela—she had to in order to lead the Brass Bulls. The face shot made Sabrina's ears ring and her vision sparkled, but she took it without staggering.

Brace readied for the return shots. Sabrina took a step forward and wrapped her arms around Brace's neck. The look of confusion on Brace's face was beautiful. The Bulls gasped at the unexpected action.

"You're right, Brace," Sabrina whispered. "I am too weak. Just helping to bolster your rep."

Brace grabbed Sabrina's arms and held her back, scanning her like she was an alien oddity.

"I don't have time for this shit, Rina. When we get back from Sector D, you're going to complete the challenge. If I feel you holding back when you hit me, you're out."

Brace shoved her aside. It was almost harder to stay on her feet than when she'd been hit, but she managed to catch herself. Brace left the headquarters in a huff, followed by Ezzie. Vela stopped in front of Sabrina and squared up. The Bulls stopped moving at the new development.

"Are you going to puss out on *my* challenge, bitch?" Vela said.

Sabrina miraculously got away with a second hug. Even having just seen her do the same, a true Bull could never expect it. It took all the willpower in Sabrina to get her arms around Vela without letting rage or violence take over her actions. Vela ripped out of the embrace and shoved Sabrina out of the way. Her legs didn't cooperate as well that time. She stumbled and flailed her arms out, catching herself at the last moment. Vela shouted that the challenge would be met when she returned, and stormed out.

Most of the Bulls and initiates filed out after her. Some shook their heads in disgust, but many more offered the sympathetic looks she'd been angling for. She took note of their faces. Regina was one of them. When those going to Sector D all exited, Sabrina didn't feel her balance loss until the floor rushed up to her face.

SALLY CLEANED OFF SABRINA'S face with stinging cleansing wipes. She gasped when Sabrina's eye opened. An awkward hug around her neck ensued. Sabrina looked around to find that all the Bulls left behind were seated around them in a circle.

"We won't tell you fell over," Sally said. The Bulls nodded. It was Erin all over again.

"Don't lie on my behalf, ladies. My time is coming."

"Bullshit," Sally scoffed. "No one, not even Vela, could have taken two hits from Brace. And your poor eye…"

Sally's eyes misted over.

"Don't." Sabrina sat up slowly, with help from Sally's hand on her back. Her whole head throbbed and pulsed against her skull.

"I think they left me behind for the same reason," Sally said. "Because Reggie made me bleed."

"Reggie's stronger than she looks. Remember when Ezzie hit her?" one of the other Bulls said.

"*I* know that, but fucking Brace and Vela..." Sally trailed off.

"They're all violence, no nuance," Sabrina said.

"What does 'nuance' mean?" one of them asked.

Thankfully another one explained so Sabrina could focus on not succumbing to the pain throughout her body. She lowered her head in her hands and massaged her scalp. She wanted to be back home, relaxing her head on Kirsten's chest, listening to Panda's excitable reading.

"Our Rina stood up to a force that knocked Erin over five times," a Bull murmured. "She'll never fall."

"Did you not believe what you just saw?" Sabrina asked. "I just fell down."

"I mean, you know, from your place in the Bulls. So many would choose you over Vela and Ezzie..."

That was exactly what Sabrina needed to hear.

"It's not about choice, ladies. It's about the rules. The rules say violence answers questions. It eliminates weakness."

"We can be strong even if we fall. Would any of you ever *want* to take a shot from Erin?" Sally asked. "Just because she fell during a massive battle doesn't make her any less of a strong bitch. All she had removed was her patch."

That was it. The logjam loosened...

"Bulls, do you all see me as stronger than the other officers?"

They nodded.

"Stronger than Erin?"

They agreed.

"Well, she didn't fall, Bulls. She didn't even waver against those impossible odds. And she took a hit from the biggest woman I've ever seen in my life. Bigger than Vela, stronger than Brace... The woman who destroyed my eye but didn't even mean to—it was an accident. The woman Erin only staggered from her hit and... Erin saved my life..." Sabrina whispered that part, then sniffed and lifted her head. "*I* fell five times. You just watched me fall here. Erin made up the same lie you did—about me standing through it all, when I couldn't."

The Bulls' murmured shock, their fists shook in their laps, and their confusion was palpable.

"Bulls, we can still be strong, even if we fall down. It was harder to hug Brace and Vela—especially Vela—than anything I've ever done in my life, including surviving the dozens of Violet Vipers trying to kill me and Erin.

"Erin chose the lie Sally just did, and you all agreed with it. Things can change for the better. Our worth can be measured by more than our fists. Let me tell you what's going on."

The Bulls leaned forward to listen to her, but before she could say more, Sabrina's eye drew to a brighter-than-normal flickering outside the door. The Bull heads moved to follow her gaze. A shadowy mass of people lurked outside with torches.

Chapter Eighteen

BROKEN DAM

THE MALE GANGS DEPLOYED on their diplomatic mission from Sector K. The returns were promising. Olive preached patience with the Queens and Rabbits, though she was a little ashamed of the method she used to bring them back to the negotiating table—utilizing Erin and the threat of the Brass Bulls as already switching to Olive's side. It wasn't technically true, yet, but Erin spoke with supreme confidence that Rina would come through on her end, and her faith infected Olive and Twill.

All Erin had to do was walk in a room. She stood only as tall as Olive, but her posture, musculature, and rancorous, boisterous demeanor silenced all chatter and focused the leaders on what Olive had to say. It helped that Erin took so completely to the Demons, despite Olive's initial misgivings. For her initiation she passed out goods to the worst-off, sometimes-dangerous gangless with a big smile. She resized a pair of jeans to be looser, then did the same for several Demons who loved the look without seeking trades for the service.

Demons gravitated to her conversations and stories of the Bulls, which she shared with glee, despite how they'd exiled her. Wine had a dangerous effect on her, though. Twill had to watch over her the first time she tried it, then kept her from drinking at the next event. Erin claimed to hate what it did to her alertness and vowed to never bother drinking again, anyway.

Twill developed a rapid, easy friendship with the newest Demon. They always tried one-upping each other in feats of strength, helping to construct overhangs or walls for the gangless. Their pats on the back caused people in their immediate vicinity to wince, but the two only ever smiled from the exchanges.

It didn't escape Olive's notice that they flirted with each other incessantly, graphically, but always laughed it off. Twill cut off any speculation by telling Olive it was all in fun, and that Erin claimed to be in love with Rina—she only joked around to keep up her spirits.

That was plausible, but Olive didn't really like it. Twill was spending more time with Erin than her. She knew how unfair it was of her to be jealous. She'd distanced herself from Twill physically, and Twill's attitude had changed when they were alone together. Their conversations turned to the mundane. Thankfully, she stopped asking Olive about what had changed in their relationship, and why. Olive needed that. But she also needed Twill to care for her in some capacity when the dam broke.

If it broke.

Each day the incidents played back in her mind, in her body; unprovoked and unwarranted. She spent her alone time in the nest, flipping through her collection of books, trying to find something that would help her. There were plenty of victims in the stories, but nothing about living with *being* a victim. Victims were often narrative tools for a protagonist to avenge. It was always framed on the protagonist or author's retribution and the way the incident made *them* feel.

No one ever asked the victim how they felt.

Yet Twill had, and Olive rejected her... Discussing it—thinking about it—only made her feel worse about everything, especially how she'd handled the aftermath.

She decided not to talk to Doctors about it. The first one had been so dismissive. Above all, she wasn't hurt physically anymore. She would be taking valuable time out of the Doctors' days when so many gangless needed help during their relatively short shifts.

No, it was *her* problem.

Her failures led to it.

Her failure to avoid more death.

Her failure to communicate with Twill.

It should have been no surprise to see Erin and Twill looking for excuses to touch each other.

It was Olive's fault.

OLIVE'S LEG FINALLY FELT flexible enough to walk without a limp, but she didn't have her old jeans re-sewn. In fact, she'd had them burned in a brazier.

She sifted through the bags of denim for something that would fit, but every pair with her waist size was too tight in the legs. She needed the fabric to stay off her skin; not *touch her* so much everywhere down there.

She remembered what Erin had been doing for some of the Demons, and brought a pair to her when she found her eating alone, sitting cross-legged against a wall.

"Little tight, boss?" Erin smiled. She offered the food scrap with only a couple bites left. Olive politely declined and handed over the jeans.

"It's still surprising to me that you Bulls sew."

"Because we're violent goons?"

"Well, my initial thoughts anyway. Do any of you read?"

"Brace does, but she doesn't go out of her way to teach. Doesn't bother me. Too quiet for my liking."

Olive leaned back against the wall as Erin finished her food, then pulled out a sewing needle and a roll of thread. Olive dropped extra scraps of denim next to her.

"So you don't want me to teach you to read? I would. Gladly."

"Nah. Plenty of us get along just fine without it."

Olive sighed but not loud enough for Erin to notice. "Apparently there used to be something called 'school' where kids were *required* to learn. Even young adults had to keep learning."

"Yeah? Where did that get everybody?"

Olive pointed to the ceiling. "It keeps them up there."

"Fuck, it's that easy?"

"My contacts say they use the fear of being cast down here as incentive to keep up with their educations and get jobs."

"Sounds horrible."

"More than being born here?"

"More than being forced to do boring shit my whole life just to end up a smear on the ground down here, fucking up the nets."

"That doesn't happen that often. That's a sweeping generalization, no better than the Upcity's derision for us."

"Your words are too big for me, boss. I can't tell if you're talking down to me or if I'm just dumb."

"That was quite a verbal catch-22 you just trapped me in, if I admitted to either."

"Huh?"

Olive laughed and slid down the wall to be eye-level as Erin continued working on the jeans, resting her chin in her palm as she watched Erin work by the light of the brazier.

"Do you have any contacts with the Upcity?" Olive asked.

"No. Well, kind of... We have a cherry Ruby Rider at headquarters who hasn't run away screaming yet."

"What's a—"

"Some Upcity rich bitch gang. We caught some of them slumming. Our Rider is brave, cute, squeamish, doesn't like women... She's a weirdo."

"She's been...allowed within the Bulls?"

"She's not *a Bull*. Brace took some kind of liking to her. A lot of us don't get it, but she was doing pretty well for herself, at least from what I heard."

"You mentioned she doesn't like women? Are the Bulls all—"

"No. Just some of us, like anywhere else. Why?"

"Just thought things would be a lot easier if they were..."

Olive explained to Erin what she did to placate the male gangs in the sectors they conquered.

"Brace keeps the men in Sector B like pets," Erin said. "There's no play-kating. They get out of line, they're dead. I can tell you Brace *is* like us, but... She's rough. Rougher than... Anyway, that's not how you're going to win against her. She's as stubborn as it gets. If she respects you after a fight, she'll bed you, but... You wouldn't survive that battle in the first place."

"Everyone keeps saying that. Like I've never experienced pain before."

"You don't look like it. Twill told me your injuries were from accidents, not battle."

Olive stared into the brazier at that, the heat accentuating the hate she held inside for herself.

"Hey, I'm not saying you're a weak *person*. I'm saying Brace's fucking hands are like concrete. The people she hits take weeks to recover, if they get up at all."

"...Twill said you hit harder than anyone she's ever fought."

"Brace is much worse. And her lieutenants would probably drop Twill. Don't get me wrong, Twill is a tough sister, but... This is our life, Olive. We live violence. Your only hope is my Rina."

Olive scratched her scalp and knocked her head back against the wall with a much deeper sigh, no longer mindful of Erin hearing her frustration.

"Would you hit me, Erin? I need to... I'm tired of hearing how I can't measure up. How can I, if no one will hit me?"

Erin punched Olive's bicep without hesitation, then went back to sewing. It was the worst stinging sensation Olive had ever experienced. Her flesh felt like it'd done nothing to protect her, and Erin's hit had bruised the marrow of her bones. The ricochet of her arm against the side of her chest rippled into her heart.

She wanted to remain stoic, but after a desperate moment of being unable to quell the pain, she curled into herself and rubbed her arm. She sniffed back a tear, but it was too late to escape Erin's notice.

"Brace is *worse*..." Erin whispered without moving her head up from her work.

OLIVE'S ARM STUNG ALL day, and she found herself unable to lift it without assistance from the other hand. Erin told her it would pass eventually.

However, Olive found herself holding her head a little higher around Twill. They were the only two Demons to be hit by a Bull. Olive started inserting herself between Erin and Twill, helping them out as much as she could. Neither of them resented her presence like she thought they would.

Her spirit lifted as they included her in more conversations, and she learned more about the Bulls and their culture of violence.

Spending a day sweating next to Twill felt good, too, along with their slow reconnection. As negotiations went smoothly with Sectors H and I (Rina's message about them being friendly rivals who would follow each other proved true), Olive finally invited Twill back to her nest one night.

They held hands and lay in silence for a long while, naked with each other for the first time in... She couldn't even remember when the last time was. Twill waited for Olive to say something first. Every time Olive opened her mouth, words stuck in her throat.

"How do you like Erin?" was what escaped, and Olive cursed her own cowardice.

"She's a tremendous asset to us."

"Mm." Since she didn't even want to ask that question, Olive had no follow up. She squeezed Twill's hand harder. Sweat built on their skin from the humid environment and her fingers slipped through Twill's like they used to before—

She cut the thought off. She didn't want anything sexual to happen between them still, at least not yet. She needed to tell Twill what happened; everything else was a distraction.

"Twill, I..."

Unexpectedly, Twill pulled Olive to her and kissed her in far more than reassurance; tongue already out, searching for hers. Olive let go of Twill's hand and pushed against Twill's chest, but she'd already wrapped her arms around Olive's back, holding her tight so Olive couldn't turn her mouth away.

Not wanting to hurt her, but not being strong enough to resist with her body, Olive bit Twill's tongue lightly, but that only seemed to excite her more. Finally, mercifully, Twill released Olive's mouth and clamped her lips on Olive's neck.

"Twill, stop! Stop! Don't you feel me pushing away?"

"Yes, every day, my love," Twill said between soft bites and licks, "I need you more than you know. It's been hell without you."

Olive pressed away, conjuring as much power as she could, but Twill's arms were too strong, and she seemed to enjoy the movement against her as Olive struggled to free herself.

"Please, Twill, you're hurting me. Let...me go...please."

Her pleas didn't work until Twill felt tears spatter her forehead. The tension left her arms within a second of realization. Olive pushed away and stood up. She grabbed her rags and jeans and sprinted out of the headquarters.

She found an alcove to pull her clothes back on, but it was in far too much haste to check for occupants.

A pair of rough hands touched her bare shoulders from behind. Something brushed against the back of her naked thigh. Without a second thought she swung around and punched. A sickening snap came from the person's neck and they fell backwards without bracing for it; deadweight.

Olive's hand throbbed while she pulled on her rags. She went outside to grab a candle and brought it back to the alcove.

It was an old woman. The thing that had brushed against Olive's thigh was an unlit candle sticking out of her rags. Olive dropped to her knees at the woman's side as her eyes fogged over. She wept through the rest of the night, holding the poor woman's rough, undeserving cold hands.

Olive's eyes were scratchy and puffy in the morning. She ignored Demons wishing her a good morning as they passed along breakfast scraps. Some complimented the work Erin did with her jeans, and Olive only stared away into a corner, her thoughts only briefly allowing the voices of others to pass through.

Twill wisely stayed away. She was the last person Olive wanted to talk to, let alone see.

A hand crossed Olive's vision to bring her back into focus.

"How's the arm, boss?"

Olive couldn't keep her lips from quivering into a sneer at Erin, obliviously disturbing her wallowing. Erin detected something while scrutinizing Olive's face and her smile faded.

"What's wrong with your eyes?"

"I've been crying all night. Something you people aren't capable of."

Erin's eyes darted away and her brow furrowed, as if she couldn't understand what Olive said.

Olive didn't know what drove her to her next chain of thoughts, but they ended with her squaring up in front of Erin, and the room falling silent.

"I guess I owe you for hitting you in the arm," Erin whispered. "Sure. Come on, hit me as hard as you can."

"No. That wasn't a challenge. *This* is."

Erin looked around at the others who were watching, uncertainty painting her expression.

"I'm not hitting you again, Olive. You can hit me, but I won't return it. I owe you that much."

"You'd better fucking hit me back, Bull."

Olive invoked the power she'd dealt the night before. She wanted to know if the old woman had died from weak bones more than Olive's strength. It wouldn't change the outcome, but it might lessen the weight on her conscience, and there was no better way to determine her fault than hitting *someone*.

Also, in a way, hitting Erin might replace the desire to hit Twill, if she just got it out of her system.

Erin's face hardly yielded to Olive's fist. It was as hard as Twill's abs, but with additional bone structure. Olive's fingers exploded in pain, but she gritted her teeth and put her hand behind her back, pressing it into the flesh to help soothe it while she kept her eyes locked on Erin's amused stare.

"Not bad," Erin whispered. A little trickle of blood ran down the side of her mouth. She began to turn around.

"Don't you turn away from me." Olive's voice cracked and her lip quivered as she fought back an unwanted sob.

Erin stopped but didn't square back up. "I can't wait for you to meet Rina, Olive."

"In the meantime, you better fucking hit me so these people can go about their day. Are you trying to discredit me; make your new leader look weak? I don't need your pity."

"Are you trying to be *Brace?* Why are we going to all this trouble for peace if you're just going to solve your problems *her* way?"

"Please, Erin..."

Erin rolled her eyes, then addressed the crowd of confused Demons.

"Listen here! I owed Olive that hit! Look at her arm!" Erin grabbed Olive and ripped open the rag sleeve. The purple bruise covered her entire bicep. "Olive completed a Bull's challenge! She's a brave sister I'll follow into any situation. There's only one path to peace in the Underfoot. *Fuck* the Bulls!"

The Demons responded with the same fervor and went about their day with a renewed sense of purpose. Olive didn't feel any better about anything, but at least she didn't have to pep up her charges when she felt so damn low.

She did, however, have to go to the Doctor to brace her broken fingers. Olive didn't feel like she'd suffered enough for her deeds, but broken fingers were a good start.

That night, she hid away in the alcove with the old woman she'd killed and drank an entire bottle of wine. She talked to the woman all night—sharing her life and everything she'd gone through to that point, and how she wished she could trade places with her.

Unfortunately, her open confessional didn't have the desired effect. She still needed to talk to Twill. But not that night. The street sweepers made weekly pickups of the dead, and the woman would be removed the next day. Olive lay next to the corpse and put her arm over the torso. She practiced all the ways she could think of to say she was sorry, and earn forgiveness—*deserve* forgiveness—from Twill, the old woman, and *all* the other dead she never intended to leave in her wake, until she managed to fall asleep.

Chapter Nineteen

Sisters

REGINA DIDN'T INITIALLY SEE the wisdom of allowing runts to do all the fighting, especially against men. But Brace explained before they entered the Iron Iguana's territory that the men weren't armed, and the Bulls didn't need them—*their* arms were literal and just as deadly. Getting her head around marching into battle proved difficult, despite her tough talk and trying to psyche herself up.

As Brace addressed the runts and her expectations for them, Regina resolved to follow them in, but only act as support. The rest of the Bulls, including the officers, set a perimeter around the territory to catch escaping Iguanas, but wouldn't enter in support or aggression.

As the runts prepared with a few peppy punches of each other, Brace put her hand on Regina's shoulder.

"I won't think less of you for staying back, Ten Stories. I already told you what I think, and that wasn't an attempt to shame you into joining them."

"You haven't guilted me into joining, Brace. I'm ashamed of what you did to Erin and Rina."

Regina jerked out of Brace's grip and went to stand among the eager initiates. They announced their presence at the territory's main entrance. The screams carried through the streets and alleyways in the vicinity. When the echoes died, the charge began, and Regina followed.

Despite the loud declaration of war, several Iguanas emerged in confusion. They didn't get far past awareness before they were laid on their backs with powerful punches from the front line. The second line cleaned up, delivering fatal hits to their necks, heads, and chests.

Regina felt a little sorry in witnessing the massacre, until more Iguanas realized what was happening and formed a counter attack. They were still *men*, and they staggered their fair share of soon-to-be Bulls, but not enough to knock them down. Regina hid off to the sides, watching the runts counter the counter. None of them teamed up. It didn't seem necessary at first—their blows were so brutal that the men didn't get a second hit in.

As Regina followed along, she could see some of them weakening. It started taking two hits to knock down the men, then three. That was when the second wave switched with the front line and reignited the ruthless rush to catch the Iguanas unprepared.

How quickly the battle would have ended if the real Bulls had been involved... Regina questioned the efficiency, but had to remind herself she wasn't a leader, and this wasn't the Bulls' first incursion in enemy territory. Surely the strategy had yielded favorable results before.

The more dead men she stepped around, though, Regina recognized a certain level of method to the madness. The *initiates* were winning their battles. They would grow to be stronger every day past that point, until they were capable of taking and dishing out inhuman amounts of damage—were there ever to be a battle that required the *actual* full force of the Bulls, it would be over in moments.

Pride swelled in Regina's chest for having survived two real punches, from *real* Bulls, including their third-in-com mand. She felt even *more* drawn to Vela's nightly embrace and the protection it offered. There was nowhere in the Underfoot she'd be safer and nowhere she craved to be more in that moment... The adrenaline of the fight infected her, even so far back from the front line.

Regardless of the pity she felt over Brace's treatment of Rina, she wondered if Brace was right, as usual—Rina *was* weaker than the others, maybe coasting off her motherly charms... Though that didn't quite make sense in their meritocracy: Rina had to be *something* as fourth-in-command.

The fighting lost steam as the initiates split up in pairs to find the last remaining Iguanas. As Regina tailed a pair, an Iguana slunk out of an alcove with a long object in his hands. He crept behind one of the initiates. Regina cried out.

The initiate turned around in time to take the hit with more than surprise. She braced, but the hit still knocked her down. Her partner pulverized the man while Regina sprinted to check on the prone woman. She knelt down and helped lift her up from her daze. It was Bridgette, the initiate who fell down at Sally's unveiling.

Finished with the execution, the partner put her hand on Bridgette's head in sympathy, gave Regina the length of pipe the Iguana had used, then ran ahead to join her future sisters.

"Are you okay?" Regina asked. She wiped away a stream of blood before it could fall into Bridgette's eyes.

"No. I just lost out on becoming a Bull."

"What? That's bullshit! You can't be expected to stand up to something like that!"

"Just leave me, Rag Doll."

Regina helped Bridgette to her feet, despite the jab of using that nickname. It grew on her—actually a bit *too* apt—the way the Ruby Riders expected the membership to take on the plastic qualities of a doll that they could pressure to dress up in finery. In the Underfoot, she'd been dressed in the local "clothing" yet was seen as the same sort of inanimate object that could never be "human" in the way they all thought of each other within their respective ecosystems.

There perception of her otherness tore her up inside whenever she daydreamed about joining them. Even as some of their practices repulsed her, she wanted to be one of them...

Bridgette regained her balance after a moment, pushed away from Regina's steadying hand, and followed the others further into the territory. Regina fell in behind, needing to skip a few steps to keep up to Bridgette's pace.

A pitched fight took place outside the Iguanas' headquarters, a last stand. Bridgette rushed into the brawl. Regina found a couple of initiates on the ground, unmoving. She knelt next to one who was still breathing shallowly. The other was dead.

Regina grabbed the dead woman's arm and dragged her over to the unconscious one. She lifted the living woman up by putting her arm over Regina's shoulders. Once she balanced, Regina then grabbed the wrist of the dead one and began dragging them back to the entrance.

It was the hardest thing she'd ever done in her life: a different sort of pain than Ezzie and Sally inflicted; a different sort of drenching sweat than what Vela coaxed from her in the nest. She couldn't move quickly, and eventually initiates began passing her on the walk back, their fists covered in blood and bone. More than a few teeth were plucked from their knuckles and tossed onto the street with a clatter.

They all ignored Regina's struggle, until Bridgette came to her and picked up the dead woman, muttering something about them both being deadweight. They were the last to exit the territory. The Bulls cheered for the conquerors and gave them hard slaps on the back and "playful" punches in the arms. Some of the initiates' arms were like noodles by that time, unable to reciprocate. So were Regina's, for her part.

Brace pointed for a Bull to relieve Regina and take the unconscious woman to a Clinic, but not before the entire gang saluted the dead woman. They put her next to a brazier, crossed her arms, and placed a Brass Bull patch under them.

While the women celebrated in the middle of the street with beer brought forth from Brace's secret stock, Regina saw Bridgette refuse a bottle and turn to leave. Regina ran to grab her arm and pull her back, but Bridgette yanked it away.

"What's going on over there?" Vela shouted and quieted the gang.

Regina looked back to see them all staring at her, and Bridgette took the opportunity to storm off anyway.

"Hey, Bridgette! Get back here!"

Regina chased Bridgette and put a hand on her shoulder. She whirled around and pushed Regina hard, sending her into a wall—in the middle of the street? Vela was there to catch Regina's fall.

"What's this all about, baby?" Vela whispered, an edge to her voice. She gave Bridgette's back a hard stare before she disappeared in the darkness altogether.

"She... She fell, but it wasn't fair. She was hit with a pipe from behind. She got back up and kept fighting."

"What do you care?"

"She wants to be a Bull so bad..."

"Everyone does, Doll." Vela put her arm around Regina and guided her back to the celebration. Vela motioned for quiet again. She instructed a Bull to bring Bridgette back, then she shared her bottle of beer with Regina as she talked to Ezzie about the situation.

The beer was warm and tasted horrible. Regina would have spit it out, but she'd grown out of showing wastefulness among people who had virtually nothing but each other.

Once Bridgette returned, her head hung low, Ezzie addressed the group.

"No one will hold someone usin' a weapon against you, Bulls. As Raggy as my witness, even *I* fell to four electric clubs from the pigs watchin' the Elevators. If they fight dishonorably, *you* are not dishonored fallin' to them. Bridgette, get your fuckin' ass over here for a beer, and share it with Regina for bearin' witness to your beautiful fists!"

Another cheer, and Vela's lips tickled Regina's ear in just the right way.

"Good job, baby."

Regina stomached the disgusting swill a little better, having a drink in Bridgette's honor, but saved most of it for her. Regina received hard smacks on the back from Vela and Brace in appreciation.

Brace's hurt worst of all, but Regina stood tall and at her side as Brace addressed the gang.

"You're all Bulls now, ladies. We'll pass out your patches back home. And I hope you all saw what I saw—the only one of you who can't become a Bull, still risked her life to bring back two of your sisters, and saved Bridgette's reputation.

"Reggie of the Ruby Riders, I will never call you a Bull, but you are now my sister, and a sister to all Bulls."

The cheer struck her hard enough to knock tears out of her eyes. Vela suddenly picked her up by the armpits and lifted her to sit on her shoulders. She carried her around to slap hands with her new sisters. When they completed the circuit, Vela brought her down and kept her arm around her waist as they all began walking back to the main street.

A mass of people blocked their path after they ambled across two intersections. It wasn't the trash cans. They were all women, all carrying pipes.

Vela squeezed Regina tight, and it was enough for Regina to not immediately break out in a sweat of fear. Brace moved to the front of the Bulls and shouted for the leader of the Crystal Crackers to step forward.

"What the fuck is this, Trina? Didn't expect us to succeed in taking care of your man problem? There's nothing to clean up, babe."

"We never doubted it, Brace. Now that you're all tired, though... We're taking over!"

"That was your plan all along, Crackers?"

Trina nodded, a bit unconvincingly, even to Regina's untrained eye. Brace spit, then gestured for them to bring it on.

The Crystal Crackers ran at the Brass Bulls and Regina recognized the full genius of Brace's strategy. Not a single veteran Bull was tired from the previous battle, and, impossibly, the newest Bulls sprinted past the seniors to meet the charge head on. Any Cracker that got past that initial wave was met with a life-altering, or life-ending, punch from a much stronger Bull.

The pipes were ineffective. Most were caught mid-swing while others took the blows strategically in nonlethal places, but they were never dodged. Crackers who had waited to attack dropped their pipes and retreated. It was over in a matter of seconds.

Vela let go of Regina and found Trina on the ground among the mess of bodies: still alive, but barely. Vela lifted her to face Brace.

"Were you pressured to do that, Trina? It sure as fuck wasn't like you."

"There's been male resistance, Sectors E through G, cos of the push from the Denim Demons. They killed the Purple Rams, and they're converting the rest to join the Demons.

"We were told by the Acrylic Kicks: we needed to help take you Bulls out, make it easier for the Demons to sweep through the Underfoot. They want the sex deals and vaccines."

"What the hell do you care about the males?" Brace asked. "We *just* solved your problem. The Maroon Mongeese in Sector C are weak drug-runners, but at least they're not raping anyone. We could have total control over A through D, and enough Bulls to hold back whatever those fucking Demons throw at us. But instead of working together, you chose to make life easier for *men?*"

Trina only stared up at Brace's hard eyes until Vela shook her out of the trance.

"Answer her, Cracker bitch," Vela said.

"She's coming, Brace," Trina mumbled, as if barely holding onto consciousness. "We don't want to live in violence anymore."

Brace rolled her eyes. "Yeah, sure looks like it with all those pipes, babe."

"Let me end her, Brace," Vela said with another shake.

Brace hunched in front of Trina.

"I don't know, Vela. I can't believe that Demon cunt has pushed in as far as she has. They're almost on our fucking doorstep. The Demons were held up around Sector K the last I heard. All this 'love' bullshit..."

"What do you mean, Brace?" Regina asked. "Love works on this side, too."

"Careful, Reggie. You're my sister but you're not an officer. But to humor you, as you continue to observe us, a little context: the Bulls have survived the longest of all other gangs. So many are falling now, giving themselves over to the Demons for the promise of a little more food, a little more medical access, a little more sex. When Olive can't provide those things anymore—and it's only a matter of time when the Upcity decides on whatever whim they want to cut her off—they'll turn on her and go back to pitching their tents in each Sector.

"The fear of the Bulls is eternal, Ruby Rider. My predecessor never fell, and neither did hers. Vela won't fall. Ezzie won't fall. Remember what Rina took? I've never hit anyone harder that I didn't want dead. She'll *never* fall. These magnificent bitches that just demolished two gangs in a day? We might lose one member a year, but we'll always be here, and we're not for sale. We make our own way, using our own contacts, dictating our terms, living *our* lives.

"What would *you* do with Trina, Reggie?"

The direct question so soon after the speech knocked Regina back a step. She scrambled for an answer, growing uncomfortable before Brace and Vela's patient stares.

"You give the initiates a second chance when they fall, right? You could give the Crystal Crackers a chance to reconcile their transgression. It looks like they learned a painful lesson, don't you think? Wouldn't grateful survivors make the most dutiful servants?"

Brace and Vela exchanged little smiles.

"What a delicious use of fear, sister.

"Trina, heal up and come to Sector B *alone*. We'll discuss the next steps then. If I don't see you in two days, I'll consider your absence as spitting on my sister's mercy, and we'll come back here to finish the job. Got it?"

Vela dropped Trina to the ground and put her arm around Regina again, leading her back to Sector B. On the way, Brace sidled to Regina's other side.

"You up for sharing Vela tonight, Reggie?"

"Excuse me?" Regina scoffed and Vela chuckled at the immediate rebuke.

"After a battle is the best time for sex," Brace stated. "I'm all amped up."

"Careful, baby," Vela said to Regina, "when you spend a night with Brace, you'll remember it in more ways than one—for *days*."

Regina shrugged out of Vela's grip. She expected to have to fight harder to get away, but Vela loosened willingly. For some reason, that boiled her blood a little more than being propositioned: did Vela want what Brace offered *more*? Was Regina's innocence worth less than a brutal experience Vela'd had countless times before?

"I only just recently... I'm not interested in... How do you even do it with so many limbs...? No! I'm not a fucking toy! You two want to fuck? Fine. Leave me out of it. And...don't come to my nest later if I'm so forgettable you'll fuck anyone else so soon after... *Fuck you*, Vela!"

Regina pushed away from Vela's reaching hands, ignored Brace's bark of laughter, and sprinted ahead to cross Sector B's border with the other Bulls.

As they came to their home street, everyone paused. Unfamiliar women filed out of the headquarters, followed by Rina, Sally, and the other left behind Bulls.

"Who are they?" Regina asked the nearest Bull.

"Onyx Orcas from Sector A. They don't cross over the border very often, though..."

While the Orcas walked away with extinguished torches, the Bulls who'd fought the battle boisterously greeted the ones tasked with guarding the place. It didn't escape Regina's notice how Rina's smile dropped when Brace and Vela came into view.

Chapter Twenty

No Escape

SABRINA'S HEART SANG WHEN the Onyx Orcas dropped their aggressive stances and doused their torches. She convinced them that they didn't need to make a move on the Bulls, because Olive and the Denim Demons would be sweeping through soon enough. If the Orcas of Sector A simply remained patient, they would be in a much better place—as opposed to being battered after an ambush attempt that wouldn't work.

The Orcas' leader shook hands with Sabrina. Even better than the Orcas agreeing to her suggestion was her Bull sisters going along with it, too. Hope for Olive's love got through without Sabrina having to convince them first—they were all swayed at the same time.

However, Sabrina's hope plummeted when the rest of the Bulls returned quicker than expected from the Iguana attack. She wished the Orcas were gone so she wouldn't have to explain why there weren't mounds of them outside the headquarters. Negotiating with them, without Brace present, was a gigantic risk, but since they left in peace, Brace paid them no heed. Sabrina's unfinished challenge must have weighed more heavily on Brace's mind.

All eyes were on her, but the only ones that mattered were Brace and Vela's. The celebratory mood picked back up as the Bulls who were left behind gobbled up all the details of the battle. They took the party inside. Sabrina expected Regina to be on Vela's arm, but she pushed through the crowd to get inside well ahead of her.

Sabrina remained outside to face Brace and Vela.

"Don't fucking hug me again, Rina," Vela said with no hint of a smile.

Sabrina didn't respond other than to meet Brace's hard stare.

"Before we talk," Brace said, "you're going to walk in there and hit me back in front of those Bulls."

"No."

Vela took a step but Brace held her back. Again. Sabrina was beyond pleased to see it. Brace never used to restrain Vela's actions. She'd stopped her *twice* that day, for Rina's sake. Was there actually a way to get through to Brace? Sabrina hadn't really considered it could be through anything but violence before that moment...

"Rina, you've proven yourself in my eyes. You stood through both of my hits. You need to complete the challenge for *me*. Everyone in there respects you. Now you're going to do me the courtesy of hitting me as hard as you *motherfucking* can."

"Then I get my—" Vela started.

"Shut up, Vela," Brace said in a low voice. "Go inside and make sure everyone watches us enter."

Vela put her shoulder hard into Sabrina's on the way past, but Sabrina didn't break from Brace's intense eyes flickering from the brazier.

"I already answered your challenge, Brace. With both of my fists, around your back."

"Don't get cute with me, Bull. Do you think I don't see what you do around here? The one they turn to when mean ol' Brace, Vela, and Ezzie are too hard on them; the one they look to for an easy solution before they have to do the difficult one *anyway*; the one who's 'above' all this violence?"

"I hit as hard as any—"

"Your physical power isn't up for debate." Brace punctuated that statement by grabbing Sabrina's rags and giving them a hard shake. "But I need to see something from you right now—that you're a fucking *Bull*."

"What are you talking about? Of course I'm a—"

"Did you think no one saw you rescue that Sapphire Snake assassin?" Brace pushed Sabrina away, letting go of the rags. "We went back to retrieve her, found the ropes but no Snake, and canvassed the gangless in the area."

"Why would you sit on that? Let me continue as if—"

"Because I fucking *need* you, Sabrina. All that soft shit? It keeps the Bulls who are on the edge from running away. They see someone who will protect them, stand up for them, and allow them to see there's something to remain with us for—*besides* fists and death. You bring out the sisterhood that's behind it all."

"...Why would you never tell me this before?"

Brace broke eye contact and relaxed her posture.

"I don't want the soft shit to go *too* much to your head—or theirs. Bulls can be more than physically strong, but they have to *at least* be able to kick some ass, or they're a liability. Soft sisters are dead sisters. That's why you're going to follow me in there, and try to lay me out. Anything less, and I'll tear your patch off myself, and burn it in this fire."

Sabrina was certainly thankful to hear that Brace valued her for more than her physical prowess, but after such an articulate rationalization of their culture, it left Sabrina wondering whether Brace could be hiding something else? Did she follow up on what happened with that Snake? If the question came up, Sabrina supposed she could use the same excuse she had with Erin: they needed a Sector guide in order to find a high-value target. But further still... Brace might already know everything about that day was a lie. Bitter Vipers had incentive to tattle: no dead Serpents, no dead Demon, that Sabrina was the one who fell... Would Brace willingly sacrifice someone as strong as Erin for the sake of keeping Sabrina around?

Brace didn't allow further conversation. She walked by Sabrina into the headquarters. She had the frantic thought that without her patch, Sabrina could simply run through the sectors into Olive's loving embrace. She could learn more about Twill. She could reunite with Erin...

But leaving Kirsten and Panda behind in such a selfish pursuit? That couldn't happen. And she couldn't turn her back on the Bulls who had potential to be something so much more than violent enforcers. Losing her patch would cut off her access to all of them, including the Sector itself. She couldn't be as effective in helping the Denim Demons from the outside.

Sabrina followed Brace, who was already squared up front and center inside. The Bulls hushed immediately. Ezzie placed her hand on Sabrina's shoulder, softer than she'd ever touched her before.

Were they patronizing her?

"Don't hold back, Rina," Ezzie whispered.

Sabrina squared up but couldn't muster any desire to strike Brace after their conversation. Luckily, Vela loomed not far from Brace's shoulder, a look of disgust malforming her pretty face. Sabrina pulled back and unloaded her hate for Vela into Brace's face.

Brace's leg shot back to stop her from a full-on stagger. The Bulls gasped. There was an awful moment when Brace's eyes blinked rapidly, like she was trying desperately to refocus her vision.

It only took a second for her to regain her posture, and a big, bleeding smile brightened up her face. Brace gave Sabrina a tight embrace where, instead of confusion as in their last hug, there was something deeper that sparked hope in Sabrina that maybe she *could* get through to the hardest Bull in history.

While the Bulls cheered for the display, Brace whispered in their embrace, "thank you, sister." Brace let go and proclaimed they would party through the rest of the night, which earned even more cheers.

Vela came around Brace and got in Sabrina's face.

"It's *my* turn, bitch," Vela said, her lips curled in a snarl.

"Let it go for today," Brace said. "Don't bring the mood down. Come to my nest and we'll—"

Vela yanked her arm away from Brace's fingers, then stomped out of the building.

"Not sure how long it'll be before she reinstates that challenge, Rina," Brace said. "But you know I can't stop her forever."

"I would never ask you to, Brace. We're fucking *Bulls*."

Brace clapped her hand over Sabrina's shoulder and guided her to the last of the beer from her celebratory stock. Ezzie popped the top, then handed it over with a clap on the back that put to bed the thought she'd grown soft, too.

AFTER THE CELEBRATION, SABRINA left for home. She took her normal route, but kept an eye out for Vela, who hadn't been seen since her abrupt departure. She checked alcoves, around corners, and behind free-standing structures. With no sign of her, Sabrina sighed in relief outside her home as she took one last glance back where she'd come. Satisfied that she wasn't followed, she stepped inside. As her eyes adjusted to the low candle light, she took in a nightmare.

Vela sat in their nest, her arm around Kirsten's slumped shoulders, the other arm around Panda's back, cradling her from the thigh. Panda's animal book was open; she pointed at animals and sounded them out for Vela, who wore an evil grin upon Sabrina's arrival.

"Mom! Your friend said bulls are the best animal, but I still think panda bears are better!"

"They're not bears, honey," Vela said without breaking Sabrina's death stare. "They're verminous raccoons."

Panda flipped the pages furiously in search of the mysterious new animal.

"Little thieves, honey. Getting into places they don't belong. A Bull works for the herd. It doesn't shy away from a challenge. They trample raccoons."

Sabrina slid her hand along the wall, to where the pipe should have been. Vela let go of Kirsten's shoulder to reach behind the nest, then lifted the pipe for Sabrina to see. She dropped it back down and put her arm around Kirsten again, who wasn't responding in the slightest, not even a shiver.

"Mm, your red-haired mommy's so soft, Panda. I remember her from a long time ago. Probably before mommy number two came along. Before you were born? I don't know. What a piece of ass she was..."

Panda flipped to a new page. "Ass... Jackass...? Looks like a mule, or donkey. A little like those bulls you showed me!"

"Not...even...close...*honey*."

Sabrina's heart pounded against her ribcage and sweat poured down her back. Her knuckles were sore from hitting Brace, and she couldn't squeeze them dramatically enough to make a cracking sound. Vela knew what was going through her head, though, and made a meal of Sabrina's disadvantage.

"Vela... Please..." Sabrina whispered while shaking her head.

"Please what? Join you and your lovely...*wife*...for a night of debauchery?"

"What does de... deb... debarchery mean?" Panda asked, looking up innocently into Vela's horrible bitch face.

"Mmm, ask me again in a couple years, honey. I'll *show* you."

Sabrina's lips pulled back, baring teeth. It took everything in her to not attack in the presence of her child. It would kill her if—

"I don't like it when Mom has that look," Panda said, then buried her face in Vela's rags.

Sabrina took a shuddering inhale of breath, her eye reluctantly growing wet with helplessness.

"Don't worry, little Panda. I'll protect you from that mean ol' mommy."

Anger collapsed into a despair so deep Sabrina fell to her knees. She held her arms out to her baby.

"Puh— Panda... Please. Your mommy needs you, baby. Please come here."

Vela let go of Panda and gave her a small push out of the nest. While Panda ran to Sabrina's arms, Vela leaned even more casually into Kirsten's body, that evil smile still on her face.

Sabrina wept with Panda in her arms, wetting her rags.

"Does your bad eye hurt when you cry?" Panda asked, putting her little hand on Sabrina's left cheek.

"Everything hurts when I cry, baby," Sabrina whispered.

Vela lazily rose from the nest and made for the door, but stopped behind Sabrina's back.

"We complete the challenge tomorrow morning, *Mommy*. No more stalling."

After Vela left, Sabrina scooped up Panda and rushed to Kirsten. Her eyes were open but she only stared. She didn't react to Sabrina's gentle touch.

Sabrina sat in the middle of the nest as Vela had, and cradled her wife, then asked Panda to bring her book over.

"Show me the panda bear again, baby. I love that one more than any of the others."

Sabrina lay awake all night, listening to Panda's light breathing on one side, running her hand through Kirsten's hair on the other. Kirsten finally closed her eyes after Vela had been gone a few hours. Sabrina took steady, controlled breaths as she savored the comfort in the touch of her family.

She wished Olive would arrive soon to relieve, and, perhaps, forgive Sabrina's violent life.

Sabrina strode into the headquarters in the morning, the last of all the Bulls. The rest were assembled for breakfast. Vela squared up immediately—Sabrina's face showed her intent.

"Well, look who graces us with her presence, Bulls! Come on, you soft-ass runt. You first!"

Sabrina paused only to square up properly, then unloaded a punch so hard that Vela's legs flew up, slapping Sabrina's thigh before hitting the cement floor.

Sabrina rolled the unconscious body over with her foot, gripped her patch with her left hand, and tore it off in one fluid movement.

Sabrina didn't acknowledge the other Bulls or Brace. They didn't gasp. They didn't cry out. Reggie made a move to Vela's prone body, but Sabrina turned around and left the headquarters before anyone else could properly respond. She threw the patch in the brazier outside the door and went straight to the Clinic in dim hope of treatment for her shattered right hand.

PART THREE
IT COMES FOR US ALL

Chapter Twenty-One

TALK TO ME

OLIVE SWEATED THROUGH THE night alone, her broken hand waking her every time she rolled over. Her dreams didn't help—all the familiar ones were overtaken by Twill, only she didn't have the decency to stop once it was clear beyond a doubt that she was hurting Olive. In the morning Olive hurried ahead to Sector G to negotiate with the Luscious Lemurs. Sectors H and I were easy enough for Demon leaders to convince, mostly because the incongruous Murder Minks of H were the friendliest gang Olive had encountered in the Underfoot, and their neighbors in I followed their every move.

Without Rina's tip, things may have gone a different way...

Olive's mood fouled considerably from the lack of sleep, her injuries (the broken nose and black eyes to accompany her broken hand), and not having Twill to consult with anymore. Erin continued gravitating to Twill, so there wasn't an alternative.

Olive learned that the male gang in Sector G, the Green Marines, grew nervous over the news of Sector D's Iron Iguanas being completely wiped out by the Brass Bulls—two complete sectors away from the Bulls' home turf. What worried Olive was the rumor that the Bulls didn't even do anything—it was their *rookies* that won the battle, and they'd only suffered *one* casualty.

Several female gangs between Olive and the Bulls were having meetings to discuss joining a side, or whether they should consolidate with each other to push both sides back. The Lemurs leaned heavily towards joining Olive. As usual, the Demons' promises of fresh supplies and virtually violence-free streets carried a tremendous amount of weight.

They warned Olive about the next two sectors—the Vipers and Snakes, who had reasons to side against the Bulls but were just as fiercely independent and favored violence over talking.

Olive knew she'd gotten lucky running into the most amenable gangs at that point in her conquest. She was proving herself to be a weak leader of late—beaten up, taking the easier way with violence, losing closeness with her top people...

Those were the rumors she kept hearing from Doctors and advance spies. Ironically, some thought she was becoming *more* dangerous because of all that: she had an iron grip on the supplies; she stole an increasing amount of supplies to fulfill her promises; she killed people for touching her; she killed them for disagreeing with her; she shut down negotiations if the gangs wouldn't agree to wear the jeans; she got into fights with her own people; and she left a trail of blood everywhere she went.

In contrast, the rumors about the Bulls were practically glowing: meeting their foes with honor; without weapons; without baiting them with empty promises; they kept to themselves, only venturing into other sectors if asked; zero tolerance for rape or placating male gangs with transactional sex; and their indomitable bond with each other.

Even with Erin to parse rumors from fact, Olive worried more and more how she was going to break through the two serpent gangs and the Bulls. The rumored threat of Olive's violence invited a forceful resistance rather than a stroll to the negotiation tables. Without the confidence of walking into a room with Twill, possibly the largest woman in the Underfoot, and her battered inability to convey any sort of physical intimidation, Olive needed to begin utilizing Erin closer to the front line.

She found the two of them constructing a new outhouse as a goodwill gesture for Sector H. Olive needed every one of those gestures as she could afford. She recruited Demons hungry for leadership positions but had been passed over when Twill made her recommendations. They couldn't afford any perception that Olive wasn't still thinking about them or that she would break her promises.

Olive watched Twill and Erin work together—they made it look effortless. They didn't notice her approach, and as their hands went to a tool at the same time, their touch lingered. Olive's face contorted, though she had no right to feel anything. She'd pushed Twill away.

Telling herself that didn't help.

Olive waited for their brief little moment to pass, then she cleared her throat within earshot. Her dark mood pushed to the tip of her tongue, and she let it escape.

"You know what *I* love? People in love with other people loving *other people*. That's the whole damn goal, isn't it?"

In the dim light of the braziers it was hard to tell the expressions on their faces. She hoped it was shame.

"What are you going on about, boss?" Erin asked like a naïve child.

"I'm 'going on about' looking forward to meeting this Rina, and attaching to *her* hip, just as you two have with each other. What a love-filled Underfoot this will be."

Erin looked over at Twill and snickered.

"Does she always get like this when she hasn't had enough sleep? Her eyes are like black holes."

Twill only remained quiet, staring at Olive's feet.

"Ah. Olive, I apologize," Erin said in a more serious tone, "I get so close to my sisters, I can't help it. We're pretty free with our love in the Bulls. I'd be so happy for you and Rina if you…followed through on that little threat—*if* I didn't think it would kill you and Twill."

"Don't talk about us like you know. And what the fuck do Bulls know about love? You all beat the ever-living fuck out of each other. That's not love."

As she'd gotten closer, Olive could see their faces a little better. Erin's lips puckered to the side and Olive couldn't tell whether it was dismissive or something was being held back. She rapidly lost her already thinning patience.

"Forget about it," Olive said to Twill's downcast face. "Come on, Erin. I need you for something."

"Okay, boss, but I'm not going to fuck you so you can make Twill jealous, or whatever the fuck's going on between you two."

"I need your bullshit violence, not your bullshit love advice. Follow me."

Erin didn't lose her infuriating good humor and shrugged at Twill before getting up. Twill surprised Olive by speaking, barely above a whisper.

"If you'd only talk to me, my love…"

"Did you just mispronounce my name? It's Ol-live, lieutenant." Olive turned away and strode in the direction of Sector F, the home of the Sapphire Snakes.

"Are you going to make more comments like that the whole way?" Erin asked as she fell in line.

"I want your muscles, Bull, not your conversation."

"I'm a Demon."

"Because I need you."

"No, it doesn't work like that, Olive. I did the initiation and joined the Demons. I shook your hand. You can't just decide to—"

"I decide everything. The moment you're not useful, I don't need you."

"Yeah, I mean, that's bullshit, but it does track with how you've been treating Twill..."

Olive whirled on Erin to punch her before she remembered her broken hand. She winced as her fingers couldn't ball up into a fist. Erin wore a bemused little smile that only served to anger Olive more. She couldn't control herself, and kicked the side of Erin's thigh.

The irritating smile didn't disappear, it simply grew larger. Erin at least had the decency to stifle a laugh.

"You know, Olive, if I thought sex would get you out of whatever's eating at you, I'd happily help you out. That said, despite what you might think about me and the Bulls, *I* have the emotional intelligence to know that wouldn't solve your problem. You need to talk with Twill."

Olive turned back toward Sector F and continued walking. "No, what I *need* is you to scare the Snakes into joining the Demons, and then the Vipers, and then the others until we get to Sector B."

Erin stopped following. Olive huffed and looked back.

"Come on, Bull. We have work to do."

Olive carried on a few steps as if that was the end of it, but then Erin suddenly came around, put her shoulder into Olive's stomach, and lifted her up like a rag doll.

"We sure do, sister," Erin said as she carried her back the way they came. Olive pounded her unbroken hand against Erin's back. When that didn't elicit any pain response from her, she pinched Erin's side and twisted. Erin gave Olive a squeeze over her arm and slapped her butt hard enough to feel like she'd been stabbed.

Twill had just finished the outhouse when Erin arrived. She set Olive down and held them both by the arm.

"Look, sisters, I don't think I can ever help you understand what I sacrificed for Rina and your ideals. She believes in you so deeply, she's betraying sisters she loves and who love and respect her more than anyone else. Pull your respective shit together so we can get this movement back on track."

Erin let go of their arms and left Olive and Twill to look at each other's feet. After an agonizing minute, Olive spoke.

"It...smells really bad here."

Twill nodded but didn't move or say anything. Olive exhaled and grabbed Twill's fingers to lead her away from the outhouse. Holding their fingers again after so long, awkward silence passed between them instead of words. Once they were sufficiently away from the outhouse, Olive stopped.

"Twill... This isn't something that can be solved. I... There's nothing to say. If you can't work with me without touching... I'll need to..."

"Take away my jeans?"

Olive's head dropped as she fought back a wave of tears she had no right to shed. She let go of Twill's hand and pressed her palms against the bruised skin around her eyes. Not too long ago she would have expected to be enveloped in Twill's big, comforting arms, but when Twill respected Olive's wish to remain no-contact, it lifted her spirits a bit. Maybe she wouldn't have to part with Twill completely after all.

"Olive... Can you tell me if there's a future for us? Maybe when things settle down?"

"If I could see the future, we wouldn't be having this...whatever is happening right now."

"You'll be direct enough to confirm you want me out of the Demons if I touch you again, but you won't just put words to it so 'whatever is happening' can continue?"

Olive couldn't meet Twill's eyes anymore. The flash of hope she'd felt disappeared as she realized she couldn't surmount the awful depression weighing her down more and more each day, and Twill wouldn't be the one to rescue her.

The problem *was* her. It would be a mercy for her not to take Twill down with her; let her be happy with Erin instead...

"'Whatever is happening,'" Twill whispered, "I'm sorry I made it worse for you the other night. I love you so much, Olive. I took more than you offered and didn't respect your signals. If you want to go about this alone, I'll make myself useful elsewhere. But I need to know... Do you still love me?"

"Of..." Olive's voice broke and an intrusive sob followed. "Of course I do, Twill. I love you!"

Their arms opened to each other at the same moment. It felt so good to rest her head in Twill's chest, and for her large but gentle hands to stimulate the wanting nerves in Olive's back. Holding each other outside the realm of sexuality relieved so much tension from Olive's body, and her mind finally relaxed. Twill wasn't the enemy, she wasn't wholly the solution either, but she was a love that Olive had been so wrongfully denying herself.

Olive sniffed and kissed the back of Twill's hand as they parted from the embrace. "I'm closer now, Twill. I'll... I'll tell you what happened later tonight."

Twill nodded, and Olive's steps were lighter as she left to continue cultivating her rebellion.

OLIVE FELT A FOOL for holding onto her pain for so long, believing she was the only one that could get her out of her drowning depression. Telling Twill what happened to her freed Olive of a lot of the festering self-hatred and guilt. Olive didn't have to worry about what Twill would do in retaliation, because the Royal Rabbits had already taken care of it. All they could do was move forward. Twill told Olive she would always wait for her to initiate any sort of intimacy, so they could sleep next to each other without Olive fearing the worst.

It was the best night of sleep she had in a long time.

There was a notable improvement in the Denim Demons' attitudes after breakfast. Olive chuckled at a stupid joke of Erin's and the joke passed along until the whole place was laughing for the first time in what seemed like ages.

The Demons, old and new, dispersed to their humanitarian and strategic tasks, all except for Senna, the Demon who'd helped rescue the Upcity woman from the crashed vehicle. Olive dismissed Twill and waited for Senna to approach with whatever was on her mind.

"Olive, I'm glad to see you smiling again."

"I wish you all wouldn't focus on my demeanor so much."

"How can we not? Without you—"

"Yes, yes, I've heard this before. I am sorry you've been affected by my moods. I'm working on remedying that—*me*. Now, is there something you needed to discuss?"

"Yes, but... I'm only here because you don't seem as depressed, as it made me a little less apprehensive to bring this to you."

"Bring what?"

Senna looked around the emptied headquarters, then pulled a wrapped bundle from her rags and handed it over. It contained an electrical gun. Olive hid it quickly and shoved it back in Senna's hands.

"What the fuck do you mean to do, bringing that in here!"

Senna twitched and held it back out. "I found it on the ground after that scrum with the Gophers and the pig who started the whole fight."

"Police officer. And they *track* these, don't they? What if they send a squad to get it back?"

Senna shrugged and pressed it back into Olive's hand. "They haven't yet. If it was that big of a deal, you'd think they'd have been here already, wouldn't you?"

"Take it back to them. Right now!"

"Fuck that! They'd fry me for getting that close, and then to find I was holding onto it all this time? And before you say it, *you* can't do that, either! You've been anything but yourself since that stunt you pulled with that Upcity bitch. Now that the darkness is pulled from your eyes, you can't put yourself, *and us*, through that again."

"So your plan is for me to *keep* this? For what?"

Senna sighed and shook her head. "Do I really have to explain? Things are about to become very dangerous, as I'm sure you well know. It might be good to have it in your back pocket. Don't pretend you don't know what I mean. If you hadn't thrown out all the electric batons..."

Olive exhaled and told Senna to go about her business.

Alone later, Olive pulled the gun out of the wrap and observed it by a brazier. It had a dial on the side with a color scale from light to dark. She held the gun in the crux of her elbow and the gun came to life with a low electrical hum that increased in volume each time she clicked the dial up.

A bar of light on the other side of the handle had the word "bat" above it, similar to the flashlights from the weekly supply drops. When the dial reached its apex, the battery indicator dropped. When she lowered the dial, the indicator filled back up. She surmised that one shot from the highest setting would zap the entire battery's life.

Did they design such an ironic display on purpose?

Olive switched it off altogether and put it in the back waistband of her jeans, covering the handle with her rag shirt. She'd toss it down into the pipeworks when she passed them next.

Later that day she found Erin working with other Demons to build nests for the old folks in some of the less-traveled streets. Once Erin was alone, Olive bopped her on the shoulder.

"What's up, boss?"

"I need to talk to you privately. Got a moment?"

Erin told the Demons what she hadn't finished yet and followed Olive out of earshot.

"First of all, *Demon*," Olive said, "thank you for what you did for me and Twill. I may not be as strong as one, but I can be as stubborn as a Bull sometimes."

"Sisters fight all the time. It's natural. Some of us are too bull-headed to get over things until it's too late. I'd have hated to see that happen between you two."

Olive nodded and ran her hand down Erin's shoulder in appreciation.

"The second matter I wanted to discuss is far more serious. Twill wanted me to ask you about this... Have any of the Bulls killed anyone with your fists? I mean, we all hear *rumors*, but is it really possible?"

"Of course it is. Someone's neck snaps, or they fall down badly... Sometimes the ground does the killing. Why? If you're going to ask me to kill someone—"

"No, no. I just... I *accidentally* killed someone. All I wanted to know was how the Bulls deal with that kind of thing."

Erin whistled and shook her head. "You know, Rina and I might have killed a couple of the Violet Vipers. But I don't know. When you're fighting for your life against that many people, you kind of don't want any of them to stand back up. We think more about surviving the encounter than how to feel afterwards."

"The person I killed didn't deserve to die, and I wasn't surviving. It was an accident, but I have to live with that... The needlessness... I was just hoping..."

"Being violent doesn't mean we know anything more about death, except that it comes for us all. We just live for our sisters until the time comes."

Olive's lips twisted in dissatisfaction. She playfully punched Erin's shoulder with her non-broken hand and went back to work.

Chapter Twenty-Two

CHINA SHOP

ONE MINUTE REGINA WAS receiving an affectionate squeeze on her butt from Vela before breakfast, the next Vela was laid out on the ground. Rina tore off Vela's Bull patch and stormed out of the headquarters, leaving the entire floor silent. It struck Regina that she was the first to react to something so horrible.

She rushed to put her hand on Vela's back; her cheek pressed into the concrete and her eyes were closed.

"Back up from her, Reggie," Brace said. Regina looked up at Brace, wearing the oddest expression of neutrality.

"She could be really hurt, Brace."

"That's the whole point."

Ezzie pushed Regina back, but it was much softer than the time she flung Regina away from Rina when she wrestled with that Snake assassin. Three other Bulls helped Ezzie pick up Vela by her limbs and take her outside. Regina followed closely behind. They laid her next to the brazier outside the doorway. The pallbearers started to go back inside when the whole rest of the herd rushed out into the street.

Only Brace stayed inside, and it was soon evident why—she threw empty beer bottles around the headquarters, the cheap glass smashing apart against the walls and the ground. Regina moved away from the door and knelt beside Vela. She put her hand on her cheek and frowned at the bloody welt on Vela's pretty, fucked-up face.

"Go get some brooms from the prisoner room," Ezzie instructed some of the Bulls. "Get the place cleaned up as soon as Brace exits. The rest of you... You don't want to be here when she does. Go have some fun with the men or each other, or help the gangless, I don't fuckin' care."

They all dispersed without so much as a parting glance for their second in command—no, *former* XO. Regina sat down next to Vela, rubbing her hand on Vela's thigh.

It seemed the last glass bottle had been broken. Regina peered up to see Brace standing in the doorframe, breathing heavy, teeth gritted.

"You remember what I told Erin, Reggie?" Brace seethed.

"Yuh— Yes, Brace."

"When she wakes up, tell Vela the same thing."

"Is there no possible second chan—"

"Reggie, if I have to repeat myself—"

"No. Okay. I got it, Brace. I'll tell her."

Brace's muscles were so flexed it was a wonder they didn't burst through her skin.

"Anyone asks, Reggie, I'm putting a stop to the drug-pushing Maroon Mongeese in Sector C."

"Oh. The men? *Alone?*"

Brace's slow turn of the head scared the hell out of Regina—worried she'd redirected Brace's wrath upon herself—but then she saw her dead-eyed stare. Brace stalked off without another word.

Regina blew out her held breath and returned to assessing Vela. Her placid face reminded Regina of fairy tales she'd heard as a child. She kissed Vela's lips, hoping to wake her from her unconscious state. That didn't work, so she settled for hugging around her hard torso.

They sat together for a few moments before Vela stirred.

"Oh, thank God," Regina said, and kissed her again. It wasn't returned.

"What the fuck happened?"

Regina's lower lip quivered. Why did *she* have to break the horrible news?

"Rina... She..."

"That fucking *cunt!*"

Vela shot up to her feet, but something caught her attention. She felt the absence of her patch.

"Where is it?"

Too scared to say anything, Regina only pointed at the brazier. Vela put her foot on the side of it and kicked it over into the street, brightening up the environs for a moment before the flames snuffed out over the wet ground.

Vela stormed off. Regina rose and scampered after her. Even in her current state, it was hard to keep up to Vela's furious pace.

"Vela, I'm sorry, I just don't want to see you... I mean, Brace said you have until tomorrow morning to—"

"I know the rules. Now get the fuck away from me, Upcity bitch."

Both her feet and heart stopped, but the latter beat again a painful second later. She thought for a moment, then continued following Vela as she was at the edge of disappearing into darkness. Of course Vela was hurt to her core—she'd just lost everything. Regina gave allowance for words Vela might not have meant if she weren't boiling in a stew of anger and grief.

Vela went far beyond the region Regina had become familiar with around the headquarters. The braziers spread out, the candles grew fewer, and the smell got worse the deeper they went. Vela never looked back. Was she heading to a second home? Regina didn't recall Vela ever sleeping outside of the headquarters. Or the others, for that matter. Except for... Rina...

Regina kicked up her pacing but she wasn't very fast. She wasn't much of an athlete back home—none of the Ruby Riders were. They were to focus on their beauty regimens and hobbies above anything else; maintain their bodies but not train them. Over the last few weeks, Regina wished she'd taken the physical education classes more seriously in school.

They finally hit a street that seemed to lead to nowhere further, and Vela stopped outside of a cardboard shack with cute little windows carved out of it. She took a quick look around before disappearing through the doorway, still not noticing Regina's slow approach.

Regina crept closer, thinking it odd there weren't shouts from either Vela or Rina. A child started crying. Regina poked her head through the door to find a couple of candles illuminating the small space and a child holding two halves of a book, torn down its spine.

Vela pressed an unfamiliar woman into the corner, one hand over the woman's mouth and the other between her legs.

"Vela!"

"Come to watch? Get in on it, or get the fuck out, Rag Doll."

Regina got caught up with indecision—not over what Vela said, but whether she should remove the child from the situation or help the woman. She picked up the child and turned to leave when she saw a pipe propped against the door frame. Regina set the child down just to the outside and knelt down to her eye level.

"Stay right here, sweetheart. Don't move."

Regina went back inside to grab the pipe. She held it like a baseball bat. She at least knew how to do that, having grown up with a baseball fanatic for a father.

"Vela, let her go."

"Or what, Rag Doll," she said without stopping, no hint of a question in her tone.

"I'm gonna... I'll fucking hit you."

Vela looked around, disinterested at first, then stopped her horrid action when she registered the pipe.

"Oh, baby, after everything we've been through?" Vela tore the rags off the woman's legs with one swift, violent motion, then pushed against her face to get up and square to Regina.

"Please, Vela, just leave. Why are you hurting these people? Rina's the one who—"

"I *am* hurting Rina, baby. Drop that pipe, and I'll forget you raised it to me. I might even let you taste my fingers after I'm done with this drug-addled cunt."

Regina took a quick glance down at the woman. A needle stuck out of both arms.

"Broken bitch must be fed up with Rina's shit. She had those in her rags. I just upped the dosage; helped her out."

"Vela, you're... That's torture. Please leave her alone."

"I love how you say please, baby. Reminds me of how you asked me to make you come a second time the other night. I'll do it again and again if you want to follow me into exile. But first, we make Rina *pay*."

Vela made for the woman again, but Regina swung and hit her thigh. The pipe vibrated painfully in her hands. Vela turned again, much slower and with far, *far* less sick humor.

"Beginning to think you don't love me, Rag Doll."

"I... I warned you. Get away from her. Now!"

Vela unexpectedly moved to rush her. Regina panicked and backed out of the doorway, accidentally falling over the child. She started bawling again, but Regina couldn't spare a moment to comfort her. She scrambled to her feet as Vela cut through the darkness of the doorframe like a nightmare.

The child saw Vela menacingly step forward and crawled away screaming. In a horrible, unexpected turn, a shape materialized by the child, picked her up, then ran out of Regina's periphery. The child stopped crying, amazingly, but it might have been that she was in as much shock as Regina. Vela didn't notice, or didn't care if she had. She kept coming forward.

"You don't have the balls to—"

Regina swung the pipe into Vela's head. For a horrible second, she stayed on her feet, but it was the second blow to the head she'd received in a short period of time. She fell over with a sickening thud.

Indecision struck Regina again—go after the child, or see if she could help the woman inside the shack? But what if Vela got up?

Regina went with the closest option, going into the shack. The woman hadn't moved. Regina took out the needles hanging from her arms and made a quick rag skirt out of a loose blanket to cover the woman's legs. She hoisted her up like she had for the woman she saved during the battle with the Iguanas, which already felt like a lifetime away.

She grabbed the pipe again as she struggled to get through the door. Vela was still on the ground. Regina looked to the street end, where a black alley tucked into the corner. Was that where the child had been taken?

Regina didn't always care for Rina, but the people Rina knew didn't deserve to suffer. She staggered towards the hole in the wall, shouldering the woman's slack weight. She took a couple of cautious steps inside before she heard a high voice screaming for her mommy. Regina went in that direction, turning into the building to her left and following the cries to a little room lit by candles. An old man hugged the child as she struggled to get away.

Regina put the woman down gingerly, then raised the pipe at the man.

"Let her go, trash can."

The man rolled his eyes and let the girl go. She ran to the unconscious woman and cried into her rags.

"It's okay. I'm her reading teacher."

"Nice classroom."

"Classroom?"

Regina raised the pipe higher and took a step.

"Wait, look! Here's the book I'm teaching her from!" The man handed over a ragged book, the cover partially torn so she couldn't see the title.

"Who's Sun Tzu?"

"I don't know. We don't have a big library down here. I read her whatever I find."

Regina relaxed her guard and flipped through a few pages.

"This is a little much for a child, isn't it?"

The man shrugged. "She does keep asking where the animals are..."

Regina came back to herself when the child stopped bawling.

"What should I do?" Regina asked the man.

"What happened?"

"She had two needles in her. I don't know what was inside. Drugs, obviously, but..."

"Let's get her to the Clinic."

Regina knelt to the girl and asked her name.

"That's the cutest name I've ever heard," Regina said, then took Panda's hand. The man picked up the woman and they all went outside.

Regina tightened her grip on the pipe when she saw that Vela wasn't where she'd left her. The shack was torn apart and scattered throughout the street. Trash cans had stolen all the semi-useful items that belonged to Rina's family, but Regina couldn't do anything about it—they had more pressing matters.

It was disorienting walking by all the dark shapes scuttling through the street, expecting Vela to appear in front of them at any moment. The feeling never left even as they approached the crowded area around the Clinic.

"How long do you think these lines take?" Regina asked the man.

"Could be a few hours, at least."

"Can she survive that long?"

The man shrugged again. Regina doused a flash of anger as she reminded herself it was unfair to expect trash cans to have much knowledge of anything.

"Okay, stay in line, please. Panda, stay here with your mom, okay? I'll be right back, I promise."

Regina strode a little too quickly to the police officer sentry near the Elevators. He lifted his electric gun to her head before she even got within talking range.

"Drop the pipe, trash can, and turn around."

Regina forgot she was still holding the pipe and dropped it, then put her foot on it to keep from rolling away.

"I'm a citizen! Scan my hand."

The officer approached but kept the gun pointed at her head. He scanned her hand and relaxed, then motioned for her to move along to the Elevators.

"Sir, I have a seriously sick woman with me. Can I take her to my family's clinic? It's on the tenth floor."

"Are you *insane*? Get hit in the head while you're down here? Oh, yeah, looks like you're pretty beat up. No, Regina Rondel, you cannot bring a trash can onto the Elevators."

"Even if I'm with her? I know they'll kill anyone who gets on without a chip, but what if she gets on *with* me?"

"Nope. Not gonna happen. Even if I *let* you get on just to die, I'd get fired for allowing it. I'll never risk my job for a trash can."

"What if I call our doctor to come down here?"

"Doctors aren't allowed in the Underfoot without applying for volunteer status, which takes months."

"Please, sir, she's going to die."

"So are dozens of other trash cans today. Either move along to the Elevators alone, or go back to your research."

Regina shook her head, turned away, and picked up the pipe on her leave. She went back to the man and Panda. They hadn't moved in the line at all. Regina took in the lines for the first time with any sort of attention. Everyone moaned or cried as they waited to be seen.

Regina's wits came back to her as fear of Vela's reappearance faded. She checked the woman's wrist for a pulse. Was it just her imagination that she couldn't feel anything? She tried the neck pulse and found it, but it was very weak.

"Sir," Regina said to the man, "Can you take Panda back to your classroom? I'll stay in line."

"I don't think she should be separated from her mother."

Regina whispered, "I don't know if she's going to survive this line. Do you think Panda should watch her die?"

The man wrestled with that for a moment, then nodded. He knelt to Panda's level to whisper something to her and she nodded. Regina put a hand on Panda's head.

"Goodbye, Panda. I'll see you again soon, okay?"

Regina had to catch herself from making a promise to bring the child's mother back to her. She didn't know if she could handle any more heartbreak in one day.

Chapter Twenty-Three

GAMBLE

WHILE SABRINA HAD HER finger bones painfully put back in place by a Doctor, she learned more about Olive's path. She was almost in Sapphire Snake territory. That would be hard enough on its own—then the Violet Vipers were next. Sabrina hoped her gambit with the Snake assassin would pay off.

She also hoped Vela would be well on her way out of their Sector by the next morning. Sabrina needed to check in with the Bulls. She wasn't quite sure if Brace would let her move up to position three after Ezzie's ascension. She'd been passed over before.

Not once did the thought occur that she'd ever be able to supplant Brace. Vela's face had shattered her hand, and Brace hardly moved when Sabrina hit her. There was no chance in Hell anyone could knock her down so Sabrina could be the leader of the Bulls.

"What are the other Upcity contacts saying about this war?" Sabrina asked the Doctor.

"Well, it's been *mostly* bloodless—except for what happened to the Purple Rams. The government doesn't care what happens to any of you, you know that. They're just looking to score Compassion points among voters for at least keeping the Doctor program and supply drops going."

"What do you mean? Those things could be voted away?"

"Indeed. The police lobby is one of the Underfoot's biggest allies, since they get overtime and hazard pay for roaming around and guarding the Elevators. The Doctors are second. We're volunteers, but once any of us spend a day down here... Let's just say it's impossible for a Doctor to turn their back to *this much* suffering."

Sabrina winced as another bone popped back in place.

"All of that is to say," the Doctor continued, "it would be really hard to vote away care efforts for the Underfoot. Many politicians try, but none of them have been voted into positions of significance."

"That's still...unsettling that our lives hang by such thin threads, held by voters who will never set foot down here."

"Eh, don't worry about it too much. Most people will be long dead before anyone manages to shut the place down."

"What would that entail?"

"What do you care? I just told you you'll be dead."

"...I have a daughter. There are thousands of children down here."

"Do you care what happens to the children in the Upcity?"

Sabrina didn't consider that a fair question, but she shook her head anyway. Why should she feel guilty for children living in luxury and light, education and safety? None of them would ever know a day of real suffering, and that was Underfoot children's first memories. Yet her lesson, handing over the tie of that suicide to the Ruby Rider rookie, came back to her and she regretted her lack of compassion in the moment.

"Do you think anyone would ever vote to integrate us—"

"Don't even dream of it. There's no faster way to get dropped off a ballot than to bring that up. Sorry, you're all stuck here until you're wiped out by a plague, or a vote to cull the Underfoot, however unlikely."

Sabrina sighed and tossed her head back as the Doctor wrapped her fingers and hand with gauze.

"Sorry I don't have any splints. Just try not to bump it. I'll give you the rest of this gauze roll, though. If you can, keep it cool and above your heart to reduce swelling. That's about all I can do for you. Keep taking your pills and you should be good in a couple months."

Sabrina nodded and left the tent. She had pushed her way to the front of the line when she arrived, so curses and furious looks greeted her. Shrinking from their rightful indignation, she placed her broken hand up on her opposite shoulder and walked along the line to leave. She'd done enough to piss off the line, she didn't want to add pressing between them to get over the barriers to the list of offenses.

As she neared the end of the line, Sabrina sighed at the realization she would need to hide out with her family for the rest of the day—until Vela's exile went through. An unexpected possibility came to her: could Vela survive the re-initiation? Would she put herself through it? Even if she somehow survived the entire gang taking a shot at her, Brace wouldn't hold back as the anchor, and Ezzie had motivation to block Vela from retaking the number two position.

Sabrina jerked her rags away from someone in the line grabbing her, too troubled as she thought about Vela's pettiness to care. A more insistent pull acquired her full attention. About to apologize for cutting, instead she found Regina.

Her thoughts reset at the sight of Kirsten slumped against Regina's shoulder.

"Panda's with her teacher," Regina said before Sabrina could even ask.

Sabrina looked her wife over quickly and found the tell-tale sign of needles. In both arms?

"What the *fuck*, K?" Sabrina pinched Kirsten's side to wake her up, but she didn't respond.

"She didn't do it to herself." Regina explained what happened.

The recounting made Sabrina nauseous. She should have had the foresight to know Vela would want revenge. She should have planned for her family to hide out with Panda's teacher before the challenge.

"Has she ever overdosed before?"

"Once. She would have died if I didn't have this Bull patch..."

"Let's use it, then!"

"I don't think she's overdosing. You said Vela was touching her—that would make her freeze up even without the drugs. Did you see if the plungers were pushed in on the needles before you took them out?"

Regina seemed surprised. "I...didn't even think to look."

"She'd probably be worse off, if they were. White foam coming out of her mouth, shaking, that kind of thing. The Bulls don't use drugs, so I'm sure Vela didn't know what she was doing. She definitely wouldn't know how to find a vein. Still... Her weak pulse... Maybe enough did go in. Let's go to Sector C."

"Why not wait here? Or use your patch and get to the front of the line!"

"I've already used that privilege today. I don't want to set off a riot."

"Even for your wife?"

Sabrina didn't want to get into her family history with Regina. It was complicated, but more so something else held her back. A couple years before she wouldn't have hesitated, but the more she focused on reframing the Underfoot as a place that needed more love and fairness in order to survive, it made her sick to use her privilege to get ahead of all the gangless who were suffering worse.

She hated herself for using privilege to get her hand looked at. How many gangless in the line would die before reaching the tent because of her non-life-threatening injury? The pain had driven her thinking in the moment, though—she'd reasoned that she was destined to improve all of their lives by helping Olive, so it was *okay* to prioritize herself. They'd all be doomed without Olive; without Sabrina to help her; without Sabrina getting her hand fixed immediately, so she could get back to that task.

Faced with the prospect of using her privilege twice, Sabrina couldn't justify it, no matter how much she loved Kirsten.

"Why Sector C?" Regina brought Sabrina back to the moment.

"The Maroon Mongeese are drug-pushers, so there are a lot of overdoses. The Clinic there should be better equipped to help her."

They shared the burden of carrying Kirsten out of the line, since Sabrina's hand was hampered.

"You're being awfully calm," Regina mused as they got onto the main thoroughfare.

"She's not showing signs of an overdose. And... I hate to say this, but I'm a little mad at her. Vela wouldn't have had those syringes, which means she found them on K."

"Meaning... You're saying she deserves—"

"No! I just... I thought we'd moved past this shit. I didn't think that Vela coming to our home last night would cause her to slip again so soon... That I had time to go back to her before..."

"You sound unsure about everything."

In fact, the closer they got to Sector C, the more rage built up in Sabrina's chest. Maybe she was talking just to talk, to shift blame onto Kirsten so she wouldn't have to follow through on her threat to the Diamond Ducks for allowing drugs across the border again, or destroy the first Mongoose she came across.

Curiously, there were no Ducks manning the border when they stepped into Sector C. Sabrina wasn't about to question the good luck. As they continued, however, Sabrina recognized Mongeese patches on others being dragged towards the Clinic. Most of them were unconscious, maybe even *dead*.

They arrived at the Clinic to find another long line, filled with Mongeese. When they saw Sabrina's patch, the conscious backed away from the line, leaving behind their fallen comrades. Their presence pushing drugs in the next Sector over put them on extremely thin ice with the Bulls. Sabrina took advantage of their fear, claiming a spot in front, then helped herself to the next open tent.

Sabrina collapsed on her butt next to the table when the Doctor said Kirsten would be okay. They gave her a shot of something and said she'd be fine when she woke up except for a headache. Sabrina ran her left hand through her hair as tears threatened to spill out in relief. Her gamble not to force her way to the front of the line in Sector B paid off. She also thanked God the Mongeese let her go to the front.

Betting her wife's health on non-violence had worked out, but the victory was tainted knowing she beat up those Mongeese so badly before. It must have spread to the others how dangerous she was...

Sabrina needed so badly to speak to Olive—to understand her place in Olive's world when she had such a hard time getting away from violence. What if, after the dust settled, Sabrina couldn't control herself again? Would Olive banish her in the same way the Bulls banished each other? What would Sabrina even do, then? What would be the options for her and her family if she couldn't wear the jeans that would one day occupy all twenty-six sectors in the Underfoot?

Would she have to go back to being gangless? Her privilege had improved their lives so much. If it was all taken away,

Sabrina didn't know how long they could survive, and she was too proud to live off of donations, begging, or stealing. But would she always have that pride? Or did it come from being a Bull? Maybe it was from becoming a mother, wanting to show her daughter a different way? Though...she had failed at that. Sabrina no longer knew where her pride came from.

Sabrina got up from the ground, helped Regina lift Kirsten, then they exited the tent. The injured Mongeese still reacted fearfully to her. She asked Regina to move Kirsten away and went to one of the men.

"What's going on here? Why are so many of you injured like this?"

"Don't you know? One of you Bulls is fucking everyone up!"

"Vela?"

"How the hell would we know?"

What chain of events had Sabrina wrought by laying out Vela? She shouldn't have been surprised her violent solution only led to more violence.

Sabrina rifled through her rags and produced a half-spool of thread and the gauze roll. She handed them to the man and apologized for cutting in their line.

Regina re-shifted Kirsten so Sabrina could help carry her. They began the trek back to Sector B, but the number of injured men going to the Clinic increased.

"Fucking Vela is probably trying to establish herself in the new sector already," Sabrina muttered.

"It's not Vela. It's Brace," Regina huffed under the strain of supporting Kirsten.

"What? Why didn't you say something?"

"I thought this was more important, Rina."

"No, you're right. Thank you so much, sister."

Sabrina laid Kirsten down gently, then embraced Reggie tight.

"I'm sorry, Reggie, but can you please take Kirsten home? I'll pay you back for everything, I promise."

"You... You don't really have a home anymore. Vela destroyed the place, and the trash cans took everything..."

Sabrina's lips pressed against her teeth upon hearing the pejorative for the residents of the Underfoot, but she had more important things to deal with in the moment.

"Take her to Panda, then. I'll return soon. Keep that pipe handy."

Regina sighed, but agreed to help and took Kirsten away draped over her back. Sabrina ran towards the Mongeese territory. Some of the men laying on the side of the street were dead. The injured and low ranks limped to the Clinic, assisting the still-breathing. They all gave her a wide berth. She followed the trail of them to their headquarters.

Sabrina inched inside the door. There were dropped torches everywhere, illuminating parts of the floor. Brace sat on a table with her head down, breathing steadily, as if she were a queen resting on a throne. Her feet dangled over the unmoving Mongoose leader.

Getting closer, Sabrina could see Brace's hands were covered in blood, and her hair was drenched.

"Brace..." Sabrina whispered.

"Who's there? Ah, Rina. The cause of... No. No, that's not fair. Fucking Vela challenged you. I told her not to and she wouldn't leave it alone. She deserved what you gave her."

Sabrina wasn't sure if everything was out of Brace's system yet, so she approached slow and steady, ready to defend herself if Brace decided to challenge her again.

"Are you... Are you hurt, sister?"

"What do you think, sister?"

"If I'm honest, I think you would have laid me out by now if your arms weren't so tired."

"I couldn't lay you out, my dear. I already tried." Brace gave a genuine smile which relaxed Sabrina. "You're a tough bitch, Sabrina. I'm so happy you're on our side."

Sabrina tensed up again just as fast. Was Brace trapping her?

Brace let out a slow breath and laid down on the table. She held her hand out. Despite a fear that the other shoe might drop, Sabrina put her left hand in Brace's. Brace still had an amazing amount of strength left in her grip, despite what she'd just done to the Mongeese and the insane swelling, but it wasn't an aggressive hold.

"I'm sorry. I... You know I loved Vela. Maybe more than any Bull I've ever been with. It made me happy when she accepted our Rag Doll. We could have... With Reggie's help in the Upcity, our lives could have improved so much..."

"Why would we need the Upcity? They don't care about us. There are... There are so many people in the Underfoot that could help improve our lives, without all..." Sabrina gestured around the room, "...*this*."

"Bulls help ourselves. I'll use the Upcity contacts until they run dry, but we don't *need* anyone else's help. Especially not naïve bitches like that Denim Demon. Who the fuck does she think she is, telling everyone how to live? We existed fine before she came along."

Sabrina hadn't expected such a conversation to present itself and was caught unprepared to uplift Olive. She had to play what she said to Brace with the utmost caution.

"You don't ever wonder what it would be like to live without pain?"

"It's not pain. It's strength. That's how we live."

"It's... It's too *easy*, sometimes. Look at what I've caused. I should have viewed it as an honor to defend the headquarters. It hurt me more than it should have when you relegated me. Instead of doing the hard thing, *the right thing*, and respecting your directive, I did the *easy* thing and challenged you to more violence. Look where violence has led us. I got my own fa— *Our* family broken apart. Vela would still be here, and we'd still be celebrating back home."

Brace let go of Sabrina's hand and sat back up. "You're telling me that you think all *this* was easy?"

"For you? Yes! It would have been harder for you to *not* lash out."

"You're talking like I should seek the hard path? Worse: you think a Bull's way of life is *easy?*"

"*Violence* is easy, Brace. Being who you want me to be? The gang's mother-figure? The one to temper our way of life so they don't all run away? *That's* fucking hard. Harder than anything I've ever done. But I feel validated that you see this side of me and still keep me around. That's *your* hard thing. People like Vela are easy. They don't listen, even when it would serve the gang's best interest."

Brace rolled her neck around, cracking it while dragging her dripping hair across her face—a sign she was thinking harder than usual. Sabrina's heart skipped as Brace got off the table and put her arm around Sabrina's shoulders.

"Come on, sister. Let's go tell the Diamond Ducks what the fuck I just did to their sector."

As they passed through the door, Brace's weight shifted into Sabrina's side. Her legs were failing her.

Brace stopped and sniffed.

"I'm okay. Just a twinge in my ankle from hopping off that table."

"I know, Brace."

"You didn't see anything."

"Of course not, Brace."

"Lying is the easy way," Brace whispered.

Sabrina remembered saving the Sapphire Snake; Erin's sacrifice and their night of intense love; Sally and the other Bull's promise to lie on Sabrina's behalf; and everything she was doing to tear apart the Bulls for their own good.

"No, Brace. Sometimes it's the hardest thing in the world."

Sabrina gave Brace a kiss on her bloody cheek, drew her in close to her side so she'd *accept* Sabrina's support, and they walked through the carnage of the former drug-pushers. No matter where their paths took them in the coming days, sharing the weight of a sister was never a burden.

Chapter Twenty-Four

SEEDS

THE INFORMATION RINA AND Erin gave to Twill and Olive proved incredibly valuable. The Sapphire Snakes were belligerent, rejecting all attempts to negotiate. They threatened to send their assassins after the Denim Demons' leadership if they didn't retreat from Sector G. If Olive had come at them with the usual spiel she may not have survived the attempt.

The Demons took on extra-vigilant guard shifts throughout Sector G, working together with the former Luscious Lemurs to clear out any nooks and crannies that could be used for assassination attempts.

Erin chomped at the bit to take a fight straight to the Snake leadership. Olive was heartened that Twill became a calming voice for Erin to be more patient and allow diplomacy its due process—before falling into the easier, far more devastating, *violent* solutions.

Unfortunately, nothing was working. All of Olive's ideas and sweetened offers meant nothing to the Snakes. They wanted no part of alliances, let alone allegiances.

Olive met with Twill and Erin in a final meeting before presenting the Snakes with an ultimatum—the last step before Olive would even begin to contemplate a battle. All their ideas exhausted, she wanted to go through one last brainstorming session. Twill started.

"Erin, can we use the Bulls' presence against them? Pose it as: 'it's them or us?'"

"No way. They hate the Bulls, but they know there's no real danger of the Bulls moving out of Sector B. We—Excuse me. *They* aren't interested in conquest or expanding. They love their lives in B. All this overtaking and allying and changing their identifiers has never occurred to them. The Snakes are nice and safe here, just as safe as the Vipers, Crackers, Diamonds, and Orcas."

"Do the Snakes accept challenges the way the Bulls do?" Olive asked.

"I don't know. I can tell you they don't fight fair. They'd rather strike out from hiding. The Vipers are similar, but they favor *numbers:* a pit of them over sending in a more deadly one."

"That's for damn sure," Twill muttered.

"I've run out of things to offer them," Olive said. "I never wanted to have another fight like with the Thirsty Thorns, but... Maybe we need to use the electric batons from the next supply drop instead of giving them to the men this time... The Rabbits would help out, gladly."

"Probably wouldn't hurt to have them at your side during the last meeting," Erin said. "Not that I'm condoning weapons..."

Olive cocked her eyebrow. "That's a strange thing—"

"For a violent goon to say? There's no honor in using weapons."

"I don't like it either," Olive said, "but sometimes it's necessary. We have no way to go around these Sectors. They join, or we make them join."

"Isn't this all enough?" Erin earned a hard stare from Twill at that. "I mean, I'm sorry, I know I'm just your muscle and not an officer, but... What's your end goal; where does it stop?"

"Speaking of strange things to say..." Olive frowned. "Why would we need any reason to do this other than easing all the lives of those in the Underfoot, decreasing such preventable deaths?"

"You really think the Underfoot needs *more* people?"

"It needs *healthy* people to run everything. Maybe one day we can figure out a way to get on those Elevators, or get through the barrier. I don't want us to just die out, like we never mattered, or worse, that we may as well have never existed."

Erin bit into a browned apple core and spit out the seeds.

"I just want to have sex and live with sisters who need me. I don't want kids and I don't care what happens around here when I die."

Olive bent down to pick up the slick seeds and held them out on her palm.

"Do you know what these are, Erin?"

"They hurt my teeth, is all I know."

"Seeds," Twill said. "Life."

"I've read books that tell of something called 'farming,'" Olive said. "In the past, people would collect these seeds from fruits and vegetables and plant them in the ground. They could sustain themselves for generations that way, as long as there was soil to grow them in."

"So what? There's no soil here."

"There is outside."

"So...your plan is to unite the Underfoot, then dig us out of here? And what, grow food with all the shit the Upcity throws out? Why take the extra step of uniting? You were all in Sector Y; you could have gotten *out* through Sector Z."

"You don't think we tried? For five years I searched for an escape route, but the area is completely sealed off. I heard rumors about there being a way out in Sector A, but no one who went in search of it ever came back. We've been probing each Sector's barriers and there are no gaps. There's never been a rumor about anywhere else but in A."

Olive placed the seeds into a pouch and handed it to Twill, who put it in a box with other pouches.

"Okay," Erin said, shaking her head, "all your preaching about peace and love is just bullshit? If you tell me I betrayed my sisters and left my Rina behind for this...rumored dream..."

"It's a wonderful byproduct: easing our passage through, and it'll make it easier to convince people to leave once we get there. Farming is hard work and takes many hands. I've already given better lives to the people from Sectors G through Z. Intoxicating as that is, I want to put this Underfoot behind us. I'm tired of living off the garbage of the Upcity, in its filth; in our despair.

"I will lead us outside, and everyone I've allied with is welcome to join."

"Lot of effort for what could be nothing," Erin said as her arms crossed.

"If it's all for nothing... At least I did something with my life. As I said, all our lives have improved because of my efforts. That could be enough, but I'll never stop trying for more, especially freedom."

"Erin, we don't really need to convince you of anything. We're doing this whether you approve or not," Twill said, an edge to her voice that Olive hadn't heard the two use with each other before.

"I already said I'm not an officer. Chill out, babe. One more thing, though. I'm guessing you haven't told everyone about this because if it *does* end up being bullshit, they'll string you up in the sewers and cut the rope?"

Olive and Twill nodded. Erin's smile was slow but full. She suddenly hugged them, startling Olive with her strength as she pulled them to each other in a squeeze.

"Thank you for trusting me with your secret, sisters. I'll take it to my death. Now let me tell you *my* secret. I wanted you to win over the Snakes your way. But since they're being such stubborn bitches, let me talk to them one more time for you. Bring your batons, just in case."

Olive had no idea what Erin planned to say, but putting her and Twill front and center in the last meeting seemed to temper the attitudes of the Snakes' leadership. Erin strode up to their main leader like she owned the place.

"I want the Snake named S-s-s-stevie brought here before we proceed."

"Do not mock us, Demon." Their leader frowned. "I can end all three of you with a snap of my fingers."

"Sorry, that's just what she called herself when my sister and I rescued her from death in Sector B."

"That...was you?"

"Yes. My sister stopped Stevie from killing the Bull leader, then they strung her up in the sewer, cutting up her back for a show of slow torture. The two of us rescued her and brought her home without the Bulls' knowledge."

The leader whispered to another Snake, who left with haste.

"Why didn't you bring this information to us earlier?"

"Because I thought you'd all have more sense in finding a peaceful solution."

"You may have overplayed your hand, Bull. Stevie failed her mission. Why would we put any stock into what she has to say, regardless of your...rescue?"

"Just relax, lady. Wait until she gets here. You might want to grab the sentry that we came upon and handed Stevie over to, as well."

While the Snake leaders deliberated, Erin went to stand back with Olive and Twill.

"Why did you hold this back?" Olive asked. "I could have used this."

"It wouldn't have meant as much coming from you, and it's not as easy as announcing we rescued her. Be patient, sister."

After another Snake went to fetch the second person Erin mentioned and they were all gathered by the leader, Erin approached for all the Snake leadership to see and hear.

"Snakes, above all the other vermin in the Underfoot, I hate you the most!"

The hissing that followed would have been comical if not for the sharp objects each one produced from their rags.

"You kill like cowards: with weapons, from hiding. You've killed my Bull sisters, and they've killed you. Your most recent attempt to kill the Bulls' leader *in her own headquarters* was thwarted by one of the officers. They punished Stevie and left her to die, but that *very officer* and I pulled her out of the sewer and brought her home to you."

The leadership murmured. Apparently they hadn't heard the story. Stevie seemed to be replaying the torture in her mind.

"I would have killed Stevie, and one of you at the border, if it were not for my Rina. She opened my eyes to mercy, of finding another way, *without* violence."

"That's prime Bull shit," a Snake lieutenant said to approving hisses. "Bulls only know violence. *Our* violence is to protect ourselves from you and your former sisters."

"Then hear me! My Rina showed mercy and has changed her entire life—for this woman *here*. Rina believes in Olive's peaceful mission so much that she's actively betraying your enemy in Sector B, to turn the Bulls all into Denim Demons. I'm the prime example—I'm here, a Demon anew!

"Without Olive's love reaching a complete stranger in Sector B, your sister Stevie would still be hanging, dying the slowest death imaginable, and your sentry would be dead, too. And...my new favorite sister, Twill..." Erin looked back with a mix of bashfulness and shame on her face, "Rina stopped me from killing her, too.

"If the love of the Denim Demons is enough to erase generations of violence from one of the most hardened Bulls in their entire existence—my Rina—you have absolutely nothing to lose by joining. As she continues to turn people like me, the Bulls and all the other violent gangs will no longer threaten any of you soon enough. AND—look at these fabulous jeans!" Erin completed her speech with a little twirl.

The sentry leaned and whispered into the leader's ear while the surrounding Snakes murmured, the hisses dissipating from their whispers.

Sweat broke out across Olive's brow. They'd either accept or things would get very bloody, and Olive wasn't sure how electric batons would fare against sharp objects. The numbers also weren't in their favor: three Demons on the Snakes' home turf. An army of Demons and former Rabbits hung back at the border and were to respond if one of the Demons' leadership didn't return in a specified time, but that wouldn't help if a fight broke out right *then*.

The leader of the Snakes straightened her back and the area quieted down.

"My sentry says the Bull with one eye said something to her about the Denim Demons."

"That's my Rina!" Erin said, clasping her hands in odd giddiness.

"I'm...at a loss for why they chose to hold onto this information, but the Bull asked that the Snakes ally with the Demons, and that it's in all of our interests to cooperate. I'll admit that information alone would not have been enough, but, in light of your admission, and learning about this Rina... Please give us one day to talk this over."

Olive nodded, unwilling to say anything further that might damage what Erin just did, and the three of them left to relieve the waiting army. When it was only the three of them alone, Olive embraced Erin tight enough to get her to tap out and complain of the lack of air. Twill grasped Erin's hand, and the two smiled as their arms shook with competitive strength and sisterhood.

"Phew!" Erin exhaled and stepped back. "I'm all worked up! Let's go scout the Vipers?"

"It's late," Twill yawned. "I'm going to bed."

"Me, too," Olive said. "Get some sleep, sister."

She punched Erin's arm playfully and took Twill by the hand to their nest.

THE SNAKES ACCEPTED OLIVE'S terms, with all the added conditions. No longer afraid of getting stabbed from hiding, Olive walked around Sector F with a lighter step. Before it was time to act on Sector E and the Violet Vipers, Erin pulled Olive and Twill aside.

"Sisters, you're wasting your time talking with the Vipers. There's only one thing they're afraid of, and that's Bulls, and they will *still* choose to fight Bulls in large numbers. I don't doubt that we'd claim victory in the end, but they would kill so many of us..."

"You don't have any inspiring stories to drop on them?" Olive asked, half-joking.

Erin's good humor didn't come through, which sunk Olive's heart a little bit. It had been such a rush, such a resounding relief, solving Sector F without violence.

"How do we avoid a prolonged battle, then? Will subduing their leader help?"

Erin shared a look with Twill, and they both shook their heads.

"It still has to be violent, doesn't it?" Olive sighed. She fingered the electric gun hiding in the back of her pants that she couldn't bring herself to throw out.

"On the bright side," Erin said, "the Crystal Crackers and Diamond Ducks should be pushovers. Then... I'm not sure. Hey, give me a day to find Rina. I'll see what the state of the Bulls is, plus, with the trip through Sector E, I'll get an idea of what the Vipers are doing—they must have heard about the Snakes' surrender by now."

Twill indicated that it was Olive's decision. She nodded approval, and they embraced Erin farewell. Erin removed her jeans and put on a set of rags, then ventured forth alone.

Without diplomacy to pass the time, Olive and Twill coordinated humanitarian efforts with the former Sapphire Snakes. As the day dragged on, Olive mulled over the possibility of a battle, far more dangerous than their previous ones.

Morbidity crossed her mind, frequent and unwelcome. In their nest that night, Olive talked about her fears. Twill listened and nodded along, offering reassurances that they far outnumbered the Vipers, and Olive would be well-protected.

That didn't soothe Olive's apprehension—half of the equation was losing Twill, and another part was Erin. She wasn't someone Olive thought only to use as a tool anymore, much in the way she saw Twill at first. They were all good friends, *best* friends; sisters.

And she had Rina to thank for it. They were already like sisters, and Olive would embrace her as one as soon as they met.

A DAY PASSED AND Erin hadn't returned. Twill assured Olive it was only natural that she would want to spend more time with her lover. Olive was so giddy to get past the Vipers and meet Rina that she became impatient and paced around. Twill calmed her down by reminding her that impatience led to mistakes, and they couldn't afford any so late in their journey.

As they lay in their nest, Olive felt something she hadn't since Sector M—a stirring for Twill. They spent the better part of the night getting reacquainted. Twill was careful and didn't do anything without Olive's insistence. It felt like their first time together, all over again. Bliss.

The good time was haunted by morbidity creeping back into Olive's thoughts, though it also had a way of focusing her to enjoy every last sensation.

Any residual feeling of pleasure disappeared as the next day passed with no sign of Erin. Olive needed to believe that Erin would come through, but she rallied her army to prepare for the worst.

She convinced nearby male gangs to lend out the electric batons for the battle, so every fighter had two. Olive planned to imprison without killing, unless the captives made earnest attempts to initiate into the Demons.

The leader of the Vipers came to the border between Sector E and F and requested Olive's presence. She and Twill arrived and were surprised that the leader didn't have more officers around her. She beckoned them to come to her, then introduced herself as Atriss.

"We're going to join the Denim Demons," Atriss stated.

Olive and Twill exchanged glances but didn't betray anything else. Olive was both confused and overjoyed.

"May I ask what changed your mind? My diplomats said you wouldn't listen to a single one of them."

"I'll show you."

Even more confused, Olive and Twill followed Atriss down the main thoroughfare, across the sector. They stopped above a brazier to find something so horrifying that Olive rushed to the wall to prop herself as she threw up. Twill rubbed her back and returned them to an amused but troubled Atriss.

A woman had been stripped bare and beaten along every part of her body. She hung by the neck from a rope over the brazier, and her toes were charring, contributing to an overpowering smell that threatened Olive with another heave.

A crude copy of the Brass Bulls' patch was nailed into her forehead, covering her face. Streams of dried blood coated the woman's neck and chest.

"This Bull announced a coming assault from the entire Brass Bulls gang, then put twenty-seven of my Vipers in the Clinics before we finally subdued her. I've seen some of the Bulls. They have many more like her and...bigger. This one... We never got her on the ground. She died on her feet.

"This isn't about our pride anymore. If the Bulls rampage, and the gangs remain individuals, they'll have no trouble crushing every Sector from A to Z, including the men. I received news the other day... Their fucking leader decimated the entire Maroon Mongeese gang. *Alone.*

"Quite simply, Olive, we're all *fucked* if we don't join together and find some way to stop them."

Olive nodded and shook Atriss' hand immediately, then went back to respectfully ponder the woman. How in the world had she managed to injure so many Vipers before succumbing? It was a sobering thought to add to the already-percolating fear of what it was going to be like to take on the Bulls.

"Did you see her, Atriss?" Olive asked. "Before covering her face? Did... Did she only have one eye?"

"No."

It was a ridiculous thought—Rina had proven herself as non-violent—but she only wanted to be sure. It troubled her that Rina hadn't convinced more Bulls to join them yet, the more she thought about it... The entire gang *couldn't* have been planning an assault...

Unless... Had they killed Rina after discovering her betrayal? And now, fully aware of Olive's intentions, they planned to snuff them out all the way back to Sector Z?

"Is... Is there anything else you learned from her? Before...all this?"

Atriss reached into her rags and pulled out a folded piece of paper.

"We found this before we stripped her. Can you read? None of us can. We haven't seen a book in this sector for years."

Olive took the paper, torn from a book. In the corner she saw strange words next to the page number. She squinted, unsure what the second word was: S-u-n T-z-u.

She unfolded the note and it was written in a child's scrawl—very difficult to read.

Olive and Twill thanked Atriss and told her to expect humanitarian goods to start flowing as soon as they crossed the border with the news.

The two leaders of the Denim Demons brought the note to their headquarters and used a flashlight to make it easier to read. Olive followed along with her finger, reading aloud to help parse it out, as Twill held the note steady.

sum bulls wif u but sum r no

iz onle wa win vipers
luv sistrs we r cd

Olive and Twill ran back to the corpse hanging over the brazier and got her down. Olive collapsed when she removed the Brass Bulls patch from her sister's face.

Chapter Twenty-Five

HOME

REGINA TOOK TO VOLUNTEERING manning the lines at the Clinic after the ordeal with Vella and Rina. If she could ease any of the suffering she'd witnessed while standing in line with Kirsten, it would lift her soul to do so, as well as lighten the guilt of not belonging in the Underfoot. Rina's heartfelt embrace—both before she went off for Brace, and when she returned to Panda and Kirsten safely—had given Regina a new sense of purpose. Rina's affection was as fulfilling as it'd been to give away expensive, unused goods from Regina's home to the trash cans.

Sally used the art supplies in secret, hoping to present a new unveiling soon. Bridgette acted as her nude subject. Regina retrieved a couple of pens from Sally and gave them to Panda. The man in the dark room had told Regina he wished he could teach her to write but had no writing implements. Regina thought it was a useless thing to learn in the Underfoot, but realized it was a much better use of the girl's time than some of the things she witnessed other children doing in the streets.

Rina didn't have anything to give in return, since their home had been ransacked, but Regina insisted she stop trying to make a trade out of a donation.

Panda's teacher welcomed the family of three into his home until they could construct another. Rina had said that *she* could stay with the Bulls but families weren't welcome—the gang was supposed to be their Family above all.

Outside among the Clinic lines, Regina helped keep order by calling out line-cutters and waking people up to move along, since the lines could be slow. The guards near the Elevators had shift changes along with the Doctors swapping. Regina noticed a guard who'd scanned her hand before. When their eyes met, he perked up. To her surprise, he left his post and approached her.

"Got a message for you, Miss Rondel. Came in on the scanner this morning. Thank God I didn't have to search around this forsaken Sector for you. Your dad wants to take you to a baseball game and discuss your research."

"Oh… Wow. He's never… Okay, let me tell my sisters I'm leaving."

"Your *what?*"

Regina waved off his confusion and signaled the Bulls' gang sign to one of the other volunteers, then pointed her intention to go up. The Bull shrugged and nodded.

"What the hell are you doing?" the officer asked.

"Nothing. Do you need to scan my hand again?"

He did, then waved ahead to let the other guards know she was authorized to board the next Elevator.

Once boarded, she hit the button for level ten. The Elevators were capable of holding dozens of citizens as they commuted up the towers to offices, interconnected walkways, and the flying vehicle garages. The baseball stadium was on the top floor and spanned across the roofs of eight towers.

First, though, she needed to go home. The Elevator stopped at each floor and took on handfuls of citizens. They all got one look at Regina and chose to huddle on the opposite end of the lift. Not one hid what they thought of her appearance and smell. Regina didn't let that get to her like it might have before she made that fateful decision to escort Tiffany to the Underfoot.

When the Elevator stopped at level ten, Regina walked past the Upcity snobs. Their whispers and condemnations of the mess she left behind with her footprints and from leaning against the wall weren't quiet.

"Not contagious, assholes," she said over her shoulder before the doors closed.

Her favorite butler bot rushed to clean up after her and print its little invoices (including the one for swearing) while passersby hugged the sides of the hallways to avoid her. She'd always dreamed of entire rooms staring at her in her plastic glory, but this amount of attention proved unsettling instead.

She knocked on the front door. Her mother already had a garbage bag ready to go. Regina rolled her eyes and stripped. She would have been perfectly comfortable going to the game as she was, but the prospect of an entire stadium of eyes on her curdled her confidence, and she cleaned herself up in triplicate.

"Much better, Regina," her mother said and deigned to give her a hug. "Ugh. Your hair still smells. Did you wash it?"

"Yes, Mom. Three times."

She sniffed again, then wrinkled her nose.

"How do they not have showers down there? There are supposed to be water pipes, right? What the hell am I paying my yearly donations for?"

"The water mostly comes out in steam, and it's too scarce to waste on bathing."

"Well, what about the cleansing wipes? I throw down one a day!"

"Mom, there are *tens of thousands* of people down there. Chill out. We're just living our lives."

"*We?*" Her mother was startled, as was Regina. She hadn't even thought about the word—it just slipped out.

"Hey, Reggie, ready to go?" George said as he emerged from his bedroom dressed in his favorite player's jersey.

"I don't know, Dad. Mom's about to throw up over here, being around me. Can you handle it?"

"Sure can. It's all going to pay off when you become a doctor. You know doctors get to move up anywhere past the fifteenth floor? Grin and bear it, Vanessa." George smiled, kissed his wife, then put his arm around Regina's shoulders and guided her to the Elevator.

No one paid attention to her when they got on. Without visual identifiers from the Underfoot, among the many lavish perfumes and colognes filling the space, no one could pin her with that one whiff of whatever smelled *off*.

George spoke with other jersey-wearing dads. On the fifteenth floor, Regina was caught off guard by Tiffany getting on with her father. Tiffany muffled herself from screaming and instead coolly flashed the Ruby Riders' gang sign. Regina returned it, then came forward, eager to pass the next one-hundred-fifteen floors with a sister, rather than listening to dad-talk.

More thoroughly than even Regina's mother, Tiffany looked her over; Regina's appearance was more important than how she managed to survive the sewer hanging.

"I can't believe you still have your hair! I would have cut it all off after being lowered into that sewer. When are you scheduled for your plastic?"

Regina shrugged and smiled, having happily forgotten how fucked up priorities were in the Upcity.

"Well, Corinne took me and Brittney to get new jackets immediately. She and some of the others are going to be at the game, too. You can give her your...measurements... Oh my

God! You've lost so much weight! I'm so jealous! How did you do that?"

"Oh, it was really easy, Tiffany. Live in the Underfoot for weeks and starve yourself nearly every day. It's faster and easier than all the dieting and exercise Corinne forces us to follow."

"I could never," Tiffany turned her nose up a little bit.

"No one's stopping you from taking the Underfoot diet."

"No, only basic decency. Hey, I caught the eye of a Bateman last week. He couldn't *believe* what we went through down there. He hung on my every word. Once you really clean up and get your plastic, that second car... You'll have to beat those Bateman's off with both hands."

Tiffany giggled at her crude joke while Regina seethed behind a polite façade. Was this what she sounded like before? Regina hated herself more the longer Tiffany went on about all the things she'd been doing in the Riders since her "escape."

The Elevator became cramped. Regina's ears popped painfully, and she didn't like so many strangers rubbing up against her. She got pressed into Tiffany chest to chest. Regina started to hate Tiffany the more she prattled on, all without a "thank you" for saving her from the sewer. Tiffany waved her hand in front of their faces, complaining about Regina's breath, but still didn't stop talking.

Regina fantasized snaking her hand up Tiffany's designer silk blouse and shoving her dirty tongue past Tiffany's perfect white teeth, shutting her up while turning her dials. They'd be punished for public displays of affection, and Regina would be flagged as an enemy of the heteronormative government, but it'd almost be worth it to shut her up and get something out of the humiliation Tiffany so casually tossed out.

When they exited the Elevator, George gave Regina her ticket and said he'd meet her at their seats—he wanted to have beers with the guys beforehand. He basically pushed Regina into following Tiffany without asking if that's what she even wanted. After the ascent, all Regina desired was to drink beer, too.

Instead, Tiffany took her to a little overhanging balcony where the Ruby Riders waited with champagne flutes, decked out in their gang leather jackets over designer ensembles. All Regina wore was a pair of jeans and a white blouse. The sneers from her sisters, who she hadn't seen in so long, were like little punches to the stomach.

The leader of the Ruby Riders, Corinne, however, gave Regina a genuine smile.

"How thoughtful of our sister, ladies! We haven't had a shopping trip in two weeks. We've been given a blank canvas! Once she cleans up, that is."

The Riders broke into excited conversation about what they thought would look good on Regina, and which shops carried the things they'd put her in. She felt more like a Doll among the Riders than she did in the Underfoot.

Regina stood with her hands in her pockets and stared past them all, out across the vast ocean of trees and the three distant metropolises that jutted up from the Forests below. She remembered Virgo saying he found a way into the Forest, but not even Upcity citizens wanted to venture between their trunks for fear of getting lost, and *they* had GPS. Besides, as he said, there was nothing to do out there.

She wondered if that was really true, or if he just didn't know any better. Regina didn't excuse herself—she simply walked away from the Riders, ignoring Corinne's consternation.

Regina oriented herself to the Elevator and did her best to guess where the Sectors would be. She strolled along the outer barrier of the stadium, getting a little nauseous as she peered out over the edges. From that high up, it was hard to see any gaps in the forest canopy, but out from where she figured Sector A was, she thought she saw patches of land that weren't covered. Were they from fallen trees? Equipment or vehicles crashing on top of them? Controlled logging?

Even if Virgo or anyone else made it outside of the Underfoot, coming across those disparate patches would be too easy to miss—they could wander to their deaths in search of them.

A hand on her shoulder made Regina jump, afraid to be pushed over the side despite the adequate railing.

"I said, 'how dare you walk away from your sisters?'" Corinne said. She could have been perturbed, but it was hard to tell with all the plastic that made up her face.

"What? I didn't! Brittney and Tiffany walked away from *me!*"

"Not that! Just now. We were sharing our proposals for your makeover and you wandered off!"

"None of you care that I've been gone all this time. What's a couple more minutes? You're all acting like nothing happened."

"Don't put yourself before the gang, Reggie. That's selfish. What did you expect, we'd drop everything and go down to that disgusting place; get ourselves lowered into the sewers for the *one member* who can't keep up with dues and surgery schedules? I was going to talk to you about this, when you returned with Brittney and Tiffany, but you've been demoted—until you make it up with surgeries and comply with our makeovers."

Regina could only stand there, dumbstruck and blinking. She shook her head and moved against Corinne's shoulder in what felt like a normal brush off, but Corinne fell to the ground and cried out as if she'd been leveled by a Vela-slap. The other Ruby Riders rushed to her and lifted her up as she furiously rubbed her shoulder.

"You—!" Corinne came up to Regina and made to slap her, but Regina easily caught her wrist. Corinne whined as if it was getting crushed when Regina hadn't even applied pressure.

A lieutenant also tried to slap Regina, but Regina put her palm out to catch it in a high-five, and the woman complained that it stung worse than anything in the world.

"Jesus *Christ*, what creampuffs," Regina muttered and left to find George. She sort of enjoyed all the impotent shouts from the Riders behind her.

George handed her a beer when she sat down, and she drank it in one chug. Her father whistled and whapped her back when she belched without covering her mouth. She remembered a time when she was younger and her father did the same thing; she'd whined like those pathetic Ruby Riders. The back slap felt good. She scooted over into his side and enjoyed the strong side embrace he gave her in return.

Throughout the game, she cheered along with him, delighting in his exuberance and stinging high-fives. Regina vibed along with the other dads in their section more than all their other disinterested children. During an inning break, the stadium pep squad brought out T-shirt cannons and fired them into the crowd.

Regina followed a shirt as it flew over outstretched hands. It was going right towards an excited boy, jumping up and down, but a grown man bulled the child over to catch the shirt. He rejoiced in his grab, ignoring the boy he'd cleared onto the ground. No one shouted at him, though when everyone sat down, there were some passive aggressive, low-volume statements tossed in the man's direction. If he heard, he didn't act it.

Regina shouted in their stead, "hey, asshole! How about you give that boy his shirt back!"

A little buzzer went off in the armrest of the chair, then printed her fine for swearing. The man only looked around like a fly buzzed around his head, oblivious.

"Hey!" Regina stood up, shaking free of George's tug at her sleeve. "You! Dipshit!" —buzz— "Get off your ass" —buzz— "and give that kid back his shirt!"

The man finally noticed her, but only frowned. No one had ever called him out on his shit before. He went back to watching the field as if Regina wasn't just an anomaly, but an impossibility.

"Don't ignore me, jackoff!" Another buzz, and an increasing murmur from the section as they realized something out of the ordinary was happening. "Are you drunk? Or just stupid?"

Regina squeezed past the men who were content to do nothing but stare at what unfolded and drank. She went down the steps to stand directly next to the rude man, hands on her hips.

"Give that boy his shirt back, or I'll *take* it from you, dickhead." Buzz.

"You're racking up quite a price for this stupid thing. I caught it fair and square. Go back to your seat, princess."

Regina grabbed it with surprising ease—no one would ever expect someone to go that far—then took it down to the boy. The section cheered for her, but hushed when the man stood to block the path back to her seat. She did the same thing she did to Corinne, shoving a shoulder to his side to get him out of her way. He took it like Corinne had, as if he'd never been touched in his life. He tumbled over the handrail splitting the stairs down the middle.

Another cheer, and hearty backslaps on her way back to George.

She loved it all.

To one last cheer, George held her hand up, as if she had just knocked out a boxing opponent.

Close to the end of the game, ushers worked up and down the stairs collecting all the partially eaten food that would be tossed over the rails to the Underfoot.

As the crowd left once the game finished, security officers pulled Regina and George aside. They explained Regina had too many unpaid fines and had new ones to issue for assaulting three citizens. Regina directed George to dip into her surgery fund to pay them all off, then asked how much she had left.

After the officers took the credit transfer, Regina held back from the line to the Elevators in search of the vending manager. She queried how much it would cost to buy all the unopened food. With the quoted figure, and perplexed manager, Regina asked George for the rest of her surgery funds.

He refused at first, but she took advantage of their dynamic to remind him it was *her* money. He begrudgingly accepted that. She wasn't sure he would have, but she'd had an epiphany that day: what big pushovers Upcity folk were. Regina directed the vendors to wheel their boxes along the perimeter of the stadium, then tossed all the food over, into the nets below.

Despite the protesting and whining, they did as they were told when she reminded them she paid for it, and it was hers to do with as she pleased.

"That money could have gone towards your education as well, Reggie," George huffed when she met him by the nearly cleared Elevator line.

"I'll figure it out, Dad."

George put his arm around her as they waited for the Elevator to get back to the top. On the ride down, she leaned her head on his shoulder. At level ten, he balked at the door when she didn't follow, and she hit the button for the lowest sub-level.

"Say 'bye' to Mom for me, Dad. I'm going home."

Chapter Twenty-Six

THE EXILE

SABRINA VOLUNTEERED TO PATROL for the Bulls, but kept her path along the streets that led to her temporary home, an ever-vigilant eye out for Vela. Kirsten had promised to stop using again, and Sabrina had an easier time believing it because Panda's teacher was always around. She couldn't wait for Olive to complete the journey so Kirsten and Panda could be front of mind.

Until then, Sabrina spread rumors of Olive's benevolence to any Bull willing to listen. Brace hadn't said anything about their talk in Sector C, after the Mongeese were destroyed. Sabrina also had to worry about Vela showing her face.

When Sabrina was about to relieve her shift and go home, a gangless resident covered in blankets approached her in the middle of the street.

"I'm sorry, ma'am, I don't have anything to give out today. Would you like an escort to the nets?" Sabrina asked.

"I'm full, my love."

"Hm?"

The blankets flew off and there was Erin with a big, beautiful smile on her face. They embraced, then covered each other's necks in kisses until their lips came together, both far less painful and swollen than the last time. Loath though she was to break it off, Sabrina grabbed Erin's hand and brought her off to the side, away from prying eyes.

"What are you doing?" she asked. "It's so dangerous for you to be here right now."

"I needed to see your progress, Rina. The Violet Vipers are next, and I'm not sure the Demons can fight them without taking heavy casualties. Have you converted any more of the Bulls?"

Sabrina nodded. "I have most of them, but it's all behind whispers and whenever Brace or Ezzie are gone. There are still quite a few that will only follow Brace no matter what. But get this: I might have gotten through to Brace!"

Erin squealed and did a little standing-in-place happy dance.

"That would be *so amazing!* How could she possibly get through to Ezzie and Vela, though?"

"Don't get ahead of yourself. I said 'may have' gotten through. But in another bit of good news, Vela is out of the picture."

Sabrina explained what happened. When she finished, Erin's eyes were wet as she cradled Sabrina's broken hand.

"I'm sorry, Rina. I know you had a lot of bad blood between you, but... I did love her."

"Well, I don't think she felt the same, if I'm being honest. She started a relationship with Reggie as soon as you were gone, if not before."

"So? I started one with *you* and I still loved her at the time. Olive was just as surprised when I told her about how free we are with each other."

"Mm. I wouldn't have quite put it that way, but obviously I see your point. How are Olive and Twill, by the way?"

Erin shared the information from her end.

"Goddamn Vipers won't budge." Sabrina sighed.

"They're pussies who only fight in numbers."

"Fighting dishonorably doesn't mean they'll lose. What's Olive's plan?"

"Probably hope her own numbers do the trick. And use fuckin' weapons."

Sabrina needed to think on it; anything that could help. But it grew late, and it was her night to collect dinner. Erin hid under the blanket as Sabrina guided her to the nets nearby.

A larger crowd than usual gathered beneath the nets. Scavengers quickly and efficiently traded goods for what looked like fully-packaged food. Women threw themselves at the scavengers seeking favoritism, so Sabrina worked together with Erin to give out more without trading, just to keep people from hurting each other in the crowd.

Sabrina also pocketed a few choice items for her family. Once the nets were cleared of their bounty, she led Erin back to her home street. Before turning around the dark corner, she stopped to face Erin.

"Say, Erin... I... My family lives in here."

"Your...family?"

"My wife and daughter. And her teacher. If you want to come inside while I think about this problem, you're welcome to, but...please don't touch me in there, in front of them."

Erin became momentarily crestfallen.

"If you're married, that means...this was all..."

"Erin, you said yourself how 'free we are with each other.' What difference does it make?"

"It... It just... You don't love me as much?"

Sabrina cupped Erin's cheek with her good hand.

"Of course I do, Erin. You validate the Bull in me, the one that doesn't need violence to be strong. You're one of the best sisters I've ever known. You saved my life. You sacrificed your reputation for mine, for Olive, for a better life for us all. If we can finally break free of violence and live in peace, it will all be because of *you*."

Erin took on a shy smile. Sabrina guessed she might ask to join with her and Kirsten in their nest, with Erin's reputation for enjoying threesomes. Instead, she kissed the back of Sabrina's hand and motioned that they could move along. Sabrina appreciated that Erin was so many things to her, but that she was also capable of *not* being her lover for the moment.

Sabrina introduced Erin to Kirsten and Panda's teacher. Erin put her hand to her mouth when she saw Panda.

"What a beautiful child, Rina," she whispered.

Sabrina brought out from her rags the unbelievable, luxurious feast—candy, potato chips, and hot dogs with fluffy buns, all sealed up in plastic, without a single bite taken out of them. While they ate, Panda explained what she'd learned about battle tactics that day. Sabrina didn't appreciate the subject matter, but she hadn't come across any other books to substitute for reading material.

Panda had been heartbroken when her animal book was torn in half by Vela, but her teacher did some investigating, found the gangless who absconded with the halves, and traded to get them back. Panda still loved learning about her animals, but for reasons Sabrina and Kirsten couldn't understand, she was also happy to read the Sun Tzu book.

After dinner, Panda's teacher brought out a new book that he'd found, and wanted to surprise her with it.

"This is called... Wait. Panda, can you read what this says?"

Panda ran her finger over the cover by the light of a candle that Kirsten held for her.

"*The...Outsiders.*"

"Very good, Panda. I wasn't sure you'd get it on the first try. You can read three pages, then it's time for bed."

"Can Panda write, sir?" Erin asked.

"She just started a few days ago, when that young Upcity woman brought her some pens."

"I like drawing!" Panda said.

"Writing, Panda. Read me the first page, then you can show our new friend here how well you can write already."

While Panda and Kirsten gathered with the teacher around the book, Erin and Sabrina sat down near the entrance, hip to hip.

"Rina... I think I know how Olive can turn the Vipers. How easy do you think it will be for her to come through Sectors C and D?"

"Considering what Brace just did to the men in C, and what the Bulls did to D, it will be easier than any other sectors she's taken, I imagine."

"What are you going to do when Olive comes through for negotiations?"

"Before that, I'm going to talk to Brace again, then see where the rest of the Bulls' heads are at. Perhaps I can convince them not to battle—at least hear Olive out before fists get put on the negotiation table."

"You really think that will matter?"

Sabrina exhaled and dropped her head.

"Erin, Brace absolutely *fucked up* the Mongeese. *Alone.* If she gets near Twill, I'm afraid of what will happen. The challenge of defeating her might seem too tempting... Does Olive have any other women like Twill? Or us?"

"The Royal Rabbits are tough bitches. They killed their men, too. There would be a lot of support, but there aren't that many fighters in Olive's 'army,' sadly. She's counted on diplomacy to save the day so much, I think she'll overestimate what her army can do, even against the Vipers."

Erin slipped her hand behind Sabrina's back, underneath the rags, and caressed her bare, sweaty skin. Kirsten wasn't at an angle to see it, so Sabrina let it go despite her request outside not to touch.

"But I said I think I know the way. That means Olive's counting on you. I mean... We're *all* counting on you, Rina."

Sabrina stared off as she enjoyed Erin's hand on her back, and contemplated her imminent role in Olive's rebellion.

"There's something else you should...well, no. I'll let Olive tell you. I know she already trusts you and will welcome you with open arms. It's not my place to tell her more personal secrets. But if you can start a good relationship with the Onyx Orcas, I'm sure it will help her so much."

"Already taken care of. The challenge is *Brace*. Please...tell Olive that I don't want Brace killed. She deserves peace, too."

Erin scrunched her face in skepticism and shrugged.

"I guess with the power my words had on the Sapphire Snakes, I should believe anything is possible."

Erin shimmied up the wall as Panda finished her reading.

"Hey, Rina, can I take Panda outside to see her writing? It's a little too warm in here."

"Sure. Have fun!"

Sabrina went to Kirsten and sat next to her, running her hand through her hair to help get out the knots while Panda's teacher read ahead in the new book.

"Do you know what that book's about?" Sabrina asked.

"No. Believe it or not, even though I can read, I haven't read every book yet."

"Jerk," Sabrina muttered, then laughed along with Kirsten.

"I wonder who we have to thank for all that wonderful food?" Kirsten said as she crunched on a chip.

"Probably one of those vehicles had an open back door and spilled its contents. How lucky are *we* that it was over our net?"

Kirsten took on a more alert look after a few minutes.

"Sibby, how well do you know that woman? They've been gone a little long..."

"I know her well enough. I'll go check on them."

Sabrina felt along the dark hallway, out to the alley where Erin held a torch next to Panda.

"Your writing is so nice, Panda," Erin said. She folded a piece of paper torn from Panda's Sun Tzu book and placed it in her rags. Sabrina smiled at the exchange; a souvenir for her Auntie Erin? "You're already the smartest person I know!"

Panda beamed and hugged Erin, then ran to Sabrina and hugged her leg. Erin handed the torch to Panda and she ran back inside, leaving Sabrina and Erin alone again.

Sabrina put her hand on Erin's shoulder, but Erin shrugged it off.

"I'm sorry, Rina. For touching you inside when you asked me not to…"

Sabrina was undeterred, her hand in the small of Erin's back, to pull her in close.

"I'm glad you did. When you come back, after we change Sector B, I'll always make time for you."

Erin put her hands on Sabrina's hips and extended her arms to create a small distance.

"It…feels wrong. That you have a family. I mean—That's not what I mean. Only that I don't want to be the reason something got between you and them."

"Don't be ridiculous. There's enough love in my heart for both of you." Sabrina leaned in to kiss Erin's lips. She took it for a moment but didn't return its fervor like when she hadn't known about Sabrina's family. "What's the matter? You love threesomes! I promise I can convince Kirsten if you want to join us."

Erin pushed away again, a little more strength behind it. "It's different, Rina. I wish I could explain why, I just…think it's *different*, is all."

"You're not making any sense, Erin. I want this as much as you did. Come on, baby, touch me like you did last time. I've been dreaming of it for so long. No one will see, if that's what you're worried about."

Sabrina put both arms over Erin's shoulders, against the wall. She used a little more force to get at Erin's lips, then rubbed her hand more roughly over her chest, as they had when they first gave in to each other.

"Rina..." Erin said breathily, which only drove Sabrina more crazy as her hands traveled all over, "you're...acting like...Vela."

Sabrina immediately stopped, then took two steps back, trying to recover from the red haze that had overtaken her limited vision. That was a stinging thing to hear about herself, almost as bad as the feelings that overwhelmed her when she'd struck Panda. What in the world had gotten into her?

"Oh. Oh fuck," Sabrina whispered, rubbing her forehead in regret. "Oh, Erin, I'm so sorry. I can't believe... I just... I love you so much that..."

"Okay, Rina. You weren't hurting me; it was the 'baby' thing and not responding to my resistance."

Sabrina rolled her neck and stared at the black ceiling.

"Hey. Hey, Rina," Erin said while reaching for Sabrina's good hand. "Maybe... I could get over it later. When we get through all this. I didn't stop loving you tonight. In a way, I feel like I have more to fight for. It just feels... I mean, you said don't touch you, now you're talking about a threesome... Do *you* even know what you want?"

Sabrina thought about it, trying to put words to her unfocused feelings. Their hands became slick with sweat as their fingers lightly clenched and unclenched together.

"I want the violence to go away. I want my family to be safe. I want Panda to lose her fear of me. I want to meet Olive and see Twill again. I want to be around my sisters without feelings of betrayal hanging over my head. And... I want to say goodbye the same way we did last time."

Erin smiled after a moment and regripped Sabrina's hand.

"I'm glad you made up your mind. Take me to our alcove."

ERIN TOOK THE RAG blanket off on the other side of B's border and handed it to someone that needed it. Sabrina had said her goodbyes and promised to do everything in her power to make the Denim Demons' passage easier once they finished with C and D.

There was something different about Erin's final goodbye that Sabrina couldn't really pinpoint. Her effervescence seemed tempered, even though she had no problem in the alcove expressing her love. Perhaps it could be chalked up to parting again—Erin was prone to tears more than other Bulls besides Sally.

Before Erin was too far away to see anymore, she turned back and waved. Sabrina returned it, and silently wished luck to Olive so Erin could come back to her home, no longer an exile.

Chapter Twenty-Seven

CHAMPIONS

OLIVE AND TWILL USED their personal collection of cleansing wipes to make Erin beautiful again, and dressed her in jeans and rags with the Bull patch sewed onto the back. They gathered supplies to construct a stretcher to carry her along to each new headquarters as they pushed closer to Sector B. Olive wished to show Rina how much she'd impacted not only Erin as an individual, but all the Denim Demons. Twill proudly spread word of Erin's sacrifice all the way back through Sector Z.

The two leaders of the Demons were putting their heads together in preparation for their first approach of Sector B when a sentry got their attention. A broad-shouldered woman, only a little shorter than Twill, came into the building followed by two more sentries.

"This woman overheard chatter from our relay network and is interested in joining," the sentry said.

Olive thanked the sentries and dismissed them. The woman's handshake was crushing, worse than Erin's, even as she used her non-dominant hand to avoid Olive's broken one.

"So *you're* the leader? Why isn't it *this one?*" the woman asked as she hooked a thumb at Twill.

"You must be another former Bull," Olive remarked.

"What do you mean, 'another former' Bull?"

"Just a little déjà vu. What's your name?"

"I'm Vela, and I want in on destroying the Bulls."

"We aren't here to 'destroy' anyone," Twill clarified. "If that's the energy you bring, unfortunately, you'll be unable to join."

"Hmmph. So, who's the Bull who turned tail and ran to you? You sound like Rina."

"Rina?" Olive asked, cautious to give away that she knew the name.

"Of course. The cunt broke up the greatest ring of leaders the Bulls have ever had, and she's poisoning the rest of them. She's the reason I'm *here* instead of bolstering our defenses against *your* push taking over the entire Underfoot."

"You sound more like an enemy every passing moment," Twill said.

Olive felt Twill tensing up from a few feet away, and her own hand drifted to the metal touching her lower back. If Vela noticed, she didn't betray any level of fear.

"What can you tell us about the Bulls' leadership, Vela?" Olive asked. "Anything that can help us get through without a battle—that's our goal."

"You'll need to kill Brace and Ezzie, but to get to them you'll be going through a lot of bad bitches."

"We'll only kill if it's absolutely necessary. Avoiding bloodshed is our top priority, in conquest and in daily practice. If that's the best advice you have, you'll need to leave," Olive said. "I've only listened to you this long because of..." she choked back a lump in her throat, "...because of how valuable a Bull has been to our cause. She took down the two most violent Sectors without killing a single person."

Vela's face darkened by the torch light, and her eyebrows knit together.

"Who's the Bull who won *your* battles? *Alone?* Only Brace is capable of that."

Olive motioned to the stretcher by the wall, covered by a blanket. Vela went to it and lifted the blanket.

"No," she whispered. "Not my... How...?" Vela dropped the blanket and raked her hand across her already swollen face. "Erin died for *you* people? How the fuck did you poison her mind to come to your side?"

"Stop saying that word," Olive said in a low voice. "She came to us of her own accord. *After* you Bulls exiled her... You have no right to call it—"

"It *is* poison. Erin was one of the purest Bulls I've ever known. Yes, she was exiled for falling, but she wouldn't have come to the Demons. Violence was in her blood. She would have joined the Vipers or Snakes, or maybe even the Rabbits. You people are nothing like my Erin."

Olive exchanged glances with Twill. Even if Vela was also exiled from the Bulls, they couldn't betray Rina.

"Maybe, Vela, that's a hard lesson in the power of what I'm doing; of what the Denim Demons can promise everyone. She *believed* in our cause. She was willing to die for it. And she *chose* to, even though I would have done everything—*EVERYTHING!*—in my *fucking* power to have kept her from doing it, had I known the sacrifice she planned to make... Your Brace would have encouraged it, using her for her own ends. She threw Erin away like she was nothing the second she didn't meet your standards. So are you a Brace Bull? Or an Erin Bull?"

"You outsiders have *no fucking clue* what it means to be a Bull, or how Brace feels about *anything*."

"I know that even the best Bull among you could see the wisdom of love over violence, and she embraced it whole-heartedly. She was so much more than the brutality that shaped her. I believe she's not the only one."

"No shit. Like I said, you remind me of Rina. That fucking *bitch* is undoing generations of the greatest legacy the Underfoot has ever seen, and *she's* the whole reason I'm... I need to tell Brace!"

Vela hadn't noticed Twill moving closer to her, and she blundered into Twill's chest, forcing Twill to take a step back to brace against Vela's granite body.

"You aren't telling Brace anything," Twill said. "You're not a Bull, and you're not a Demon. In fact, you're *nothing*. Olive, we can't let her—"

Vela punched Twill, sending her staggering into the wall. Olive grasped the handle of the electric gun, but Twill pushed off against the wall and matched Vela's strength with her own punch. Vela flailed her arms but caught herself from falling. Olive's mouth hung slightly open at the overwhelming power of the exchanged punches—she'd felt the air move with each hit.

"Is the challenge over?" Olive asked in mild desperation. "That's enough, right?"

"I'm not a Bull anymore. That wasn't a challenge," Vela growled. "Let me pass or you're going to die, you gargantuan freak."

"I don't want to hurt anyone," Twill sniffed blood back into her nose. "But you are *not* going to ruin what we've fought so hard for."

"You don't know the meaning of the word 'fought.' That was your one warning."

Twill caught Vela's incoming punch, then gave one back. It didn't seem to affect Vela, and that terrified Olive. Vela put her shoulder into Twill's stomach, lifting her up, then charged outside the building, taking Twill with her. Olive ran outside to see the two wrestling on the cement, rolling and punching and holding.

Demons gathered around in a circle. One tried to get Vela off but received a punch that sent her sprawling into other Demons. Olive faced an agonizing paralysis—she knew Vela would break Olive based on the power in her fists, but Vela seemed to be getting the upper hand on Twill. Using the gun could inadvertently hurt Twill as the two wrestled close, and the precedent Olive would set by using the gun could be dangerous, unraveling everything they'd fought to achieve through non-violence.

A Demon to Olive's side pulled out an electric baton. Olive grabbed it from her. If the electric charge transferred to Twill, it would at least be nonfatal. Olive pressed the baton into Vela's shoulder. She acted like it was nothing more than a bug and swatted it off.

Olive immediately regretted intervening—it distracted Twill and Vela got in another hard hit to the face. Olive raised the baton and cracked it across Vela's head, increasingly desperate, and horrified at the damage Vela was doing to Twill. Vela pushed off Twill and popped to her feet in a blink. She snatched the baton out of Olive's hand and broke it across her knee, then flung the pieces down the street.

"Dishonorable *cunt!*" Vela punched Olive in the shoulder, only missing her face because Twill got her arm around Vela's neck and pulled her away.

The hit to her shoulder was the hardest she'd ever been struck, harder than Erin. Considering what Erin had been capable of casually, and what she did to the Vipers, it alarmed Olive to imagine more clearly what it meant to face Brace. Nobody propped her up with rumors. If Brace was stronger than Vela, and if Rina couldn't turn Brace, the Denim Demons were doomed.

And Vela was killing Twill.

"All of you! Now!" Olive yelled at the Demons, pointing at their batons.

Vela convulsed as multiple batons electrocuted her back, but she wouldn't let go of Twill. Olive did the only thing she could think of and inserted herself between the two of them. The shocks weren't as bad as when the guards had punished her by the Elevators. She used all the strength in her body to separate the two titans.

Somehow Vela still had enough control to squeeze her arms together, and she wrapped Olive up while she trembled from the electricity. The arms became tighter and tighter, until Olive feared her back would break. She screamed but couldn't move an inch, and she couldn't tell the Demons to stop trying to subdue Vela.

Twill pushed the assisting Demons aside, then smashed a pipe into Vela's head. Olive felt a slight easing of Vela's grip, but it took two more hits for her to let go. Olive rolled away and Demons lifted her to her feet.

Vela and Twill's faces were covered in blood. Twill stood above Vela with the pipe in her hand, catching her ragged breath. Miraculously, Vela *was* still alive, her head slowly rolling back and forth as she glared into Twill's eyes.

"You...didn't win...dishonorable...*bitches*..." Vela coughed out as blood sputtered from her lips.

Twill lifted the pipe, and Olive looked away, resisting the urge to demand that she stop. Vela was a wild animal, but Olive still winced and cried as the horrible, wet sounds of pipe-on-skull repeated.

Olive shook off the residual energy of the shocks and half-walked, half-stumbled away from the group. She vaguely heard Demons asking if she was okay as she passed, but she didn't respond. Her feet carried her to the border between Sectors B and C.

Across there were Bulls at various points along the street. They noticed her jeans. One ran away while the other two came forward. Olive couldn't meet their eyes, so she stared at their feet. She opened her mouth but nothing came out. She swayed in her stance. Where the hell did she start? Would they even consider it a tragedy befallen a sister, or was Vela just another gangless to them?

"The fuck do you want, Demon? Is this the attack?" one of the Bulls said.

Olive's arm lifted and waved back in the direction of Vela.

"I... I just..." she said, her voice low and cracking, "Do you know Vela or Erin?"

"Of course! They're not Bulls anymore, though. What do *you* care?"

Olive raised her head to meet their eyes, then dropped her gaze again, thinking of Erin and Twill, and how she would feel if anyone were to show up and tell her that her loved ones were dead. Would it be worse than coming upon Erin as they had?

"They're... they're..." Why couldn't she speak?

Two more pairs of legs arrived. Olive looked up and was taken aback by the one with a rag covering her left eye. Would she know who Olive was?

"Fuckin' Demon said something about Vela and Erin," one of the Bulls said to Rina.

Rina's eye flashed and she tensed up.

"What is it, Demon?" Rina asked. "What about them?"

"They're... Back..." Olive simply couldn't get it out. "Can you follow me?"

"Fuckin' trap, Rina. It's started. We need to tell Brace."

"Wait." Rina put her hand on the Bull's arm to stop her from running off. "Let me go see what's going on. You all stay here in case any other Demons approach." Rina stared pointedly at Olive. "If I'm not back in an hour, *then* you can tell Brace."

"Okay, sister. Don't take any shit from those pussy Demons. Erin and Vela aren't even Bulls anymore."

"You don't need to tell *me* that, sister."

Rina crossed the border. She put her hand on Olive's upper arm and guided her back in the direction Olive had pointed. After they were out of sight of the border, Olive stunned Rina by embracing her tight and sobbing into her.

"Are you...?" Rina whispered. Olive nodded, unable to lift her face off of Rina's hard shoulder.

"Sister..." Olive whispered back. "I'm... I need to show you something."

Rina seemed to understand that conversation would be too difficult in Olive's state, so she wisely followed instead of asking a bunch of questions. Olive didn't have the energy for them.

When they got to the site of the battle, the Demons were wrapping up Vela's corpse.

"That's... That was Vela," Olive whispered.

Rina nodded, but surprised Olive with the lack of concern over her former sister's death. Would she be so callous to the one that always called her "my Rina?"

"Where's Twill?" Olive asked one of the sentries to the headquarters.

"Inside. She's..."

The words trailed off and Olive ran inside. Twill was upright, but sitting against the wall, next to Erin's stretcher. She was still having trouble catching her breath. She wheezed and rasped with each one.

Olive crouched down and put her hand on Twill's shoulder.

"Oh my...God..." Rina said from behind. "Twill, did Vela do this to you?"

Twill nodded slowly. Rina knelt and put her hand in Twill's.

"I'm so glad I could see you again, sister," Rina whispered. "I'm...so sorry a Bull did this to you. I'm so fucking ashamed..."

"Rina," Olive said, then motioned to Erin's stretcher.

Olive was instantly ashamed for her mean thought about Rina's callousness when she was quickly overcome with sorrow, sobbing into Erin's chest. Olive didn't have time to comfort Rina as her worry for Twill increased alongside each wheezing breath.

"Twill, let me take you to the Clinic."

Twill shook her head slightly. "Not...going to...make it."

"Yes you are, my love. Wait here, please. Rina, I'm so sorry, but...can you wait here with Twill? I'll be right back."

Rina didn't lift her head up from Erin's chest but she nodded. Olive ran outside and gathered a few Demons to follow. They ran to the Sector's Clinic. Olive burst into a tent that a patient exited. The Doctor told Olive to get her rags off for an exam.

"I need you to follow me, Doctor. Someone is dying, but she can't move."

"That's not my problem, trash can. We volunteer to work these tents, nothing else. I'm not risking my life to go any deeper."

"I have an escort. We'll protect you, *I promise* you will be safe."

"No. If you don't leave right now, I'm calling the guards over."

"You don't *understand*, she's everything to me! She needs your help!"

"So do all those people outside in the lines. Step away from me."

Olive brushed by the Doctor, grabbed his bag of supplies, then pushed him aside to exit the tent. She and the Demons ran down the street. Guards shouted for them to stop, but the deeper they got into the Sector, the officers' bravado weakened and they turned back.

She burst through the headquarters to find Rina on her knees, her chin on her chest and her hand on Twill's unmoving cheek. Olive dove in front of Twill, letting the bag contents spill over her and Rina's laps.

"She's gone," Rina whispered.

Olive put her hands on Twill's head and shouted at her to wake up. Rina put a warm hand on Olive's back as Olive cried for Twill to answer her.

Demons filtered into the building at the sound of all the wailing.

Many hands touched Olive's back and shoulders, and sobs broke out from different areas of the building.

Rina leaned to Olive's ear.

"I'm...I'm so sorry, sister. I need to get back; the hour's almost finished. Please, mourn our losses, don't rush into Sector B. Let me do all I can to put an end to this, so we never lose another sister again."

Rina squeezed Olive's shoulder and left.

Olive spent the rest of the night with her sisters, mourning and celebrating the lives of their two champions.

Chapter Twenty-Eight

Power Shift

REGINA APPROACHED THE BULL Ranch alone, yet the men reacted as they had when all the real Bulls showed up—lining up and standing at attention. It was almost cute. She asked for Virgo, to which the men hooted and pushed him forward, exhorting him to bring back a new tale to share of 'sex' with an Upcity girl. Regina led Virgo away from the loud idiots, towards the main street of Sector B.

"Are we going on another date?" he asked with no subtlety.

"Maybe. I need you to take me to that hole you were telling me about. In Sector A?"

"There are alcoves everywhere, if you're looking for privacy."

"My, how bold you've grown since we last met." Regina guided him to a wall and put one arm over his shoulder, and her hand on his stomach, fingers teasing his treasure trail. "Take me to the hole, and we'll go from there, okay? Don't act like a begging dog just because a woman is talking to you. It's a real turn off."

"Turn off?"

"Just... Shut up." Regina sighed, pecked his cheek, then backed away from him. "Now let's *go!*"

As they walked, he grabbed her hand. She didn't yank it away; she would put up with it if she could see the place. Her heart pounded as they turned onto the street that would take them to Sector A.

"You remember I said I only fit through as a child, right?" Virgo asked.

"Yes. That's not important. I just need to know where it is."

Since Regina didn't wear any patches or colors, the Onyx Orcas didn't react to them walking through their sector.

"Do you think the Orcas know about this spot?" she asked.

"I don't know... I heard about it from someone else, so I'm not the only one that knew about it."

"How has no one acted on this before?"

"I already said... It's small!"

"I *get* that. I mean, why not *open it up* with tools or something?"

"What tools? There are small tools sent down with supplies but nothing that could break through the wall and ground."

"Mm."

When they arrived, Regina was dismayed that he wasn't exaggerating. The hole between the concrete siding of the building and the cement sidewalk was indeed too small. She got down on her stomach and stuck her head through it, but everything was pitch black. They searched for a nearby torch and lit it in a brazier, then Regina put it inside and pushed it in. She looked in again but that didn't do anything other than show that the hole opened into a wide pipe.

She pulled the torch out, handed it up to Virgo, then stuck her head in one more time. Now that she had an orientation, she focused on the direction of the pipe leading to Sector A's outer walls. Far away, there was a pinprick of white light.

After getting up, she asked Virgo if the hole was the only pinch point, to which he nodded.

"So we'd only need to make this hole bigger, then a regular person could crawl through..."

"Didn't we already talk about this? There's nothing out there but trees."

"There are empty patches, places to grow food... The trees are perfect shelter... If there was a supply drop to those patches..."

"You're mumbling. Are you trying to say something to me?"

Regina shook out of her trance.

"Sorry. Come on, let's get back home."

"Wait, you said—"

Regina cut him off with a glare.

"When was the last time you cleaned...everything?"

"Every day since our date... Just in case you dropped by..."

It was nice to be wanted, but Regina had more important things to do. Still, with the speed Virgo finished last time, and his excitement to be around her again, it probably wouldn't take more than a tiny bit of effort.

"Okay, Virgo, over there in that dark corner. Come on. This needs to be quick."

She stood partially behind him and slipped her hand down his pants in the front. He was already stiff as a pipe. Her guess was right—it didn't take long at all to make him gasp and shudder.

"I feel like you could have done that yourself," Regina muttered.

"Can I do you again? It felt good to make *you* shake."

Regina smiled. "That's sweet, Virgo, but we don't have time. You can do me next time, okay?"

She grabbed his hand for the hike back to Sector B. Outside the Bull Ranch, she knew he was going to say something. She didn't give him the chance and kissed him in front of the other men. They whooped and hollered. Regina let him have his ego stroked, then told him "until next time" and jogged back to the Bulls' headquarters while using a cleansing wipe on her hands.

Brace was inside talking with Ezzie and others. Regina knew better than to interrupt them, and hung back until they finished their talk.

Someone tugged on her sleeve, and Regina turned to find Sally.

"Hi, Reggie! Do you want to see my art before I show it off to everyone?"

Brace's meeting didn't seem close to ending, so Regina nodded and followed Sally outside to where she did her work.

"Silly, did you know there's a way out of here?"

"Yeah, we just walked through it, *silly*." Sally laughed at turning her nickname back on someone else for once.

Regina punched her shoulder and matched her smile.

"I meant out of the Underfoot!"

"Reggie, is this state-the-obvious day? Of course *you* have a way out. In your dumb hand."

Regina stopped Sally by putting her hands on Sally's upper arms and addressed her face-to-face so she'd listen.

"For *us!* Fuck, not *us*. I mean, for *you!* All of you!"

Sally only cocked her eyebrow and shrugged out of Regina's grasp.

"I don't really care about anything but my art, Reggie. Thanks to *you!*" Sally turned around suddenly to give a quick, hard embrace. It was so unexpectedly charming that Regina returned it and let the topic drop.

They got to the new canvas, covered by a blanket of white fabric. Sally checked that no one else was around, then brought a torch while Regina lifted the blanket.

It was much easier to tell it was a naked woman than the last one. Sally spent little time on the body, though, and focused more on Bridgette's face. It was pretty exceptional for only Sally's second try. The art supplies improved the presentation immensely, but it was still quite ugly overall, if Regina was being honest.

"It's beautiful, Sally. I hope your unveiling goes better than last time."

"I'm only sharing it with my sisters. Fuck those gangless assholes."

"Those trash cans need to be educated in what art is. They're going to be confused for a long time, but you should keep trying. I saw smiles on some of their faces last time. You'll earn more with each piece."

Sally shook her head and fingered the artwork, then spoke without lifting her head.

"Why does the Upcity call us 'trash cans?'"

"I wasn't calling *you* a trash can."

"Just answer me."

"I think it's pretty simple. We throw out all our garbage down here. That's all."

"Why do you keep using it, when you've heard us say 'gangless?'"

"It's…" Regina frowned at herself. It was a shit excuse, but, "it's just a habit, Sally. I'm sorry."

Sally punched Regina's arm, then wrapped her up in another embrace, even warmer than the quick one a few minutes before.

"Do you really think I can educate people, Reggie?"

"They need you. You can make so many people happy."

Sally sighed. After a moment, Regina heard sniffling and felt shaking.

"I miss Erin and Vela."

Regina ran her hand through Sally's knotted hair, careful not to snag or pull.

"Me, too. Can't we visit them, though? They're just not allowed in the Sector, right? You could look for them when you take your light bath."

"I guess. I've been so absorbed in this piece… Will you go with me to find them?"

"Sure, but I need to talk to Brace first."

They pat each other hard on the backs as they parted from their embrace. Regina flashed the gang sign, then returned to headquarters.

Brace stood outside, leaning against the doorframe. She was just staring off into space.

"Brace, are you free for a while?"

"Not really. The Demons are on our doorstep, and… I've heard some absolutely shit news that I…"

Brace was usually so sure of everything she said, never hesitating, that it surprised Regina to hear it, along with the little shake in her voice.

"What is it?"

"Erin and Vela… They're dead, sister."

Brace's face hinted at turmoil until she reeled it back to neutrality. Regina remembered their talk about not allowing anything to be personal; that Brace had to constantly hide her feelings. Regina did the same, only because she didn't know *how* to feel. Vela had shown her true colors, but she'd also shown a softer side and gave Regina pleasurable nights. She didn't know Erin much, except for the sympathy she'd felt over her unfair exile.

Something told Regina the news didn't hit Brace the way it would have if lower Bulls had died—Brace probably presided over many deaths. Regina remembered what Rina did after taking Brace's challenge—she *hugged* her, and Brace took it. Maybe she wasn't such a hard ass after all…

Regina put her arms around the Brass Bulls' indomitable leader and squeezed as hard as she could, hoping she could show physical strength—the only strength they seemed to respect—in her time of certain sadness.

Brace's hard body didn't yield, but Brace snorted a little at Regina's effort. Brace laid her face against Regina's upper shoulder, then shocked her with another kind of snort—a *sob*, of all things!

It was an ugly, wet sound. Brace put her arms around Regina, nearly suffocating her while she pressed her tears into Regina's rags. It only lasted a moment before Brace pulled away and composed herself.

"Thank you, sister," she whispered. "I know you liked being with Vela. If you ever want to..."

"Brace, please don't..."

"Okay. But my nest is always open to you."

"Why are you thinking about that now?"

"Affirmation of life—or some shit. Maybe it's fear. Fear that the second hardest Bull in our history was killed by the Denim Demons. I'm told it was a single fighter, too, not like those cowardly Vipers. That...worries me. Maybe Olive actually has the strength to get through us, and my time is coming.

"I'd love for my last time to be with *you*, Reggie, but I can be with a Bull, too. I just...wanted to thank you for everything you've done here. I never expected you to stay past those first couple of days. Sentries told me you've come back to us *twice* after you've gotten on the Elevators. You're a true sister, just like I thought when I first laid eyes on you. I like being right."

Brace smiled at that, a rare sight indeed. Regina reached out and hugged her again. She cleared her throat and backed up when that one wasn't returned.

"Um... Maybe this is a bad time, but... Could you come with me to Sector A? I need to show you something."

"Yeah. Ezzie is planning our defenses and won't be back to share for a while. Gives me something to take my mind off things."

"You know, it's okay to keep thinking about them," Regina said. She grabbed Brace's iron-like hand and led her down the street towards Sector A.

Brace never let go as they ventured across the border. The Onyx Orcas certainly took notice, unlike Regina's last sojourn. Brace waved one over and told them they were only there to scout in case the Denim Demons managed to get through.

Regina knew that was a lie—Brace wouldn't let them pass, or she'd die keeping them out. The Bulls didn't make escape plans. How could anyone ever believe they'd get past?

They came to the hole and Regina showed her where it led.

"So what?" Brace shrugged when she got back up on her feet.

"It's... It's *outside!* The entire Underfoot could get out! The children... No more trash food, no more garbage, or bodies raining down on you from the Upcity. Maybe...no more wars between the gangs..."

Brace seemed unmoved, her arms tightly crossed.

"Where would we get food? What about Doctors? Weather? I've read things in books... We've lived here forever. Why leave for the dangerous unknown?"

"Brace... I... When I was up there, I decided something. I'm going to dedicate my life to helping the Underfoot. I'll get better supplies, better food, as much as I can possibly do. I can arrange transport of supplies out to the forest, instead of everything coming from the nets. You don't have to live like prisoners anymore!"

"Prisoner? I'm no one's prisoner, sister. And we have more important matters to worry about. Come back to me with this once we've turned back the Demons."

There was no question in her voice—the conversation was over.

They went back to Sector B and found Ezzie going over defense plans with several senior Bulls. Brace joined them.

Regina didn't know what to do with herself, so she decided to do something she hadn't attempted in all the time she spent in the Underfoot—talk to the gangless.

She posed questions about their hopes of getting out. That was the wrong way to go about it. "Outside? Escape?" What was she talking about?

Regina passed among them, gauging their reactions to the idea of leaving the Underfoot, without explicitly stating there was a solution.

Hours later, she realized that for every person who expressed a hope to leave, there were five others, comfortable living as they were, and all the promises of a "better life" landed on deaf ears.

However, Regina did learn of a nearly universal hope—that their children could grow up in better conditions—away from the violence, hunger, disease, and, most of all, the darkness.

As Regina walked back to headquarters in the evening, still unsure if she would join Brace in her nest or not, her focus drew to the back of her hand. It struck her in that moment: she had more power in her hand than all the Brass Bulls and their anvil-like fists combined.

Regina changed course and boarded the Elevator.

Chapter Twenty-Nine

BETRAYAL

SABRINA FINISHED A MEETING with a section of Bulls who were contemplating allowing the Demons to take over. She sold them on the sacrifices Erin and Twill had made for the cause. An added bonus was that the means of their martyrdom, enacted by fists, only proved the Bulls' strength would still be needed, no matter what the patches on their rags said, or the articles of clothing they wore.

Their plan would be to isolate Brace and Ezzie, then show them that fighting their own sisters wasn't worth their obstinate beliefs.

Most of the Bulls grew up the way Sabrina had—abused, abandoned, orphaned—and the Bulls offered a home if you were tough enough to live by their code of physical strength. Sabrina reached them by explaining they would still have homes and sisters that loved them for themselves, not their strength alone. They could in turn have families and lives outside of the gang.

The next step was to arrange a meeting between Brace and Olive.

When she wasn't busy with her schemes, Sabrina wept in the alcove in which she'd joined with Erin. She couldn't grieve with Kirsten about the situation, and didn't want to break down in front of Panda. She couldn't grieve openly with the Bulls—they weren't supposed to mourn exiles. She couldn't grieve with Olive and the Demons because it would ruin her efforts to unite the gangs in nonviolence if she were found out by Brace, crossing the border.

That hurt the most—not being able to help poor Olive in her grief as well. Twill would have been a true sister to the Bulls, and would have likely been the only one to knock down Brace if it came down to a physical battle.

Sabrina had been a little bit shocked at Olive's stature, but she realized that was stupid. Size didn't matter. Erin was the same size as Olive but still leveled waves of enemies. However, in Olive's embrace, Sabrina despaired that everything would be for nothing... If Brace only allowed an end to the conflict with a leader-to-leader final challenge, Olive was *frail* in comparison to even the scrawniest Bull.

That she got Twill and Erin to die for her cause was reason enough to let that go, though. Perhaps she had a magic pitch that'd swayed so many Sectors to her side without violence?

But *Brace*... Brace was like no one else in the Underfoot. No one could bring her down, and she had no reason to listen to a single person if she didn't want to. She was content with Sector B. She was content with only helping when asked. She had no reason to conquer or bend. She was a bulwark of stability and strength for her sisters, and under the Bulls' rules, she was as fair as could be expected.

It occurred to Sabrina that with Twill gone, Olive might need another at her side who embodied the strength needed in dire situations. Could she convince Brace to join her side as an officer; a partner? Sabrina would fill that role if she wasn't so injured—a dead eye, broken hand, and a face that would wear the scars of getting hit by Brace and slashed by that Snake for the rest of her life—scars better suited for intimidation rather than negotiations.

No, if Sabrina was to help Olive, she needed to whittle away at Brace's support structure, and continue to hope Brace could somehow be turned so they could avoid a whole bloody battle.

A DISGUISED DEMON RELAYED a message to Sabrina about the meeting request and Sabrina convinced Brace to meet with Olive, if only to hear her out. Brace loved to be right, but not through blind decisions. Sabrina appealed to her need to know all the information, before they reached a point of no return.

Sabrina trailed Brace and Ezzie to the border of B and C. A terrible sight greeted the three Bull leaders—an army of Demons with electric batons in their hands, and Olive the point of the spear.

"Very 'honorable,' Demon bitch," Ezzie said.

Sabrina used her eyebrows to ask Olive *"what the fuck are you doing?"* Olive didn't respond in any way, only locking eyes with Brace. She did, however, betray fear at seeing Brace for the first time, despite the arsenal of weapons behind her.

Brace laughed derisively, and Ezzie followed. Their mirth in the face of such overwhelming odds actually caused several Demons to waver—their faces dropped and their stances weakened.

Sabrina had no clue how to de-escalate before things tipped, but she had to do *something*. She stepped to the border.

"Why would you bring your army like this, when the Bulls come to you unarmed and open to a meeting?"

Olive shook out of her uneasy stare with Brace, then did a double take that it was Sabrina who'd spoken.

"Bulls are never unarmed. This is for *our* protection. We won't attack unless we're attacked first."

Brace laughed again, then came forward.

"You're right to bring this many, dearest Olive. It wouldn't take long for the three of us to wipe out your entire effort to subjugate the Underfoot."

"Subjugation is not the goal, and it never has been. It's a united sisterhood—a goal to live better, not selfishly for ourselves, but for all who reside in the Underfoot. Disease and hunger die behind me, not *people*. I *empower* people; I educate them; I provide for them; I support them; I *love* them. All that: *without* violence, *without* intimidation, *without* fear, *without* a legacy of *death*."

Ezzie spit and smirked. Brace continued wearing an amused mask.

"You lie pretty good, Olive. You killed Vela. Wiped out the Purple Rams. Killed those two Upcity citizens. I even heard a couple of Thirsty Thorns didn't live long after your conquest. You're not better than us."

"Vela and the Rams were self-defense. One of those citizens was already dead when they crash-landed. I saved the passenger and returned her to the Upcity. The Thirsty Thorns... I will live with their deaths for the rest of my life, and I deserve the pain of remembering their faces every time I close my eyes. I'm haunted by all the needless death because that's exactly what it was: *needless*.

"I've seen death since I started—*too* much death—that's true enough. But my goals haven't changed. They're worth dying for, as your own Bull did. Erin was a true Bull *and* a true Demon. She showed me that we can coexist, when I believed violence was the only thing a Bull was good for."

"Erin wasn't a true fuckin' Bull," Ezzie growled. "Don't use our exiles against us, bitch. I don't even care that you killed Vela, probably just like you showed up with all these Demons—with fuckin' weapons and numbers. I dare you all to try that on *me*."

"Hold off, Ezzie," Brace said. "I haven't even heard a proposal in all this nonsense."

"Don't listen to anythin' the lyin', misguided cunt says. Let me take 'em, Brace. Let me earn Vela's spot."

Sabrina needed to convene—Brace's expression indicated she might let Ezzie off the leash. She put herself between them and the border.

"Wait, sisters. I... I can't let you believe that about Erin any longer. I planned to tell you the truth...after all this, but... Erin never fell. Not once. She was... She covered for *me*. *I* fell five times. She was a pure Bull to the end. She didn't stand up for herself when you stripped her of her patch because she was being a sister to me, above all else. If I'd been there—not dealing with my eye—I would have spoken the truth, but once you'd made your decision, Brace, there was no going back.

"I just...wanted you both to know. Erin wasn't an exile."

"The Vipers' leader, Atriss, told me she never fell. She died on her feet." Olive choked up, then shook her head back to the task, "—for *us*. For the idea of Bulls and Demons coming together in sisterhood," Olive said, but Brace cut her off further with a raised hand, not looking away from Sabrina.

Ezzie's lips curled in a sneer, hardly able to contain her fidgety rage.

"You're tellin' me I stripped my sister's patch for *no fuckin' reason*? What the *fuck* for, Rina? Why would she take the fall for *you*? She was *Vela's* girl."

"She was my *sister*," Sabrina shrugged as a tear escaped her eye. "I didn't ask her to do that. She valued me above herself. I... She taught me that I can do the same. I value you both so much that I have tried everything I can to keep this conflict from becoming bloody. I want to join the Demons, and I want every one of our Bull sisters to live through it, including both of you. If we join Olive, nothing has to change but the pants we wear.

"She still needs enforcers. It's a dangerous world we live in down here... We don't have to change anything about ourselves except this insane drive to commit violence against others. On *each other!* Our own *sisters! Love* is the answer! Not more violence!"

Sabrina heard a step behind her—Olive. Ezzie went around Sabrina and straightened her back on the border line.

Brace grabbed a fistful of Sabrina's hair and pushed her towards their headquarters.

"I *dare* any of you to take one step further!" Ezzie yelled. "I'll *fuck* you up!"

Strong as Sabrina was, the pain in her scalp prevented her from fighting back—she could only use her left hand to squeeze between her roots so Brace didn't tear her scalp off. Brace's hold never weakened during the whole grim march. Right before they arrived at the headquarters, Ezzie caught up.

"They're all a bunch of fuckin' *pussies!*" she said. "I signaled for all the Bulls to get here right away, Brace."

Sabrina smiled despite herself—the spectacle to come, no matter the outcome, would ensure that Olive could slip into Sector B with no resistance. It was too bad Sabrina hadn't managed to deploy the brightly colored tape that Twill had given her.

Ezzie slapped Sabrina.

"Get that smile off your face, Rina. You don't have anythin' to smile about the rest of your fuckin' life—I'll make sure of it."

"That's enough, Ezzie. Go inside and get everyone ready."

Brace pushed Sabrina into the wall and let go of her hair. She stood in front of her while many confused Bulls went into the headquarters from their various duties.

"Sabrina…" Brace whispered, "did you sell us out?"

"No, Brace. I'm not getting paid anything; no resources, or the promise of a position in the Demons' leadership. I just want a safer world for my daughter to grow up in, and to live in peace with my wife. I love my sisters, and I want the same for them. We can live together, with *Olive*. She's… She's wonderful, Brace. She's the Underfoot's salvation. I'd… I wish you'd give me a chance to show you, starting with Erin."

"You may yet get that chance. But first, you need to survive *this*."

Brace grabbed Sabrina's neck and directed her into the headquarters, where every Bull had gathered. Ezzie took Sabrina by the back of her arms and centered her in the room, then moved to the side.

"You run, you die, Rina," Ezzie whispered.

Brace addressed the floor: "Brass Bulls, we have a very important matter to work out, more important than those limp Demons. Rina has dishonored our former sister Erin. Erin's dead. She wouldn't be, if Rina had fessed up to who *really* took the falls during their mission to assassinate the Sapphire Snakes.

"Rina, you didn't kill anyone over there like you were supposed to, did you?"

Sabrina shook her head.

"More lies. Rina has committed a terrible crime, Bulls. Erin would not have been exiled but for Rina. If we'd have known, Erin would be back here, her patch reinstated, and she wouldn't be *dead*."

Murmurs rose—not everyone had heard that news yet. The worst part for Sabrina was that Brace wasn't even lying. Erin *would* be alive if it wasn't for her.

Brace continued, "Rina has earned her own exile…"

Ezzie tore the patch off Sabrina's back.

"…but she's going to gain this patch back on *Erin's behalf*."

More murmuring, and Sabrina couldn't believe her ears. Earning a patch back was impossible—so impossible no one in their history had ever lived through it. It was rare for anyone to even try it—better to live in exile than attempt re-initiation.

"For our newer Bulls," Brace announced, "there's only one way back from dishonor—Rina must survive a punch from all of us, including me and Ezzie. You cannot hold back; you cannot choose to not participate. If Rina survives, she will meet her fate as a Bull. If not, she dies in disgrace, and we'll dump her at the feet of the Demons, who poisoned her and Erin, and killed Vela."

A disquieting hush settled over the Bulls.

"You're first, Ezzie." Brace took a few steps to stand between the door and Sabrina. "No escape, Rina. If you try to run, I'll end this whole thing. You *know* I will. Turn to your former sister. If you fall from any hit, I'll end you on the ground.

"Good luck, Sabrina."

It stung to hear her name spoken aloud in front of all the other Bulls. Some of them knew it, most didn't. In the moment, it served to "other" her, to ensure they wouldn't hold back from hitting an "outsider."

Sabrina expected a big, evil smile from Ezzie, like Vela would have given, but she only seemed neutral.

"Sorry, Rina."

Ezzie's hit was almost as hard as Brace's had been the night before Vela got laid out. Two objects slid over Sabrina's tongue. She spit out teeth, and they made a wet clatter next to Ezzie's feet. Ezzie stooped down and picked them up.

"Much respect for standing, Rina," Ezzie said quietly as she pocketed the teeth. "Good luck."

Sabrina's vision blurred after the hit, and she couldn't really see who shuffled to the center to be the next to strike her.

They took a step forward, but a familiar voice called "wait" and hurried to square up instead.

Sally took a big inhale, drawing on her strength and courage. Her fists raised, then her arms swept past and squeezed Sabrina's back. She tapped one of her fists into a back shoulder, whispered she loved her, then parted.

"You can't hold back, Sally," Brace asserted.

"I'm not anymore, Brace," Sally said casually, then went back to the floor of Bulls.

The next Bull did the same as Sally. The one after that struck Sabrina in the stomach. Knowing it was coming helped her absorb the energy into her abs, but it still stung like crazy. Ten Bulls after that all hugged her. Then came another hit across the face, causing a new laceration along her cheek.

More hugs than hits followed, but by the time the last Bull before Brace finished her hug, Sabrina's face dripped with blood, and she felt her life slipping away as she swayed on her feet.

"Look at me, Sabrina," Brace said from behind.

Sabrina shuffled her feet, barely registering their existence. She even took a few steps in Brace's direction, but that was all that was left of her energy. She couldn't bring one more foot forward. Ezzie materialized behind Sabrina and held her shoulders steady.

"You can do it, Rina," Ezzie whispered. "Just one more. For Erin."

Something Sabrina wasn't used to hearing in front of the leaders broke through the haze of pain—sniffling from many of the Bulls. Sabrina slowly turned her head, but couldn't see anyone from her blind left eye and blurred right.

"Stop...crying...Bulls," she said.

Brace's face betrayed that the proceedings were killing her. She was always so neutral that any other expression was noticeable; something to treasure when it was joy, something to mourn when it was, for once, pain.

"Never thought you'd survive this long, Rina," Brace said, giving her back her Bull name.

"I wanted...to see you...one last time," Sabrina whispered.

Brace cocked her executioner's fist back.

"Why's that, my dear?"

"Because...I love you. I love all of you. I loved Erin, and I'm glad you gave me this chance...to regain her honor as a Brass Bull. I just...wanted us to...live without...pain. Olive will love you like I do. She wants...to be your sister, not your enemy. I...hope you'll see that...after I'm gone..."

After a strange moment that stretched on with no movement, Brace's fist loosened. Her arm dropped an inch. Sabrina made to smile, to speak, when Brace stiffened like a board. Her head shook so violently that sparks ignited in her hair and smoke billowed out of her ears and eyes. She fell face first at Sabrina's feet.

Sabrina looked up to the hazy vision of Olive holding an electric gun. Her entire army stood outside the headquarters.

Sabrina dropped to her knees. Brace's burning hair wafted into her nose. Sabrina felt Ezzie brush past her shoulder and heard footsteps charge at Olive. The sound of more electricity crackled throughout the room. Shouting and a rush of air swirled, but Sabrina couldn't see anything. She laid her head on Brace's back, and smeared tears and blood into her Brass Bull patch.

Chapter Thirty

OUTSIDERS

THERE WAS A TENSE moment when Olive believed she was about to die as the wild-eyed Bull charged for her at the door, but a number of Demons pushed her aside and shocked the Bull into submission, though it took six batons to get her down. More Bulls rushed towards the entrance, but they didn't attack the Demons other than to push them off of the wild Bull and pull her away. Why weren't they attacking?

She went to Rina, bent over Brace's body and sniffling. The Demons swarmed into the building and circled around the Bulls, all the electric batons activated to shock and subdue if needed.

Olive knelt and put her hand on Rina's shoulder.

"Are you okay?"

It seemed like she tried to get up, but she had trouble lifting herself. Olive assisted her to sit on her calves. Rina's face was covered in blood, with little clear streams breaking apart the red mess.

"How could you?" Rina whispered.

"She was going to kill you. Did you want me to let her?"

"I... I got through to her... How... *Why?* You've been patient for so long..."

"I just told you. How could I come this far with your help and just let you die?"

"You just proved me...full of shit in front of all my sisters, Olive. If you'd...waited just a minute longer... I *had her!*"

"I don't like how I got here, either, Rina, but here we are. And with your help, Brace will be the *only* one. Help me talk down the Bulls that are rearing up to fight."

"They won't...listen to me. I'm not a Bull anymore. I've...sacrificed everything for you. I have nothing more to give, now that I...can't deliver Brace into your sisterhood. It's your time now, Olive."

Olive caressed Rina's shoulder, then stood to address the Bulls.

"That was... Regrettable is an understatement. I did not *want* to kill your leader. But Rina has been everything to me since we reached the halfway point of our push through the Underfoot. We couldn't be here to bring you a better life without her and...your sister, Erin, who became *my* sister. She *chose* to join me, and I quickly came to love her.

"Erin sacrificed so much for Rina and the Demons, all in the hope that the two strongest gangs in the Underfoot would come together peacefully. So, in a way, she sacrificed herself for *you*, as did Rina. My most trusted advisor, friend, protector, and lover, Twill, wasn't originally a Denim Demon. We were enemies who met on the battlefield.

"Rina and Erin met Twill on the battlefield, and fought together as sisters even though all three weren't in the same gang at the time. Segregating ourselves is no longer necessary! I've ended so much suffering in the Underfoot, prevented so many avoidable deaths, and none of it would have been possible without the help of all the gangs that joined us.

"I regret to my very soul the losses I've caused. I'll pay for it the rest of my days. But the unfortunate way we got here doesn't mean we must all be denied that better life. It's there for the taking, in honor of their sacrifices.

"The Sectors we've absorbed are so much safer now. Better food is spread to more people. We have vaccines to prevent disease. We're collecting books so we can teach anyone who wants to learn to read.

"We bring better medical supplies so many can avoid the lines at the Clinics. We bring jobs to keep you busy, and build homes for the gangless and ourselves out of more than soggy cardboard and soiled blankets. We have clean clothes, more cleansing wipes, better hygiene items.

"I ask you, Bulls, with all of that available, who wants to trade the life we offer for one filled with pain and violence, punching and challenges, disease and hunger?"

A Bull took a step forward from their gang.

"What choice do we have? If you've already taken over the entire Underfoot, it doesn't sound like we'd have anywhere to go otherwise?"

"You can always join the gangless. But we won't allow anyone to start up new gangs, or hold onto old ones. Not after everything we've gone through to get here, after all the sacrifices that have been made for this better life as a collective, a governing body that works for the whole rather than itself."

"So, it's put on the jeans or live in the streets?"

"Yes. But we will never deny access to our supplies."

Bulls looked around at each other, exchanging uneasy expressions. One of them left the group and walked slowly to the front. Some Demons got a little closer to Olive, ready to attack if needed. Olive waved them back.

The Bull put her hand on Rina's shoulder.

"I'm with you and Rina. I'll join the Demons."

Rina put her unbroken hand over the Bull's.

"Thank you, Sally," she whispered.

Soon more Bulls followed Sally's example, until there were only about a dozen Bulls left in the middle.

"Get these ladies their jeans and vaccines, Demons."

Olive took a couple steps closer to the remaining Bulls.

"I don't expect everyone to immediately join. Please come with us and see all the things we do in our organization.

"Please allow us the chance to *show* you a better life."

Everyone filed out of the headquarters, leaving Olive and Rina alone.

Olive got back down on her knees immediately and cried into Rina's shoulder.

"Oh Rina, I'm so fucking sorry. We had a hell of a time finding this place, or I could have stopped them before they nearly beat you to death. I'm so sorry, sister."

Rina hesitated, then put her hand on Olive's back.

"Stop...crying."

Olive pulled back and was heartened to see a small smile crack out from the blood crusting over Rina's face.

Something stirred behind them. The wild Bull got up groggily, moaning. Olive didn't have a baton, and all the Demons were outside. Rina put her hand over Olive's.

"Ezzie?" Rina asked, unable to move her neck far enough to speak over her shoulder.

"Move away from that dishonorable bitch, Rina. Let me fuck her up for Brace."

"Ezzie, help me up, please."

Surprisingly, the wild Bull complied, put her arms beneath Rina's and lifted her up.

"Ezzie, please take me to the Clinics."

"But this bi—"

"Ezzie. It's over, sister. I'm..."

Rina collapsed into Ezzie's embrace. Ezzie repositioned Rina and lifted her over her shoulder. Olive moved to support her head from moving too much.

"Hands off, Demon. I've got her."

Ezzie carried Rina away, leaving Olive alone with Brace's dead body. Rina's words that Brace was about to turn sides stung horribly. The least Olive could do for her and the Bulls was give Brace a ceremony alongside Erin and Twill, now that their push had completed. The Orcas would join by the next day.

After the ceremonies, her true quest would begin: finding the exit to the outside world.

THE FORMER BULLS AND new Demons attended the funeral for Twill, Erin, Vela, and Brace. Their bodies would be respectfully set aside for the death collectors in the morning, all with their patches or denim—in Erin's case, both.

Bandages covered Sabrina's face as she stood with her wife and daughter, no longer afraid to be seen with them for fear of Vela. She also told Olive her real name after returning from the Clinics.

The Upcity citizen named Regina had come upon the scene right before it started, and she openly wept with Sally and Ezzie at her sides. Olive had never seen a citizen that deep in any of the sectors voluntarily, and couldn't wait to talk with her, but there was no need to distract her from her grief. Many more Bulls cried than Olive would have imagined—likely pent-up tears from years of suppression. It could also have been from losing their way of life, but Olive would do everything in her power to ensure the Bulls were eased into the Demons. They had the chance to be the most important allies she had, if any more of them had the heart of Sabrina and Erin.

After the sobering, solemn event, Olive had the Demons bring forth wine and quality food. As she met the more affable former Bulls, she noticed Sabrina's child reading a book off near a brazier.

Olive knelt to her eye level and smiled.

"I know your mom, but she didn't tell me your name."

"Panda."

"That's so cute! What are you reading?"

"*The Outsiders.*"

"What's it about?"

"A poor gang fighting a rich gang."

"That sounds...*heavy.*"

Panda lifted the book up and down. "It's not heavy."

"Do you have a flashlight, Panda?"

"Flashlight?"

Olive reached into her back pocket, then handed one over.

"Come talk to anyone in these jeans if you want different books, okay?"

Panda thanked Olive, then moved to a dark corner and sat down to read without the burn of the brazier ruining the experience.

As the funeral broke up, Olive sought Regina. She asked her how in the world she ended up befriending the most dangerous gang in the Underfoot. Regina shared everything about her experience, not even leaving out her relationship with Vela or what happened after that. She cried several times, much like the Bulls getting their pent-up feelings out in the open for the first time in their lives. Olive supposed that in some ways, the Upcity might have felt the same.

Regina didn't know much about Olive outside of Brace's casual derision, but it didn't take long to form a solid comradery once Olive explained her humanitarian reasons for taking over the Underfoot—still excluding the ultimate goal. She was worried, no matter how friendly Regina seemed, that the wrong people could hear about the hole, and her quest to find it would be over before it could even start.

Before they parted for the night, Regina asked Olive to meet her at the border of Sector A in the morning. That was the next course of action, anyway, so Olive agreed to wait for Regina to join her.

OLIVE WASN'T PREPARED TO see Regina coming to her with a large mallet resting on her shoulder. She motioned for Olive to follow along beside her as they went into Sector A.

"I told Brace about this, and she didn't want to do anything about it until after the battle. I have no idea what she would have done if she was still here. But I can't go back to the Upcity without letting you know. Whether you act on it or not, I can't control, but I wouldn't be able to sleep if I kept it to myself."

Olive's heart sped up.

"What are you talking about, Regina?"

"Just a moment. It's right up there."

Regina stopped in front of a small hole where the wall met the sidewalk, then put the mallet head on the ground and leaned on the shoulder-height handle.

"This leads outside. I tried to slip through but I could only get one arm and my head in. So, I went home and bought one of these before coming back to the funeral. It arrived at my parent's home late last night. I also arranged for another delivery, but I can't show that to you yet."

Olive covered her mouth and closed her eyes. Tears spilled out that had been welling up since she saw the hole. She hugged Regina tight, rendered speechless.

"You should have seen how hard it was to smuggle this mallet down here without the guards seeing it."

Olive laughed and backed away, sniffing and wiping off her face.

"Do you want to do the honors?" Regina asked, holding out the end of the handle.

The mallet head was far heavier than Olive expected, and she didn't get it far off the ground at first. She put her hand closer to the head and used her legs to lift, then started tapping it against the edge of the hole to get used to the weight. After that, she put more power into it, but the angle was awkward, and she didn't seem to be doing much damage.

"Choke up on it, like a baseball bat," Regina offered.

"Baseball?"

"Here, let me show you."

Regina held the further end of the handle with both hands. She wasn't much stronger, though, and the head wobbled as she brought it above her shoulders. A full swing put a small crack in the concrete, but she dropped the mallet and complained about the vibration stinging her hands.

"Thanks, I'll try again now," Olive said. She mimicked Regina's stance and swing.

It hurt like hell.

They worked the hole together, taking breaks. The handle eventually smeared with their blood; their hands had painful blisters.

They tore off pieces of their rags to wrap around their hands, then got back to work.

Regina volunteered to find water for them and Olive kept hammering away. They were both dismayed once they found metal rods supporting the concrete inside, so they were fighting against more than the hard surface alone.

Their stomachs reminded them it was time to eat dinner when the last piece that would allow an adult to pass through crumbled.

Olive went back to Sector B to get food while Regina cleared away the chunks of concrete and bent the metal rods out of the way with the mallet. They wolfed down their food, then completed the operation by pulling the last loose chunk out of the pipe.

Covered in sweat and blood, the two grinned at each other.

"Like hell I'd go first. Get in there, Olive."

Olive hugged Regina, then took a deep breath before lowering herself into the pipe. She couldn't look behind to see, but she heard Regina follow. The pipe was a little tighter than she expected, for the size of the hole they made. She didn't have her flashlight, but she could see the pinprick of light, far ahead of her.

A strange sensation compressed her chest, and she started having trouble breathing, which led to hyperventilation and an overwhelming need to escape. She tried scooting back but her legs got caught up around Regina's arms.

"Olive, settle down!" Regina sputtered. "Get your butt out of my face!"

The intense desire to turn around was all-encompassing. The pipe grew tighter.

Regina ran her hand along Olive's calf.

"Hey, Olive, it'll be over soon. The only way to get out is to move forward. You've been doing it for so long. This isn't the time to turn back. Take a moment and breathe."

Olive shut her eyes and concentrated on her breath.

"That's it. You can do it. Do it for the Underfoot. Do it for Erin and Twill."

Olive's hand reached out and she dragged herself a little bit. She opened her eyes and decided to keep her head down, rather than staring forward, to that far away light.

The motions became so repetitive that she thought she had fallen asleep, and when her eyes opened, they stung. She stopped again, and Regina's hands found her foot.

"What's wrong, Olive? Why'd you stop?"

"My... My eyes are on fire!"

"Okay, I get that. Close your eyes. Close your eyes and keep pushing forward. I'm right here, Olive."

"The smell... It's... What if I can't breathe?"

"Hey, Liv, I can't smell anything but your feet. *Please* move ahead before I throw up all over your butt."

Olive chuckled at that, and it infected Regina. It also seemed oddly fitting to hear her old nickname. Eyes closed, Olive pulled herself forward foot by foot. The heaviness of the air relented the closer she got. Even with her eyes closed, light increased and felt like an actual weight pressing into her face. The smell was indescribable, but pleasant. She could feel the end nearing as the fresh air *pushed to meet her*, cooling her skin.

Her eyes still burned, so she resisted the urge to open them. As Olive's arms extended in another body-dragging pull, there was an absence of pipe. Her hands brushed something soft. She squinted.

Grass. Just like it was described in the books...

She still couldn't take it all in with the light burning her eyes, but she wriggled out onto the soft ground.

Olive rolled around like she was a kid again. Regina appeared next to her. Olive rolled back and wrapped her arm around Regina's torso.

"What does it look like, Regina?"

"It's all trees. And the sun is setting, so you should be able to open your eyes in a few moments."

"The...sun? Help me up so I can feel it on my skin."

The warmth from the sun was miles different from the humid, heavy warm air of the Underfoot. She felt *clean* for the first time, or at least as close to it as books described. As the light lowered down her face, she opened her eyes to see the top of the sun disappear over the forest canopy.

She thought she was cried out, but a waterfall spilled down her cheeks as she took in the forest, grass, and *sky* by the dying light of *day*.

"Over here, Liv," Regina said. Olive was struck by Regina's skin color from the hand she used to shield from the brightness. Her own skin was gray, ashen by comparison.

Regina stood over a box that hugged the outer wall of the city. Inside were strange tools and fabrics that Olive had never seen before, along with some general things like containers of water and food.

"Gardening tools and tents. I bought them and arranged delivery to this spot. It was quite expensive, but I think if I find a better company and make it a steady gig, I can get supplies dropped out here on a regular basis for less money.

"Another thing, Olive. I've seen this forest from the top of the towers. It's... It goes on forever. You could easily get lost. There are patches of clearings, but it would be easy to pass them and never find one."

Regina leaned down and pulled out a large bag full of thin metal stakes with ribbons tied to them.

"So as you search for a clearing to plant in, you can use these to mark your path. If you run out and haven't found anything, pick them up on your way back and go in a different direction. I wish I could get in my car and guide you from above, but that canopy is too thick, and I can't bring any attention on you by hovering so far down here. The deliveries are easy to pretend like a box fell out and they're just retrieving it, if caught."

Olive grabbed the bag, then rubbed Regina's arm in thanks before turning back to the sight of the rapidly darkening forest. Regina pulled a large flashlight out of the box and handed it over.

Olive switched on the light, which cast a wide beam and lit up the trunks. On the ground, a small thing scampered across the light and disappeared into the forest.

"Was that a—?"

"A rabbit," Regina affirmed.

Olive clutched the bag of markers to her chest and took in a deep breath, absorbing the essence of the trees and dirt into her lungs.

She followed the path of the rabbit with her first steps into the new world.

EPILOGUE
ALTERNATE PATHS

Regina Rondel sat in front of the makeup mirror as three women glammed her up for the cameras. Her wardrobe had been impeccably curated for the video audience. The women grumbled over her lack of plastic—their cosmetics weren't designed to be applied to real skin.

Regina was nearly broke. She'd sunk all of her money into building wells out in the clearings, and doing it on the sly increased the costs five-fold. According to the messages the delivery and construction drivers passed back and forth from Olive to Regina, they were nearing self-sufficiency, and almost all the children from the Underfoot had been evacuated. Only a fraction of adults followed them into the Forest, and the ones that remained were presided over by the Denim Demons who worked weekly shifts inside, so they all had their chances to live outside if they chose to.

The campaign manager came to Regina after the cosmetologists scattered. He laid out her talking points, confirming that she'd practiced them in the mirror all week.

"You're not going to bring up the bullshit about the Underfoot, are you? You're fucking *ahead* in the polls. If you so much as *mention* the Underfoot, you'll be removed from the ballots altogether."

"Donors have been very receptive to my pleas to help."

"Those are *private* donors! If you make it public, they'll all freak out. This topic is verboten, Reggie. Do *not* waste all our hard work to get you here."

Regina sighed and leaned her elbow on the arm of the chair. She nodded and the campaign manager went out to check on her microphone and podium among the row of three.

Staring at her reflection, she questioned whether running for office was a good idea. She struck many populist tones, all in hopes that she would one day convince the government to integrate the Underfoot population into the Upcity. But she knew it would feel like she lied to her constituents if she were to drop that bomb on them *after* getting elected, and she could easily be removed from office.

The only chance it had to work was to get people on board before the election, just like she'd done with the rich donors who'd admired her for "tending the zoo" and being "such a humanitarian," freeing their consciences to continue enjoying their lavish lifestyles while earning tax deductions. Well, Regina wasn't above using *those* people to help the Underfoot.

But she couldn't lie to her voters.

Out on the debate stage, she didn't even have a chance to ease into the topic—her opponents dug up her history of visiting the Underfoot, and accusations flew over what she did down there. There were even rumors that she was against the heteronormative agenda. Some theories were so outlandish that Regina didn't even have an intelligent response for them that wouldn't get reduced to insult-slinging.

Given her chance to speak, she dug deep in her soul to convey how much the Underfoot affected her in a positive way; how she was a better person for the experience; how people truly suffered down there; how they were *people*.

All of it was met by audience derision and snide comments from her colleagues at the podiums.

After the debate, the campaign manager's head hung low, shaking back and forth with his hand covering his forehead. He tossed a stack of paperwork over his head and said his invoice would arrive shortly, along with his resignation. Regina checked her communication device and the live polling results dropped flat, erasing all of her gains over the previous two years.

The next day, Regina presided over a meeting with the charity she ran, explaining she would be putting one-hundred-percent of her attention back into it, having abandoned the office race. She instilled in them the importance of what they were doing, and how it meant more than any other job in the Upcity.

During a private virtual meeting with a major donor, in which they appeared to waffle their support after the debacle of a debate, Regina's most trusted partner laid out a convincing pitch. Even if the pitch didn't work, Regina was heartened that there really were people around her that believed in her mission.

In the break room for lunch, she leaned against a counter sipping synth-tea and listened to her employees chatter inanely about sports and shopping. They were all good at their job, but most of them only saw it as a job and didn't necessarily believe in the charity's mission.

Regina reflected on the previous five years, up to the disastrous debate and the conversations going on in the breakroom. Her gaze settled on a knife lying on the table, then, while lowering her mug, she looked extra long at the back of her hand, exactly where the citizen chip resided.

5 YEARS LATER

Blank white paper was ultra-rare in the Forest and Underfoot, but there were plenty of books. Panda reclined in her family's tent, scrawling her thoughts into the margins of her ancient copy of *The Art of War* as if it were a diary.

She absent-mindedly peeled a sheet of skin off the back of her arm. Her parents scolded her for running around outside without protection from the sun, but Panda loved her darkening skin. The girls in her gang, the Ebony Owls, set up once a week in an unclaimed patch of sunlight in an attempt to make their skin colors match. Naked, they oiled and peeled each other's backs depending on the stage of skin transformation.

The previous week, however, a gang calling themselves the Crimson Bunnies found the patch, and staked a claim to it. Panda's girls planned to attack later in the day. When the Bunnies were crispy and vulnerable, they'd suffer the open palms of the Ebony Owls.

Panda kept her gang's violent tendencies quiet, for fear Momma Sibby would find out and send them back to the Underfoot. She'd threatened it for years as Panda and her friends learned how to survive in the Forest, not always in the "right ways" according to her parents and Mistress Olive.

Well, they didn't read as much as Panda did. There were more ways to live than any of the small-minded adults could possibly imagine, though Mistress Olive routinely stumped Panda when her rebuttals were too reasonable.

A shadow darkened the tent flap. Panda tucked her diary in the back of her jeans, and slid the pen over her ear, into her hair. Her best friend and first lieutenant, Mira, greeted her with their gang sign outside the tent.

"Ready to fuck bitches up?" Mira asked. "Those Bunnies are gonna have handprints on their pretty pink bodies for days."

"Yep. Let's go—aw, shit. Just a sec."

Momma Sibby and Momma K came back from the vegetable field with a basket of salad makings.

"Where's your shawl, Panda?" Sibby scolded. "The sun is intense today."

"We'll stay in the shade, Mom. Promise."

Sibby side-eyed the response. K took the basket, kissed Panda's cheek, and went into the tent. Panda met Sibby's good eye and smiled, but lost it when Sibby didn't return the gesture. Mira shifted on her feet in Panda's periphery.

"You need to come up with something else besides hand signals. Olive will sentence you to the Underfoot if she catches gangs starting up again, and I won't fight her."

"We're just friends."

Sibby nodded, then revealed a rare smile from her scarred face.

"I know. Just don't hurt anyone. Please. We sacrificed—"

"—so much for us. You don't need to keep repeating yourself, Mom."

"Apparently I do. *Don't hurt anyone*, Panda."

"We weren't going to, but *okay*."

Panda hugged Sibby as hard as she could. It was always a fun challenge to attempt to get her to grunt, but it never happened. Sibby only ever made Panda gasp when she'd return *her* strength.

"Love you, Panda."

"Love you, Mom."

Mira and Panda went into the forest.

"Are we really leavin' the Bunnies alone? They took our fuckin' sun spot!"

"We're not leaving them alone, but we're not touching them today."

"Are you pussin' out? Because of your *mommy?*"

"No, Mira, because it would be really *stupid* to hurt them right after we were warned. You don't think they'd figure things out tomorrow? I'm not going back to the Underfoot. We need to come up with something that won't leave marks, is all."

"What are you thinkin'?"

"You know how Laurel's parents clean meat all day? If we hurry, we can get the blood buckets before they're transported to the disposal site."

"Holy shit. I never would have thought of that!"

"I know."

Mira punched Panda's arm and they gathered at their gang's secret meeting place. Two dozen women between eighteen and twenty-two years old saluted their leader, and Panda instructed them all to go to the meat processing area. She went ahead to the sun spot to verify the Crimson Bunnies were there.

They all laid out in the sun on their stomachs or backs, the sun baking their beautiful, reddening skin. They gabbed quietly or dozed, except for one girl who was reading a book on her back. That had to be their leader.

The Ebony Owls arrived at Panda's back, and she signaled for them to encircle the clearing. Panda angled to cut off their leader if she tried bolting.

Another look at the book, though, gave Panda pause. She imagined how she would feel if someone ruined one of her books. She'd probably lash out violently, especially if it was done on purpose. Books were everything to her, after her sisters. It was rare for anyone to bother to learn to read, instead of relying on Mistress Olive or some of the older Demons to tell them stories.

She recalled the heartbreaking smile and tears of her old teacher when she and Momma K helped him shuffle through the long, liberating journey of the pipe. Not many older folks left the Underfoot, but he'd said he needed to see the outside before he died. Before they made the journey, he passed all his books to Panda.

She had just finished reading his collection for the third time the year before, nine years after he died of happiness at the edge of the Forest.

"Panda," Mira hissed low, "we're waitin' for your signal! Yell when you want us to cover them!"

Panda nodded, then walked into the clearing, straight for the Crimson Bunnies' leader. Murmurs and shouts grew as Bunnies took notice. A couple of brave lieutenants tried to get between Panda and their leader, but she easily pushed them aside.

Panda snatched the book away and looked it over.

"Cover's torn; what's it called?"

"*Watership Down.*"

"Never heard of it. What's it about?"

"Leadership. Finding value in allies. Fighting to build a better society."

"I'd love to read it." Panda turned away and took a few steps.

"What the hell are you doing?"

"Protecting it. I'll give it back to you in a minute. Now, Owls!"

The Bunnies were drenched in blood and entrails, and the Ebony Owls laughed their asses off at the horrified reactions of the sun spot usurpers.

Panda forced the truly-crimson Bunnies to agree to a schedule so the two gangs didn't clash or hog the sun. Then she instructed her Owls to retrieve rags to help clean the Bunnies off so they could all go home.

Panda caught up with their leader after all was said and done and handed back the book.

"How many books do you have, sister?"

"Only a few. Mistress Olive reads to me sometimes. She gave me this book over ten years ago, back in the Underfoot."

Panda whistled. "You want to see *my* collection? I'll let you borrow one of mine if I can read your book."

"After what you just did to us?"

"Hey, we were going to slap your naked, sun-baked asses. You bitches will sleep easier tonight thanks to my change of heart."

"Mm. I guess it wouldn't hurt for the Forest's rudest gang leader to learn a little something about leadership."

Panda pulled out her copy of *The Art of War* and waved it in front of her face.

"I know *plenty* about leadership, Red Rabbit."

"Crimson Bunny. And *war?* That's not all leadership is. Jesus, you really *do* need to read my book. Have at it."

"Come over to my place. You're going to take one of mine. You can't have my *Art of War*, but the others—anything you want."

At her family's tent, Panda emerged with a stack of books and her flashlight. The sun had set only a few moments before, but the Forest darkened everything incredibly fast. The Bunnies' leader brought out her own flashlight and perused the stack. Panda sat cross-legged beside her and opened to the first page of the tattered book.

THE END

Special Thanks

Thank you to my editor, Ollie Ander, who's read all my books and hasn't dropped me yet!

Thank you to my beta readers, especially Richelle, for giving me the confidence to keep going.

Thank you to my bookdragon fan, Ivy, who I appreciate for stepping outside typical genres and championing indie authors in multiple niches. Every indie author should have such a world-class fan for motivation and support.

About VB Scott

I'm an unassuming Pacific Northwest elder millennial, writing in several genres, and would love nothing more than for you to follow me as I release more stories that I hope you'll enjoy.

My handle is vb_scottwrites on Threads, Instagram, Facebook.

Feel free to contact me through my email address at vbscott.writes@gmail.com

ALSO BY VB SCOTT

Revenge of the Bakeneko

A historical fiction, action-adventure novel set in the early 1700s of Japan's Edo Period.

A dice game in the hands of Takana Gozen is anything but a matter of chance. Takana covets golden *ryō* coins almost as much as she hates yakuza, and she is a master at manipulating both as she hosts backroom gambling events to pay off her deadbeat father's debt. She's spent the last eight years wandering the *Nikkō Kaidō* highway, living the life of a homeless vagabond—stealing, cheating, and killing—all in the never-ending pursuit of coin.

Instigated by the lowliest of prostitutes in the brothel Takana's mother runs, a series of brutal, deadly events break Takana out of debt, and she earns the power to oppose the very structures that bound her. The found family she collects along the way looks to her for leadership, and together they form their own *yakuza* clan—the most prosperous and feared in all of Eastern Japan: The Bakeneko Clan.

Takana has trained her whole life to survive deadly encounters, but the risks that come with being a clan head come in more forms than *katana* and *kunai*. Protection, love, compassion, friendship, and sacrifice will all be necessary if she is to survive her new life—a life that proves to be more dangerous and unfulfilling than the old one.

Black Aura

A horror/metal mashup novel that will take you straight to Hell.

Led by the sibylline Auranna Korpela, the world-famous metal band "Black Aura" is soon rendered infamous. Devoted fans vanish at every show. Auranna's inaction stuns the community and raises suspicion, birthing a stained reputation which precedes them. And through it all, Auranna suffers increasingly dark and perverse dreams of the netherworld.

But Auranna's visions morph into a hideous reality. Her foremost fan has contacted her from the abyss, and Auranna can no longer ignore her deepest fears taking root. As her bandmates and unlikely allies unite at her side, she must contend with a corrupted girlfriend, doorways to damnation, and a soul contract she never signed.

Despite the threat of Hell itself, most painful of all lurks the threat of dissolution: Black Aura disbanding at the height of their glory. Must Auranna sacrifice herself to win their salvation, or has their grim fate already been decided?

A masterful celebration of sixty years of metal, Black Aura's vivid characters and horror-rich immersion pave the road to Hell like never before.

They Will Surprise You

Tera wants to enjoy one last party with her cheerleading squad without coming out of the closet.

Katie wants to start a whole new life after she's pulled off one last gig with a scumbag crew.

Timothy wants to spend a nice weekend camping trip with his family one last summer before his sons grow too old and unruly to care anymore.

And Slater wants to kill them all... But he promised his family they'd refrain during their vacation to Diamond Lake. Unfortunately, someone else at the campgrounds is beating him to it and having all the fun.

They Will Surprise You is a campy slasher horror with all the fixings: hedonistic high schoolers, boat shenanigans, forced isolation, wicked traps, a seemingly unkillable serial murderer, unexpected heroes, final girls, scenic vistas, and of course, family values!